A SAVAGE JOY

A SAVAGE JOY

LUIS E. ROSAS

A Savage Joy

Copyright © 2021 by Luis E. Rosas

Editing by Rooted in Writing, www.RootedInWriting.com
Cover image by L1 Graphics
Book design by Amber Helt

ISBN hardcover: 978-1-7365184-2-7
ISBN paperback: 978-1-7365184-0-3
ISBN e-book: 978-1-7365184-1-0

www.LuisRosasBooks.com

Only a fool wants war, but once started it cannot be fought half-heartedly nor with regret. It must be waged with a savage joy in defeating the enemy, and it is that savage joy that inspires our bards to write their greatest songs about love and war.

– BERNARD CORNWELL

CONTENTS

San Francisco, California
15 May 2013

Joseph Donovan's suspicions for being summoned to the presidential suite of the Gran Coronado Hotel cemented the moment the laptop screen came to life. A lanky, pale man strapped to a metal chair in a steel-walled room or prison cell stared, his body and dark hair layered in sweat. Donovan felt a chill down his spine, his rotund body shifting uncomfortably in the turquoise-and-ivory-colored Louis XV chair. The man's face was broken and ruined, one eye swollen shut, blood oozing out of his broken nose and split lips, and crusted blood running down his left ear and down his neck. All the while, the silhouette of a man sat just right of the camera, calmly watching the man quiver.

With a spark, raw electricity coursed across bare copper wires that were jabbed into the man's fingernails, and Donovan jumped as the man let out a bloodcurdling scream. Donovan gripped the carved armrests and cringed away from the headphone's shrieks, only loosening his grip at the sight of the seared flesh of the index and middle fingers.

Donovan exhaled and sagged for a few blessed seconds when the screaming ceased. His muscles relaxed in unison with the man who tilted his head forward and sucked down precious air in between sobs. The silence was jarring in the compartment that seconds earlier echoed with screams. The man's broken jaw quivered while whimpers and pleas fell onto unsympathetic ears.

Why the hell am I watching this? I did as I was told! He peeked left, turning his head ever so slightly toward the man behind him, who stood casually smoking a cigarette. The stench from the smoke he would normally ignore was now sickening.

His attention went back to the screen as the shadowed man leaned forward on his chair. Donovan heard a Russian accent: "Yuri . . . Yuri, do not pass out on me now, you piece of shit, or I will start cutting off your fingers knuckle by knuckle." He held up a sharpened blade, turning it to catch the light and reflect it on Yuri's good eye. Yuri could do no more than mewl pathetically.

The man sighed. "Let us try this again. Who tipped you information about Mr. Fedorovich's operations, hmm? Who else knows about Syria? About the Western girls? If you tell me now, I will put a bullet to the back of your head. Easy. And after all the articles you have written about Mr. Fedorovich, you should be thankful I feel merciful."

Donovan tensed as the Russian reached somewhere off-screen and retrieved a handheld blowtorch. He lit it and regulated the flame until it formed a perfect, sharp blue cone.

"But if you lie to me again, I will burn your flesh to the bone"—he waved the blowtorch in a slow, methodical arc—"centimeter . . . by fucking . . . centimeter."

The lanky man—Yuri—sobbed. His eyes followed the dancing blue flame with absolute fear. "I told you, Antonin. It was a woman, b-but she never gave me her name! I never met her, believe me! I—I don't know anything about her!"

Donovan squirmed as Antonin moved the torch forward, downward, until it fell from view of the camera. He gripped the armrests tighter as he watched the unfiltered terror etched on Yuri's contorted face, heard the savage screams as the torch contacted flesh. Yuri bashed his head against the chair repeatedly.

Antonin's voice was barely audible above the screams. "I want names, Yuri! Give me names, and this can stop!"

An unintelligible string of words and bloodied spittle exploded from Yuri's mouth. But it was the one coherent thing he said that terrified Donovan to his core.

"Joseph Donovan!" Antonin pulled the torch back, allowing Yuri to continue in between sobs. "Joseph . . . Donovan! An American banker in San Francisco. He—he works with her! He knows who she is! If . . . if you find him, he will tell you. Sh-she told me they worked together at Pacific Bank, or something."

The man behind Donovan lit a new cigarette.

Antonin pondered for a moment, then pressed the torch below the screen once more. "Stop lying to me, Yuri! Who is this Joseph Donovan? Are you covering for him? How does he know this woman? I want to know everything."

Donovan ripped the headphones off, nauseated by the brutality—and of being implicated as a snitch—and ran to the bathroom, barely making it to the toilet before heaving the last of the vodka and tonic he'd drunk earlier.

For years, he'd been complicit in laundering money for the Russian mob, all the while reaping the many lavish rewards. But he would never dare cross the mob. He was far too aware of the consequences. They were animals, and the video proved it. Now he feared facing the consequences for something he hadn't done. His mind raced as he caught his breath. *Who is this Yuri, and how the hell does he know me? What woman is he talking about?*

He flushed the toilet and groaned as he lifted himself up,

stumbling to the sink. He rinsed his mouth and washed his portly face, desperate to wash away everything he'd just witnessed. His face was pale in the mirror, and his double chin quivered with fear.

He didn't want to end up like that guy, and he would do anything to avoid it.

His hands trembled as he patted his face dry with the towel. With a deep breath, he walked back to the suite's living area, returning to his seat like a scolded child.

Konstantin Yuldishev, the man he'd worked for from a distance for many years, closed the laptop, to Donovan's great relief. Konstantin casually pulled his long jet-black hair back, took yet another cigarette from a sliver case, and returned the case to the pocket of his leather jacket.

Donovan flinched when Konstantin flicked the lighter and brought the flame to the cigarette. The man's dark eyes locked on his. The tip of the cigarette glowed red as smoke rose and the stench of burning tobacco hit Donovan's nostrils. He was sure he was going to vomit again.

Konstantin tapped on the laptop and said in his thick Russian accent, "This is what happens to those who betray Sacha Fedorovich." From the duffel bag on the bed, he pulled two bricks of hundred-dollar bills. "And this is what happens to those who help him." He took a drag of the cigarette, still holding Donovan's stare as he sent the smoke in his direction.

Donovan's jowls shook as he coughed, still unsure of what, exactly, he'd been implicated in.

"You, my friend, are somewhere in the middle, and that is not a good place to be." Konstantin squinted and pointed the cigarette in Donovan's direction. "How is it that a Russian journalist knew your name, hmm? Better yet, who is this mystery woman that seems to know who you are and what you do for us?"

He let the question simmer as he took another drag.

The silence was excruciating, but Donovan didn't know if

he should say something or keep quiet. So far Konstantin hadn't accused him of anything. Was he supposed to wait to be accused of something or claim his innocence? *Or is that just in cop shows?*

"I don't know how that guy knows my name, Konstantin. I swear! I've never seen him in my life. As to the woman . . . I—I have no idea who she could be. You have to understand, I work with a lot of women." He pulled a handkerchief from the breast pocket of his white jacket and dabbed the sweat off his forehead. A thought came to him. "That's it! Maybe he said that to throw you off! Maybe he's making it all up!"

Konstantin ran his hand through his hair. "And he made up Pacific Bank, too? I don't think so, Joseph. You don't convince me. Maybe I've been too generous with you, and you are playing me." He pointed the cigarette at him again. "Is that it? You think you are smarter than I am, and you're playing both sides?"

"Oh, God no, Konstantin. I would never betray you or Mr. Fedorovich." A fresh bead of sweat ran down Donovan's balding head. His voice was high, pleading. "I've never told anyone about this, I swear! Not a single soul. I don't know how that woman or Yuri learned my name."

Konstantin leaned back, took another drag, and squinted at him. "It is better if you tell me the truth now, Joseph. If you lie, I'm going to have to bring you to Antonin, that deranged psychopath. And believe me, that was not the worst that happened to Yuri."

"I'm telling you the truth! Maybe I slipped up and mentioned something, but nothing that would tie you to me!"

Konstantin opened his arms in a gesture of confidence, like a Venus flytrap inviting its prey to rest within its sticky jaws. "Joseph, you can tell me if you use our connections to get laid. It's fine. I do it all the time." He gave Donovan a sly grin. "Is that what happened? You impressed some girl and had a little pillow talk? Tell me her name, and maybe we can make this disappear."

Donovan's fat body jiggled as he shook his head vigorously. "No! Never! I would never talk about our relationship in public, Anto—Konstantin." He corrected himself, praying he hadn't manifested his fear. "Please, believe me!"

Konstantin stepped in front of him and pinched his fat cheek. Donovan winced.

"I want to believe you, Joseph. I do. I don't want to have to take you to Antonin. I like you, so I tell you what. You find out who this mystery woman is and we do the rest, okay?"

Donovan nodded heartily without a second thought. He jumped from his seat and made his way to the door. "I'll do that, Konstantin. I won't let you down. I'll find her, I promise." He pawed at the doorknob and looked back, relieved to see Konstantin gesturing for him to exit.

"I'll keep you to that promise, Joseph. Don't let me down, okay? We will stay in touch."

Joseph Donovan hurried down the hall to the elevator bank, desperate to reach the sanctuary of the executive lounge and unwind from the madness his life had become. He reached the elevator and jabbed the call button again and again, cursing the elevator's slow ascent.

The doors opened and he stepped inside. *Don't follow me, don't follow me.* He hit the E button and groaned as the doors took an eternity to close. At last, the elevator descended. He leaned his rotund body against the elevator wall, patting the sweat off his high forehead and fat cheeks. His gasps filled the silence inside the elevator car.

His mind scanned the faces of the women he knew at Pacific Bank & Trust. Could he pin this on any one of them? It was no secret that all the women hated him, but how many could have learned about his involvement—or who would even know to contact a Russian journalist? No, Konstantin would never buy it. Whoever this woman was, she had to have working knowledge of international finances. Specifically the laundered accounts. The faces continued scrolling across his mind to no avail. *Who the fuck is this woman?* He'd have to build a list and investigate each one individually. It would take some time, but he'd find this mystery woman, even if it killed him.

The alternative was far worse than death.

1

Leesburg, Virginia
Friday, 2 May 2014

Hector Vidal lifted the mug and sipped, careful not to gulp the last of his beer and speed the unavoidable return home. *Home.* He sneered at the word. More like a mausoleum for his failing marriage. He lowered the mug to the coaster, let out a heavy sigh, and rubbed his face. A glance at his watch told him it was quarter to six. *Fuck.* He was late—very late—and there was sure to be some calamity when he returned. *Fuck it.*

He gulped the rest of the beer down and raised the mug in the air. "Hey, Brenda! Another round."

The supermodel thin, pale blonde bartender, who barely filled out her black tank top and jeans held up with a spiked black belt, shot him a disapproving teacher stare as she poured from the tap. That didn't faze Hector. He'd known the twenty-two-year-old since she was in diapers. She walked the mug over, ignoring the waves of patrons cramped around the curved bar.

"Don't you have a party to get to?" she warned. "I don't

want to get a nasty call from Kelly chewing me out for not kicking you out sooner."

Hector took the mug and winked. "Last one, I promise."

He and Kelly were hosting a party tonight. Well, more like Kelly was hosting while he was forced to smile and listen to her coworkers bloviate about their overinflated accomplishments. "I closed this deal." "I sold this much." "Last week at the country club . . ." Blah, blah, blah. The boring, obnoxious, and over-detailed hours of inhuman civility could wait a little longer.

Brenda propped her hands on her waist and cocked her hip to the side. "So where's your partner in crime? You two are practically inseparable."

"Chuck?" Hector took a drink. "He's at the party with Betty, missing out on the fun down here."

Brenda's jaw dropped. "Are you telling me that he's at your *house*? Where *you* should be? Right *now*?" She threw her arms in the air. "Jesus, Hector! No wonder she's pissed at you. I would be too."

Hector held his arms up in surrender and let out a long, hard sigh. "I know, I know. I'm already gonna hear about it tonight. I don't need to hear it twice." *Especially from someone not much older than boys I've led into battle,* he thought sullenly.

Brenda dropped her arms to her sides and shook her head. She leaned on the bar and put her hand on his. "Did you two have another fight?" Behind her, a gathering crowd of impatient customers called out to get her attention. She turned and barked, "Just a minute already!" then turned back to Hector.

"Jesus Christ! Does everybody know about our fights?"

"My dad's been your bartender since I was a kid, Hector. Of course I know about your fights. Besides, it's not like you hide it very well after a couple hours here."

Hector raised an eyebrow. "I know I'm a regular, but did you just insinuate that I can't hold my liquor?"

Brenda chuckled and slapped him on the shoulder. "No,

you knucklehead." Her smile slid. "But when you and Chuck toast a lost friend, you sometimes crawl into a bad place and say things I never hear you say out loud otherwise . . . And it's okay to let them out sometimes, you know? I'm here for you. We're here for you."

She glanced over her shoulder at the other customers. Jason, her older brother, was now handling the bar. With the pressure off, she turned back to Hector. "So I hear you're getting a promotion. That should help with Kelly, right?"

Hector chuckled, then pointed at her. "Your old man *cannot* keep a secret." Brenda eyed him, not letting him off the hook. He sighed in resignation. "Not exactly." He took a deep gulp.

Brenda frowned. "What do you mean 'not exactly'? You either get a promotion or you don't."

"Well"—Hector rubbed the back of his neck—"it was more of a job offer than a promotion. Chuck wants me to take over as Chief of Global Operations."

"Holy shit, Hector! That's friggin' huge! I mean, I don't know exactly what that is, but it sounds like a big deal."

Hector squinted and swayed his head from side to side. "Eh, it sorta depends on how you look at it."

Brenda raised an eyebrow.

"Jesus, Brenda! Stop it with that stare. God, now I know why your dad can't keep a secret."

"I learned it from my mother. Don't change the subject."

Hector chuckled. "It is something of a big deal. Essentially, I would be in charge of all Parabellum's operations world-wide. Yes, it would mean I would spend more time at home, which everyone agrees I need more of, but . . ."

Hector took a long sip from the mug. Why hadn't he taken the job yet? Chuck Masters, his best friend—and, conveniently, the CEO of Parabellum Risk & Security Enterprises—was offering him a position that *could* end his troubles.

He put the mug down and looked Brenda in the eye.

"Look, it's not just that things between Kelly and me aren't good. Our marriage isn't a real marriage anymore. It isn't what it once was, and me taking this job just to be home longer isn't going to help any. In fact, it'll probably make things worse."

After all, what was his life without his team or the missions?

Sometimes he wondered which was the mistress: Kelly or the team. The bond he shared with his team was as sacred as his marriage, perhaps even more. The fear, excitement, camaraderie, and adrenaline generated a rush unlike any other. More importantly, living and fighting alongside his team brought them closer to each other in more existential ways, to the point that they anticipated each other's thoughts and carried the same burdens. To the uninitiated, it would be like looking over a precipice on a windy day and having nothing to keep you from plummeting to a certain death, save those that you trusted implicitly. It was intoxicating, and he wanted that rush. No, he *needed* that rush.

He took a deep breath, thinking about his fights with Kelly since his last mission four months earlier. "Kelly hates it that I still go on missions after all these years, but I just feel like I would die inside if I didn't go out with my team any longer."

It was Brenda's turn to let out a long sigh. She looked up at the ceiling and blinked repeatedly as she shook her hands. After a deep breath, she pointed to a stack of bottles in an island behind the bar. "You see that bottle up there? The half-empty bottle of Staggs bourbon?"

Hector lowered his head, knowing where she was going with this, and nodded solemnly as he looked up to the stack of bottles.

"That is the bottle I pull when you toast a fallen comrade, and it kills me every time I do." Her voice cracked. Hector averted his gaze as she wiped her eyes. "I'm afraid for you when you go on those missions, Hector. I don't know where you go or what you do, and I don't dare ask. I think I'd lose my mind."

She put her hand on his. "I can't even begin to imagine what Kelly goes through each time you leave."

Brenda was right. Lord Almighty, she was right. The scrawny Avril Lavigne–wannabe kid was wise beyond her years. The Parabellum position was his to take anytime, even now. He'd be a damned fool not to take it. But that, in the end, was the problem. By taking the job, he'd freely surrender the bond and that rush for the rest of his life, and he just wasn't quite ready to let go.

He took another gulp. "I know. I've been thinking about that too. Maybe I'll do this next last mission and then hang it up. Who knows?"

He'd do this mission, and maybe another after that, then call it quits. But there was no doubt he needed to go on this next mission. He'd already invested time training and planning the mission where he and his team would be on their own, and he wasn't about to put their lives in the hands of someone who didn't understand the mechanics and nuances that made the team a unit. He absently sipped the last of the beer and set the mug down.

The double doors of the Downtown Saloon swung open. Hector's eyes snapped up at a group of urbanite, carefree twenty- or thirtysomething couples sauntering in. This place in the not-so-little town west of Washington, DC, that looked like a biker bar every other day of the year was today replete with the likes of them. The newcomers blended with other couples at the overcrowded semicircular bar. Guys in designer sports coats and polos shook hands while the girls in sleeveless dresses pecked cheeks or air-kissed, a scene that had been repeated countless times tonight. And, God willing, would be *only* tonight.

As expected, the group got a mix of beer mugs and

colorful drinks that clashed with the setting and moved to the rear of the bar. Hector swiveled in his stool to watch as they walked past him to the honest-to-God, floor-to-ceiling polished brass dance pole set at the rear of the bar. The women giggled and pointed to the banner that hung behind the pole:

Cinco de Mayo Weekend Amateur Pole Dancing Contest
Saturday, May 3, 2014. 9pm – Midnight
Must be 21 and over

Brenda reached forward and slapped him in the back of the head. "Yo, Hector! Quit gawking, dude. You're married!"

Hector swiveled back and raised his hands in surrender.

The salacious dancing around the pole by two of the girls, blatantly intended to tantalize, got more than just the attention of their guys. The gyrating and sensual movements brought a wave of drunk revelers like moths to a flame, crowding terrifyingly close to the girls. The boyfriends, in a poor effort to confront the drunks, tried to placate the group and defuse the situation.

Hector instinctively gripped the mug tighter as muscle memory took over. In his hands, the mug could be turned into a lethal weapon. He swiveled around once more with mug in hand, keeping his back to the bar. A habit. It never surprised him to see the lengths people would go to in order to avoid violence or aggression when that was exactly what was required.

He wanted to ignore the situation, to distance himself from what he knew was about to happen. Maybe, just maybe he wouldn't need to get involved. The last thing he needed to do was explain to Kelly why he'd been in a bar fight when he was supposed to be at her side. But just in case, he decidedly took larger gulps of beer to empty the mug, all the while praying he wouldn't need it.

And then it happened. One of the girls slapped an offender so hard that the sound resonated over the loud music, and she yelled, "What the hell is wrong with you, asshole?"

He held the mug at the ready and waited. A moment later, grunting led to glass breaking and wood splintering as the drunks threw the boyfriends against the back tables.

"Hey!" Jason shouted from behind the bar.

That was his cue.

Hector found the two boyfriends getting pummeled by three drunks—but more importantly, he saw three other drunks forcing themselves on the women pressed against the pole. He recognized the fear in their eyes. The fear of being helpless to stop what was about to happen, the fear that no one would come to their aid. The same fear he'd witnessed countless times across the globe, the same fear that haunted him when all was quiet and still.

This was something his warrior ethos could not let happen. Not again. Not where he lived, and sure as hell not in his bar.

He advanced on them. A voice not entirely his boomed, "Knock the shit off and leave them alone!"

They all stopped and stared at him, surprised that someone would actually bother to get involved. The thug closest to him countered, "Fuck off, or you'll be next, asshole."

Hector felt the violent darkness build up with explosive force. Without warning or thought of consequence, he smashed the thick mug against the drunk's face. Blood and snot erupted from his nose. The man's eyes rolled back and he fell, hitting the floor hard.

Before the nearest thug could react, Hector grabbed him by the back of his head and yanked him forward, smashing his face against the pole—once, twice, three times. The reverberant sound of the pole was comical, though the pure violence of action was all but. He let the drunk's head bounce back, his eyes unfocused and blood oozing down his nose, then yanked again, and again, and again.

The raging beast inside Hector roared a battle cry, demanding to be let loose and destroy.

Then, as if waking from a daze, Hector found himself holding the bloodied drunk by the hair. Something had snapped inside him. The beast that only saw the light of day in faraway places had been let out where it was forbidden—and it liked it.

He let go, and the guy dropped like a sack of potatoes. He turned his attention to the third drunk, blood-rage radiating from him like an aura of ferocity. The others cowered as if they'd seen the angel of death reveal itself, and they scurried far away from him, leaving their friends to speed their escape.

Hector turned to the women to ask if they were all right, but they, too, hurried away, terrified at the savagery glowing behind his eyes. The beast was restless, and it worried him. He needed to go on that mission and satisfy its hunger.

Hector turned back to the bar. Brenda stood frozen in shock. She'd seen less than thirty seconds' worth of a side of him that he wished she hadn't, but the damage was done. He took a twenty from his wallet and put the bloodied mug over it before leaving the bar. "Tell your old man I said hello."

2

Kelly Vidal adored everything about hosting evening parties. From choosing the right catering that flaunted her sophisticated palate to choosing the perfect lighting that softened the atmosphere and spending hours shopping for that perfect dress to balance elegance and femininity, the art of hosting was something that gave her an air of class and sophistication. This level of party planning was not for bargain hunters —and the importance of this party demanded she spare no expense.

She relished the silky sensation of the fuchsia strapless dress against her skin. Every head turned her way as she navigated the sea of guests, socializing with the inner circles of the powerful and influential. Knowing that she had orchestrated all this was a rush of excitement that made her skin tingle.

The list of guests from Columbia Investment Bank and Norton-Allied Energy was an enviable assortment of magnates from the financial and energy commodities worlds, and she applauded her instinct to host the party at her home. The wooded half-acre backyard was extensive enough to offer space and privacy without having to go from room to room to check on her guests. She made the rounds, glancing from the rose garden at the far corner to the stone patio at the rear of the house, then from the stone path at one side of the house to the outdoor kitchen and firepit on the other. Something wasn't right, and it was gnawing at her.

Where the hell is Hector? I told him how important this is. Ugh! He'd better not be at the bar. She took a deep, calming breath and found her center. *It'll be fine.* This was her night.

They'd had another fight last night that led to a screaming match, and the worst part about it was she couldn't remember why. The pressure of getting this merger done had turned her world upside down. She spent days and nights worrying about every detail, even those she had no control over. Hector had his own work issues to worry about, whatever those were. *Couples therapy. Shit!* That's what the fight was about. It had been weeks since they had gone to therapy, so Hector had insisted they cancel it altogether. Typical. They both agreed it was important, and she *really* wanted to make the therapy sessions work. Not just because it felt good to have someone else understand—no, validate—her feelings, but because they could actually communicate for a change. *So why does he fight me on this?*

A gentle gloved hand tapped her shoulder, snapping her out of it. Kelly turned to see it belonged to Denise.

"Fabulous party, Kelly."

Denise . . . Clarkson! From HR. "Thank you, Denise! I'm glad you made it."

Denise leaned close and whispered, "I hear they've settled on a new name after the merger. Any chance you happen to know what that is? I mean, you're the one that made it happen, right? I just don't think I can wait until July to find out."

Kelly relished being in the sacred inner circle and knowing things that the likes of Denise could only hear about in gossip. And yet it killed her not to share the secret that only a handful of people knew. "I'm sorry, Denise. I'm not at liberty to say. They've sworn me to secrecy. I'm sure you understand."

Denise pouted. "Aw, come on, Kelly. Just between us."

Kelly feigned regret and rubbed Denise's arm. "I wish I could. Why don't you go get another drink? I'm sure it'll take your mind off it." She walked off before Denise could say anything else.

Before she could get to the patio steps, she was stopped again.

"Kelly!" Andrew McCarren, the founding partner of Columbia Investment Bank, waved her over to join his lively discussion with the senior partners from both firms. His breath reeked of whiskey and soda. "Your husband's a military man, is that correct? What does he think about this nasty Syrian civil war business and these damned ISIS fellows causing a ruckus in Iraq?"

What's his *opinion? Why? Because he's a man? The nerve!* She took a deep breath to speak her mind.

"He *was* military, Andrew. An Army Ranger, at that. But that was ages ago. Now me personally, I think we should just leave those savages to kill each other off and make less of a mess when our new partners move into place." The senior partners turned to her expectantly.

Kelly smiled politely, careful not to show her irritation. "*I* think the situation out there isn't going to end anytime soon. *I* think we should have our new partners at Norton-Allied hold off on taking over that oil field until it blows over. That would be the sound financial decision. That's *my* opinion."

Light, condescending laughter broke among the group, like adults laughing at something cute a child might say, and it made her blood boil. *These macho pricks! Laughing at* my *opinions, at* my *party, and in* my *home? I'm a senior vice president, for fuck's sake!* She remained civil and put on her empty smile, one well practiced from dealing with condescension and chauvinism on her rise to the top—but she was about to lose it.

She scanned around in search of something or someone that would get her away from this situation and spotted Betty Masters at the patio. *Thank God.* She prayed Betty would look her direction and notice her distress call. If there was one ally who could save her now, it was Betty. Betty and Andrew had been friends, and she was probably the only person here not from either firm that he showed deference to.

Betty Masters mingled among the guests, drawing attention with the charm of a southern belle and the allure of a Hollywood actress from days long gone. Betty caught Kelly's stare and smiled, touching up the complex bun of sandy blonde hair and pesky slivers of gray she paid a fortune to cover up before making her way over. Her form-flattering red dress flowed through the crowds. Kelly had always admired her youthful and attractive appearance; it belied the fact that Betty had turned fifty-two this year.

Betty injected herself into the group with an air of superiority and said in a well-spoken Southern Virginia drawl, "Gentlemen, please! Let our hostess have some breathing room."

Kelly smiled. Betty was far more than a socialite. She was a commanding woman with a benevolent nature, fierce character, and ironclad convictions, and she never judged a person by their station.

"Mrs. Masters," said Andrew, joining in a nod from the others. "Always a pleasure to be in your good graces." He raised his glass to her. "And thank you for the invitation to Heather's engagement party. She's grown to be a lovely young woman."

Betty glimmered at the mention of her oldest daughter's engagement. "You are most welcome, Andrew. I look forward to seeing Gloria again. You must bring her next time."

She hooked her elbow around Kelly's arm. "Kelly dear,

Hector walked north on King Street and eventually reached St. John the Apostle Catholic Church. The way back along the historic street was at an incline, but that worked to his favor. He needed to work off the adrenaline after that episode at the bar. He walked another block past the church and turned right onto Bridgette Lane. Now nearly home, he had the beast under control. He grimaced at the idea of *home*; he'd have to socialize with people he had nothing in common with but who were an integral part of his wife's world. For that, he'd have to put up a façade for Kelly's benefit and pay some forced lip service. That was how her world worked, but he'd never understood the importance of it. Hector would never expect exaggerated or undeserved recognition in his line of work. After all, every mission was a team effort. No one man was better than the whole of the team, unless he laid his life down for another.

You shouldn't be rewarded for doing your job. And yet it seemed to him that people in her world demanded recognition for just showing up. *God, is this what it would be like as the Chief of Global Operations?*

As he reached the middle of his block, he found high-end

luxury cars lining both sides of his street, occupying most spaces that weren't a driveway—and it wouldn't have surprised him if there were cars parked all the way around the block.

He stopped at the end of his driveway and considered. This was *his* home, and if he didn't want to walk in through the front door, then goddammit, he didn't have to. Besides, if Kelly was there, he'd be compelled to give some explanation and make things more awkward than they should be, and she certainly didn't need to know about the bar fight.

Pussy, he berated himself. He took out his phone and texted Chuck.

Coming in through the side door. I'll meet you at the grill.

The response came back immediately.

Already there.

The first thing that caught Jessica Beaumont's eye on entering the Vidal home was an oil painting depicting a Mexican charro serenading his love during a full moon. The moonlight masterfully shone on the two lovers in some hacienda in old Mexico. A young woman with braided black hair and a peasant-top dress leaned on a balcony rail, her chin resting on her bent wrist, her lovestruck eyes cast on a charro dressed in black regalia and white sombrero, strumming his guitar and professing his love in song. Jessica was moved by the art. She wondered if such romance still existed.

"Jessica?" She slowly turned to the voice, reluctantly tearing her gaze from the painting. "Oh my God, I'm so glad you made it."

"Kelly?" It took her a moment, but Jessica quickly recognized her estranged stepsister. "Oh my God! Hi!"

Kelly giddily hurried over and wrapped her arms around her. Jessica had last seen Kelly seven years ago in San Francisco, before each went her separate way, and the reunion was long past due. Kelly gripped Jessica by the shoulders and looked her over with sheer joy. "You look amazing! God, it's been too long."

Jessica beamed. "And you look fantastic, Kel." She pointed to the painting and asked with a tinge of jealousy, "Is that supposed to be you and Hector?"

Having missed the wedding and all, she had never gotten to meet Hector. Everything she knew of him was from Kelly's social media. When she first found out Hector was of Mexican lineage, she thought their dad would have an aneurism. It wasn't until later when she saw his photo that she knew Kel had hit the jackpot. The lucky bitch had landed herself a ridiculously handsome dark-haired and fair-skinned hunk, like one of those leading men from a steamy Mexican telenovela.

Kelly blushed and waved at the comment. "No, the painting has been in Hector's family for generations." She led the way to the interior of the house, occasionally looking back to ask a question or two. "So, do you still keep in touch with Mom and Dad?"

Jessica forced a chuckle. "Oh, I let them know I'm still alive every now and then. I send gifts during Christmas, Hanukkah, and the usual holidays. But I just don't always have time to talk much, you know? I mean, look at us. We didn't get in touch until I moved here. It's hard to slow down and make the time when we're as busy as we are."

Kelly nodded in agreement, giving the impression she, too, had sacrificed much for her career. Though she doubted Kelly's sacrifices haunted her and kept her up late into the night, like her own.

"But we should catch up after the party, what do you think?" Jessica asked. "Just you, me, and a bottle of wine."

"I'd like that!" Kelly beamed.

Jessica followed Kelly until they reached the French doors leading to the backyard. Jessica had to pause to take in the ridiculous number of guests just on the patio, wondering how many more she couldn't see from here.

Holy shit, Kelly! Was there anyone you didn't invite?

Kelly gently touched a woman's shoulder, older but still very attractive and stylish, and said, "Betty, I'd like to introduce you to my stepsister, Jessica Bradford."

"Beaumont," Jessica corrected. "Jessica Beaumont."

Kelly did a double take. "Yes, sorry. Jessica *Beaumont*." She took a deep breath. "This is Betty Masters. Betty is a very close friend and, I would dare say, mentor."

Jessica extended her hand. "It's a pleasure, Betty."

Betty smiled and took the hand. "The pleasure is all mine."

They locked eyes, still smiling cordially, but Jessica noted a hint of suspicion in her eyes. The woman was sizing her up. She knew this because she was doing the same thing. The old bat wasn't some rich socialite. No, this one had experience behind her. A lot of experience. She'd have to keep an eye on Betty, because she would obviously be doing the same.

In the short seconds where all of this transpired, she vaguely heard Kelly going on—something about Hector and Betty's husband. She was too focused on getting a better read on good ole Betty. "Anyhow," Kelly concluded, "it turns out Jessica is a lawyer for Norton-Allied and was reassigned here from New York."

Betty smiled. "Oh, so how did you get in touch, if you thought her surname was Bradford?"

"I legally took my mother's name a few years ago," Jessica answered a bit too quickly. She turned to Kelly and added, "I found you when I got the news about the merger. Great job on that, by the way."

Betty nodded in understanding. "I see. So have you finally settled in?"

"I have. I found a beautiful place in Old Town Alexandria."

Betty nodded in approval. "Excellent! I'm sure you've already discovered what a wonderful area it is. Especially that gorgeous view of the Potomac."

Jessica followed Kelly and Betty onto the patio. Kelly gushed about the party's details, pointing out the recent home renovations they'd made just for the occasion. An older man with two cameras strapped across his chest stepped in front of them. "Can I get a photo of you lovely ladies?"

Before Jessica could respond, Kelly pulled her and Betty by the waists and smiled. The cameraman snapped a series of photos in quick succession. "Thank you, Ms. Carlyle," he said, then gave a small bow to Betty and went off into the crowd.

"Well, that was exciting," said Betty. "I guess I'd better go find my husband before the photographer does. I'm sure you two ladies have a lot of catching up to do." She flashed a gorgeous white smile at Jessica. "And welcome to Virginia." She turned and blended into the sea of guests.

Jessica watched her leave, awed in spite of herself. "Is it me, or does she seem like someone straight from the cast of a southern soap opera?"

"Betty *Carlyle*-Masters is a true southern belle from an honest-to-God American dynasty."

Jessica scowled. "How? I've never heard of her."

"For starters, she's the heiress to Carlyle Maritime, a ship-builder in the Norfolk area. And I guess it's a mid-Atlantic thing, probably why you don't recognize the name, but the Carlyle family goes back to the Jamestown colony. The woman belongs to everything from the Daughters of the American Revolution to the VFW Auxiliary. If you're running for office or want influence, you make sure to be seen with Betty Masters."

Jessica grabbed Kelly by the arm. "Wait—so then who took that photograph?"

Kelly winced at Jessica's grip and rubbed her arm once she let go. "Oh, that guy? He's with the Style section of the *Washington Post*."

Jessica felt her heart sink into the pit of her stomach as a cold shiver coursed through her.

"Jessica, honey, are you okay?" Kelly asked, fanning her face. "You turned pale all of a sudden. You want to sit down?"

Jessica shook off the comment, her mind racing. "No, no. I'm fine. I just haven't had anything to eat yet," she lied.

"Well, let's get you some appetizers or something first, and then I'll introduce you to some of the guests."

After getting some food and water in her, Jessica followed Kelly around as her stepsister introduced her to some of the more powerful and influential people on the East Coast. With each introduction, Jessica had to be careful not to reveal a growing jealousy. Or was it resentment? In the near decade since they had parted ways, Kelly had compiled the life that Jessica coveted. She couldn't blame Kelly for the choices that resulted in her own path, but her resentment only grew as Kelly introduced her to magnate after magnate of the financial world, including Alex Portman, the senior managing partner at Columbia Investment Bank.

"Hi, Alex. Thanks for coming."

Alex Portman, a man with a full head of silver hair and a distinctive trimmed moustache reminiscent of the Hollywood stars of the '40s, pecked Kelly on the cheek. Jessica's eyes bugged at the familiarity. "I wouldn't dare miss it. You were a central piece of this merger, and everyone here knows it." His eyes then drifted expectantly to Jessica.

Kelly motioned to Jessica. "Alex, I'd like to introduce you to my stepsister, Jessica Beaumont. She's with the legal office at Norton-Allied and recently moved from New York to DC, so we'll be seeing a lot of her, I'm sure."

Jessica resisted the urge to cringe. *Jesus, Kel. Just with the legal office? Really?* She felt the introduction was demeaning and diminutive, particularly since she had worked just as hard to make sure the merger went without a hitch . . . and then some.

"Is that so?" Alex smiled brightly. He turned to an older man talking with other distinguished guests. "Gregor! Look over here. This young lady will be sitting across the table from you."

A hunched, balding octogenarian with thick horn-rimmed glasses turned slowly with the aid of a cane as a young assistant whispered in his ear. Jessica shot a quick glance at Kelly. *Gregor Solomon? The Columbia chief counsel? Does she fucking know everyone?*

"Wonderful, wonderful," Gregor said indifferently. "I am sure you are doing a fantastic job." He gave an obligatory smile, then slowly returned to whatever more interesting discussion he had been involved in.

Jessica looked with muted envy at the girl who at one time had followed her around like a lost puppy. It had become painfully apparent that Kelly wasn't just more successful than she was; she had gained influence leagues beyond her own and risen among the social elite. In her mind, it was an aberration—their roles should be reversed. Sure, Kelly was technically the older sister, but only by mere months. It should be Kelly who envied her as she had done so before . . . and for lesser things. Jessica had always been the more attractive, fashionable, outgoing, and adventurous of the two. Fine, she could be intimidating, manipulative, and coercive—but Kelly could have been, too, and in fact she had. After all, the Kelly who used to follow Jessica around couldn't have accomplished all this. In the end, none of that mattered. A single choice in Jessica's past had ensured her visions of grandeur, of a life in the spotlight, never came to fruition, and fooling herself that she could have a better life than Kelly's was just a dream.

The parading went on and on, from one guest to another, always introducing her first as "the stepsister." *As if my achievements were predicated on that.*

Just once, she'd like to be introduced by her position or by one of her many significant achievements—which Kelly hadn't even bothered to ask about. Like discovering one of the most extensive sex trafficking rings in the Western Hemisphere and one of the largest crime syndicates in the continental United States. *And then it would be all about me. Wouldn't it, princess?*

Jessica shook her head and sighed at the futile thought. God, she could never speak of that. It was her secret to keep. And so, she resigned herself to being shown off like a birthday girl's new puppy.

Before long, though, the reunion started wearing thin. "So, Kel, are there any *regular* people at this party?"

Kelly blinked, then covered her mouth. "Oh my God, I'm so sorry. I haven't introduced you to Hector. As soon as I find him, I'll grab him for you. Promise."

Jessica folded her arms and pursed her lips. She didn't have to take the humiliation. She could walk out right now and drive to wherever she pleased. *Just take a deep breath and calm down. Stay in control.* She spotted a group of associates from her firm clustered at the far end of the backyard. "You know what, I'm gonna go say hi to some friends, all right?" She turned and walked off without so much as a wave. Right now, her ego demanded attention, and she knew exactly how to get it.

The young associates from Norton-Allied had gathered in the small rose garden, arguing about whether the Giants or the Redskins had a better chance of dominating the NFC East. Jessica interrupted them. "Pardon me, gentlemen, is this seat taken?" She pointed at the chaise at the end of the garden.

The associates were beside themselves, befuddled by her

presence, each looking at the other to see which of them would be the first to say anything.

With no objection, Jessica leisurely reclined on the chaise, extending her legs and crossing them in one smooth motion. Pleased with their reaction, she asked, "Would one of you gentlemen fetch me a drink? A cosmo would be lovely, thank you."

Three perked up, aiming to please the hot girl in their group, and raced off to get her a drink.

Jessica shook her head and smirked. *Boys, boys. As if you really had a chance with me.* With that taken care of, she next played the role of an Egyptian queen while men with Ivy League pedigrees ogled and jostled for her attention. Everything her demanding ego needed was almost perfect except for one thing—or rather, one man.

Paul Monroe.

The Scandinavian perfection of a man was leaning against the lamppost illuminating the garden, drinking his neat Scotch and talking with his fellows—never once glancing her way. He was somehow immune to her charms, and that was something she intended to change. To be fair, she wasn't trying *that* hard, though he did catch her eye when she first moved to DC. Ever the diligent stalker, she made it a point to ask around about Paul. As it turned out, she had missed him in the New York office by just a few months. The ambitious Paul had transferred to the Washington office for an opportunity to finesse his political skills, escape his father's shadow, and expand his own network. After all, nobody did this job for selfless reasons—she should know.

She was trying not to be miffed at Paul's indifference by relishing the other men's attention, but that wasn't working. Fortunately, Kelly showed up and saved her from doing something stupid. Or worse yet, something desperate.

"Excuse me, gentlemen, but I need to speak to Jessica for a moment."

Jessica rolled her eyes and handed her drink to whoever was closest. "Is everything okay?"

Kelly waved her hand. "I want to introduce you to Hector and Chuck. Now just so you know, Hector is the strong, silent type. So, don't be offended if you can't get him to string together more than three-word sentences. Just asking an open-ended question isn't going to cut it."

"Intriguing," she said with feigned interest. "Let me put these boys out of their misery." She turned back to the group. "I'm sorry, gentlemen, but I must leave you all for now." She tipped her chin to her shoulder and added, "It's her party, after all."

As they exited the garden, Jessica passed Paul, who grabbed her by the arm, stopping her mid-stride. "When you're done, come find me." His voice was strong and confident, and Jessica could have melted on the spot.

Kelly glared disapprovingly, but Jessica didn't care. She kept glancing back over her shoulder even as Kelly dragged her away.

5

Hector and Chuck popped open fresh beers when Betty found them in the outdoor kitchen. "Well, hello, gentlemen," she called out, like a teacher finding students in the hall during class. "How nice of you to make it easy for me to find you."

Hector chuckled and tipped his beer to her. Chuck swaggered to Betty, wrapping his muscular arm around her slim waist and pulling her to him. He lifted her chin up to his and lowered his head for a kiss. "Hi, love."

She sighed like a girl with a teenage crush. "Oh, Chuck, what am I going to do with you?" He winked and stroked her face with the back of his fingers. She closed her eyes and held his hand in place, savoring his gentle caress a few precious seconds longer. Hector looked away, uncomfortable.

Betty extricated herself from Chuck's embrace. She looked back to the crowd, which they were clearly not being a part of, and turned to Hector. "Kelly has an impressive guest list, doesn't she?"

"I suppose. Not bad for the vice president of . . . something or other."

Chuck laughed heartily. "Jesus Christ, Hector! You don't

know your wife's job? She's the Senior Vice President for Mergers and Acquisitions, for fuck's sake! *And* the reason why everyone is getting drunk here instead of at the Ritz. From what I've heard so far tonight, she might make partner this year."

Hector scratched his head. "Well, I've never had much of a head for business. Good thing we have you for that, old man." While he said it in jest, Hector was really alluding to the fact that he didn't have the head or the heart for the new job. And that was the crux of it. It wasn't that he didn't want to move up their version of the corporate ladder; he just wasn't ready to move on. At least not yet.

He often wondered what it was like for Chuck to hang it all up. He could see the longing in his eyes during the mission briefs, wanting to feel his pulse quicken and the rush of adrenaline all over again. But in the end, he knew Chuck did it for Betty and the girls. He could see it in the way he talked about them. The way he watched Betty, the way he kissed her, and the way she did the same with him. Chuck and Betty had true love. The kind that comes around once in a lifetime and lasts twice as long. Sadly, he wasn't sure if he and Kelly still had that.

Chuck looked from the crowd to Hector, then asked, "Not to press the subject, but have you given more thought about the offer?"

Hector shifted uncomfortably, hoping to derail the topic, when he caught movement in his peripheral vision. He turned, instantly drawn to a tall, gorgeous woman in a white dress heading in his direction—nearly missing the fact that she was carrying on a conversation with Kelly. Her raven-black hair cascaded over her bare shoulders, bouncing with each step, making it seem as though her movements should be in slow motion. Though only slightly taller than Kelly, her slender figure and long, shapely legs in high heels gave her a statuesque appearance that towered over Kelly.

His eyes traced her form from her stiletto heels to her athletic build beneath the sleek spaghetti-strap dress, hypnotized by the rhythmic, smooth swagger of her hips. She laughed at something Kelly said and tilted her head back, giving him an exquisite view of her luscious neck. Hector rubbed the nape of his neck and gulped at the sight of her red lips as they slightly parted. His heart raced as her long lashes fanned slowly over her full, expressive blue eyes.

He broke from her spell just as the women reached them, and his eyes instinctively went to Kelly. She'd clearly seen him gawking at the other woman, and guilt surged through him. *Ah, shit.*

Kelly cleared her throat. "Jessica, this is Chuck Masters, Betty's husband. Together they run Parabellum Risk & Security Enterprises." She left Jessica's side and hooked her arm around Hector, overtly claiming him as hers and leaving no doubt in anyone's mind. "And this is my husband, Hector. He works with Chuck—"

"Well, technically, he works *for* me," Chuck interjected half-jokingly, earning him a murderous glare from Kelly. Getting the clue, Chuck cleared his throat. "I mean to say that he's a team leader in our company and . . . yes." He stopped talking.

Jessica slowly stirred the straw in her cosmo, smiling at Hector and daring him to look away.

He didn't.

"So, what's your work like, Hector?" Jessica cocked her head with a playful grin, swiveling her torso back and forth. "Are you like one of those tough bad boys from romance novels? The one that always takes the girl in the end?" She brought her drink up to her lips and sipped. Her cheeks lightly drew inward. It was . . . suggestive.

Hector smiled politely, desperately trying to hide the physical effect she was having on him. "We're not like Kevin Costner in *The Bodyguard*, if that's what you're asking. We specialize in hostage rescue operations and war zone security. We keep bad people from hurting our clients."

Jessica smiled, as if she knew something he didn't. Hector coughed, repositioning himself.

Kelly tugged Hector's elbow. "Would you mind helping me in the kitchen?"

Hector snapped from Jessica's trance and sighed inwardly. He recognized that tone. It was Kelly's trying-not-to-cry voice, which meant that whatever it was she wanted to discuss would result in an argument—probably either his lateness or gawking over her stepsister, or possibly both. He nodded, then followed her unquestioningly.

6

Syria: Fifteen miles east of Tartus

Konstantin's radio squawked, and on cue he brought the night-vision goggles to his eyes. In the distance, he picked up a dust trail and followed it to the source. He spotted three armored Mercedes-Benz SUVs moving his way on the winding, desolate road, just as the intel had said. Moonlight blanketed the terrain with an iridescent glow reminiscent of a lunar landscape, making the conditions for Boris Soklov's Syrian Army security team a nightmare. Soklov's convoy was visible for miles, driving slowly on a narrow road with a deep drop-off on one side and a steep slope upward on the other. If this part of the war-torn country wasn't controlled by the Assad regime, the convoy would be an easy target for the regime opposition forces. Who knew? Maybe there was an ambush already in place. Syria was a very dangerous country.

Soklov was returning from an assignment directed by Sacha Fedorovich himself. Soklov's regular duties included providing entertainment for Syrian Army officers who could afford top-shelf Western girls—but this assignment had been a special case, arranged for the pilots and crew of a helicopter unit responsible for dropping barrel bombs on opposition forces. With Sacha's quiet approval, Konstantin had seen to it that Soklov spent the night there with two girls and kept them for entertainment so the men had their fill.

The real purpose was to give Konstantin the time he needed to prepare the ambush. He waited until the vehicles reached where the road widened, then keyed his radio and said, "*Iditi*."

On his command, a bright flash lit up the night sky, and the lead vehicle catapulted into the air. Seconds later, the report from the blast reached Konstantin, and the deafening explosion broke the silence. The second vehicle skidded on the loose gravel and crashed into the burning wreckage. Konstantin smiled as the wrecked SUV's engine revved but went nowhere.

Muzzle flashes sputtered from Konstantin's position, and swarms of bullets pelted the remaining vehicles. The low crackling of gunfire echoed from the other side of the ridge, giving the impression two ambushes were coinciding.

The follow vehicle drove up alongside at an angle that provided some cover from the gunfire while still allowing for an escape, but its progress was cut short when a flash streaked down from the mountain, striking the vehicle and engulfing it in a massive fireball. Meanwhile, brighter flashes joined the blinking constellation as the louder thuds of the more powerful PKM machine guns pounded the last surviving vehicle, steadily wearing through the armor.

Konstantin barked into his radio in Russian. "Assault team, move forward now!"

Konstantin watched through his binoculars as dark figures closed in on the remaining vehicle and fired their weapons. The windshield crumbled under the intensity of the machine-gun fire, and the attackers fired on the driver and commander, shredding the driver's upper torso and bursting his head like a watermelon. The commander managed to raise his short-barreled AK-74 and fire, killing two attackers before suffering the same fate.

The two rear doors opened, and muzzle fire flashed from the door gaps in a futile effort to repel the assault, but the attackers had greater numbers and maneuvered beyond the guards' line of fire. The passenger-side guard exited the vehicle to fire at the men advancing on his position, only to have his shins splintered by a hail of bullets. He dropped to the ground and was soon ripped to shreds with bullets.

The last guard continued firing his weapon until he emptied all his ammunition. At the final click of the empty magazine, he let out a primal scream, unleashing his rage, knowing he wouldn't live through the night. With his rage exhausted, the guard dropped his weapon, raised his hands, and slowly exited the vehicle. The guns all went silent as attackers quickly moved in and forced the remaining occupants from the vehicle, leading them on a death march to the edge of the road, facing the steep drop-off. Two men, Middle Eastern and Caucasian, were forced to kneel in wait for the choreographer of the ambush to appear.

Konstantin leisurely made his way from his watch position and strolled up to them. His jet-black hair shimmered in the moonlight as the breeze blew past him. He pulled a Makarov pistol from his holster, pressed it against the back of the guard's head, and squeezed the trigger without hesitation. The sound of the gunfire echoed in the mountain pass as blood and brain matter exploded from where the man's face had been a second earlier. His lifeless body tumbled over the ledge.

Soklov screamed hysterically, urinating on himself as the body rolled into the ravine like a discarded rag doll. His body quivered with fear as Konstantin grabbed him by the hair, pulled his head back, and hissed in Russian, "Where are you running off to, little mouse?"

"Konstantin! Wh . . . what is this? What is happening?"

"Boris, please. There is no need to keep up this song and dance. You were lucky that Yuri—you remember Yuri, yes?"

Soklov's eyes widened at hearing the name.

"You're lucky he didn't give you up—but your luck finally ran out."

"Wait! What about the girls? Y-you killed the girls! Sacha will never forgive you for this! He—"

"I don't care. They had outlasted their use anyway. All Sacha wants to know is, who is the American, the woman who talked to the FBI? You can tell me, or you can tell Antonin—and you know what that Chechen psychopath does to traitors." He drew a combat knife from its sheath and pressed the razor-sharp edge against the left side of his throat. "My way is faster."

Soklov blubbered incoherently, not daring to move his head in the slightest. His luck had run out. No matter what, he was going to die. All that mattered was how.

He sniffled, took three deep breaths, and said, "I . . . I don't know. The last I knew of her, she was in San Francisco, but she left some years back. Neither Yuri nor I knew where she went! Sh-she just vanished!" He began whimpering again. "I swear! I don't know where she is now. I would tell you if I knew. Please don't take me to Antonin!"

Konstantin nodded, satisfied with the answers. "I know you would." Without another word, he drew the knife back in a slow, deliberate motion, slitting Soklov's throat. Blood pulsated out in thick sprays, and gargling replaced the screams. Expressionless, Konstantin kicked the back of Soklov's head forward, sending him over the edge. One more unknown name claimed by the war.

He wiped the bloody knife on his pants and put the knife back in its sheath. One of the attackers handed him a satellite phone. He dialed a number and waited for an answer. "It's Konstantin. I need to talk to Mr. Fedorovich."

7

Leesburg, Virginia

Hector leaned against the granite counter and stared out at the soft light of tiki torches and string lights stretched across the backyard. *So what's it gonna be tonight, Kelly? Being late, the job again, or catching me checking out your sister? Hell, maybe all of the above.* A fight was bound to happen. He was just surprised she wanted to ruin her precious party with one.

She came up next to him and looked down at the counter. "So, what do you think about Jessica?" she whispered.

Hector scanned the backyard, finding Jessica in conversation with some of the guests. He watched her as he considered his answer, careful not to reveal what she stirred in him. Her flirting was like a breath of fresh air in a stale room. He cleared his throat. "Um, she's something else, all right. She livened up the party a bit, that's for sure."

"Yeah, she has a talent for that." There was a hint of jealousy in Kelly's voice. And maybe something else? "She's beautiful, isn't she?"

He felt her stare. *Way to set the trap. How the fuck do you answer that?* If he said yes, it was sure to start a fight. If he said no, she'd know he was lying. "Um . . ."

"It's okay if you think so."

A tsunami of relief flushed through Hector, like getting a pardon just as the executioner reached for the switch. But the long pause that followed filled the air between them with an awkward silence. This was something Kelly wanted to talk about. *Or even argue about*, he thought. He, on the other hand, wanted to avoid the topic like the plague.

"I see how you look at her. How they all look at her. She puts on this flirtatious act and mesmerizes everyone she meets." Her face flushed as concern became evident, a concern she directed at him. "She always does this when she wants something"—her voice broke—"and she always gets it."

Hector didn't say anything. Kelly sighed deeply. "She's always been the prettier of us. Ever since middle school. She was always the popular one, you know? The queen bee of the popular girls," she mocked, fluttering her eyelashes. "She was the first one to kiss Kevin Donaldson and the first one to dump him." There was unmistakable resentment there. "She's still that kind of girl, I suppose."

She gave him that look, the one she used when she wanted to know what he was thinking, but he wouldn't bite. The stare remained.

Fuck. At the risk of opening Pandora's box, he asked, "Is that why you don't have any pictures of her? Or why she wasn't at the wedding?" The statement was a gamble, and he braced for her to lash out or give him some long-winded tirade, but the answer surprised him.

"No, not entirely. We had a falling-out back at Stanford."

"But she's here now," Hector said, his voice quiet. He met her gaze cautiously; he was treading on a mine field. "You can have a fresh start with her."

"I don't know." Kelly sighed. "Growing up, we had the same friends and shared the same toys. I think it was in middle school that things changed." She paused, recalling some distant memory. "Anyway, after graduation we both worked in San Francisco, but we never really saw each other. And now we're working in the same area again. I don't know. I was hoping things would be different now." She searched his eyes with a sadness that pierced his heart. "But I see that was all wishful thinking."

Kelly blinked and shook it off, now focusing her attention on Jessica. "Something happened to her. I don't know what brought her from San Francisco to New York and now here, but it wasn't an accident. I can feel it. She's the one who reached out to me, and I don't think it's because she wants to reconnect. I don't know if she's in trouble or something, but she's not the type to just reconnect after so many years. She wants something."

Hector turned to reassure her, enveloping her in his arms and smoothing her hair. Kelly melted into his embrace.

"So when do start your new job?"

The question came like a punch to the chest and hurt just as much. He let go and staggered back, facing the window and again leaning on the granite counter, feeling her eyes on him. *Goddammit, Kelly.* He felt as if Atlas had shrugged and shifted the weight of the world to his shoulders.

He took a deep breath. "I'm still considering it."

He paused, trying to find a way to say the last thing he wanted to say. "I just need to get this next mission done, and I'll probably take it after that."

Kelly crossed her arms, choked back the tears, and said tersely, "I don't want you going on another mission, Hector. I mean it. I can't take it anymore."

The beast inside Hector grunted. Hector balled his hands into fists, ready to pound through the countertop. He was sure she was manipulating his emotions, using his guilt against him, and he fucking hated it when she did that.

"I have to go, Kelly, it's already arranged. The team needs me."

"I need you, Hector!" Kelly shouted at him, causing heads to turn in their direction. "What about me, huh? What about my needs?" There was ferocity in her stare. "I need you here with me. Alive!" She threw her hands up. "Why does it always have to be *you*? Why can't you let someone else go? I don't know how else you want me to explain it! I'm scared *every day* you're gone!" She pounded his chest with both fists. "Why can't you let someone else's wife be the terrified one with the sleepless nights?"

She pressed her head against his chest, the truth taking the fight from him and leaving her exhausted. Her words lingered in the air. A few guests entering the kitchen paused at the door, casting intrigued looks their way. *Great. A freaking audience.*

Hector needed her to understand that, as the team leader, he was responsible for everyone else's lives. He *had* to go. But the honesty in her words disarmed him, leaving him with no choice but to wrap one arm around her and once again stroke her hair.

"This all would be different if we had a family," he said softly. Letting the words out felt good, like a wave of relief, but he hated them the moment he said them.

Kelly lifted her head, the shock of his words etched in her face. She pushed herself away from him. "Are you seriously bringing that up right now? How dare you!"

They glared at each other, paying no mind to the servers and guests who abruptly stopped at the kitchen entrance, then kept walking.

"You're an asshole, you know that? That was a cheap shot, even for you." Kelly wiped her tears with the tips of her fingers and sniffed. "I'm telling you right now, Hector—if you go on this mission, don't bother coming home."

She smoothed her dress at the waist, fixed her hair, and let out an exhale. "We better be getting back to our guests. And that actually means talking to other people, Hector." She walked out without another word.

Hector deflated. He leaned back against the kitchen island and exhaled hard. *Well done, dumbass. That was fucking epic.*

Hector nodded mindlessly as the guest droned on about how this merger would better the global economy, or some shit like it. In truth, he couldn't care any less. He couldn't get past the fact that the guy had an air of arrogance that made his blood boil, compounded by the fact that he went on without a pause.

Jesus fucking Christ, man! Do you ever shut the fuck up?

His mind went back in the kitchen, Kelly's last words swimming around his head. Not caring any longer, he interrupted Diarrhea Mouth mid-sentence. "Yeah, that's fantastic." And walked off, not bothering to look back.

He lost count of how many of these fucking idiots he'd "mingled" with, and he'd had enough. He'd been polite to the point of exhaustion, suffering through conversations with Artie Fuck-nuts, Professor Plum and Mrs. White, Corner Office Barbie and Metrosexual Ken, the Monopoly guy, and Howard "Can I Get Any Fucking Fatter?" McBucks.

He spotted Chuck and Betty and rushed over to them. He grabbed the first glass that still had any liquor in it, poured it into his mouth, and refilled the glass. He shook his head at Chuck with a look that said, *You have no fucking idea . . .*

With the liquor still burning his throat, he let loose. "Fucking hell! I was about ready to throat punch someone!"

Chuck's raspy laugh filled the air around them.

"Are you quite done, Hector?" Betty admonished, unamused. "Just imagine how poor Kelly must suffer every time you boys get together and tell your war stories and tales that would make a pirate blush."

Chuck and Hector stared at each other, then laughed.

8

The few lingering guests were finally gone, leaving Kelly and Jessica alone on the patio with two pairs of heels and two bottles of wine between them. Kelly uncorked the first bottle and poured into stemless glasses as she told Jessica about her first year with Columbia Investment Bank in San Francisco.

"I liked the work and my friends, but it was the junior VP who was a real asshole and made it rough." She rolled her eyes as a cold shiver ran down her spine. "He had an overinflated sense of importance and wanted us to believe the partners sought his advice on the happenings of the lowly junior associates and analysts." She took a sip and continued, "He barely interacted with us, and when he did, it was usually to hit on the women. He tried being smooth with me, but always came across as slimy and gross. Ugh! I just wanted to go jump in the shower to scrub off the ickiness."

Both laughed, and Jessica nodded. "Oh my God! I know just what you mean."

"Anyway, after many failed attempts, he changed tactics and tried to convince me he could guarantee me a job with more responsibility if I *took care* of him."

Jessica snorted and rolled her eyes. "So what did you do?"

"I saw an opportunity," Kelly said matter-of-factly. "It just so happened that a competitive position opened here in DC, so I told him that if he submitted anything less than a stellar performance review and a recommendation for that position, I would file a sexual harassment charge against him and personally tell his wife."

Jessica raised an eyebrow and her glass. "You go, Kel!"

Kelly shrugged. "I would've been happy to stay in San Francisco, or maybe even go to New York like you did, but I knew I could move ahead here in Washington."

Jessica pointed. "You would have liked New York. It would suit you." She sipped and asked curiously, "So what happened then?"

Kelly laughed. "The asshole didn't squirm at the mention of a sexual harassment claim, but he did at the thought of his wife knowing." She smirked triumphantly. "Turns out he tried the same thing later, but the next girl actually *did* file a claim against him. He resigned his position before any formal action occurred, and as far as I know, that was the end of him." She refilled their glasses. "So, what about you? Why did you leave San Francisco? I thought you were happy there."

Jessica fidgeted at the question. She had so far kept quiet the details of her life all these years, not even having an active social media account Kelly could find, under Beaumont or Bradford.

"After law school, I got a job in commercial banking with Pacific Bank and Trust. It was a shit job, but I figured I could use my finance minor and law degrees there. Turns out I got hired more to be gawked at than to do real work. Their legal department was a joke. I mean, even the department head would pat my ass!"

"Ew! Gross!"

Jessica took another sip. "I mean, I was a Stanford graduate, for fuck's sake! And the manager—a pig of a man, literally and figuratively—told me to my face that he wanted me to dress all slutty."

Kelly snorted, imagining a cheesy plot from some '70s porn movie. "Please tell me you didn't!"

"I wish. I ended up wearing shorter skirts, tighter blouses, and heavier makeup. I even went so far as to go platinum blonde!"

Kelly snorted. "No! You didn't!" She couldn't imagine Jessica, the high school queen bee who eviscerated the bottle blondes with her razor-sharp barbs, to go blonde herself, much less platinum blonde.

"I'm serious, Kel! I considered filing a sexual harassment suit and quitting, but I didn't have a backup plan. So, I focused on building up my résumé and . . . waited for something better to come along."

Kelly detected hesitation, and that was definitely not in Jessica's character. It piqued her suspicions. "Well, that can't be everything. What took you to New York? Come on, don't hold out on me. We still have a second bottle to get through."

Jessica chuckled. "Jesus, Kel. When did *you* get so bossy?"

"Well, I *am* the senior VP, don't you know?"

"Yeah, I know," Jessica retorted. "You haven't let me forget."

Kelly covered her eyes. "I know, I know. I'm sorry!" They both laughed.

Jessica let Kelly refill her glass. "So you remember how Mom and I would drive Dad crazy whenever we started talking in Arabic or Hebrew?"

"Oh my God! Yeah! You two used to make him livid." Kelly sipped and tucked her feet under her legs, now starting to feel the evening.

"Well, it turns out that came in very handy after all." Jessica grinned and added with a sultry tone, "My tongue has *many* great talents."

Kelly laughed. "Slut."

"Whore."

"Tramp."

"Skank."

They briefly stared each other down but broke character and laughed like they'd done so many times in their shared bedroom back in Julian, California. The place that both would forever call home away from home.

Kelly uncorked the second bottle, and Jessica changed the discussion. "So, Kelly, you married a soldier! You swore you'd never date one, much less marry one. What happened?"

Kelly grinned and took another sip of wine. "We'll be needing another bottle before I'm through, but I'll say this. The marines we'd see at the mall in Carlsbad were still boys. I'll just leave it at that. Oh, and by the way, you're staying here tonight. It's settled. I don't need you driving home drunk, okay?"

Jessica rolled her eyes. "Fine! Just, come on. Give me the meet-cute."

Kelly thought back to that winter evening. "I was at the bar at Uncle Julio's in Arlington with a group of other girls from the office when he walked in, wearing his dress uniform with the rows of colorful ribbons and badges, and an air of confidence and ultra-masculinity that . . ." She sighed. "It was so damn sexy. I thought he was going to start hitting on us or offering to buy us drinks because, well, that's what every other guy at the bar did. Except he didn't. He ordered his drink and kept to himself. He was so mysterious, which only made him that much more intriguing."

Jessica nodded fervently. "I know, right?"

"After a while he looked up. He looked directly at me, as if we had some connection. I wasn't looking to get hit on, especially with someone doped up on adrenaline rushes, alcohol, and loose women. But he wasn't any of those things." Kelly took another sip. "One of the girls waved him over while the rest of us giggled like teenage girls—then the others suddenly needed to powder their noses when he arrived."

"Mm, those bitches."

Kelly giggled. "So it was just him and me, and I asked him flat out if he was in uniform to get lucky. You know, to deflate his ego and let him know I wouldn't fall for any of that bullshit."

"Yep. You know guys love to be put in their place."

This time Kelly didn't reciprocate the banter. She took in a deep breath and exhaled hard. "That's when he told me he had just buried one of his friends in Arlington Cemetery."

Jessica reached for her. "Oh, honey."

Kelly's eyes belied her smile. "I felt like such an idiot, but I dug my hole deeper when I stupidly asked what it was like to be in a war, not connecting that he had just come from the cemetery." A lump grew in her throat, and she choked out, "God, when I think that could have been him . . ."

Jessica wrapped her arm around her. "No, honey. Don't think about that. That's in the past."

The past. Yeah, right. Kelly composed herself and pulled away from her sister.

"What about kids? Are you two planning, or . . . ?"

Kelly flinched and looked away, the question touching a frayed nerve.

"We tried several times," was all she managed to say before she felt her throat closing again. "I miscarried each time, and I've been scared to go through that again."

Jessica was quiet for a moment, then said, "But surely you and Hector can—"

"I don't want to go through that again." Kelly snapped. She took a deep breath and exhaled. "I'm sorry. It's just . . . Hector wants to try again. Rather, *wanted* to try again."

That was her breaking point. She pressed her hand to her eyes and let everything out.

"Oh, honey," Jessica soothed. She moved to Kelly's chair

and cradled her, stroking her hair. "I'm sorry. I didn't mean to pry."

Kelly shook her head. "It isn't just that. Hector really wanted a family, and I pushed back. He kept pressing and pressing until he stopped. But he didn't just stop pressing. He also stopped loving me."

Jessica hugged her tighter, rocking as her sister sobbed.

Kelly nodded, and Jessica released her. "Our lives got busier and we drifted apart. I was promoted to Senior VP and spent more time at work while he traveled more. But the truth is that I didn't want to fail again at the one thing that mattered to him. How is it that I can be successful at everything except motherhood?"

She wiped the tears from her eyes. "Now, we're mere strangers who share the same bed." Her tone was thick with regret. "The unintended consequence is that we've stopped doing the things that reflect a couple being in love, like asking about each other's day or holding hands at an endearing moment." Kelly gulped and then confessed, "Even intimacy has become less frequent. We used to fight about trying again. Now it seems like we fight about everything."

She dabbed her eyes and stared into the heavens. "But I was determined to save our marriage. Still am. So I did the little things that couples in love do. I touched him when he passed, kissed him in the mornings, and snuggled up to him when he came to bed at night. I even went so far as to buy toys and lingerie from an adult novelties shop. Do you have any idea how embarrassing that feels?"

She shook her head and snickered. "In the end, the clothes and toys did work for a while, but it wasn't enough. I made time in my schedule to go to the gym or run in the mornings to keep him interested in me, but all my efforts gained me only empty compliments and gestures. The only thing that matters to him is the next goddamned mission."

Kelly looked up, wiping the tears away with her fingers and dabbing her nose with a wadded-up napkin.

"But I think the worst part of it is that I'm terrified for him every day he's gone, and that doesn't seem to matter to him at all. The few times he's called, I end up doing all of the talking. I may as well be talking to a wall." She sniffed and wiped her eyes again. "I don't know what to do anymore, Jessica. I'm just done with this. I love him, but I don't deserve to be treated like this. I want to be happy too. I told him flat out—it's me or the missions. I'm not going to be the other woman. I won't compete with a fucking job."

They sat still, letting the moment linger, quietly sipping their wine. So much had happened between them all these years, and it would take time to come to terms with it all.

9

Any other night that Hector and Chuck enjoyed by the firepit, they'd be talking up some old war story over beer or bourbon. Tonight, however, they sat across from each other, leaning over the table as if they were in the middle of a high-stakes chess match. On the table was a map of northern Iraq and some files detailing a proposal from none other than Norton-Allied, the new client they'd meet officially on Tuesday morning. The irony wasn't lost on Hector that the people he'd tried desperately to avoid all night would be the same individuals he'd most likely be working with at some point. Another example of why he just wasn't suited for the life of a businessman.

He shook off the thought and focused on the map. It depicted Irbil and the Kurdish controlled region to the north, Iraqi-controlled Mosul and Kirkuk to the west and south, and the Iranian border to the east. In the middle of it all was Taq Taq, a small city lodged between Irbil and Kirkuk, its small footprint highlighted in blue. This was the location of Hector's next mission. Norton-Allied had won the bid for an oil field nearby, and the American energy firm was ready to invest a significant amount of manpower, equipment, and capital in northeastern Iraq.

That was great and all. But what he was most concerned with was the area west of that small footprint. A sea of red on the map represented ISIS advances from Syria and the extensive captured territory so far. The group with no homeland or regular army was the most effective, ambitious, and dangerous of all factions in the region and was rapidly gaining ground against Kurds and Iraqis alike. To the trained eye, the blue spot on the verge of being swallowed by a wave of red was a chilling reality.

Chuck peeked over his readers and asked, "What do you think?"

The question was a loaded one. Chuck didn't just want to know what the tactical plan for this mission was. He was curious to know how his future Chief of Global Operations would handle a less-than-ideal situation. Hector met Chuck's eyes, then he looked over to Betty as she sat on the armrest, one arm wrapped around her husband. Hector leaned back, stroking his chin as he pondered the degree of risk Norton-Allied was willing to take and the limits of Parabellum's capabilities.

"Iraq is a really nasty place right now," Hector said, keeping his eyes on the map, "and I just don't know if we have the manpower to support the site long-term without putting our other commitments at risk."

Parabellum provided quality worldwide security services by experienced former Rangers, SEALs, and Air Force PJs. The company boasted an array of equipment that included commercial Level 7 armored vehicles, helicopters, transport aircraft, and even a boat service—all conveniently staged at various depots around the globe. But they weren't an army, and this job would require a full complement of personnel, equipment, and infrastructure. Hector rubbed his face and exhaled, shifting his eyes around the map.

And just like that, he sprang forward and snapped his fingers in a stroke of genius. "Then again, maybe we don't need an army. The key is to gain the loyalty and support of the tribes in the region, right?" He looked to Chuck and Betty. "Norton is sending a negotiator with us to leverage the Iraqis. Why don't we also have the negotiator work out a deal with the Kurds and some of the more influential sheikhs in the area? We'll just take him with us when the patrols take us through those areas."

Chuck nodded slowly, putting the pieces together in his head. "So you think we could get the Kurdish Peshmerga to be our army?" He tapped his finger north of the dot. "The Norton guy can work something out between the embassy and the Kurds to hire or subcontract the Peshmerga outpost here, where they have roughly two hundred fighters. Sure, it's putting a lot on the Norton guy, but what the hell. It's their oil field."

Hector leaned back triumphantly. "The facilities team can set up containerized housing units and generators for the Peshmerga, and we can use the site as a base. They get air conditioning and electricity, and we get experienced shooters." *Checkmate.*

Chuck removed his reading glasses and pinched the bridge of his nose. He leaned back on his chair and looked up at Betty. "And what do *you* think? There's a lot of moving pieces to this project, but I like it."

As the real money behind Parabellum, Betty wasn't just a "silent member" of the team. Besides the fact that her name carried significant weight with the political and business classes, Betty was pretty tactically sound and had a knack for reading the situation ten steps ahead. "I think that's a great idea, Chuck. From what I've heard, Bill Carson isn't a timid CEO. He likes to take the bull by the horns, and expects all his people to do the same. And he doesn't suffer fools lightly."

She rubbed his scalp gently and added, "How do you think they won the bid in the first place?"

Chuck, rarely taken aback, now raised an eyebrow at her. "Well, aren't *you* full of surprises?" He pulled her to him and tilted his chin for a kiss. Betty was an asset in the planning meetings. Having fresh eyes and unbiased clarity on things made her opinions a valued commodity. "All right, I'll shoot him an email tonight and see what he has to say on Tuesday."

Chuck shifted in his seat then, turning to Hector and saying, point-blank, "So, about the position."

Hector became rigid and raised his hands.

"Wait—before you cut me off, I know how you feel. I've been there. But you can't do the grunt work forever. Eventually, you'll have to leave it for the young and bold. The *teams* are going to need more guidance than just learning the ropes. They're going to need a leader who can see the big picture, and that's you."

"I know." Hector chewed his lip. "I'm not that old yet. I've got time."

Hector caught the glance Chuck threw at Betty. "But Kelly needs you more, and she's not going to wait around for too long. I hope you can see that. Hell, I'm just glad Betty saw the writing on the wall and made me see what it was doing to us before it was too late."

Hector again felt the heaviness of his situation. He wiped his face, taking in Chuck's words and Betty's nods, and let out a long exhale.

Betty spoke up. "We don't want to pry too much, but I hope you understand that Chuck and I care about you both. You're practically family to us." She paused, then cleared her throat. "Kelly and I are good friends. Best friends, really, and while she hasn't said anything specific, she's worried."

"I know, I know." Hector threw up his hands. "But I have to see this mission through. I can't just walk away so far into the planning." He gulped his beer, thinking about their earlier fight. "I know you understand this, Betty, but I can't seem to make her see why it's important that I go. Can you talk to her about it? Make her see reason?"

Betty shook her head. "Hector, I've given her my point of view, but it's not my place to make her think one way or another. If you want her to understand you, then you need to *communicate* with her, not just talk to her." She adjusted herself on the armrest and pressed her lips together, her expression becoming more serious. "I'm sure you're aware of the incredible amount of stress she's been in with this merger. But what I don't think you've realized is how much more stressed she's been about the two of you. She loves you very much, but . . . sometimes she feels like you don't love her anymore." Betty held his stare. "Is she right?"

Jesus Christ, I don't need to talk about this now. In Hector's mind, he was convinced that no matter his decision, the abyss between Kelly and himself was too big to bridge.

Then, out of nowhere, Jessica appeared in his mind. The picture came like a bolt of lightning that quickened his pulse and stirred him inside. It was the same feeling he had when he first met Kelly—but no, he didn't want to read too much into it. He had *always* been faithful to Kelly, even when the opportunities were plenty and no one would have been the wiser. But something was different now. Was it that he knew his marriage was over? Was that why he felt this?

Snap out of it and get a fucking hold of yourself. He felt a sudden cold sweat come over him. He shook it off. "Of course not." Was it a lie?

Chuck took that as a cue and slowly rose to his feet. "All right, we're gonna call it a night. Thanks again for letting us stay over. Are you okay here?"

Hector inwardly sighed and nodded. "Yeah, I'll shut down here, and I'll head up with Kelly shortly."

Chuck let out a low grunt as he stood up, knees creaking.

"Good night, old man!" Hector stared into the fire,

swirling the last of the beer. No matter how bad things had gotten between him and Kelly, he'd never had feelings for another woman. This worried him.

Fuck it. He downed the last of the beer, shut off the gas to the firepit, and turned the outdoor kitchen lights off. He paced back toward the elevated patio, using the distance to clear his head, and climbed the patio's stone steps. There, asleep on the lounge chairs with two empty wine bottles between them, were Kelly and Jessica. Each was curled up under a light blanket that left their feet exposed. He gently shook Kelly and whispered, "Hey, wake up. It's bedtime."

She shrugged in response. *Wonderful.*

He went to Jessica and lifted her up, surprised at how light she was. In turn, she instinctively wrapped her arms around his neck and smiled, even though she was dead to the world. He was keenly aware of how close their mouths were as he carried her up the flight of stairs into the second guest bedroom, and it sent his pulse racing. Her perfume was enticing—earthy, as opposed to Kelly's usual floral aroma. Her body was light and athletic, and little of her was soft or flabby. The toned definition of her thighs and the silky smoothness of her skin was arousing, reminding him that weeks had passed since Kelly and he had been intimate. Or was it months? Jessica's body and scent awoke a hunger in him that demanded attention but couldn't be fulfilled.

He reached the second guest bedroom and laid her down on the full-size bed, unable to keep himself from looking her over as she lay on the purple-and-gray diamond-pattern quilt. He let his hand caress her exposed shoulders and back as he pulled the quilt from beneath her. *God, she feels good.* Her skin was smooth and taut, making it almost impossible to draw his hand back. He let his hand linger there, far too long, and pulled the quilt lower.

His pulse quickened as his hand slid down her toned back, allowing himself to feel the softness of her skin and the light contours of her muscles until he reached the hem of her dress. His hands trembled as he slipped her legs under the covers and took in the sensual manner in which she raised her arms over her head and nuzzled against one arm. *Even asleep, she's sexy.* His eyes took in the way her dress hugged her slender shape, following the contour of her curves and dipping between her—*Jesus Christ, Hector. What the fuck are you doing?*

He pulled the quilt over her, leaving only her shoulders, head, and arms exposed, then looked away. *Good Lord, what is it with this girl?*

He stole one last glance as he reached the door, then forced it closed, lest he be tempted to do more than just watch. Hector's heart was racing. Even now, on the other side of the door, he could still smell her perfume. He fought hard to clear his mind of Jessica on his way to retrieve Kelly, but she occupied every aspect of his conscious thought. He paused, allowing himself to let the moment pass before exiting to get Kelly—*Kelly, you know, your wife.*

As he reached her chair and bent to pick her up, she asked in a slow, slurred voice, "Wh . . . where's Jess . . . ?"

Hector cleared his throat. "I put her in bed," he said, the smoothness of her skin still fresh in his mind.

Kelly grinned and accused, half joking, "Hector Vi . . . dal. Did you take another woman to bed?" Her head slumped back as she passed out once again.

Hector gulped. "That's cute, Kelly."

He retraced his steps up to the second floor, now entering their bedroom. God, he wanted so much to remove her dress and attend to his desires, but that was not going to happen. Not tonight. No, instead he laid her gently on her side of the king-size bed and unzipped her dress. He lingered there. He felt her skin from her neck down to her exposed shoulders, allowing himself the pleasure of his wife's body. He traced the contour of her shoulder blades and spine. She twitched at his touch, which brought a smile to his face, giving him encouragement to keep sliding down. She was firm and smooth in all the right places, just like Jessica, and—

He pulled his hand away, as if he'd touched fire, and rubbed his face. *Goddammit! Why is she in my head?* He wanted to appreciate what he had, to convince himself that he and Kelly were still in love, still desired each other. But more than anything, he was just hoping to quiet his thoughts about Jessica.

He pulled the covers over her and went to brush his teeth and change into his sleep pants. Jessica was still in his head. Rather, the yearning she stirred in him. She made him feel vibrant in some respects, but that wasn't where he wanted his mind to go. Jessica was the forbidden fruit, and he had to resist, no matter how tempting. So, when he finished, he climbed into his side of the bed, staring up to the ceiling, an ocean of sheets between him and Kelly. He took a deep breath, almost smelling Jessica's scent, exhaled, and closed his eyes.

But that didn't last long. He opened his eyes a second or two later and stared at the ceiling, then looked at the door. Too much lingered in his mind. Jessica, the mission, the feel of Jessica's skin against his, the job, Jessica's eyes and red lips, and, of course, the fight. Kelly's words in the kitchen were still fresh. Would she really throw it all away if he went on the mission? Or was she giving him an out without saying it?

I bet Betty didn't know how willing Kelly was to throw it all away. He wondered how many more fights he could stand, if he cared anymore, and if he could feel Jessica's touch again. One thing was certain, though: sleep wouldn't visit him anytime soon.

10

Jessica lazily stretched the length of her body, from the tips of her fingers to her toes, with a satisfying exhale. When she opened her eyes, she scanned the unfamiliar setting. Drinking late into the night wasn't foreign to her, and neither was waking up some place other than her own. The dreaded "walk of shame" was an occasional hazard, but this wasn't that. Kelly had invited her to stay the night, but Jessica didn't remember getting herself into this room. She bit her lower lip and shut her eyes hard as she retraced what she could remember. Her face relaxed and she sighed with relief. *Nope, nothing happened.* Though the opportunities had been plentiful. *Stop it, Jessica. Behave.*

She took in the décor, deciding that the royal purple and gunmetal gray of the duvet were the inspiration for the colors on the walls and furniture. She pulled the covers away and sat up on the bed, taking one more stretch for good measure. The clock on the nightstand read 8:07 a.m. It was Sunday, so why couldn't she sleep a little longer? She puffed out a big breath. Nope, she wouldn't be able to go back to sleep. *Of course*—her mind began to wander—*I could always accept*

Paul's invitation . . . She grinned at the thought. *No, that would come across as desperate. Let him come to you.*

She hopped off the bed and made her way to the dresser and rummaged through the drawers. Kelly had to have something that would fit. Sure enough, she found a pair of yoga pants and a tank top. They weren't flattering, but they did the job. Next, she pulled out a pair of rolled-up flats from her purse and put them on.

Fresh clothes did wonders for her, and after changing, she faced herself in the mirror. *What's one more night of sleeping in my makeup?* She felt an urgent need to go for a run and sweat out last night's toxins. If she stayed for breakfast, she'd for sure get a hangover.

She pulled her cosmetics kit from her purse and took out all the necessities she'd learned to carry with her over time. She splashed warm water on her face and once again practiced her routine of removing the old makeup and reapplying. Satisfied with the result, she made her way downstairs. Finding no one else stirring, she left a note apologizing for ducking out so early, promising to stay in touch and offering to host Kelly next time and show her around Old Town Alexandria—even if she was the new girl in town. She signed it, posted it on the refrigerator, and made her way to her car, but not before retrieving her Louboutins from under the chaise lounge. The fact that she'd left them outside was its own travesty. No need to add another one by forgetting them.

There were drawbacks to living in the nation's capital area, but the cost of living was definitely not one of them. It was considerably less than the Bay Area or New York's outrageous rentals. Still, it wasn't home. California would always be home.

But this corner of Virginia did have a unique kind of

charm. Jessica had found a townhouse at the edge of the Potomac River in Old Town Alexandria with a gorgeous view of the DC skyline and the lights of National Harbor. The view of the Woodrow Wilson Bridge and the Potomac River paled in comparison to that of the Golden Gate or Brooklyn Bridges, but the Capital Wheel—the giant Ferris wheel in National Harbor—more than made up for it. And the plentiful restaurants within walking distance and the nightlife in King and Union Streets would have been a cab ride from her apartment in Soho. Old Town was as good as it would get. Her housing community in Harborside was flanked by the Potomac River on the rear and ornamented with colonial-style architecture on the front, and the scenic Mount Vernon trail was the perfect running trail.

That morning, she extended her running distance by zigzagging in and out of the various side streets on her way back along Union Street, deliberately running uphill at Captain's Row, a cobblestone street that hadn't changed much since the colonial era. Jessica rounded the last corner and fell into a cool-down walk, panting. She was checking her pulse when she arrived at her townhouse and found a visitor on her doorstep.

Paul Monroe was waiting at her door, two cups in hand. She pulled her earbuds out and smiled. "How did you find out where I live?"

He shrugged indifferently. "I'm a resourceful guy."

She watched him quite openly undress her with his eyes—not that her fluorescent racerback sports bra and black compression capris left that much to the imagination.

A devilish grin spread across his face. "I know how to get things that I want." His boastful remark earned him a smile reserved for those she intended to win over and make hers.

She walked up the steps to her doorway and pulled out her key. Paul remained leaning up against the frame, forcing her to come as close as possible to him. She caught the scent of his cologne as she moved closer, and she resisted the urge to swoon. She met his eyes and said mischievously, "I'm sweaty. You might get that nice Orlebar Brown polo wet if you stand too close."

Paul pinned her between him and the door. "You promise?"

She felt her knees weaken, and it wasn't because of the run. He was aggressive and wanted her to know it. In turn, Jessica engaged him with the same flirtatious stare and wagged her finger at him. "Now, now. Don't be getting your hopes up. I'm not that kind of girl." She pressed the same finger against his chest, feeling the resistance of his muscular chest, and pushed him back.

She reveled in the degree of sexual tension they generated as she turned around and inserted the key. She felt his eyes on her, admiring the muscle tone she'd worked hard to develop. She gasped as he slipped his finger inside the thin racerback strap and slid it sensually up and down between her shoulder blades.

Jessica froze in place, biting her lower lip and relishing the shudder that raced down her back. She rested her head on the door and uttered a soft, stuttered exhale.

Paul leaned forward and whispered in her ear, "Your tag was sticking out."

She mustered enough self-control to open the door and step through. Paul sauntered in after her, uninvited, and handed her one of the paper cups, letting his arm caress her sweat-slickened shoulder. "Low-fat chai latte, no foam, no water, with cinnamon and nutmeg sprinkles."

She dropped her keys on the breakfast bar and squinted suspiciously. "How did you know?"

Paul stepped closer with a triumphant expression. "Like I said. I know how to get what I want."

Jessica cocked her hip and gave him a disapproving look.

When he didn't immediately answer, she tilted her head and raised an eyebrow.

"Okay, okay," he said, smirking. "I asked the barista from the coffee stand at work." The answer wasn't as cool as his prior one, but it did get a laugh out of her.

"You're right." She smiled. "It's my favorite morning drink. Not only are you a bad boy, but you're a clever one too." Then, said with a sly, sultry tone, "Such a dangerous combination."

Paul winked and recited a line from *Top Gun*: "That's right, I am dangerous."

She rolled her eyes and laughed. "So, I'm sure you didn't just find out where I lived to bring me a drink." *Let's get down to your real intentions, pal.*

He took a sip of his coffee. "I wanted to see you again, but you didn't come back. And since you're new to the area, I figured I'd show you around. There's a lot more around here than just Alexandria and DC."

"Oh, really? What if I already have plans today?"

Paul approached her, slow and deliberate, his gaze never leaving her. "Then change them."

Her arms loosened as her defenses caved in. She searched for a retort but found herself unable to find one. "I . . . Let me just go shower and change." Jessica turned to her bedroom, then added, "No peeking, bad boy," though she expected Paul would be watching her the entire way. *Well, this is going to get interesting.*

Minutes later, a cloud of steam spilled out from the bathroom as Jessica opened the door. She stepped out, a bath sheet wrapped around her, drying her hair with a towel. She stopped mid-step, startled at what she saw—but not outwardly revealing it. To her disbelief, Paul was under her covers. His clothes were on the floor. She watched him study her appreciatively, from her bare shoulders glistening with water beads to her glossy red toenails.

A sly grin formed as she raised a single, perfect eyebrow. "You really do get what you want, don't you?"

His eyes met hers. "Why don't you climb in and find out?"

Jessica let the bath sheet drop at her feet, sashayed to the bed, and climbed in.

11

San Francisco, California
Sunday, 4 May 2014

Joseph Donovan bit into the whole wheat toast spread with apricot preserves and sipped his freshly brewed coffee as he chewed, appreciating how the preserves sweetened the black coffee and gave it a unique taste that lingered in his mouth. For the first time in a year, he felt confident his luck was changing. He had slept terribly the night before, his sleep plagued by nightmares of Konstantin's compounding wrath at the cold trail. This wasn't supposed to be a good meeting. A year of searching, and all he'd found was an alias. But then the *Wall Street Journal*'s Sunday paper had come out, and Donovan's salvation was at hand.

He had a name.

He again picked up the morning paper and continued reading the article about a merger between Columbia Investment Bank and Norton-Allied Energy. The writer cited an expert who argued the merger would create a financial juggernaut that would tilt the delicate balance of the energy commodity market. As a counterpoint, he cited another expert in favor of the merger who stated the merger was a welcome change, bringing freshness to a market that was becoming stale with the added benefit of expanding green energy sources.

Donovan set the paper down, took another sip of coffee, and glanced out the windows of the executive lounge of the Hotel Gran Coronado. The high, clear windows offered a spectacular view of the Golden Gate Bridge, Alcatraz, and the Pacific Ocean. This, and the five-star service, was why he paid the exorbitant club membership fee. The serenity of the view always helped him clear his head and find a solution to whatever ailed his thoughts at the time.

And today he needed that serenity more than ever to finally put an end to his living nightmare. The peacefulness was short-lived, as his phone began buzzing in his jacket pocket.

He pulled his phone out and recognized the international number. He drew in a deep breath and slowly exhaled. This was one step closer to ending this yearlong nightmare. "Hello?"

"Your diligence paid off, Joseph. Boris Soklov is one less problem for all of us. This has made Mr. Fedorovich very happy." Konstantin's voice came through the speaker with a slight crackle. Donovan knew the Russian was somewhere overseas, hunting down another mole Donovan had uncovered.

Donovan let out a sigh of relief. He thought about asking if Sacha could find a way to show his appreciation, but that would be pushing his luck. "Glad to hear it. It seems like today is a day for good news all around."

Donovan gestured to the breakfast table, and a smartly dressed young lady in a black tie, white shirt, and fitted black slacks rushed over to the table with pad and pen. "Yes, Mr. Donovan?"

He pulled the phone from his ear. "Would you bring the menu, please?"

"Right away, Mr. Donovan." The young lady smiled and strode to the hostess station, her ponytail swaying side to side.

"You are getting closer to finding this bitch? How many more names are on the list?"

Donovan waited for the clip-clop of the waitress's block heels to fade before putting the phone back to his ear. "It seems we may have finally struck gold. We may be done with this insufferable business soon."

"Go on, Joseph. I'm listening."

Donovan pulled the phone away again as the waitress returned and handed him the brunch menu. She left without a word.

"There was one name that I couldn't locate, and it just kept gnawing at me. It took me some time to find her because she changed her name once she left San Francisco . . ." Donovan pulled out his tablet from his leather satchel and unlocked it, revealing a social media site he had been studying. "Jessica Bradford was this little tart that worked for me a few years back. She had a perfect ass and a set of tits on her, but she came across as a bitchy ice queen."

He waved the waitress over as he continued. "She was placed in the legal department, but without any real duties. Apparently, that was beneath her. I mean, she was getting paid well to be eye candy. How much easier could a job be?"

The waitress returned with a smile. "Are you ready to order, Mr. Donovan?"

"Yes, sweetheart. I'll take another coffee and the eggs Benedict. Extra runny." He winked at her and patted her ass in her form-fitting black trousers.

The waitress gritted her teeth, plainly trying to keep a pleasant smile, and said, "Right away, Mr. Donovan."

"Are you eating *again*?" Konstantin's voice was disgusted,

but Donovan ignored it. He was much less intimidating over the phone.

"Yes, sorry about that. As it happens, this young woman was cleverer than we gave her credit for. Somehow, she managed to find our hidden books, and that's how she came up with the information. She changed her last name to Beaumont before leaving San Francisco—which is why I couldn't find her before—and recently moved to Washington, where she reconnected with her stepsister, Kelly Bradford. Now Kelly Vidal."

"Excellent work, Joseph. I knew we could count on you."

He clicked on a link to the *Washington Post's* Style section shared by Kelly Vidal and swiped the screen in search of what he had discovered earlier. "I'm sending you a photo that will help explain it all." He pulled up a photograph, magnified it with his portly fingers, and grinned. It was of three women standing hip to hip, arms interlaced at the waist, with a caption that read, "Sisters reunited at last, enjoying the company of Betty Carlyle-Masters."

He lowered his voice and added, "We find the sister, we find the bitch."

The waitress returned with the coffee tray. As she bent at the waist to put down the tray, Donovan put his hand on her ass again, feeling the material stretch over her pleasantly firm butt. "Don't go too far, honey, I'll need you later."

The young lady shut her eyes in disgust. She hurried off, nearly trotting, to go hide in the kitchens. The corners of Donovan's mouth curled at her response.

Konstantin came back on the other end. "Mm, yes. Very nice. I see what you mean about her tits. Such a shame, though. She would be a lot of fun." Donovan was about to speak but was interrupted. "Good, now for next part. We'll have to find her and then get her."

Donovan was apoplectic. "What? What do you mean? You

said you needed me to find her! I did! I was only responsible for finding her!"

Konstantin breathed into the phone. "Perhaps it is that you don't understand how this works. You find where she lives, and you lead me to her. You don't have to do dirty business. I have someone for that, but I need your help to execute it."

Donovan broke out in a sweat. "I thought my work was done."

Konstantin's voice was ice. "Your business with Mr. Fedorovich ends when he wants it to end. And he wants it to end slowly and painfully. Make no mistake. Someone will suffer. It can be her, or it can be you." He paused for a moment. "I do not care who, but I should hope that you do."

Donovan tugged at his tie, like loosening a noose tight around his neck, his jowls shaking like jelly. He pulled the handkerchief from his breast pocket and patted the sweat from his forehead and the back of his neck. His deal with the devil was getting worse. "I do. I just want to be done with this."

"Of course you do, Joseph," Konstantin said sympathetically. "We all do. Just do this, and you can enjoy your rewards with no more worries. Just be quick about it, for your sake."

The line went dead.

Donovan locked the tablet screen and tossed his phone to the table. He took the utensils, ready to start cutting into his breakfast, but stopped. His appetite was gone. He instead pushed the plate away and exchanged the utensils for his phone, giving the extra-runny eggs Benedict a second glance —but no. He waddled himself away from the table and left the lounge, not bothering to look back at the scenery.

12

Leesburg, Virginia
Monday, 5 May 2014

Hector left early Monday morning, hoping to avoid the worst of the commute to Tysons Corner on Route 7. He turned on Westpark, following the road to the Parabellum Risk & Security Enterprises complex, and parked in the open parking lot. One sure benefit of taking Chuck's job offer would be having a reserved space in the underground parking area. As important as the team leader position was, not to mention being responsible for others' lives, he still didn't rate a privileged parking spot.

Aside from the arched glass portico over the main entrance and a mirrored-window exterior, the high-rise wasn't much different from others in Tysons Corner. Hector swiped his badge at the lobby turnstiles and made his way to the two columns of elevator banks. He pressed the call button, and the doors to the elevator behind him opened immediately. That would change in a few hours, once the elevators were jammed with people making their way in. He walked in and selected the fourth floor.

For some reason, the elevator ride took him back to the day he decided to transition from soldier to private security contractor. He was midway through his umpteenth deployment when he got an email from his former Sergeant Major in the Rangers. Chuck had retired a year or so earlier, and now was asking if they could meet when Hector returned. They ended up meeting at J. Gilbert's, a steakhouse in McLean off Route 123, which gave him the impression Chuck was about to butter him up for something. Turned out that wasn't the case. Chuck just figured that after six months of food downrange, a nice juicy steak would be a welcome change. The rounds of eighteen-year-old Macallan whiskey, however, were another story. He had known other operators who went the way of private military contracting, but what made the difference with Parabellum was Chuck. He knew and trusted him implicitly. If Chuck was at the helm, his company would operate outside the ambiguous middle. The hefty paycheck helped with the decision, but what brought him over was Kelly's support and enthusiasm for something that would keep him home more frequently. It was the best of both worlds. He'd still get to be out in the field doing the job that fed his adrenaline addiction, and he'd be keeping Kelly happy.

He leaned against the elevator's back wall and blew hard. Kelly had an instinct about things like this. It was kind of freaky, actually. So why was it that he was still ignoring her?

You know why, the beast grunted.

The doors opened and he exited right, following a short hall to a metal door with a sign that read OPERATIONS CENTER. He pulled the badge attached to a lanyard around his neck and pressed it against the badge reader with a keypad next to it. He entered a passcode and pulled the door handle after a buzz. It was from here on that all similarities with the surrounding high-rises ended.

At the core of the building was an extensive operations

center that oversaw Parabellum missions worldwide. This was the brain, the center of operations he had helped plan and execute. Manned around the clock by three work shifts, the Tactical Operations Center—or TOC—was active year-round. And because of that, it housed a full kitchen, twenty single-person dormitory rooms, a common area game room, and large bathrooms that offered homelike comforts. He was glad for these on more than one occasion, like those times when he had the late shift or was snowed in. His dorm room was fully stocked for those reasons.

The TOC was bustling with activity, as usual. Hector helped himself to a cup of coffee from the break room. He filled the mug to the brim because, well . . . who would bother to drink anything other than straight black coffee?

Mug in hand, he approached a man who looked out of place in his white dress shirt, his rolled-up sleeves revealing hairy, muscular forearms. Moose was the Ops Chief—an important job, but a position disliked by most operators since it kept them from being in the field. Hector tapped him on the shoulder. "Morning, Moose. Got anything for me this morning?"

Corey "Moose" Elliot fit the call sign: big as a moose and just as hairy. His baritone voice rumbled, "Nothing different since the last update." He tilted his head toward the operations center and added, "But then again, the situation hasn't improved, either. It's dicey, brother. Everything could go to shit at any moment."

Hector nodded in agreement. "Roger that. It would have been nice to get the job months ago, but oh well. It is what it is. All right, I'm gonna head up and see the old man."

"Go easy, brother."

Hector made his way up to the fifth floor and to the east wing of the building, said good morning to Sylvia, Chuck's executive assistant, and walked into the conference room. He found Chuck leaning back in a leather chair at the end of an expansive polished Brazilian cherrywood table surrounded by writing pads, pens, and collated copies of their briefs for the meeting.

"Anything new?" asked Chuck without looking up, still flipping through pages in a binder.

"Nothing," Hector said, picking up a binder, ". . . yet."

Chuck nodded. "Well, let's keep our fingers crossed. Bill will be here soon, so we have some time to look things over. Let's hope that nothing sudden happens between then and now."

A light knock on the conference room door snapped them from their reading. Hector looked up to see Sylvia ushering in Bill Carson, the tall, strong-jawed Norton-Allied CEO with full silver hair and a self-assured appearance that perfectly complemented his slender build and tailored suit.

And then—*holy shit*. Hector's heart skipped a beat.

Next to him was none other than Jessica Beaumont—or maybe Jessica's evil twin, by the looks of it. She was dressed in a fitted black suit jacket with a white button-up blouse, form-fitting knee-length skirt, and black patent leather stiletto-heeled pumps that somehow made her legs look sexier than at the party. But it was her raven-black hair pulled tight in a ponytail that made her appear like a different woman. Her eyes seemed bluer, if that was even possible. This version of Jessica projected a commanding business aura, softened by the flattering feminine qualities of her perfect makeup and sculpted eyebrows that he had somehow missed the night of the party. He gulped and glanced over to Chuck, who either didn't remember Jessica or was one cool customer.

Chuck and Bill clasped hands with a viselike grip that turned their knuckles white. "Good to see you again, Bill. I hope the flight in from New York wasn't too bad."

"Not at all," he said with a Texas drawl. "I'm just sorry we couldn't make the party. Gretchen is dealing with some house remodeling business, but she did want me to ask when you and Betty would come up to the Hamptons."

Chuck smiled. "I'll let Betty know. I'm sure they'll figure something out."

Bill motioned to Jessica. "I'm sure you met Jessica Beaumont at the party."

Hector coughed. "Yes, we met briefly."

"Good. Then you'll be glad to know that she'll be the negotiator traveling with y'all. I'm glad you sent that email when you did, Chuck. I must admit, I was concerned you might object to her gender, but I'd be hard-pressed to find anyone else who can get you what you need from the Kurds."

Hector raised an eyebrow at the comment and exchanged looks with Chuck. He gave Chuck the slightest shake of his head with a gentle scowl. *Did you know?*

In turn, Chuck gave a barely visible shrug. *No, did you?*

Detecting doubt, Jessica spoke. "Gentlemen, I assure you that I can handle myself and will not require special accommodations." Her voice was strong and determined and bore nothing of the sultry tone Hector recalled from the party. "I am proficient in Arabic, I speak Kurdish, and I'm familiar with the regional customs. In your email, you asked for someone to negotiate terms with the Peshmerga? Well, that someone is me. I will still conduct an outreach program with the tribes in the region, per our agreement. I will gain their trust and loyalty and counter any bribing or strong-arming from Tienjing Petroleum. But just as important, I can work with the same tribes and have them be our human form of early warning detection if ISIS crosses east of the Mosul-Baghdad highway." She crossed her arms defiantly and cocked her hip. "And I'm not afraid to break a nail, if that's a concern." She made eye contact with each of the men. "Of course, if I misunderstood your needs, then please let me know. My feelings won't be hurt whatsoever."

Hector studied her, weighing her remarks.

For his part, Bill slowly nodded in agreement. "I've made up my mind about this, Chuck. She's the right choice for the job. She's a spitfire, and I think you'll find her extremely valuable over there."

Chuck looked to Hector for an opinion and got a simple shrug. She definitely hit the right notes on what they needed from Norton-Allied. Satisfied, Chuck motioned to the table, and each party went to their own side.

Hector clicked a remote control, and the large screen at the far end of the room showed the map he and Chuck had studied the previous weekend. "The Iraqis couldn't have picked a worse time to award oil bids, but there isn't much we can do about that now. Fortunately, the site you bid on is in the northeast, near the Kurdish border. The area is relatively stable in comparison to the rest of the country, and you've got Mosul to the west. As the second largest city in Iraq, Mosul is home to two divisions of the Iraqi army, including an armored division with M1A1 tanks. They will provide a buffer against an ISIS incursion to the east, but we're monitoring the situation for any changes that would affect our predictions or course of action while we set up.

"The near-term objective is to send Alpha Team to sync up with a Peshmerga unit at the Taq Taq outpost and set up a Forward Operating Base. It'll be a quid pro quo situation, but we're confident that we can operate long-term from there. We'll link with Alpha Team at the training site, but that's more of a formality. They'll ship out ahead of us and have things ready for us when we get there. We, Bravo Team, will deploy once the infrastructure is set and will assist you in conducting your outreach. Once we are satisfied with the external buffer provided by the Iraqi army and the success of the outreach program with the nearby villages, and we've established a good security posture around the site, we'll give you the green light to send your people and start operating that oil field. Once Alpha Team departs, we anticipate this phase will take as little as two months but no more than four."

Next, Chuck stood and walked to the screen opposite Hector. "Now, I know you still have some questions about how we operate and are able to secure and protect your investment, so this is where I'll answer that. Parabellum Risk and Security Enterprises isn't just private security. We provide an entire security package that includes a cadre of former special operators from across the military, like Hector. He spent ten years as an Army Ranger before joining us. We provide armored vehicles, helicopters, and boats, if necessary, to safeguard our clients, but we don't stop there. For austere locations, like your oil field, our logistics branch will provide your people with containerized housing units to live and work in, as well as a full suite of military-grade communications systems. We'll even set up in-room Wi-Fi and satellite television. I think you're going to find your people will be quite comfortable, considering the location."

The next hour of the presentation involved Chuck and Hector taking turns rattling off a precise list of the security personnel, support equipment, armored vehicles, and armaments that would be utilized. Chuck provided the why, Hector the how.

"Finally, the exfiltration plan, if an evacuation were to be necessary, would be to move south to Baghdad, if time allows, using the Iraqi army to cover our movement. If the situation is more dire, we'll move north to Irbil." Chuck scanned the room. "Are there any questions?"

Jessica's expression was stoic, unimpressed, and condescending. *Well, that's annoying,* Hector thought. Her piercing light-blue eyes went from Chuck to Hector. "You still haven't addressed the fact that competitors like Tienjing are actively paying off militias to harass other energy companies—the ones trying to access the regions not controlled by ISIS."

"That's because we can only control the area you intend

to operate in and safeguard those supply lines," Hector said. "We are aware of what Tienjing is doing on the ground and that ISIS is still pushing farther in, but there's nothing we can do about that. We are hired to defend your area of interest." He motioned to the map displayed on the presentation screen. "Besides, given Tienjing's losses to ISIS, they have more serious problems than harassing the competition."

"One more question, if you don't mind."

He took a deep breath. "Not at all."

"From a quasi-legal point of view, how are you able to take so many weapons into Iraq? Or any other place, for that matter?"

Hector turned to Chuck, who gestured for him to go ahead.

"I won't bore you with the details, but essentially when we are hired by, say, the state department or Norton-Allied, the host government allows us to act within the limited role of the purpose we were hired for. We can use weapons for self-defense or protection of our clients, but nothing more."

Her mouth curled at one corner. "I'm a lawyer, Mr. Vidal. I live for the details."

Hector was annoyed, for sure—but he thought he detected a hint of that sultriness from the party.

"Well." Bill closed his binder and gathered his things. "Is there anything else, Jessica?"

Begrudgingly content with the answer, Jessica nodded to Bill.

"There's one more thing," Hector chimed in. "As the team leader, I'm entirely responsible for ensuring the success of this mission and protecting the lives of everyone who goes on this mission." He met her serious poker face in a corporate version of a Mexican standoff. She was stone-cold and confident. Bill was right to have her on his team. "You seem to know your stuff, and you're sure of your abilities. That's commendable, but now I have one stipulation for you, Ms. Beaumont."

Jessica rapped her glossy red almond-shaped nails on the table, still holding Hector's stare. She leaned back on her chair and cocked her head, probably curious to know what this knuckle-dragging ape could want. "All right, let's hear it."

Hector leaned forward, interlaced his fingers, and rested his forearms on the table. "We will be traveling to a war zone where the situation can change in the blink of an eye. This is not combat tourism, Ms. Beaumont. We aren't going on a fact-finding mission. If you are to go, you will need to train for and pass our qualification requirements. You don't have to train for everything, but I expect you to take our exfil and tactical combat casualty courses and to qualify with the weapons you'll be issued. Because if it gets real, we'll need everyone to be a shooter."

He poked his index finger on the table and said, "We leave on six June." He dragged his finger back and added, "So we need three weeks to bring you up to speed before then. Since you are aware of the dangers, you'll understand why I want everyone on the same page." His face hardened. "My bottom line is this." He jabbed his finger on the table again. "You don't pass, you don't go. Simple as that. It's not an ego thing, Ms. Beaumont. I want to bring everyone back in one piece."

Her demeanor softened, and he could tell that the reality, and possible finality, of what she was signing up for was sinking in. She broke his stare and turned to Bill, who again nodded in agreement. She turned back to Hector, all arrogance and defiance evaporating from her voice. "Very well, Mr. Vidal. We have a deal."

"All right, then. We'll see you in San Antonio at the end of the week."

Jessica gasped, her full eyes widening at the comment. "Wait, what?" She opened her mouth, then closed it, and let out a sigh. "I guess I'll have to hand off my merger tasks to someone else in the department."

"You can split them with Paul Monroe," Bill said. "You should be back before the merger gala this summer. No need to hand off everything. Besides, I've been meaning to have him be more involved."

Jessica blushed. "Yes, sir. All right, Mr. Vidal. See you at the end of the week."

Chuck put his hands down on the table. "Perfect! Hector, why don't you walk Jessica to the TOC and go over the training schedule with her."

Hector nodded and escorted Jessica to the elevator, shaking Bill's hand again on the way out. *Jesus Christ, why her? As if it weren't bad enough that she's still in my head,* now *I'm gonna spend the next four months with her.* He subconsciously rubbed his face. *Kelly is gonna friggin' lose it.*

13

An awkward silence filled the hallway as Jessica waited for the elevator with Hector, but she couldn't stop herself from grinning. The thought of training to shoot guns was exhilarating—especially if they trained her to know if she was being followed. She could only trust the FBI to protect her identity from the Russian mafia for so long.

"You think this is all a cute joke, don't you?"

She turned to Hector, unsure of the question. "You mean the training?"

"No, I'm talking about playing me at the party," he said with gritted teeth. "You *knew* you were working with Parabellum and my team but didn't say anything, leaving us to look like idiots in front of Bill."

The doors finally opened, and they walked in. She waited for the doors to close. She raised both eyebrows and asked, "Would you have preferred I said it in front of Kelly?"

Hector stabbed the 4 button with his finger before turning to her. "Of course not. Don't play games with me, Jessica. But you had all night to find some time to tell me."

"Oh, *please*, Hector! Kelly took you away by the arm and scolded you in the kitchen like a child and then sent you out to be a good little boy and mingle with *her* guests." Hector opened his mouth, but Jessica went on. "She saw how you looked at me. Can you imagine what would have happened if she saw me with you, 'talking' about work? If your wife is anything like what she used to be, she's got a *really* ugly jealous side to her, and you *do not* want to feel that wrath."

The elevator chimed and the doors opened, giving both of them much-needed relief. "For what it's worth, I'm taking all of this seriously. Yes, I recognize I can be a flirt at times, but when it comes to work, I'm all business." She stepped out of the elevator, tipped her shoulder to her chin, and said innocently, "Well, most of the time."

Hector led her down the hall to the metal door, obviously trying not to glance at her. She grinned at his efforts. *Play nice, Jessica.* She hadn't lied; normally she *was* all professional when at work—if you want to get to the top, don't let the boys think you're willing to slut your way there—but this was different. This wasn't a coworker, this was a friend, kind of. Better—it was *Kelly's* husband. She smirked to herself. She should take it easy on him. He had vowed to keep her safe, and she didn't want to be a bitch to Kelly. She really wanted to have a sister again.

He brought his badge to a box and punched some numbers in. The door buzzed, and he led her inside and through a second door. "Welcome to the TOC," he said.

Jessica gasped. It was like something from a movie. The open-concept interior with desks and partitions in clusters was expansive, with signs overhead that read MIDDLE EAST/NORTH AFRICA, SUB-SAHARAN AFRICA, CENTRAL ASIA, MEXICO, and other signs too far away to read. Within each cluster were radios, mounted monitors, maps of their respective regions, and computer desks with multiple monitors. The back wall was composed almost entirely of large television screens showing a medley of network news channels from across the globe with a series of red digital clocks showing the exact time in Washington, Zulu, London, Abuja, Baghdad, Amman, Kabul, Kuala Lampur, and Canberra.

Am I in S.H.I.E.L.D., or what? Jessica thought.

"Right this way." Hector snapped her from her trance, and she followed him to an upraised Plexiglas-lined office in the center that overlooked the floor. The door closed behind them, and she was surprised when the sound was drowned out. He logged into a computer station and began clicking the mouse repeatedly. Then the large printer came to life.

While Hector printed the training registration and requirement files, she gazed out the Plexiglas, getting a better view of the operations center. The floor brimmed with activity as radios crackled and people gathered over large-print maps, while others walked from one point to another with a sense of urgency. It reminded her of some movie—every movie—where everyone raced to stop a devastating event before it was too late.

Hector came up beside her. "Inside are forms you'll need to fill out." He handed her a thick folder. "You'll need your physician to clear you before training begins. You'll get inoculated when you get to San Antonio, but you'll need your doctor to prescribe enough doxycycline to last through the deployment."

"Doxy-what?"

"Malaria pills," he clarified. "You'll also need to fill out the form for an Iraqi visa. Scan and send it back as soon as possible, and we'll expedite it." He tapped on the folder. "You'll also need to fill out next-of-kin forms and an ISOPREP form in the event you are captured, and—"

"*Captured*?" A long, cold chill ran down her spine.

Hector sighed deeply and nodded. "Yes. There is always that possibility."

A horrible feeling surged through her body. It was fear. Not sitting-in-a-roller-coaster-car fear, but that of the Russians catching up with her and . . .

"Jessica, are you okay?"

She shuddered an exhale but waved him off. "Yes, sorry."

Oh, God. What am I getting myself into?

He handed her more forms, gentler this time, and said softly, "You'll also need to sign some liability waivers saying you understand the risks of the mission." He handed her a folder with the newly printed forms. "Finally, you'll need to fill out the training package paperwork so we can process you for the pistol and rifle training course, the TCCC, and others. There's a training information packet inside and a packing list you'll want to pay close attention to. Any questions?"

Jessica felt the weight of the large stack of paperwork. She hadn't expected this to rival her normal legal counsel work. She gulped. *I could be captured.* Her mind started going to a very dark place, and another long, cold shudder wracked her frame. *Get out of your head about it, Jessica.*

She shook if off by glancing through the multiple forms, and she fixated on a medical form. Her jaw dropped. "I need a smallpox vaccine?" It wasn't so much the fact that she'd need one; it was his nonchalant nod that troubled her. She exhaled hard and said, "All right, Hector, I'll have most of these ready for you by the end of the week. Hopefully." She placed the forms inside her soft-sided briefcase and followed him out.

Before exiting the TOC, he said, "Expect an email from me today or tomorrow with information on your travel to San Antonio. Please be sure to read and follow the guidelines. And for God's sake, please don't tell anyone about this or go posting it on your social media. These are safety procedures in place for your security and ours."

A smile cracked Jessica's otherwise stoic demeanor as her mind conjured images of participating in some super-secret spy training. She was going to enjoy this.

Jessica collapsed onto the bottom step outside her townhouse, covered in sweat. Still panting, she took her phone out from her armband and went through the messages and prompts she'd received during her hour-long run. She had missed a call from Paul, but the follow-up text made her smile.

Tried calling you.
Are you busy tonight?

Jessica's heart stuttered at the memory of their last meeting.

I am now. Come by at 8. Don't be late ;)

14

Washington, DC
Friday, 9 May 2014

The Metro's Blue Line was thick with the morning rush. A clash of humanity ensued when the doors opened at the Foggy Bottom station. Jessica elbowed her way out of the train while those in the platform tried wedging in; it was a scene of controlled chaos that repeated itself each workday, but that was all right. Today, she wouldn't let that get to her, because tomorrow she would start a new journey.

As usual, she exited the station and walked to the Starbucks in the George Washington University Hospital. She stood in line with doctors, nurses, and other commuters as she waited to order her daily latte. The image of Paul at her door with drinks in hand crept into her mind. She shook her head at the memory and giggled—not that the other robotic customers in line would pay any mind to her gleeful outburst.

The barista called her name. Jessica retrieved her drink and proceeded north on 23rd Street to Washington Circle, her usual route to the Norton-Allied offices on Pennsylvania Avenue. On a whim, she crossed into Washington Circle with its landscaped area inside the traffic circle itself and the commanding statue of George Washington, then headed east on the bustling K Street. It was a beautiful morning after a fun-filled week with Paul; she didn't see the harm in arriving a few minutes late. Not even the panhandlers who aggressively begged for handouts could sour her mood.

Having enjoyed her brief exploratory detour through the traffic circle's small park, she entered the Norton-Allied building and stepped into one of the crowded elevators. She pressed the button to the seventh floor, which announced to the others that she was among the firm's higher echelon, and made her way to the back of the elevator. The doors were closing when a folded newspaper was wedged in at the very last second, forcing the doors open.

Paul entered the crowded car and unmistakably made eye contact with her. He kept his eyes on her, like a predator stalking its prey, and cut through the crowd to the rear of the elevator. He reached the corner and pressed up next to her. With eyes locked, they shared a knowing smile, filling the air with their pheromones. He had spent each night with her for the past week and had wanted to commute with her that morning, but she'd asked that they arrive at work separately to avoid any suspicion.

His singling her out after his arrival, not to mention his aggressive invasion of her personal space, was a deliberate violation of their agreement. But it did make her breathe harder, and she felt the back of her neck tingle. She wagged a finger at him and mouthed, "Now, now."

The doors closed and the elevator ascended. She smirked and muttered, "You didn't press a button."

Without missing a beat, Paul retorted, "Oh, I did. Multiple times, as I recall." His grin widened as her cheeks filled with color. He leaned closer. "But I can press it again. As many times as you like."

Jessica felt her temperature rise but resisted the urge to fan herself. Despite the elevator emptying with each stop, they kept to the corner of the elevator, facing each other, their proximity dangerously close.

The elevator chimed as they reached the seventh floor, and the doors opened. Paul said, "This is where we both get off, don't we?" His ice-blue eyes were penetrating, his tone sultry and direct.

Jessica's knees weakened. She mustered as much resistance to his wiles as she could and brushed past him, giving a slow wink, to sashay ahead of him, not once turning to look back. She walked past the reception desk and the phone banks, past the junior associate hub, and stopped at the double doors leading into the executive office. She sensually tipped her chin to her shoulder, a gesture she was sure he would recall from the party.

She went to pull on the door but was stopped abruptly. She recognized Paul's cologne and his strong hands on her bare shoulders. She turned her head and whispered with feigned urgency, "I need to get to work, Paul. I'm late enough as it is."

Paul leaned in closer, using his chin to brush aside the raven-black hair she'd worn loose lately, and grazed his nose against her exposed neck. *Oh . . . God.* He tightened his grasp on her toned shoulders, pulled her back against his chest, and whispered, "I need to see you again, tonight. Before you leave."

Jessica sensed the anticipation in his voice and deliberately let his grasp linger. His breaths became more forceful. She let his desperation build up, then said, "But I have so much to pack, Paul." Which wasn't true at all, but he made it so easy to string him along.

His grasp tightened, like a savage taking something and making it his by virtue of wanting. The intensity of his action sent a jolt through her body. Her heart pounded against her chest.

Paul gritted his teeth and forcibly turned her to him. "Don't lie to me, baby. I saw your bags set in the closet. Is it someone else? The guy you're gonna be spending three weeks with?"

His fury was so raw, like a wild animal. It took everything in her power not to melt on the spot. She shook off his grip. "Of course not, Paul! You don't have to worry about him. It's purely business."

She surprised herself by defending Hector, something she never intended. She traced her fingers along Paul's shoulders and down to his arms. In a playful voice, she asked, "Why, Paul Monroe, are you jealous?"

Paul eased off, grinning. "Not at all. Those guys are always trying to pull this 'oh, baby, you don't know the things I've seen, have some pity on me' shit on hot chicks. I don't want you to be just another one in a series." He took a step toward her, slid his hand onto her exposed shoulder. "With me, if I use my mouth, you know *exactly* what I do with it. Don't you, baby?" He gazed into her eyes as his hands caressed her arms up to her shoulders and back down, inching closer to her.

Jessica shuddered, her knees wobbling. She was suddenly mindful of the whisker burns between her legs. Despite that, she willed herself to regain control. She parted her lips and whispered in his ear, "And you think that's getting you anywhere, hmm?"

She let the words linger as she slipped from his grasp and disappeared through the double doors with a conniving grin.

15

Friday afternoon, Kelly had gone with Alex Portman and the Columbia Investments merger team to the Norton-Allied building to discuss post-merger details. She was about to give a brief explanation of the meeting's agenda as they stepped off the elevator when she spotted Paul and Jessica walking into the seventh-floor conference room together, dangerously close to one another. He kept his hand at the small of her back, and Jessica laughed at whatever cute or stupid thing he said. Kelly seethed at the sight of his hand sliding down to Jessica's butt, as if by mistake. The sisters had talked on the phone several times in the past week, and Jessica's "thing" with Paul had become more than just flirting, as she had referred to it each time they had talked. Deep inside, she was incensed. There was something about him she didn't like, but she was committed to making her reunion with Jessica work —no matter the unintended consequences.

Two hours later, the meeting was nearing its end. Kelly had barely engaged in the discussions once her presentations were over. She was distracted by Jessica and Paul sitting in the back row, far too close. Whispering in each other's ears. Quietly laughing and flirting, as if they were in the back corner of some hook-up bar. It infuriated her. Jessica was supposed to be a professional, for fuck's sake. Maybe Jessica hadn't changed at all. A tinge of worry gnawed at Kelly, and she feared that perhaps she expected too much from her stepsister.

"All right, everyone," said Alex, snapping her back to earth. "I suggest we break for today." He looked at the clock on the wall. "Let's reconvene tomorrow morning and hammer out these last details before moving on."

Kelly should have followed him, but instead walked up to Jessica, still escorted by Paul. Even with her Senior VP status, Kelly was still intimidated by Jessica, and the thought of standing up to her sent shivers down her back. She took a deep breath. "Jessica, do you have a minute?" Her voice was so soft, she almost had to repeat herself.

"Hey, Kel," Jessica said casually. "What's up?"

"Do you mind if we talk in private for a bit?" she asked quietly. "It'll be quick."

Jessica looked to Paul, who shrugged and put his hand on the small of her back. "That's fine. I'll wait for you at the elevator." He left without acknowledging Kelly.

Once Paul was out of hearing distance, Kelly gathered her courage and leaped off the deep end. "Jesus Christ, Jessica! What is it with you and him? We're at an important meeting, and you two are acting like you're in the back of some sleazy bar."

Jessica's retort came like a serpent's strike. "What do you care, Kelly?"

"Because you're my sister and it reflects poorly on me!"

Jessica sneered. "Worry about your husband and the shit on your end."

Kelly's blood hit a boiling point, and it took everything she had to keep from pulling Jessica by the hair and throwing her to the ground. "You're supposed to be a professional, Jessica. Not some middle-school cheerleader. Start behaving like it." To her discomfort, they were drawing looks from others nearby. She lowered her voice. "Is it too much to ask that you focus on the merger instead of hiding in the back and playing footsie with Paul?"

Jessica pulled her arm from Kelly's grip. "Yeah, it is! Don't come into *my* office and tell me how to behave. I have far more important issues to focus on, Kel. Life-or-death issues."

"I'd hardly call your workload life-or-death issues, Jessica."

Jessica crossed her arms and scoffed. "You mean Hector hasn't told you?"

Kelly became rigid, afraid that her fears about Hector and Jessica were true. She gathered her courage. "Told me what?"

"Oh my *God*, Kel. Do you *ever* talk to your husband? He's taking me to Texas with him, for three weeks. He's going to train me to do the things he does. Has he *ever* taken you to Texas?"

A rage coursed through Kelly that she'd never felt before, and she fought not to lose control. *This fucking bitch!* "Why? Why would he bother training a little shit like you?"

Jessica threw her head back and laughed. Kelly wanted to just slap the living shit out of her. "Oh, this is too rich." Jessica feigned catching her breath. "Because, honey, we're going to be together for *months* in Iraq. For the acquisition of the oil field. Why the fuck do you think I'm in all your boring merger meetings?"

Kelly's body trembled out of control. Her eyes started to well up, which only fed the queen bee with the acid tongue.

"But don't worry, Kel. I'll be sure to take good care of him —just like Kevin Donaldson."

Jessica spun on her heel, laughing as she made her way back to Paul at the elevator.

Kelly ran to the nearest bathroom, making a quick search of the stalls, then launched herself at the sink and let all the hate, hurt, and fear out. She hated herself for welcoming

Jessica, for inviting her into her home, and for fooling herself into thinking that she had changed. Kelly bawled without a concern for her appearance.

When she'd let enough of the pain out, she confronted herself in the mirror and didn't like who was looking back.

So he was going on this mission anyway. And he was taking her stepsister with him.

Why? Why hadn't Hector said anything? She was trying, dammit! She was honestly trying to keep their marriage together, only to feel it falling apart at every turn. She could barely stand for Hector and Jessica to be together for five minutes at the party, and now they were going to be spending months together.

She would've confronted him the second she got home, if he were still here, but no. The coward had left two days ago without a single mention of Jessica or the mission.

She stumbled into one of the stalls, closed the door, and sat on the seat. She tugged on the roll until she had a wad of paper in her hand. *Why couldn't he tell me? Does he not trust me?* She sobbed into the ball of paper. *Does he want to leave me for her? No, God, please. Please not that. Why can't he see that I still love him so much that it hurts to breathe?*

16

San Francisco

Donovan was up later than he probably should have been, but his eyes were burned into the small television screen. The network news was playing a segment of a series based on the continued violence in Syria, with this one focusing on the release of the "Caesar photos" and the implication by the Assad regime. The anchor gave a brief background on how a former Syrian military officer known only as "Caesar" had smuggled out thousands of photos of torture victims in regime prisons. "As a viewer caution, these pictures may disturb you."

Donovan changed the channel without a second thought. He examined the glass of whiskey in his hand, his heart now racing at the thought of Yuri. His stomach churned.

Fedorovich is one bloodthirsty son of a bitch.

He flipped channel after channel, unable to find some-thing to soothe him. His phone buzzed. Donovan forced his body to roll forward, and he grabbed the phone from the coffee table. He recognized the international number and cursed Konstantin.

"Hello?"

"Your email got my attention, Joseph. So, you said you knew how to get the bitch. Please, do tell."

Donovan flopped back on the couch. "No, I said I *found* someone who can get her to us. But I'll need your help if he refuses."

He heard Konstantin take a drag off a cigarette, then blow the air out. "Of course. I am at your service. So, who is this person?"

Donovan thumbed the screen a few times and found a photo of Jessica with a tall blonde guy at some bar, both smiling without a care in the world. He fixated on Jessica, clenching his teeth as he stared hard at the woman who was ruining his life. "I just sent you a photo. That's who I need you to 'convince,' if he doesn't play ball with us."

"Interesting. Who is he?"

"That's Paul Monroe, an aspiring senior associate at Norton-Allied."

He hadn't noticed it before, but the way the bitch looked at the man was telling. She was all dreamy-eyed about him. That was good for him—bad for her.

Konstantin chortled. "This kid is your contact? Have you gone mad, Joseph? How is he supposed to help us?"

Donovan shook his head disapprovingly. He swiped the screen several times until he got to Paul's profile, highlighting some of entries and posts Paul had commented on, and sent them to Konstantin. "You see that? Not only does he work with her, but they've seen each other daily. He can't stop posting photos with her and commenting about her. What matters is that he's ambitious. With the proper motivation, he'll practically deliver her to us. If he doesn't . . . Well, that's when you play your part."

"He looks like little bitch. He will tip her off."

"That won't happen if you make it clear that if he so much as hints anything to her, Antonin is going to make sure he regrets that decision." Donovan took another sip of his drink. "Besides, Paul won't be able to refuse a strong recommendation from influential senior partners at some very prestigious banks and lose the opportunity to skyrocket to the top."

"I like this side of you, Joseph! I was worried I was going to have to deliver you to Antonin. It has been so long since you made that promise to me."

Donovan felt the trickle of sweat rolling down his forehead and his fat cheeks. "No need for that, Konstantin. I made you a promise and I'm working hard to deliver."

"You are, Joseph. You are. Just keep that in mind, be productive, and everything will be fine. Have a good night, Joseph."

The call ended, and Donovan plopped back onto the sofa. He wiped the sweat off his forehead and considered his next move.

17

Old Town Alexandria

Paul woke to the sound of his phone buzzing. His free arm patted around the nightstand until he felt the sleek screen. He answered it, not bothering to look at the caller ID. "Hello?" he slurred groggily.

"Sorry to wake you up so late, Paul, but there is a matter of some urgency we must talk about, and it would be better to do so now than later." The voice on the other end was upbeat and didn't appear to want to wait until the morning. "Can we talk?"

Paul wiped his eyes and looked at the alarm clock on the nightstand. The gentle blue neon numbers read 1:45 a.m. He closed his eyes and laid his head back on the pillow. "Who is this and why can't this wait until the morning?"

"My name is Joseph Donovan, senior partner at Pacific Bank and Trust in San Francisco. I work with your supervisor Alex Portman from time to time. Your future could very well depend on the outcome of this conversation. I should think you'd be rather interested in that."

Paul peeked at the naked back of the woman lying next to

him, ignoring the way the moonlight highlighted the curvature of her feminine features beneath the sheets. "I am interested," he whispered. "Give me one minute."

He slid his arm from under her head and slowly got off the bed, keeping his eyes on the woman and pausing whenever she moved. Once out of the bed, he picked up his boxers from the floor and put them on, quietly walked to the living room, and sat on the end of the sofa. "All right, Mr. Donovan. You have my attention."

"I'm glad to hear that, Paul, because quite frankly your future from this point on can only skyrocket with remarkable success at Norton-Allied . . . or come to a very finite and quite possibly tragic end." There was a long pause. "At least now, with your interest, you can assure the better of the two outcomes become a possibility, instead of . . . Well, no need to bring that up now."

Paul leaned forward and responded with an equally stern tone, "I don't respond to threats, Mr. Donovan. If you know who I am, then you also know that my father sits on the board of directors at Mid-Atlantic Trust and has very powerful friends. So how about you drop the bullshit and tell me why you are waking me up in the middle of the night to talk about something that can't wait for tomorrow?"

"Straight to the point, I like that. This is about Jessica Beaumont."

Paul's breath hitched in his throat. He glanced at the bedroom door.

"There is an issue I need your help with," Donovan continued, "and it must be sooner rather than later. You see, some time ago she made some very powerful enemies. The kind of people who don't like unnecessary scrutiny into their business, if you get my meaning. Quite frankly, she backstabbed the wrong people, Paul. Me included. And I need your help in making sure she is made an example of."

"What exactly do you mean, Mr. Donovan? I don't

follow." Paul rubbed his eyes with his thumb and index finger. His mind spun as he imagined being asked to forge documents, alter financial numbers, or even ask his father for some unsavory, illegal request that literally came in the dark of the night.

"Must I really have to say it, Paul?"

A cold shudder ran down his spine as his half-asleep mind took in the meaning. "Are—are you taking about killing her?"

"*Killing* is such an ugly term." Donovan answered coolly. "But you shouldn't concern yourself with that. The fact is, she made an enemy of a very powerful man with no scruples and a very long reach, and she'll pay dearly for that, Paul. The question you need to ask yourself is if you want to be at her side when she goes down or make an opportunity of it. Those are the only two outcomes. There is nothing in-between."

Paul's heart began racing. He jumped to his feet and paced the room. "Whoa! Wait, just wait." He ran his hand through his hair, trying to think. "Why do you want her? I mean, what did she do? This is some serious shit, man! What are you gonna do to her?"

"You're damned right—this is some serious shit, Paul. So, you better think hard about the next words that come out of your mouth." This was the real threat. "Don't worry what's going to happen to her, just be grateful it won't be you. Now, you asked what she did. That's a very long story, but let's just say Jessica is not the woman she says she is. Nor is she as sweet as she makes herself out to be."

Paul paced nervously. The threat was nothing like anything in the past, where the consequence was expulsion, or a lawsuit easily countered by the mere mention of his father or his intervention. Nothing during his years at Columbia, or even observing his father, the master of manipulation, had prepared him for an actual threat upon his life.

"Look, man, this isn't funny. Jessica isn't a threat to

anybody. There's got to be something else you want from me, right?"

"You're correct, Paul, this isn't funny, and it sure as hell isn't a joke. Ask yourself this—how long do you think your little fling will go before she plays you on her way to the top?"

Paul's pacing slowed. "She wouldn't use me like that. And even if she did, I'd see it before it even happened."

"Paul, please. I thought you were smarter than that. Please don't make me reconsider telling you all this. But fine, I understand. She's an attractive girl, Paul. It's so easy to fall under her spell. I don't blame you at all."

"I'm not under her spell, Mr. Donovan!"

"Fine, you're not. Keep telling yourself that. But just in case you still doubt me, ask her who Jessica Bradford is. Or who Yuri Kamarov is. Better yet, ask her about her past. Ask her about San Francisco. She hasn't told you about that, has she? She'll use you just like she used me. Besides, you still haven't even heard what's in it for you. So sit your ass down, and listen." He paused a moment. "Are you sitting, Paul? Are you ready to listen?"

What had Jessica done to this man? Come to think of it, Jessica had never really explained how'd she'd gotten her promotion to DC in the first place . . .

Paul sat. "I'm listening."

"Good. Your part is quite simple, really. And once you've done your part, I will give you the information of five individuals representing the largest banks and investment firms in Russia and Europe, along with very high referrals and recommendations from a silent partner who will insist they do business with Norton-Allied. Then you and I will travel to Zurich and have a face-to-face meeting to ensure that they work exclusively with you. You'll easily bring in over half a billion dollars in investments to the firm. When the old man sees what you did, you'll be on track to become the youngest senior partner in the firm's history. More importantly, you'll have your father's approval. Now, does that ease your worry?"

In the same conversation, Donovan had threatened Paul's life and offered him something his own father wouldn't give him willingly. Paul refused to believe his father's sermon about "paying one's dues" before reaping the rewards of hard work. In today's corporate environment, making the right connections and tapping the right networks was what got you on the fast track to success.

Donovan was now offering that fast track—but with significant strings attached. It was a Faustian deal, for sure, except this one would offer someone else's soul.

As Donovan spoke, Paul crept to the foyer, grabbed Jessica's purse from a hook, and sneaked back to the sofa. His hand trembled as he began going through her purse. He went through her wallet, pulling out every credit card, insurance card, and identification he could find. There, deep in the card sleeves, were a California driver's license issued to Jessica Bradford and an American Express card with the same name.

Un-fucking-believable. He tried to keep from imagining all the possible things she was keeping from him, or worse, that she already knew about him. *This is insane! She would never! But could she? Would she?*

Come to think of it, he hardly knew anything about her, whereas she knew more about him than she was letting on. He put everything back in the purse and said in a meek tone, "Can I think this over and get back to you, Mr. Donovan?"

"Of course, Paul," he said condescendingly, "although I can't imagine why you would even need to think more on the issue—but sure, go ahead and take the rest of the night to think it over. Just don't take too long." Paul was about to hang up when Donovan added, "And Paul, don't go around thinking out loud, either. I'd hate for you to suffer horribly for a mere lack of judgment. You have until tomorrow night to give me your answer." Donovan hung up without waiting for Paul to respond.

Paul rested his head between his hands, shaking his head. *This can't be happening!* His mind was still trying to wrap around what was being asked of him, trying to think of some alternative to exploit. He could hear his father admonishing him now: "That's what happens when you get mixed up with a girl like that and take your eyes off the prize, boy!"

He hadn't realized how little he knew about Jessica. From the moment he laid eyes on her, he could tell she'd be a challenge. But this was so different. She was like him in a sense, driven and relentless. And then there was his ultra-ambitious ego that demanded he rise to the top without delay. And if he did this, he would.

His pride and sense of self-preservation made the decision for him.

"Paul? Where are you?" The half-asleep question came from the naked woman in the bedroom. "Come back to bed." He deleted the call from his phone's history and went back to the bedroom. He dropped his boxers and slid into the bed. The woman turned and draped her arm across his body, laying her face on his bare chest. "Where were you?"

He tilted her face up to his and kissed her lips. "Sorry, baby, I just went to get some water. Go back to sleep. You have an early flight." She nestled her head against his shoulder and fell back asleep.

Paul stared into the ceiling and let out a deep sigh, dragging his fingers along her back with long strokes.

18

San Antonio International Airport
Saturday, 10 May 2014

Jessica strutted the length of the terminal, making every effort to avoid eye contact with anyone. Still, she stole peeks through the corners of her black-and-gold Dolce & Gabbana sunglasses with their oversize gradient lenses. She needed to be incognito, even if the sleeveless white blouse and the black leggings tucked into knee-high stiletto-heeled boots she wore clashed with the more casual attire worn by so many other travelers. Not to mention the hard-sided rose gold carry-on she towed.

The excitement of this "secret" training had kept the butterflies in her stomach active since she left her place. In her mind, it equated with agent commando training that would transform her into a lethal international spy. The packing list dictated she bring personal items, hot weather clothing, two leather or webbing belts, and two pairs of hiking shoes for walking over rough terrain. But surely that couldn't be all.

She rode the escalator down to the baggage claim and was met by Hector at the carousel. She was surprised to see him wearing a faded brown cap with an American flag on the front, a light-green button-up shirt, lightweight khaki cargo pants, and hiking boots. Not the black suit with dark aviator sunglasses she had envisioned.

"Jessica, how was your flight?"

"It was awful. Getting out of Reagan National was a nightmare, as usual. The flight was overbooked, and the layover in Chicago—that was the worst. My connecting flight was delayed *two hours*," she said, emphasizing with two fingers, "and I was stuck at an overcrowded gate waiting to be let on the plane."

Hector laughed. "That's just terrible. I thought you'd be flying business class or better. What happened?"

Jessica lifted her sunglasses over her head, revealing her resting bitch face. "I did fly business class, thank you very much." He was obviously having a laugh at her expense, which only infuriated her. "Are you laughing at me?" she asked indignantly. "I'm not some spoiled princess, Hector. I've had a very bad day so far. I've been traveling since I left my place at seven, and it's now five." She crossed her arms and cocked her hip. "It's been a very long flight, I'm tired, I'm hungry, and I really need a drink."

Hector flipped his wrist down and looked at the large face of his black digital watch. "Actually, it's four here in Texas."

She glowered at the comment.

"While I'm sure you had a terrible flight," he mocked, "you should know we'll be traveling for forty-eight hours in an aircraft not intended for the comfort of the passengers. So please excuse me if I'm not empathetic to your complaints."

Jessica huffed.

They stared at the empty conveyor belt in silence. Finally, after a long and quite uncomfortable wait, Jessica spotted the unmistakable larger version of her rose gold carry-on making its way to them.

Hector lifted it up from the conveyor belt. "All right, let's get going." He started walking to the exit.

"Wait! There's one more." She pointed to an even bigger version of the other two.

Hector stopped in mid-stride, mouth agape, and palmed his face. "You *do* know we're only training for three weeks, right? You read that packet I gave you?"

Jessica's resting bitch face, complete with cocked hip to the side, reappeared. "Of course I did. And this is three weeks' worth of clothing, just like the packing list prescribed. Plus some personal items."

"Are you kidding me? Jesus Christ, Jessica! The Lewis and Clark expedition didn't take this much baggage!" He took a deep breath and exhaled slowly. "Fine! Let's just go." He stalked to the exit, not bothering to look back and see if Jessica was following.

"Hector, wait!" She struggled to pull the heavier bag off the belt and raced after him. When she stepped outside the sliding doors, she was assaulted by the heat from all sides. She'd regret bringing some of the things she packed. *Ugh! Even the wind is hot!* She stopped after a few paces to fan herself, already panting and sweating profusely, and repeated the process until they reached the elevator.

On the ride up to the third level of the parking garage, she tugged the damp blouse from her skin with thumb and index finger in a vain effort to cool down. She felt gross underneath and worried her makeup would melt off her face any moment.

The doors opened, and Jessica was relieved that the blinkers of a silver Toyota Land Cruiser nearby flashed. Hector loaded her luggage in the back while she climbed into the cab.

She immediately leaned forward to the air vent and let the slightly-less-hot air blow inside her blouse. She sighed, wiping the sweat off her brow. "Oh my God, I had no idea it was so hot here."

Hector reversed from the parking space and gave her an unamused stare. "It was in the packet, under 'acclimatization.'"

She sneered and was about to retort, but she decided differently. There was no point in continuing the bickering and making the rest of the three weeks a nightmare. The only saving grace was that the air conditioning finally turned cold.

The drive north on scenic Highway 281 was splendid as they traversed the green Texas Hill Country. The sun was getting low on the horizon. The last blinding rays of sunlight accented her dimples, exposing her infectious excitement for what the next three weeks would bring. Hector smiled with her and said, "You're gonna have a blast, no pun intended. But just know that it's going to be a lot of hard work. I'm going to push you hard and test your limits. There will be times you'll hate me, but we'll get you ready."

Jessica noted the warnings, which did little to dampen her child-like eagerness to learn real military and survival things. She giggled, unable to contain herself. *I'm going to learn spy things!* She imagined herself back in the office, shooting down any man who tried to pull his fake macho poser crap on her.

She admired the vast clear sky and the bands that brushed it in yellow, orange, and blue hues that grew darker the farther they stretched from the sun. In the deeper shades of blue, the first few stars started to appear. "So how much longer until we get there?"

"A couple of hours more."

"Jesus, Hector! Are we driving to Oklahoma?!"

He grinned. "Texas is a big state."

Okay, so he was funny. Jessica would give him that. When

she had threatened Kelly with taking care of her husband like Kevin Donaldson, she hadn't really meant it. Hector was *not* her type. He had no sense of society or style—as his outfit suggested. She had just wanted to get back at Kelly for what she'd said. Jessica had *earned* her job, dammit, and nothing she did was any of her bossy sister's business.

At the thought of her sister and the fight Jessica's words had probably started, Jessica's mood dampened. "So, I don't mean to pry, but . . . have you talked to Kelly since you left?"

Hector gripped the steering wheel tighter and checked the mirrors as tension filled the cabin. "No. Why?"

She took a deep breath. *I hope you know what you're doing, girl.* "Hector, I have a confession to make." She hesitated, then said, "I . . . told Kelly."

Even with sunglasses on, she felt the daggers he shot at her. "You did *what*?"

She winced. "I told her. About my coming to Texas . . . with you. And going on the trip to Iraq . . . with you."

"Goddammit!" He hammered his fist into the steering wheel, and she caught a glimpse of a part of him she wished she hadn't conjured. "Why the *fuck* would you tell her that, Jessica?"

"I'm sorry! We got into a heated argument at work and . . . she just made me *so* angry that I couldn't help myself. I just lost it and lashed out at her!"

She quaked as he hammered the steering wheel, again, and again, and again. As if some primal beast were trying to break out from inside him. The tendons in his neck flared out. He shot her a look that made her wish she could melt into the seat. She sat perfectly still, not daring to move a single muscle.

He rubbed his face from side to side, then rubbed the back of his neck. He checked the mirrors once more, then put both hands on the steering wheel. She noted his more passive demeanor, giving the impression that the anger had taken its course, and she sure as hell wasn't going to change that.

"Yeah," he exhaled. "She has that effect on people."

At the risk of infuriating him, she considered probing further. *Girl! Are you serious, right now?* She waved off the comment and turned to him. "Do you mind me asking why you didn't tell her?"

"Yes, I fucking mind!"

She quickly turned forward and looked down at her feet. *You just can't help yourself, can you?*

"I didn't tell her because of the same reason you lashed out at her."

She gulped. "How do you mean?"

"I'm sure she's told you about our fights."

"Yeah." Her tone was sincere. "She told me about it the other night."

"So then she probably told you we're not in a good place?"

"Yeah, but she also told me she's trying hard."

"Well, that's the thing." He rubbed his mouth. "I know she's trying, but at the same time, she wants me to stop doing what I love and take a job that I'm not sure I want. I understand why she keeps bringing it up, but she's just so goddamned pushy about it that she infuriates me, and I forget about everything she's done up to then."

"Oh, yeah." She nodded. "That's Kelly, all right. She's been like that ever since we were girls."

"Then there you go."

Jessica saw him in a new light. Sure, she'd had her fun with him at the party, been irritated by his machismo at the meeting, and now been scared at his outrage. But this was something entirely new, something she didn't have with anybody outside of her parents. In a way, he understood her. Understood what it was like to be under Kelly's shadow and rip apart something special because of her ill-placed doggedness. Okay, maybe not all that, but enough to form a bond over. Maybe three weeks with him would be good. It could give her an insight into Kelly that maybe she hadn't seen before.

They got off Highway 281 and headed west on a dirt road, driving directly into the sun as it disappeared below the horizon. A slight chill came over her, and she crossed her arms and hugged herself.

"Would you like me to put the heater on? We still have another ninety minutes to go."

Jessica shook her head, even as she rubbed her arms. "No, I'm all right. I love this scenery and the road is rocking me to sleep. I was just getting cozy." She rested her head against the door, exhaling softly, her eyelids growing heavier.

19

It was pitch-black when Jessica opened her eyes. The only light came from the instrument panel and the ocean of stars that stretched across the night sky. She hadn't realized she'd fallen asleep and was both disoriented and uncertain about her surroundings. She was about to ask Hector where they were when she noticed him focusing on something directly ahead of them.

"Where are we?" she whispered.

Hector leaned over to her, still keeping his eyes fixated in the darkness ahead. "We're at the entry checkpoint," he said with calm reassurance. "The guard is just making sure everything is in order before letting us proceed."

Jessica squinted, leaned forward to peek into the darkness. "What guard?"

"Right over there." Hector pointed with a knife-hand, something she had seen him do back at Parabellum headquarters but only now picked up on.

A disembodied red light flickered three times, and Hector turned the headlights on. In front of them was a man in a black uniform with a rifle slung across his chest, standing in front of a metal gate.

Jessica gasped. The guard had been standing in front of them the whole time, and she never knew it. How did he do that? Just . . . stand in darkness. She wasn't sure if she had ever been surrounded by such darkness back home, even during a blackout. The city's ambient light always made it possible to see most things. Her introduction to the experiences of the next three weeks was exciting, and the training hadn't even started.

The guard opened the gate, and Hector waved. "Thanks, Sheepdog, have a good one."

"You too, Gung Ho." He nodded at Jessica. "Miss. Have a good night."

As the car crossed the checkpoint, Jessica heard the guard talking into his radio through the open SUV window. "Guardian, Sheepdog. Spartan Two-Zero and one pax crossing the wire, over."

She was unable to make out the response. Silence settled back over the SUV. Jessica suddenly turned to Hector with a skeptical grin. "Gung Ho?" She raised her eyebrow. "What was that all about?"

"My call sign."

Jessica laughed with equal amusement and disbelief. "Gung Ho? That's your call sign? Please tell me you didn't choose that."

Hector turned his attention back to the road, hesitated, then said, "When I first came to Parabellum, I was around guys who had done far more things than me and were better than I could ever hope to be. These guys were the best of the best. Special operators, Navy SEALs, PJs, and Marine Force Recon . . . titans in their profession."

He slowed as he turned the wheel to follow a sharp right turn. "So, to prove myself to them, I did everything at full throttle all the time, no holding back. This, of course, did little to impress them and only ended up wearing me down by the end of the first week." Completing the turn, he again picked up speed, making the drive bumpier. "That first Friday, I damn near killed myself trying to do something as simple as fast-roping, something I had done hundreds of times before."

She gave him a quizzical look.

He glanced at her and explained, "Fast-roping is when you slide down from a hovering helicopter by a static rope. Somehow I got it in my head that this had to be the best fast-rope slide I ever did. I started sliding down but didn't get a good grip and ended up falling on my ass. So, for my troubles, I got a bad rope burn and a heavily bruised ego. After a long laugh at my expense, my team leader came over to me, slapped me on the shoulder, and said, 'Easy there, Gung Ho, you don't have to save the world all on your own.' Anyways, the name stuck, and that's how I got my call sign."

Jessica doubled over in laughter, holding a hand to her chest. "I'm sorry, Hector—I mean, 'Gung Ho.'" She laughed harder still. "Sorry, I just had to."

He laughed as well. "It's okay, I deserve it."

"Will I get a call sign?"

"Everybody gets a call sign."

She perked up. "Really? Even me? Can I pick it?"

"Hell no, you can't pick it!"

"Please!" She thought of all the cool-sounding spy-like call signs she could come up with. "I could be Black Widow or Huntress"—her voice sped up and grew more animated—"or maybe even something out of a James Bond movie!"

"Easy there, killer!" Hector said, waving a hand. "First of all, *you* don't pick your own call sign. Second, it sure as hell ain't gonna be something out of some James Bond movie or a comic book hero."

Jessica pouted as her hopes deflated.

Hector let out a laugh. "Don't get ahead of yourself there, killer. First let's get you signed in and settled in your pod."

Minutes later, the ambient light of the training facility lit up the night sky. When they crested the last hill, the Parabellum training facility in the valley below materialized. It was much bigger than what she had imagined. Though, to her disappointment, it resembled nothing from a James Bond movie or the *Avengers*.

The walls around the facility were at least twenty feet high, and the front stretched the length of a football field. It was impossible to tell how deep the facility went, but the fact that the lights kept going farther was a good indication this place was no joke. The steel door at the entrance of the compound slid open as they approached, letting them drive in. The interior was formed by a *U*-shaped formation of shipping containers converted into living units, stacked in twos, with metal railings and stairs linking the three sides of the upper housing units. Beyond the makeshift courtyard, she could make out what seemed like an obstacle course on one end and a warehouse on the other.

"Jesus Christ, Hector! It's huge!"

"That's what she said," he snickered.

Jessica rolled her eyes. "Very funny, Hector. Very mature." She chuckled. "Yeah, I guess I did leave myself open to that. That's what I get for working with blood-sucking lawyers day in and day out."

In the center of the *U* was a makeshift courtyard. A firepit with benches and chairs around it was the focal point, with a wet bar on the far end and string lights stretched across to top it all off. They parked next to other Land Cruisers and walked the short distance to the courtyard.

Sitting by the fire and at the bar were a group of twenty or so rugged men that could easily be mistaken for bikers or pirates. In any case, they seemed to be drinking and laughing like either of those. Tending the bar was a woman with loose dirty-blonde hair who wore a sleeveless denim top. Even from this distance, Jessica could tell that she didn't put up with any of the machismo from the men drinking and joking under the Texas night. She smiled. This was what she was hoping for. The scene reminded her of the old westerns she used to watch with her father. It was easy to imagine herself in the midst of banditos, gunslingers, and desperados.

"Come on, let me introduce you first." Hector led her to the bar, passing the group around the firepit, and called out, "Listen up!" Everyone stopped talking and turned their attention to him. "I'd like to introduce you all to someone."

"I'll be damned! Gung Ho got himself a pretty girl he wants to show off." The comment came from a white man with a long golden beard and matching ponytail. "Why don't you give us a little turn, darlin'?" He got a round of laughs and catcalls.

Jessica was immediately taken aback. She'd faced machismo and sexist attitudes before, but never so . . . blatantly. And yet, it was such a turn-on. *Oh my. The fun a girl could have with a group like this. Don't all come at once, boys. I'm not that easy.*

"Don't you worry about Cujo, hon." The woman behind the bar had a low and raspy voice with an unmistakable Texas inflection. "He's just unhappy because he ain't watching *A-Team* reruns with the dog wonderin' why he put the peanut butter there."

Mocking laughter ensued.

"Thanks, Vicky." Hector chuckled. "Listen up! This is Jessica Beaumont, the negotiator who'll be training and flying downrange with us. Her boss is the one flipping the bill, so get your minds out of the gutters." He turned to Jessica. "All of us here, except for Vicky and a few of the permanent party folks, make up the country team that will be traveling downrange."

Jessica looked around the men again, studying them as Hector made introductions.

"Alpha Team, where you at?" About ten men stood up or raised their hands. "Alpha Team will be traveling ahead of us and linking up with the Peshmerga to establish a FOB—the forward operating base. They'll set up the infrastructure and make sure there's power, water, and food when we arrive. Bravo Team . . ." The remaining group formed to the right of Jessica. "This is Bravo Team. We'll be your security detail and travel everywhere you go. Nothing happens without getting the thumbs-up from Voodoo or me. If I'm not there, Voodoo speaks for me, and vice versa. Voodoo, come on up."

A tall, muscular black man with a shaved head and thick beard stepped up. "*Bonsoir, ma chérie*," he said with a Cajun accent. "I'm Jacques."

Jessica shook his hand and winked. "*Merci, monsieur*." This earned her a kiss on the hand.

"Slow down there, Voodoo," said Hector. "We already have one Romeo. We don't need a Casanova. How about we let the rest of the team introduce themselves."

Voodoo winked back and gently let her hand go.

A taller redheaded man with beard stubble came next. He wiped his hand on his jeans and licked his lips, eyeing Jessica. "Hi, I'm Eric, call sign Penguin." His stare lingered a little too long. And . . . was he blushing? She liked that.

"Move over, *ese*!" Eric was pushed aside by a Latin man with a light complexion and a thick Spanish accent. He also took her hand and kissed it. He winked and said, "I'm Fernando"—making sure to roll his R—"but you can call me Romeo."

Jessica giggled.

"Knock it off, Romeo," said a man who, of all the ruffians around her, reminded Jessica most of Captain Morgan. "I'm Jason, call sign Pirate Face, or PF. And before you say it, it's not because of Urban Dictionary!" All except Jessica laughed. This must be some inside joke.

Next was an olive-skinned man with a short beard and Middle Eastern features. "I'm Yousef, call sign Megatron." She detected a hint of Arabic accent. *Levantine?* she pondered. *No, and not Iraqi either.*

"*Assalamualaikum*," said Jessica, surprising everyone around. She raised an eyebrow. What did they think "negotiator" entailed? Italian?

Megatron nodded approvingly and responded, "*Wa alaykumu as-salam.*"

And then there was Cujo. "Hi. Sorry about before. I'm something of the comic relief around here."

"You wish!" came a call from somewhere.

"Go pound sand!" he responded. "Anyway, since you already know my call sign is Cujo, may as well know I'm Vincent."

After Cujo was another Latin man with a strong accent, though a darker complexion. "Hi, I'm Francisco, call sign Guapo." Jessica snickered, recalling the *¡Three Amigos!* movie. Guapo rolled his eyes. "Yeah, I know, I know. I really hate that movie."

The last in line was a shorter black man with a distinct New York Italian accent that took Jessica by surprise. "Hey, how you doin'? I'm Samuel, call sign Guido."

Jessica smiled with relief at the fact that there was someone she could relate to. "Are you a New Yorker?"

Guido responded with a head nod. "From the Bronx. You?"

"Used to live in Soho."

Guido nodded appraisingly. "It's all good, girl. New York's gotta represent, am I right?"

Hector tapped Jessica on the shoulder and walked past her, heading to the bar. "Come on, we'll get a few drinks and then get you all settled in afterwards."

The team gathered around the bar as Vicky pulled bottles from the ice chest and popped the caps in rapid succession. Jessica wasn't much of a beer drinker, but if that was part of the team dynamic, she could stomach a Bud Light or two.

Hector passed them around and toasted, "Here's to a successful training evolution. Let's make it memorable."

Jessica heartily clinked her bottle with Penguin's. She'd only just arrived, and she was sure it would be one of the most memorable adventures of her life. Vicky turned up the small PA speakers, letting AC/DC's "Thunderstruck" wash over the night.

20

Sunday, 11 May 2014

Jessica woke the following morning to someone banging at her door.

"Jessica, are you up?"

"Yeah," she answered groggily. "I'm up." She wiped her eyes and stretched her arms out.

She looked around the spartan eight-foot-by-ten-foot box and let out a soft whimper. Her only consolation was that she had a small bathroom with shower, toilet, sink, and mirror that somehow managed to fit on the opposite side. *But it's so atrocious.* Between the bed and the bathroom was a small desk next to two high school lockers, which she assumed were to be her wardrobe. She dropped her head between her hands and shook her head. *I'm going to be living here for three weeks.*

The morning light was muted by the small frosted-glass windows that flanked the door. She pulled away the thick Mexican blanket that served as her bedcover and groaned. The aluminum bed frame creaked as she forced herself up, cursing every mattress spring that had jabbed her throughout the night.

The banging resumed, and Jessica at last stood, frowning with disgust as her feet touched the cold, dirty linoleum floor. "All right already!" She forced herself to walk on her heels all three steps to the door. *Ugh, yuck!* She turned the knob to open the door and had to shield her eyes from the blinding morning light.

"Well, good morning, sunshine!" said Hector cheerfully as he handed her a travel mug. "Jesus! You look like hell. Did you sleep all right?"

Jessica's resting bitch face was far more fierce in the early morning, especially before caffeine hit her system. "Gee, thanks, Hector. And a good morning to you too." He was way too sprightly this early in the morning for her taste. She took the travel mug. "What time is it?" She perked up at the taste and said, "Oh, wow! What is this? It's good."

"That's a cardamom-infused latte that Chef made for you, and it's seven in the morning. You're already late," he said matter-of-factly. "I need you to get ready in the next ten minutes and meet me at the truck. I got some breakfast tacos for you to chow down on."

"Ten minutes!" she shrilled. "I can't be ready in ten minutes! I need to shower, brush my hair, and—"

Hector raised his hand and cut her off. "We don't have time for you to get all dolled up, princess. We're already behind schedule. Besides, no one is gonna care how you look. Now hurry it up."

Jessica clutched her hand to her chest and gasped. "It isn't getting dolled up, *Gung Ho*! A *lady* must look her best at all times." With the mandatory dramatics out of the way, she asked, "What's a breakfast taco? Is that like a breakfast burrito?"

Hector nearly chocked on his coffee as he laughed. She made it impossible for him to remain in disciplinarian mode. "Fine, go shower and get yourself all ladylike. Just please make it quick. We're really behind schedule."

Jessica smiled sweetly. "Thank you, Gung Ho. I'll make it quick. I promise." She shut the door quickly.

Hector lifted the mug to his mouth and murmured under his breath. "Maybe her damn call sign should be *Princess*."

"I heard that!" Jessica shouted through the door.

Thirty minutes later, they were on the road to the firing range, with Hector again murmuring to himself something about the Queen of England taking less time to prepare.

"I heard that too," said Jessica, but she didn't care. She was solely focused on how amazing her chorizo-and-bean breakfast taco tasted. Why couldn't she find this in Old Town?

When they arrived, the team was already lined up on the firing line, facing turned silhouette targets that didn't seem that far away.

Aren't these guys supposed to be good? Jessica wondered. *Why so close?*

Hector handed her what looked like a pair of old-school, bulky headphones. Everyone else was wearing similar pairs. "Put them on."

She was about to put them over her ears, but she hesitated. She was curious to know what a gunshot sounded like —was it anything like in the movies?

Suddenly, the targets turned and the team drew their guns, firing with lightning speed. Jessica started with a small shriek, covering her ears as the sounds sent sharp, piercing pain to her ears. Then, as quickly as they had started, the targets pivoted and the team stopped shooting.

Hector looked at her. "I did warn you to put your ear-pro on." At Jessica's puzzled look, he tapped at the headphone-looking things. "Ear protection."

Jessica put them on at last. "I was expecting something different. Is it always that *loud*? Or are they using special bullets?"

Hector laughed, then stopped with an abrupt cough.

"You're serious? Oh. That's Hollywood for you. Making shit sound and look a hell of a lot sexier than in real life. Those were regular bullets, but the stuff we're going to be firing later this week is much louder than that."

Jessica's eyes widened.

Hector grinned. "I told you, you're gonna have a blast."

That first day, Jessica was put through a compressed course that taught what felt like everything anyone would need to know about guns: military terminology and jargon, the principles of marksmanship and gun safety, the mechanics of the Glock 19, ballistics, and how to identify and remedy various weapon malfunctions. She also learned how uncomfortable a concealed weapon was on her hips. But the most draining part of her day was the actual practice of drawing, aiming, and firing her pistol. She had never held or fired a gun before. Despite all her fantasies, when the moment came, the thought of standing on the firing line with a loaded weapon at her side terrified her.

She was quickly learning how most everything she knew from the movies was wrong.

The afternoon sun was low behind her, making it easy for Jessica to study the silhouette target in front of her. She wiped her palms against her pants. It was nearly the same distance from her townhouse door to her sofa. Shouldn't be too bad, right? She jumped when a pair of hands touched her shoulders.

"Relax and breathe," a voice whispered calmly in her ear. "You know what to do and how to do it. Remember, you're just getting acclimated to drawing your weapon and firing it, okay? We'll do it together."

Jessica slowly turned around immediately felt at ease at seeing Penguin's smile. He winked at her. "You're good, just keep your eye on the target, all right? Always keep your eye on the target."

Jessica nodded.

She adjusted her shooting stance—which was almost like her tennis stance, minus the hoping back and forth. On the command to fire, Jessica slapped her hand to her side, searching for the holster and fumbling with the grip while trying to feel the backstrap against her thumb and index finger. It was taking too long. Her brain was long past where her hand's movements were. She hurried, anxious, pulling the gun out and consciously going through the motions of presenting the gun, closing her left eye, seeing the front dot centered in the rear notch with the target in the background, and squeezing the trigger. *Bang!* She startled at the recoil, then opened her other eye and scanned the target to see where she had hit.

What the hell? The silhouette remained entirely black. *Seriously!*

She began to turn around to ask Penguin if he'd seen where she'd hit when he jerked forward and pressed against her, forcing her arms forward. "Keep your muzzle downrange!"

Jessica was mortified. Her body trembled from adrenaline, and the fear of nearly forgetting several of the cardinal sins of gun safety. *Jesus, Jessica! You want to get yourself killed or some-thing?* In all, she had kept her finger on the trigger, didn't look where she was aiming when she turned, and had nearly pointed her weapon at someone she had no intention of killing.

At least Penguin was there. He coached her finger off the trigger and gently guided her hand until she holstered her weapon. She let out an audible exhale.

"See, that wasn't so bad, was it?"

Jessica smiled at his second wink. He sort of felt like the big brother she always wanted.

"Ready to try again?"

An epiphany came to her. The next three weeks were going to be long and *draining*. She didn't know what to expect from the training, but she knew it would be intense. After all, this was how they started her off on *day one*. She needed to sit down. More importantly, she needed a drink.

From there on, her daily routine that first week was to load, reload, and fire three fifteen-round magazines over and over. The repetitions were working but came with a price: her soft, manicured hands now had calluses anywhere the grip or trigger guard rubbed against them.

Luckily, when she wasn't shooting and reloading, she went through classes with Hector that were more in line with her profession: international laws of armed conflict, judicious use of deadly force, and what to do if she was ever detained while in her capacity as a Parabellum employee.

During dinner, the team would often ask questions about her company and other places they did business, but most questions were related to the mission.

"How well are you going to be able to communicate with the people in the area?" asked Penguin—Eric, as Jessica preferred to call him. "Are they Kurdish or Iraqi?"

"It really depends on which villages we go to." Jessica took another bite of her burrito. "The ethnicities can be very intermingled, or they might be one or the other. As for communicating with them, yeah, we should be good. I have full professional proficiency in both Arabic and Kurdish."

"Look at you," replied Eric. "Just full of surprises."

Jessica shook her head. "No, just lucky. My grandparents on my father's side were Jordanian and Kurdish. How about you, Megatron?" she asked the bearded man across the table.

He raised his hands. "Oh, my family's Egyptian. I can understand Iraqi Arabic, but don't know shit about Kurdish."

Eric smiled across the table. "Well, then I guess we're in good hands."

At the end of the second week, after dinner and drinking with the guys, Jessica found herself in the middle of a rather heated argument between Pirate Face and Guapo. PF shook his head and jabbed his grimy finger at Guapo. "That's a total bullshit answer! So what if Superman is the 'Man of Steel' and all that shit? He's a fucking Boy Scout, dude! He doesn't have the balls to do the deed, and you know it." He took a pull on his beer. "Wolverine doesn't have that problem, and that's why he'd be on my team." He again pointed his finger at Guapo. "You need to stop picking Superman."

Jessica reached for a bottle from the bucket between them and interjected, "Wolverine? Really?" She raised an eyebrow. "The guy carries more baggage than the Titanic! That's his problem. Sure, he has adamantium claws and an overzealous healing factor. But the man has no finesse." Her words took a sophisticated tone. She may be sitting in their compound, but they were talking about *her* world. "And please, he's constantly brooding over Jean Grey. I mean, seriously."

The rest of the team, who usually steered away from that kind of discussion, now gathered around them. "Now, do you really want to have to listen to that every day? Yeah, he might 'do the deed,' but how many times can you hear about Jean Grey before you want to either puke or punch him?"

Guapo slapped his knee. "Man, she told you!"

PF smirked and shook his head. "All right, miss know-it-all, who would you choose to be on your team? Let me guess —Batman." He took a drink of his beer and cocked his head, gazing at her expectantly.

Jessica took a long, slow swig of her own beer, peered up at the night sky, and rapped her nails on the glass bottle for a few seconds. "No, not Batman." She scrunched her face and swallowed. "Superman, Batman, and even Wonder Woman . . . They all are either way too serious or lack that something that would make a difference in a fight." She stopped her finger-rapping, meeting their curious eyes again. "Me, I'd choose the Flash."

Both Guapo and Pirate Face froze, bottles partway to their mouths, gaping at Jessica as though she had just declared the world was flat.

Guapo coughed. "The Flash? Seriously?"

Jessica sighed and explained. "Think about it. He has superhuman speed, which means instant recon. He can outrun bullets and explosive shockwaves, so if you find yourself on the wrong side of a gun or standing on a land mine, you've got yourself a guardian angel. Plus, the guy is a friggin' scientist! I mean, think about all the MacGyver shit he could come up with when he's not racing around disarming the bad guys or saving your ass."

She paused, studying the beer in her hand, then declared triumphantly, "Not to mention making beer runs."

That last comment gained her the raucous approval of the rest of the team.

Hector came out of one of the meeting rooms and joined the courtyard gathering. "Are these two apes bothering you with their comic book fantasy teams?"

Jessica shook her head. "Not at all."

"Oh, she can handle her own," said Guapo with a wink. "She shot down PF's Wolverine argument pretty quick and threw in a completely unexpected choice of her own."

Pirate Face nodded in surprised agreement. "I have to admit, she had some good points. Though I'm still not sure I'd go with the Flash."

"The Flash?"

Jessica shrugged, returning Hector's sly grin.

Guapo snapped his fingers. "I think we got your new call sign, hard charger. Flash!"

"No!" Hector waved his finger. "We are not giving her a comic book hero call sign. No way."

Jessica's eyes lit up like a child on Christmas morning. The men all chuckled. Guapo thumped his fist on the bench. "I like it!"

Jessica reached over and hugged them both. "Oh my God! That's awesome!" She then turned to Hector with a smirk. "I'm the Flash."

Hector palmed his face. "Jesus Christ."

21

Hector clicked on the mouse and sat back as the Skype chime played. He turned his head from side to side, running his fingers through the two-week-old beard. It was coming along nicely, all except for the white patch at his chin that had doubled in size since the last time he'd grown out his tactical beard—a favorite term used by anyone downrange who was not conventional military, which these days could be anybody from an analyst to an operator.

The call connected and Chuck's face appeared in the screen, though he seemed uncertain. "Oh, there you are! Sorry, Hector. I couldn't figure out if I had answered or hung up. I still can't figure this damned thing out."

Hector chuckled. "Don't let it kick your ass, old man. It's just a computer."

"Yeah, well, easy for you to say. So, how are things with the team coming along? That negotiator shaping up for you?"

"She's on top of things. We're wrapping up week two and she's got the weapons training down nicely. Next week, we'll wrap up the Combat Lifesaver course and finish the Crash and Bang. Before you know it, she'll be zigzagging her way through DC like she owns the place and shoot her way out of Anacostia like it's nothing."

"That's great to hear, Hector. How's the team taking to her?"

Hector noted the trepidation in his tone, which was understandable, considering her gender. But he was glad Chuck brought it up. "Jessica is like a little sister to them. Yeah, they banter back and forth, but she can dish it out as well as take it."

"Really?" Chuck was pleased. "Does she have a call sign yet?"

Hector groaned with mock annoyance. "Oh yeah. It's Flash."

"Flash? As in the comic book character?"

"Yep, the same."

Chuck scratched his head but left it at that. "I'm sure that'll be a hell of a story at the firepit."

"That it will be."

Chuck readjusted in his seat. "So how well do you see her doing downrange? Do you get the sense that she'll freeze up if shit goes sideways, or do you feel that she'll step up to the challenge?"

Hector leaned back in his chair, not exactly liking where the conversation was going but not sugarcoating the topic either. "She's had a few hiccups. This is her first time firing a gun, but she isn't shying away from having to use it, if that's what you're asking. As to how she'd perform in a firefight, I'll have a better sense next week after the Kobayashi Maru."

"Gotcha."

A pause stretched between the two friends.

"Chuck, what is this really about?"

Chuck took a deep breath and let it out, long and loud. "It's ISIS. They've made more gains out west in Anbar and in the north. We're keeping a close eye on things, but no one can predict what will happen next. You have those who swear that they'll take Mosul and Baghdad by next month and those that believe they'll just fizzle out. I just wanted to get a sense from you as to whether she's up for this if it gets real." He interlaced his fingers and leaned forward on his desk. "I heard back from the Regional Security Officer in Iraq this week, and he told me that even though the embassy is on board with the mission, they won't hold it against us if we decide to pull the plug now. In fact, I think he was hoping we did."

Hector took his cap off and ran his hand through his hair. This wasn't good. But then again, when had any mission gone as planned?

"Look, I get it," Hector said. "If I wasn't around to assess her myself, I would be hesitant too. But everything I've seen about her tells me that she'll be up to the task. And besides, we'll be close to the Kurdish lines if ISIS breaks through. By the way, is there any word about subcontracting the Peshmerga unit in Taq Taq? Jessica has been out of comms with Norton-Allied."

"Yes, it looks like it'll be a done deal. But Hector . . ." Chuck hesitated, something Hector couldn't recall the last time he did. "I just want to make sure that your head is clear on this and you're not letting your desire to go on one more mission cloud your judgment."

Hector leaned back on his chair and rubbed his face. *The fucking job again. Goddammit!* He came forward again, rubbed his hands vigorously. "Chuck, do you really believe that I would jeopardize the team's lives for the sake of having one last mission before hanging it all up?" *He's not wrong, you know.* He inhaled deep. *You shut your fucking mouth!* "Look, we still have time before we leave. If the situation worsens, then sure, we'll reconsider. But for the moment, let's just keep our head in the game."

"All right, Hector. You're the guy on the ground."

"Thanks, Chuck." Something occurred to him. "This wouldn't have anything to do with something Kelly told Betty, would it?"

Chuck rolled his eyes. "Thank you, Lord Jesus. I'm glad you brought that up instead of me." He pointed his finger at the screen. "You put me in a difficult position, you know that? Kelly was livid about the Jessica thing. Naturally, she shared it all with Betty, which means I've had to hear about it almost every day for the past two weeks." He spread his arms, at a loss. "What the hell were you thinking?"

Hector rubbed his face again. "Goddammit, I'm sorry, Chuck. I just had so many other things going on."

"That's not an acceptable excuse, Hector. We all have issues to deal with. But I am worried that your desire to remain as a team leader is affecting your decision-making. I'm worried your priorities aren't in the order they should be." He paused. "Am I wrong about that?"

"No. I mean yes." Hector averted his eyes from Chuck's on the screen. In the little window view in the bottom corner, he saw his own face looked guilty. "Look, I'll step down and take the position once I get back. I'm not happy to feel I'm being forcefully retired, but you're not wrong about my priorities. It'll be easier once I get this mission out of the way. I promise."

"I'm not the one you should be telling this to."

Hector again leaned back on the chair, removed his cap, and ran his hand through his hair. "Yeah," he murmured.

"Listen to me, Hector. This is me talking to you as your friend and mentor. As if it weren't bad enough that Kelly is scared for you, now she has the fear of you leaving her for Jessica on top of it. Now before you say anything, I know you're laser-focused when you're downrange. But from what Kelly has told Betty about Jessica, I'd be worried for you too.

She's a very attractive woman, and she isn't afraid to show it. So even if you're one hundred percent dedicated to Kelly, she may not see it the same way. I'm just saying."

Hector tried to think of an excuse, to say Jessica was unattractive or that the thought had never crossed his mind, but . . . he couldn't lie to Chuck. He rubbed his face. "You're right. You're completely right. I'll talk with Kelly when I get back—about everything."

"That's good. It'll make things easier on you both. Trust me." Chuck smiled.

They went over a few more details on the upcoming mission and a few other projects in the works. When they were about ready to sign off, Hector said, "And now to put the focus on you, is Heather's engagement party still on for next Saturday?"

It was Chuck's turn to lean back and run his hand over his balding scalp. "Son of a bitch, you just had to remind me, didn't you?"

"Hey, fair's fair."

"Yeah, it sure is. I have my bank statements and the girls reminding me every waking moment."

Hector laughed out loud. "How's Veronica taking it?"

"It's crazy! You'd think *she* was the one getting married instead of her sister. I can't figure out who's been doing more planning, Heather or Veronica. By expense of some things, I'd guess it was both!"

"Well, I'm looking forward to seeing you there. Please give my best to Betty and the girls."

"Sounds good. And Hector—" There was another long pause. "Talk to Kelly. The sooner the better."

"I will. Thanks, old man."

The call disconnected, and Hector rested his face in his palms. His mind was trying to decide what to process first. The progress ISIS was making, his need to make a *real* decision about the job, how he was going to *eventually* talk to Kelly, or the fact that each time Jessica was around, he was reminded of that night at the party—and the old feelings would return.

You are all kinds of fucked up, aren't you?

22

Undisclosed Location
Thursday, 23 May 2014

The meeting went better than Jessica expected. At first, she had expected the village elders to be mistrustful, but her friendly overtures and near-perfect adherence to their customs won them over. She adjusted her hijab, pressed her hand to her chest, and said, "*Ma'a salaama*" before stepping outside. She looked at her watch and cursed. The meeting had gone longer than her timetable allowed, and she'd have to hurry to get to base before curfew.

Standing in the doorway, she paused to scan the area and let the environment show her anything out of place. She felt something was off but couldn't quite put her finger on it. It was an unidentifiable sense of dread, like the night in New York when she'd missed her train in Columbus Circle and was alone on the platform . . . or so she thought before catching a glimpse of the three figures appearing from the corner of her eye.

A cold chill ran down her spine, and she shook off the memory. *Stay focused, Jessica.*

She approached her SUV and walked around it, looking for any signs of tampering, like wires or objects protruding from the chassis or undercarriage. She sighed in relief. Nothing was amiss. The sun was starting to dip into the horizon, and therefore fewer people were out. But, she noted, the café was empty.

Okay, that's not normal. The *Salat al-Maghrib* wouldn't be called for another ten minutes or so, so why wasn't anyone out having coffee? They still had time to make it to mosque for the call to prayer. *You're overthinking it, Jessica.* She shook it off and proceeded to enter her vehicle and drive.

The street vendors and pedestrians made the traffic in the narrow streets congested, leaving her to the mercy of *inshallah*, or "God's will," in Arabic. If someone crossed the street and was hit by a bus for not looking both ways, it was *inshallah*. If their house burned down because they fell asleep with a lit cigarette, it was also *inshallah*. Basically, anything that happened because of stupidity or lack of common sense was *inshallah*. And as the call to prayer sounded, it was *inshallah* that she was stuck in traffic.

When she finally made it to the intersection, she found a car accident blocking the right turn she needed to take. *Jesus Christ, enough with the fucking inshallah!* The drivers were now out of their cars, shouting over one another as their voices rose steadily and arguments became more heated. *I need to get the hell out of here, right now.* She idled the armored SUV forward but found there wasn't enough room to fit through. The car behind her blared its horn and she whipped her head around.

Behind her, the driver honked impatiently, gesturing for her to move on as he yelled, "*Yalla! Yalla!*"

"What do you want me to do about it, buddy?" She pointed to the accident—not that the guy would hear her through the bulletproof glass.

Time was ticking, and she didn't like to think what would happen if she was stuck off base after curfew.

Her heart hammered faster, as if her world were collapsing around her. She had to do something. Without another thought, she turned the wheel as far left as she could and stepped on the gas, knocking down a makeshift tobacco stand and forcing onlookers to jump out of her way.

The road narrowed as waves of pedestrians crossed in between cars and street vendors pushed oxcarts that blocked the sides of the road. She strained her neck, trying to get a better view of what was in front without rolling the windows down.

Suddenly, the driver behind her—the same as before—leaned on the horn again. He was too close, leaving her little room to maneuver as he encroached. *Son of a bitch!* She swiveled her head, frantically searching for a way out. There wasn't one. *Dammit, Jessica, why didn't you study the map better?* The horn again blared behind her, causing others to stop and take notice of her, the lone Western woman driving without a man at her side. No matter how well she tried to dress, speak, and act like the locals, her gender and appearance would *always* make her stand out. A gap opened ahead of her and she took it.

Jessica idled through traffic and sped ahead to the inter-section just as a car screeched to a halt in front of her. The four men in the car were all glaring at her with fire in their eyes. Time slowed to a crawl as the men lifted rifle muzzles from below their windows, extended their AK-47s, and aimed them at her.

She froze. The loudest sound in the busy street was the blood pounding through her ears as her heart tried to beat out of her chest. Jessica gripped the steering wheel, shaking uncontrollably. She was so focused on the two men exiting the back seat of the car ahead of her that she failed to notice the revving of a vehicle behind her.

Her neck whipped forward from the impact as her SUV lurched forward in a bone-jarring crunch.

The sound of the men screaming *"Allahu Akhbar!"* was followed by the staccato of automatic gunfire.

Bullet after bullet struck the windshield, turning Jessica's world a lurid shade of yellow. Unhindered, the driver and the third passenger moved in to flank the SUV, firing at the side windows.

Jessica shrieked. Tears blurred her vision. She couldn't do anything, not even blink.

And then the training kicked in.

A jolt of adrenaline broke her from the paralysis. She slammed the gas pedal, revving the engine as the SUV shuddered in protest before launching forward. She steered left, ramming the rear wheel of the enemy vehicle and crumbling the blockade as the armored hulk pushed past the smaller sedan like a bull charging through a crowd. Jessica focused on nothing save escaping the kill zone.

Bullets continued peppering the SUV, bursting in yellow splatters that obscured her view. She groped for the wipers, but the pumping adrenaline made her fingers clumsy. *Come on!* She finally got the wipers on, only to smear the yellow mess further, making it impossible to see ahead. But that mattered little right now. She needed to keep moving and get off the X.

Her heart pounded harder as cold sweat dripped down her forehead. She wiped it off, but that made the grip on the steering wheel slick. She pulled her hijab back and glanced over her shoulder; the side mirrors were too coated to use. The distance between her and her attackers was opening. She got her first breath of relief, but the moment was short-lived.

Her SUV slowed down, crawling to a halt. She pressed the accelerator and felt the engine revving in protest, but the vehicle refused to move.

"Shit! Come on! Please! Go!" She tried shifting to different gears, even reverse, but nothing.

She looked back. Her attackers were now running to her. Jessica reached for the door handle, but her clumsy sweat-slicked fingers failed to get purchase. "Come *on*!" The last two attackers were catching up to the first pair. Cold sweat poured down her face, and she focused on the door handle. She curled her fingers around it and pulled, feeling the resistance break as the door unlatched.

She pressed her left leg to push the heavy armored door open and lurched forward to exit the vehicle. The seatbelt locked and dug into her shoulder, snapping her back. She groaned in pain, tears of desperation running down her face.

"Fuck!" She reached for the seatbelt release, but she couldn't get her fingers steady enough to press the orange button. Too much shaky adrenaline, too much slippery sweat. She wiped the tears and sweat from her face and at last managed to release the seatbelt.

She lurched forward, finally escaping the vehicle. A primal scream assaulted her from the left. One of the attackers was running toward her and screaming in a mad fury. Jessica locked eyes on him, which sent another jolt of adrenaline through her body.

She instinctively swept her jacket away, reached for her weapon, and clasped it with both hands. She squeezed the trigger twice. *Pow, pow.* She missed. She squeezed faster, but missed again and again. Her attacker was about to launch at her when she at last locked her elbows, focused the front sight on him, and squeezed twice. *Pow, pow.*

The attacker dropped to the ground, a blotch of blue paint, instead of red, splattered on his chest. Jessica's arms quivered. *Threats! Search for threats!*

Jessica lifted her gaze to find the second running attacker now raising his AK-47. She climbed into the seat of the SUV for cover. More yellow splattered against the rear window.

She waited for a pause, then leaned out, aimed her weapon, and squeezed twice. *Pow, pow.* The second attacker fell back with blue blotches splattered on his chest.

Now, unable to get a visual on her last two assailants because of the yellow splatter, Jessica exited the SUV and went around the front of the vehicle. She crouched low and scanned the area, panting heavily as she again wiped the sweat from her brow. All she could hear was her heartbeat battering her ear drums. She kept scanning, hoping that the last two had run scared, but she couldn't afford to be over-confident.

Her peripheral vision picked up movement to her left. She turned to find one of the attackers approaching from the narrow alley. She pointed her weapon at him and squeezed the trigger.

Pow, pow, click.

"Shit!" She retreated back behind the front quarter of the SUV and pulled the gun back to her face, keeping the attacker and gun in sight as she pulled the magazine release and reached for a fresh clip.

She slapped the magazine in place and grasped the slide with the full palm of her hand. Her hand slipped from the sweat, but she had enough grip to send the slide forward and chamber a round. She peeked out from the SUV and fired at the attacker about to reach the SUV. *Pow, pow.* She dropped this attacker, only to see the fourth one right behind him.

She adjusted her torso and arms to aim at him, and again fired. He fell back and stumbled, but he didn't fall. She squeezed repeatedly until the attacker at last dropped back and was no longer moving.

Her entire body was shaking. She breathed heavily, sobbing with each exhale. Her legs felt like spaghetti, and cold sweat dribbled down her back. God, she was exhausted, even if only ten or so minutes had passed. She gasped as her senses picked up movement to her left. She instantly revved up to action mode and drew her weapon.

A coarse voice broke out over the gunfire. It was Hector. "Cease fire! Cease f—!"

She squeezed the trigger, twice. Her reflexes were two steps ahead of her brain. Horrified, Jessica gasped as Eric bent forward, clutching his chest.

23

"What the hell, Flash! You just killed a friendly!" Hector screamed as he rounded the corner, gritting his teeth.

"Ooww! Mother . . . *fucker*!" Penguin groaned, lying on the ground.

"Oh my God, oh my God, oh my God!" Hector watched as Jessica holstered her weapon and raced to Penguin, apologizing and rubbing his back as she helped him up.

Penguin stood up, still clutching his blue-splattered chest, and nodded to Jessica as he drew a deep breath and let it out slowly. Jessica looked mortified, confused, and exhausted. "It's okay, the exercise is over," Hector heard Penguin tell her. He knew she needed to be eased out of her shock. She was oblivious to the reality of the situation, her mind still trapped in the scenario.

Jessica let out a long, stuttered sigh, then turned and wrapped her arms around Penguin's neck and sobbed, clearly unable to hold back the flood of emotions coursing through her.

Penguin held her, stroking her soaked back and reassuring her like a child waking from a nightmare. She was shaking uncontrollably. "Shh, it's okay," Hector heard Penguin tell her.

"It's all right now. No one is going to hurt you, no one is going to judge you. Everything is okay."

Hector's throat closed. He'd been in this situation many times over, to the point of becoming desensitized to the physiological effects and compartmentalized emotions. But seeing Jessica break down reminded him that normal people didn't become desensitized. Normal people reacted like Jessica, like he had done too long ago.

"I'm sorry, Hector." Jessica spoke up, but her voice was muffled. "I thought I would be able to do this, but I was scared. I was really scared."

"It's all right. You froze, but you snapped out of it and got out of the X. That's what really matters. We can work on the rest."

Jessica quickly pushed Penguin away. Without warning, she bent over and vomited.

Hector muffled his laugh. "Oh yeah, I forgot to tell you that part. It's all right." He walked over and patted her on the back. "We'll get you cleaned up."

When she stopped heaving, he asked, "Feeling better now?" She nodded and tapped on his hand, but the shock of the moment was still fresh. "Come on, let's get back to the classroom and go over the exercise."

Jessica leaned on the hood of the SUV for support. She was still trembling, her legs wobbling dangerously.

Hector was about to offer his assistance, but Penguin reached forward first and gently helped her grab purchase. "Fine motor skills are one of the many things affected by the jolt of adrenaline rushing through your system," he said. "Are you okay to make it the rest of the way yourself?"

Jessica nodded, but her knees buckled and she dropped to the floor as soon as Penguin let go. "I can't! I can't do this." She sobbed on the ground. "I'm sorry, I thought I could do this, but I can't go through with this. I'm just not good enough."

Penguin knelt next to her and stroked her hair. "Sure you can, Flash."

Something stirred in Hector. Hot, electric, consuming. Penguin shouldn't touch her like that. He stepped forward, his looming shadow drawing Jessica's attention away from Penguin. "We've all been through this. This is all part of the package. This is why we train. You will only get better from here."

Penguin chimed in. "It's true. Hell, I'm scared every time."

"How?" she asked, wiping her tears and sweat. "I mean, you all are soldiers. I don't get it."

"This isn't a normal experience," responded Hector. "It's terrifying . . . every time. It's why we designated it the 'Kobayashi Maru.'"

Despite the situation, Jessica chuckled and rolled her eyes at the name.

Penguin shook his head, smiling. "Don't worry about it. We'll talk about it in the classroom."

"We call this exercise the Kobayashi Maru, after the Starfleet Academy exercise in *Star Trek*." Hector leaned against the instructor's desk in the classroom. "And there's a reason for that. Just like the scenario in the movie, there are no right answers. Regardless of what you do, the outcome will be disastrous. But the intent is to put you in a rapidly deteriorating situation and force you to react to it, to figure a way out."

Behind him, the video of the exercise was playing, showing Jessica exiting the meeting location. Jessica rubbed her temples as she watched herself on the screen. "But I did everything you taught me!"

Hector paused the playback. "I know you did. The fact is that we can plan for every possible event, but the enemy always gets a vote. Sometimes the bad guys think up shit we never imagined. And when that happens, all you have is what you know, what you can do, and what is beyond your control."

Jessica opened her mouth, then closed it.

Hector resumed the video and pointed out the details Jessica had missed or was oblivious to, like failing to notice how the street kids only went to her vehicle and not to the other cars. He explained, "The first thing they saw was you, a woman driving herself without a man. That's what everyone noticed—not that you were a Westerner. Second, your hijab was halfway back on the crown of your head, exposing locks of hair. I know you're aware of the customs, but what you didn't consider was that, fashion-wise, it pegged you as someone with money."

Jessica squinted. "What does that have to do with anything?"

Hector pointed at the screen. "Because *that's* how the bad guys spotted you from afar. Those kids trying to sell you things gave you away."

The lesson went on to talk about how she took too long to react when she saw the rifle barrels peek up from the assailants' windows—and that was just in the first hour. The hot wash went on for two more grueling hours.

24

The team returned to the villa and gathered around the firepit to let loose, each member reassuring Jessica that no one had ever come out unscathed.

"You all have been through something like this?" asked Jessica.

They nodded in unison, and Hector spoke for the group. "We've all been in an ambush at some point."

That surprised her. "So, none of you are scared anymore?"

Laughter erupted around the firepit. "Every fucking time, Flash!" Voodoo said in his deep Cajun accent.

"Just because we do this job doesn't mean we have a death wish," said Hector. "We do it for each other, and for the people who want to do good in a fucked-up world and who just need protection from the real monsters. The fear will always be there. It's what you do about it that counts. You can let it consume and control you, or you can push it out of the way."

Jessica was quiet for a long time. "I think I know what you mean."

"How so?" asked Pirate Face.

She looked around, meeting their eyes and considering.

"If I share something in confidence with you guys, can you keep it a secret?"

The men exchanged looks, then nodded in agreement.

She took a gulp of her beer, then two, then three, and steeled herself. "When I was still living in San Francisco, I came across some information about the bank I was working for." She took a deep breath, as if about to step off a high dive. "The bank was laundering money for the Russian mafia, but what made it worse was that they were laundering money made from trafficking young women into Syria. God knows how long they'd been doing this, but I was only able to get proof for three of those years." She drained the rest of her beer, her hand shaking visibly.

"I should have gone to the cops or the FBI, but I didn't. I didn't want to have to testify or be one of those witnesses who are forced to disappear into a protection program. So . . ." She sighed heavily. "I sent the information to a Russian journalist who had been writing exposés on the Russian mafia. He assured me my information was promising. He wrote back asking for more, but I didn't have anything else to give. So when I didn't hear from him, I got scared. I legally changed my last name to my mother's and moved to New York."

A cold chill came over her. Penguin moved closer, and she looked at him and forced a smile. "Anyway, I've been scared ever since. Always feeling as if I have to look over my shoulder, you know? And I don't know if I'm paranoid or if I'm actually being followed."

She looked around the team, taking in each attentive face and getting a genuine feeling that all these men would protect her without question. She smiled. "One of the things I hoped to learn here was if I was indeed paranoid or not."

No one spoke. The fire crackled as the team members took it all in, each in their own way. Finally, Hector spoke first.

"That's very brave of you, Flash," he said. "Not just to tell us, but what you did. Too many people would have looked the other way and gone on with their life." A few of the others nodded. "However, I hate to have to say this, but if you never heard again from that reporter, then chances are he's dead. Did you say or give him anything that could be used to track you down?"

"No! Oh, God, not at all!" Jessica couldn't bear the thought of a man losing his life because of her. "No, I . . . I never used my name, I used a made-up email, and I never physically saw or talked to him."

Romeo shifted in his seat. "How long ago was this?"

"Almost three years ago."

The team again exchanged looks. "I don't know," said Hector. "Maybe that trail went cold. But I'll say this—if you're ever in trouble, count on us. You're now a part of the team, and we never leave a man behind."

"Or woman," said Penguin. A much-needed laugh ensued.

As their last night together went on, the discussions changed as the rounds of drinks came and went, often turning to tales about the kind of shenanigans they got themselves into when not working.

"Then there was that one time we were in Tijuana," said Cujo. "We finished a job there and decided to blow off some steam."

Pirate Face rolled his eyes and threw his hands in the air. "Goddammit, Cujo!" He turned to his friend. "Are you seriously going to tell that story again?"

They all laughed, and Hector slapped PF on the back.

"What happened in Mexico?" Jessica asked.

PF grinned at the invitation. "We were at some bar—I can't remember the name—but we started doing shots around noon and didn't stop until almost six, when we met co-eds from San Diego State and followed them to a dance club . . . because we were drunk and wanted to get laid." They all laughed. "All was going well until some friggin' frat boys got their panties in a wad and wanted to thump their chests at us to impress the girls. Guido, tell Flash what you did."

Guido took a big swig of his beer and shook his head, laughing as the details came back to him. "I got in their faces, said a couple of things in my best mafia accent, and finished with a 'badda-bing.'"

Jessica covered her face, laughing hard as she imagined the whole scene. After living in New York, she could envision Guido's Bronx attitude blooming in all its glory.

"Anyway," Cujo continued, "those little pricks ran off, but I guess we scared the college girls also. Oh well, their loss, right?" He took another drink of his beer. "Now, by this point, we were all totally shit-faced. I mean, we'd been drinking for almost eight hours, and there was no way in hell a smart decision was gonna come out after that. So naturally, we ended up at a strip joint."

Getting a laugh from all but Pirate Face, Cujo feigned a memory lapse and asked, "Hey, PF, what was the name of that place? I forget."

In turn, Pirate Face squinted and pointed his finger at him. "Fucker, you damn well know the name of the strip joint." He turned to Jessica, chuckled, and said, "It was Bambi's."

Jessica choked on her beer. "Bambi's? Seriously?"

"Anyway, the place was sketchy as hell. A no-frills, complete nude joint. We must have been there for a few hours, drinking and giving our money away like candy with lap and stage dances when all of a sudden PF turns his chair back against the stage and sits down facing us."

Pirate Face wiped his face with both hands, his already ruddy cheeks deepening. Cujo continued. "The girl on stage looked at us, trying to figure out what the hell this joker was up to, when all of the sudden he tilts his head back until he's looking right up at her and opens his mouth!"

The whole group roared in laughter. Jessica covered her

mouth and squealed into her hands. She caught Hector's gaze, and he gave her a wry shrug with a wink.

"Goddamn you, Cujo!" Pirate Face shouted, laughing and wincing.

"So the girl, as if on cue, spreads her legs over his head, squats *all* the way down, and PF starts eating her right fucking there!"

Jessica shut her eyes and shook her head, as if she had just bitten into something bitter.

Cujo slapped his knee, almost wheezing with mirth. "I mean, he was just going to town on her, and she was loving it!"

Jessica gagged. "Ew." She shook her head, wanting to unhear everything. "Ew, ew, *ewww*!" The sour expression returned. "Oh God, PF!"

Pirate Face shrugged. "It seemed a good idea at the time."

Everyone chimed in with what they remembered from that night, each memory more crass than the last, so Jessica took the opportunity to go to the bar to buy the next round.

Vicky was filling a fresh bucket with beer bottles. "Did Cujo tell that stripper story again? I swear, he tells that story every time someone new joins the team."

"How long have they been together?"

"Much longer than I've been here, hon," Vicky said while popping the tops. "You'd swear they grew up together, but that's how my boys are." Her tone was maternal, like a mother watching her kids play, but there was also a tone of sadness. "They've been through some rough times, those boys, but they always stick with each other through thick and thin. You're lucky to be with them, you know," she said, looking Jessica in the eye. "No matter how bad things get, they've got your back, so you be good to my boys, all right, hon?" She winked.

Jessica smiled. She felt the weight of some high responsibility tossed on her shoulders. "I will, Vicky, thanks."

She grabbed the buckets of beer and walked back to the group. She saw them in a new light now. They were all bright smiles and laughs, joshing each other, but never taking it to heart. She announced her arrival with an appreciated, "All right, boys, here's my round."

She smiled as she passed the bottles around. She'd left a mark with Parabellum, something she'd cherish for the rest of her days. It was the perfect end to her three-week immersion into a world rarely seen in her circles. Tomorrow, she and Hector would fly back to DC and prepare for the real thing. In one week, she would rejoin the team in San Antonio and be on her way to Iraq.

25

Georgetown, Washington, DC
Friday, 24 May 2014

At long last, a stressful week was coming to a blissful end. Kelly was spending Friday helping Betty and the girls with Heather's wedding plans. It was nice to forget about the constant merger meetings. But that brought on other worries. She hadn't spoken to Hector about the mission since their fight at the party, and that was nearly a month ago. He'd been hiding with his "team" down in Texas ever since. *Coward.* He couldn't even face his wife after a fight—but now he was coming home. She'd seen his flight itinerary pop up in her iCalendar. It took a lot of conscious effort to ensure she didn't sour the mood for Heather.

She had met Betty and Heather for brunch in Georgetown, where they waited for Veronica to be let out of George Washington University for the Memorial Day weekend. They had filled their day in boutique shops, helping Heather choose flower arrangements, settle on invitations, and sample the main courses and cake selections for the reception. They were ending the outing with Heather trying on wedding dresses at a high-end boutique on M Street that Betty frequented.

"That's a beautiful dress, Heather," said Kelly. Heather's pearl-white strapless dress had a long train that perfectly complimented her lithe and statuesque build.

"You think so?" Heather's question was laced with the excitement and nervousness of the occasion. "I don't know. Maybe I should try on the halter one again."

"Don't you dare, Heather!" erupted Veronica. "That one made you look like a prude."

Kelly agreed. With Heather's wavy, shoulder-length chest-nut-brown hair up, the strapless dress accented her beautiful long neck, petite shoulders, and striking collarbones. It would be a shame to cover her natural beauty.

"Veronica! It's a wedding dress. It's not supposed to be, you know . . ."

Veronica cocked her hip. "You mean, 'sexy'?"

Heather raised her eyes at her sister, as if warning her not to say that too loudly.

"Oh my God, Heather. Get over it." Veronica stepped behind her sister and raised up on her toes to rest her chin on her shoulder. She looked into the mirror with her, the younger blonde and taller brunette looking back at them. "Aunt Kelly is right. You look *beautiful* in it."

"I know." Heather frowned. "And I love it too. I just don't want to freak Dad out when he sees it, you know?"

"Why, are you worried he's going to think you look like a slut?"

"Veronica!"

"Girls, calm down," Betty said, annoyed. "And Heather, your father isn't going to think that. I promise. In fact, I think he'll be very disappointed if you choose your dress based on whatever he may think."

"See, I told you."

"Aunt Kelly, what do you think?"

"I think your mother and sister are right." Kelly smiled as Heather beamed. It reminded her of her own dress-shopping experience from what felt like a lifetime ago. And now she wished she hadn't remembered that. A wave of doubt enveloped her. She shook it off and forced herself into the moment. She leaned over to Betty. "I don't even want to ask how much it is."

Betty whispered back, "Neither do I." They shared a laugh while the girls argued over which veil to choose.

"I just can't believe she's getting married already. It wasn't too long ago that she was standing in the same place getting fitted for her prom dress." There was melancholy in her voice. "How time flies."

"I know, she's grown so quick. I remember walking her to Kindergarten like it was only a year ago." Betty smiled and reached for Kelly's hand. "Thank you for being here today. It means so much to us."

Kelly's eyes welled up. "Oh, stop. You're going to make me cry. I wouldn't dare miss this moment."

"There's nothing like watching your baby grow up."

Kelly clasped Betty's hand as her lips trembled and tears streamed down her face.

Betty cleared her throat. "Oh, honey, I'm sorry. I didn't mean to. I just wanted—"

Kelly shook her head, dabbing her eyes. "I'm okay, really." Her voice was shaky and broken, but she braved through it. "I don't think it's going to happen for us. Hector wanted to try again, but . . . I just can't go through that again." *Not after three heartbreaking miscarriages.* She calmed as she talked through it, looking at Heather and Veronica. They were so happy.

Betty patted her hand. "I'm sorry, dear, I didn't mean to bring that up."

"I just . . . I don't understand! Why is it that I can be successful at everything and fail at the one thing that I can be as a woman? It's not fair." She wiped the tears before they ruined her mascara. "Besides, as busy as we are, and him choosing others before us, I just don't know . . ." Her voice trailed off, unable to believe her own words. The fact was, she feared her marriage was coming to an irrevocable end, and she wasn't ready to accept it.

Betty faced Kelly. "You and Hector are going to get through this. I know you're worried about your sister and him being together, but Hector's a good man. Once they get back this summer, he'll accept Chuck's offer and everything will be better."

"But she's going with them, Betty! And for all the things that he does, he didn't even have the courage to tell me that my slut of a sister was going with them." She rubbed her temples. "I mean, how the hell does that even happen? What makes her so fucking special?"

Betty tried to calm her down, nervously looking from the girls, still squabbling over accessories, to the attendants, and back to Kelly. "Because, honey, she's the negotiator and understands Arabic. That's all."

Kelly's eyes narrowed. She studied Betty. "How do you know she's the negotiator?"

Betty released Kelly's hand and clasped her own together, trying to find the right words. "I think you told me. The other night, remember?"

Kelly straightened in her seat, growing more rigid. "No, Betty. I didn't even know that. This is the first I heard about it."

All this time, Kelly had thought Jessica had wormed her way into Parabellum as a blow-off excuse for an international field trip—just to rub it in her face that she could. Kelly trembled, her blood boiling as her anger rose to a new level. Apparently, she was the only one not in on the dirty little secret. "Are you telling me that you knew? This whole time? And you never thought about telling me?"

Oh, God, it hurt. Jessica was prettier, sexier, and now she was more interesting to Hector than her. The growing void between Kelly and her husband would now surely be filled by Jessica. The thought sickened her. Jessica would win him over with her usefulness. Her talent. Their shared experiences. Why wouldn't Hector want someone like that? Kelly's eyes began to water as she clutched at her chest, the feeling of betrayal hitting like a punch. What made it worse was that the betrayal was not Hector's alone. "Am I the only one who didn't know?"

Betty's mouth was open, but no words came out.

It was like Betty had signed off on an affair, on their divorce. She'd known, and she'd said nothing.

"I see." Kelly sniffled. "Apparently everyone thinks I'm an idiot." She rummaged through her purse for a tissue but found none. "I'm always the last one to know, but no more. I won't be made a fool of any longer."

Betty straightened and cocked her head with a sympathetic stare. "Oh, honey, no. No one thinks you're an idiot. But you have to understand that this mission—"

"Fuck the mission!" Kelly's outburst caused Heather and Veronica to go quiet, both staring at her. She didn't care. "It's always about the goddamned mission, Betty! What about me? Am I to sit back like a good wife and just let my sister fuck my husband because the mission demands it?"

She paced back and forth, rubbing the bridge of her nose. She gestured with her index finger. "I begged him to not go on the mission, and he can't do that one thing for me. For his wife. For our marriage. But he's perfectly okay with taking that slut because she can speak fucking Arabic. Great. Just great!" She dug her fists to her sides and nodded in contempt. "I guess he made his choice . . . and I'm the last to know. Thanks, Betty." There was fire in her words as she wanted to lash out at anyone and anything, only to unleash her pain on her closest friend.

Betty turned away with a flinch. "Girls, why don't you look at the shoe selection. It'd be nice if we could find the whole outfit at one store." Heather and Veronica walked off, casting glances over their shoulders at their mother. When they had gone, Betty turned back to Kelly and said in a soft voice, "You're right to be angry. I should have said something. But this doesn't have to be the end of you and Hector. You can still recover from it. I know you can. What you and Hector have is special. You both can overcome this."

Kelly was beginning to believe that Betty was wrong. She didn't blame her for believing in that. After all, what she and Chuck had was truly special. A love that seemed to conquer all. But unfortunately, she saw Kelly and Hector through a prism that skewed reality.

Kelly grabbed her purse and shopping bags. "I think it's best if I leave now before we say—no, before *I* say—something I'll regret." She forced a smile. "Thank you again for inviting me. It really did mean the world to me."

She left Betty's side without another word and walked over to Heather to say goodbye.

Betty remained seated.

"Aunt Kelly, you're leaving?" asked Heather in alarmed surprise. "But I thought we were all going to dinner!"

Kelly gave her a long hug, keeping her close and tight. "I'm sorry, sweetheart. I just can't stay longer. You look absolutely beautiful, though. You deserve this. I'll see you tomorrow."

Heather frowned. "All right. Thank you for spending the day with me."

Kelly smiled, then turned and exited, choking back her tears.

26

Hector sipped his bourbon and placed the glass back on the desk of his home office. He was going over their household finances and comparing his current earnings with what he would bring home once he took the position of Chief of Global Operations. The difference was remarkable—not that they were strapped for cash or anything. Kelly's pay alone could let them live comfortably. But living wasn't much if he didn't feel alive. He needed a purpose for living, and the job filled that need.

More than that, if he was truly honest with himself, he needed the distance from Kelly. He hated to admit it—deep down, he still loved Kelly—but their marital disarray over the last six months gave him reason to doubt. And now he needed to find a way to tell her how he felt and how he would hang it all up after one last mission. Chuck was right; he just wished he hadn't waited so long to tell her. These thoughts weighed heavy on his shoulders, so he took another sip in hopes that the heaviness would lighten with each swallow.

He perked up at the faint rumble of the garage door clos-ing, followed by the sound of Kelly's purse being tossed on the kitchen island and the clip-clopping of her heels growing louder. He quickly closed the spreadsheets and bank statement PDFs as a jolt of adrenaline rushed through him.

It was his body preparing him for a fight.

"Hector? Are you home?" Kelly's tone sent a shiver down his spine. The clip-clopping continued.

"I'm in the office." He looked at the computer clock and saw it was only a quarter to seven. *Why the hell is she home so early?* She was supposed to be out with Betty and the girls until at least nine or ten. At least that's what she jotted down in her iCalendar.

Seconds later, Kelly appeared at the office door. Her eyes were puffy, the eyeliner and mascara smudged away without care. She stood with her arms crossed, and he knew a fight was about to happen. A big one.

"We need to talk."

Hector rose from behind the desk and let out a heavy sigh. It was never good when she started with those words. "Okay, let's talk."

Kelly stalked off to the sitting room by the parlor and Hector followed, his steps slow and heavy, like an inmate walking to his execution. She sat on the love seat with her knees together and hands clasped over them, giving him the visual cue that this indeed was going to be a long, drawn-out fight. He sat across from her on the wingback chair, subconsciously putting as much distance from her as he could, and leaned forward, resting his forearms on his knees. "So, what do you want to talk about?"

Kelly fidgeted with her thumbs, crossing one over the other and back. She was about to speak, but first she reached into her coat pocket and pulled out a wadded tissue. Evidently, the one she'd used to wipe the mascara and eyeliner with. She looked up and sniveled, "You lied to me."

"Lied to you?" Hector squinted, unable to comprehend her accusation. "About what?"

Kelly rolled her eyes and dropped her hands on her lap. "About the mission. About Jessica. You lied to me about it all."

Hector sat back with a start. "Whoa! Wait a minute. I never lied to you about that. I never said anything about her going on the mission."

"It's the same damn thing, Hector! You lied by omission!" She clenched her jaw, baring her teeth. "You're still going! With *her*! Even after I saw how you looked at her! And how she flirted like . . . like a whore with you!"

Of all the fights he had mentally prepared for, this wasn't it. This wasn't how he had wanted to broach the subject, on the defensive instead of the offensive for once. Hector spread his hands in front of him. "I have to go! It's not like I can just step away now, Kelly! Come on, you know this. I have to see this through. Lives are at stake here! And as for Jessica, she's the client! I don't have any control over that. I'm telling you there's *nothing* between us." He ignored the small twinge of guilt at this last part.

Kelly stood up, as if she were about to charge at him, pointing her finger hard in accusation. "That is *bullshit*, Hector! For one, you could have stepped away from this long ago. It wasn't like Chuck offered the job to you last week! You've been sitting on this fucking thing for weeks— months even—so don't give me that! And second, I *know* my sister. I know how she is and what she can be like when she sees something I have. She'll do *anything* to take it just because she can! And third! If you hadn't lied to me in the first place, maybe I could believe you, but not now. Not after this."

Hector clenched his jaw and balled his fists as his blood rose to a boiling point. He felt the primal rage about to erupt like a volcano. The beast thrashed against its cage with a fury he feared he couldn't control. A shock of recognition struck him as Kelly cowered away from him. He watched the lump in her throat bob and constrict, and he knew she saw the beast within.

He looked away, breathed deeply, and exhaled three times, then slowly turned back to her. The fear remained etched in Kelly's face. He cleared his throat. "You're right. I'm sorry. I should have told you this and so many more things. But please, just support me in this one last mission." His voice was now slow and soft. "Please, and then I'm done."

Kelly let her body fall back on the love seat, and she dabbed her eyes, folding the tissue over with each wipe.

"I can't," she said, her voice cracking. "I can't do this anymore. I know you hate me, but please don't take it out on me like this. I can't bear it." She covered her eyes, shaking her head. "Don't you understand? I love you with all my being, but I feel like you use the missions to punish me, and I just can't take this anymore. I'm scared every time you go. And if that wasn't frightening enough, now you're taking that slut with you. She ruined everything that brought me joy in my life, and now you're going off with her."

Hector sagged and dropped his face into his hands. He took a deep breath, rubbing his face with both hands in an attempt to keep all his emotions from bursting out. "I don't hate you, Kelly. I don't . . ." He let the words linger, unable to add more to them.

"Yes, you do," replied Kelly. Her voice was low, broken, and defeated. "Ever since we found out we may have missed a chance at having a family. I can tell because"—she broke down—"because you don't touch me anymore. You choose the missions and the danger over me, and it makes me feel cheap. Like being cheated on."

Hector clenched his fists. *Damn this woman and her insecurities.* "I'm sorry I make you feel that way, Kelly, but I've never cheated on you. Never! All that time Jessica was with us, I *never* cheated on you."

Kelly burst out, "But you have, Hector! You cheat on me

with the missions! You care more about them than me because you hate me!" She stood up, pacing back and forth in front of the love seat. "I used to wish you did cheat on me with another woman so that I could finally hate you! But I can't. I can't hate you because I *love* you. And now all of my worst fears are coming together. She is going to ruin us because I love you. You're going to cheat on me and leave me because you look at her the way you should look at me! If you don't die over there first."

She knelt in front of him. "But you can change it all, sweetheart. You can change it by not going."

Hector's heart strained with compassion. He took her hands into his, gazing into her eyes. "Look, I've always been faithful, and I will always be. But please understand that I can't not go. I promise you, this will be *the* last mission."

Kelly wept harder. She took her hands from his and shook her head. "No, I don't believe you. It's always going to be one more mission, and I can't trust you with her."

She dabbed her eyes again, then her nose. She looked away, steeling herself, then turned to Hector. A look of resolve emanated from her eyes. "No more missions, Hector. Especially this one. I'm done. If you still love me, if you still value our marriage, you will not get on that plane."

Hector felt a rush of anger rise through him, the beast stirring again. "Jesus Christ, Kelly! I just explained to you that I have to go! I can't explain it any other way, all right? I. Have. To. Go! But I'm telling you here and now that this is it! This is the last one, and Jessica won't get between us." He breathed hard, his chest rising and falling like a bull about to charge.

Kelly nodded slowly, understanding his final decision. "I see." Her voice was calm and eerily casual. "If that's your decision, then get on that plane. Go with that whore, but don't bother coming back here. You'll not be welcome." She stood, towering over where Hector still sat, glaring at him with a raised eyebrow. "I mean it, Hector. It's the mission or me."

She turned and walked away, leaving him with those last words.

Hector remained seated, a thousand thoughts racing in his mind, a multitude of emotions battling for supremacy. The punctuated finality of his marriage came as a shock, bringing back the heavy feeling from earlier. Yet at the same time, he felt a huge sense of relief. She'd left an open door for him. An easy way out of the hell that their marriage had become, with no strings attached. So what if he wasn't welcomed back home? He would be free to do as he wished . . . to deploy as many times as he wished.

The ultimatum stayed with him for the rest of the night as he lay on his side of the bed, the all-too-familiar ocean of sheets swimming between them.

27

Concord Manor, Middleburg, Virginia
Saturday, 25 May 2014

While countless parties had been hosted at Concord Manor
over the years, even Hector had to admit that the elegance
and attention to detail at Heather's engagement party
surpassed them all. The Carlyle family home was seated in
the wine and horse country of Middleburg, with its green
pastures, rolling hills, and gorgeous horses prancing majesti-
cally in the manicured paddocks. Guests were treated to a
collage of light spring colors feathered across the grand patio
and backyard in the form of table and chair covers, streamers,
and banners that hung from the windows. The violet, green,
peach, and pink colors blended with the picturesque scene of
the sun setting behind the Blue Ridge Mountains and softened by the glowing amber from the strands of light fixtures
that stretched from the patio, over the assembled wooden
dance floor, and to the stage where a band would be playing
later in the evening.

Hector sat with Chuck, Heather's fiancé, David, and
David's father at a table overlooking the vast Concord estate.

It was at Concord Manor that Heather and Veronica had first learned to ride, and it was there where Heather first met David when his family arranged to have their stallions breed with Betty's mares.

Chuck poured the cognac into the snifters and raised a toast. "Welcome to the family, David. You've made your father proud and my daughter happy. May all your days together be carefree and filled with happiness."

Afterward, the group broke into smaller segments, leaving Hector with time alone to think. All the talk of marriage and eternal happiness soured within Hector as Kelly and their marriage weighed heavily on his mind, especially after last night. In truth, he couldn't blame her for being upset, but Kelly's vicious assault, doubting his commitment to her and dramatizing his self-destructive addiction, had only stoked the fire.

"I hear you're in the doghouse again." Chuck had walked up behind Hector. "You want to talk about it?"

Hector shook his head. "Nah, there's nothing to talk about."

Chuck came alongside, also looking out in the distance. "Back when the girls were still very young, Betty confided in me that what troubled her the most wasn't so much the fact that I was away. I mean, she always worried about me, of course." He sipped his cognac. "But what kept her up most nights was the fact that I looked forward to going back out." He put his hand in his hip pocket and looked down. "She felt as if she was competing with the missions and the teams. That she'd almost prefer I was having an affair instead. At least that way she'd have known what she needed to confront."

"Well, it sounds like the women have been talking."

Chuck put his hand on Hector's shoulder and looked him in the eye. "I understood then what she was fighting. I had to reassure her that she and the girls were more important than the army. I couldn't imagine my life without them, and that's what made the decision for me very simple." He paused, letting the words sink in, then added, "You need to reassure her that she's more important than the missions. If you can't imagine your life without her, then take the job. Today. I won't lie to you, Hector. It'll make things harder out there without you, but we can figure it out. Voodoo is a good leader, and the team *will* understand. I can't make the decision for you, but I can make it easier if you choose to stand down."

Hector took in Chuck's solemn stare, soaking in his advice, and then looked away. "I get it, Chuck. I really do. But . . ." He hesitated. "What if I can't stop going back? What if going out is more important?"

Chuck puffed his cheeks and blew out hard. He scratched his scalp as he thought about it. "Then you need to tell her," he said finally, "because it isn't fair to her either. She's got a bright future ahead of her. And maybe she won't find anyone else she loves as much as you, but there will be someone else."

He breathed deeply and sighed. "Sooner or later, the missions will come to an end, Hector. You can't go on forever. And when they end, Kelly won't be there anymore. You have to look past the missions and remember why you married Kelly. Who will be there for you then? The job is yours any time you want it. You just have to decide if you want it now and save your marriage, or later and risk her no longer being at your side."

Something caught his attention, and Hector turned to see Betty waving at them as if signaling a ship. "Guess it's time to make the rounds," Chuck said. "Anyway, just think about it." He tapped Hector on the shoulder and made his way to the love of his life.

Hector took in the words of his friend and mentor and nodded somberly. His eyes drifted to Kelly. She and the bridesmaids were clustered around Heather, each radiating excitement for the engagement, but hers was dimmer than the others. No doubt their troubles weighed heavily on her mind, as they did on his. He should have told her how beautiful she looked today. He should have zipped her dress up. He should have held her hand when they arrived. But he'd done none of those things.

He searched deep inside himself for the things that had made him fall in love with Kelly so long ago. The memories that surfaced brought life back to his face. Like the times she'd put her hair up in different ways while making sexy faces in the mirror when she thought he wasn't looking. The way her nose wrinkled like a squirrel's just before she sneezed. And the times he'd pretend to be annoyed when she'd snuggle up to him and press her cold feet against his legs.

Those memories seemed so long ago. He didn't need to ask if she still loved him. He knew she did. But the fact was that there was no turning back now. He *needed* her to understand that he'd never forgive himself if his absence was the reason someone didn't make it back. But the things that were said last night made it clear she couldn't—no, she *wouldn't*—understand. He hated it, but it was a gamble he had to take. In one week, he'd fly down to San Antonio and be underway.

28

Chuck sauntered over to Betty, wrapping his arm around her waist and lifting her chin for a kiss. "Hello, love."

"Hello, handsome," she replied with a glowing smile. "Heather asked to spend some time with you before the formal announcement begins."

"She did?" Chuck asked with genuine surprise.

He found Heather with her bridesmaids near the dance floor and stood back and watched with his own subdued smile. The little girl he remembered from long ago was now a beautiful young woman with her whole life ahead of her. The smile on her face was brighter than the ring she showed off on her extended hand. He waited to approach her for fear of interrupting her. It was a bittersweet moment he would forever treasure.

When the girls were little, he never had the kind of father-daughter relationship that Heather's friends had with their fathers. A great deal of fault lay in the fact that Chuck spent more time away than he did at home. In a sense, even when he was home, he wasn't. Too much followed him home. He thought of this as a normal aspect of his life, and since Betty accepted it, his assumption was that the girls had accepted it as well. He had never given a thought to the fact that both were young and understood nothing about the greater evils that were oceans away. What a fool he'd been for so many years.

It wasn't until he became CEO of Parabellum that he became aware of all the moments he had missed. By then, it was too late to develop that kind of relationship with his girls. They were women by then, forced to mature far too early. Not only had he missed birthdays and holidays, but he'd also missed their first bicycle rides, their first horse rides, their first scrapes, first crushes, first kisses, and first heartbreaks. Betty had been both mother and father during those times, and when he had offered his advice, they had dismissed it without a thought, seeking their mother's advice instead.

Somehow Heather had found it in her heart to make amends with him and wipe the slate clean. Veronica would come around; she was still in school and wrestling with finding herself. He would give her time. But for Heather, now, on the eve of her engagement party, he'd be damned if he would miss one more special moment.

Serendipity would have it that Heather looked up just then. Her smile glowed brighter, seeing her father standing there, and she called out, "Daddy!"

His little girl ran to him and gave him the biggest hug he'd ever had. The lump in his throat hardened, and he was overcome with emotion.

She got up on her toes and wrapped her arms around his neck. "Thank you for this, Daddy. I love you so very much."

Holding back the ocean would have been an easier feat than holding back the tears that now streaked his weathered face. "Me too, princess. Me too."

Heather gently slipped her arms off his neck, and her feet were again firmly on the ground. She took his rough hands, locked her fingers between his, and led him to the dance floor. "I can't believe you made this happen, Dad." She waved to the band, still doing sound checks, and on cue they took their place on the stage.

The band struck up "I Hope You Dance" by Lee Ann Womack, and the lead singer swayed back and forth with the melody. Heather took her father's hands in hers, closed her body to his, and together they danced. Guests joined them, and with so many others on the dance floor, the sea of bodies enclosed the father-daughter dance in privacy.

"This day wouldn't be the same without you, Daddy." She let the moment sink in. "I wouldn't have been as happy if you weren't here."

Her words pierced his heart like a bayonet.

"I'm sorry, princess." His voice strained. "I'm sorry for having missed so much." He again failed to hold the ocean back. "But I promise I will never miss another moment."

Heather lifted her head, looking with great distress at her father. She alone had broken the hardened warrior who had been her protector all these years. "No, Daddy, no." Her own tears now streamed down her face. "I didn't mean it that way. Please don't cry, Daddy! I just wanted to say how happy I am to be sharing this moment with you."

She wiped the tears off his face. "I know why you were away all those years. I understand now. I understand why you couldn't be home, and I understand why you spent so much time with Uncle Hector. I didn't get it for a long time, but there was a night, years ago, when you left after I had begged you to let me go with Tony Jeffries to the prom. You said no . . ." She pursed her lips and dabbed the tears from her own eyes. "And I had told you I hated you." She pressed her head against his chest, trying to hold back her own tears. "I am so very sorry for that. Mom sat me down that night. She told me about the friends you lost and why we went to so many funerals of people I never knew."

In that moment, they aired their collective pain, lifting the weight off their shoulders, neither knowing this was the precise healing they had needed all those years ago.

Chuck kissed the crown of her head. "Please don't cry, princess. Your mother's going to blame me for ruining your makeup."

They both chuckled with great relief.

Heather sniffed. "Oh, Daddy."

It was that moment, where father and daughter embraced with precious care, that his nightly prayer was finally answered. *All is forgiven.*

29

San Antonio International Airport
Friday, 6 June 2014

Jessica felt the butterflies in her stomach as the plane touched down and the flight attendant welcomed the passengers to San Antonio. This arrival was worlds different from the last time she was here. She wore a light moisture-wicking blouse, form-flattering cargo pants, Merrell hiking shoes, and Ray-Ban aviator sunglasses over a New York Yankees baseball cap. She still had her metallic rose gold carry-on, but hey—it was cute.

She practiced the observation skills she had learned and used her best judgment to identify potential threats or surveillance on her. Other than the one guy doing a terrible job of checking her out, nothing more nefarious spiked her alertness on her way to baggage claim.

Hector again met her at baggage claim, nodding with approval. "Look at you, hard charger! You look like you're ready for war."

Jessica smiled and rolled her eyes as the two hugged. "It's good to see you, Hector." She breathed in the leathery scent of his cologne and felt the tickle of his short beard with the extra salt-and-pepper mixed in, and she held their embrace a little longer. The lumberjack look had never appealed to her, but she had to admit she found his short-sleeved checkered button-down and chocolate hiking pants ensemble very becoming. If only he wasn't married. Kel had to be an idiot to be willing to give all of this up.

"Good to see you, too, Flash. I hope you didn't bring a full luggage set this time," he said, half-jokingly.

Jessica laughed and shook her head. "I'm never going to live that down, am I?"

Hector shook his head. "Hell no. Besides, it's a damn funny story, and we're going to need a few laughs while we're out there, so may as well have some good stories to make the time pass."

She put her hands in her back pockets and asked, "So, are we going back to the training site?"

"No, actually we're going to the other end of the airport. Our L-100 is there. All we need to do is load our gear, and we'll be set."

Jessica had no idea what an L-100 was, but she was relieved that they didn't have to drive for hours. A short while later, her two large luggage bags made their way around the conveyor belt. They grabbed the bags and were on their way.

They left the passenger terminals and drove the perimeter road to the side of the airport where private, charter, and air freight cargo aircraft were located. She expected to see a cargo jet with PARABELLUM RISK on the fuselage nestled among the others with FedEx, UPS, and DHL signage. Instead, Hector drove to a much smaller white airplane with four turboprop engines and generic-looking numbers on the tail.

"Are we getting in *that*?"

Hector turned to her with a curious smile. "Yeah. That's

an L-100, a commercial version of the C-130 Hercules. What were you expecting?"

Jessica's jaw dropped. "I don't know—" She pointed at the larger UPS jet. "How about one of those, with PARABELLUM RISK AND SECURITY on the side!" His laugh only made her furious. "It's not funny, Hector! This thing has propellers!"

Hector stifled a laugh at her reaction and explained, "Look, we can't be advertising who we are wherever we go, and our clients appreciate that degree of discretion. Well, most of our clients." He smirked. "Plus, this is a perfectly good aircraft for the mission we're going on. It's not as comfortable, but it doesn't draw attention and gives us the flexibility to land in less-desirable places, if needed."

His explanation went unappreciated. He parked near the aircraft and left the keys inside. "Come on, let's get our stuff on a pallet."

The rest of the team was at the rear of the aircraft, each meticulously completing their assigned tasks as discussed at the training facility. Voodoo and Guapo were at one pallet overseeing the transfer of ammunition, crew-served weapons, small arms, and explosives into their special crates. On another pallet were Pirate Face, Cujo, and Megatron crating the communications equipment, bottled water and pre-prepared meals, and medical equipment. On the third pallet was Guido, checking vehicle-related items like spare tires, lifting jacks, and tools.

"How's it going, Voodoo?" Hector asked as they walked up to him. "You got everything under control?"

"Too easy, Gung Ho. We're palletizing the last of the gear." He motioned at the two modified white Land Rover Defenders arriving from the same direction as Hector and Jessica. "Romeo and Penguin are driving the vehicles in."

The two vehicles parked behind the pallets. Penguin exited one of the vehicles and jogged to them. "Hey, Flash! Are you ready to do this?"

Jessica half smiled, wishing she could show the same enthusiasm and eagerness. A sinking feeling had come over her when she'd seen the vast quantity of bullets, machine guns, and medical equipment in the many crates. Her stomach tightened. This mission was really happening, and she was getting ready to travel to a war zone.

With everything loaded, the engines roared to life and the propellers began to spin as the crew chief cleared the team to enter. They each grabbed a boxed meal and a green wool army blanket on their way in. Jessica followed Hector and Penguin to the front of the cargo area, squeezing past the pallets and vehicles until she reached rows of interlaced red cargo straps on either side of the aircraft.

She patted the red canvas that was the seat with a grimace. They were going to spend many hours sitting on these. She shouted over the sound of the engines, "Seriously?"

Hector nodded with a smile.

The vibrations at her feet made their way up her calves, her butt, and along her spine. In all, it was quite relaxing. *Though it would be better if this were a plush leather chair.* Curiosity got the better of her, and she opened the boxed meal to examine the contents. Inside were orange foam ear plugs in a small packet, a Clif Bar, a plastic-wrapped sandwich, a bottle of water, a chocolate chip cookie, and what she assumed was a barf bag. She opened the earplugs package and rolled the orange foam with her fingers until they were nice and thin, then inserted each one. Next, she pulled out the sandwich and examined it, discovering that it was a ham and cheese sandwich. She let out a long sigh, showed it to Hector, and called, "You know I'm Jewish, right?"

He looked at her, then the sandwich, and shrugged with an apologetic smile. "It is what it is."

"Seriously? Ugh. This flight is going to suck."

Penguin sat on the other side of Jessica, chuckling with each voiced annoyance. He tapped her shoulder and pointed up at the top of the aircraft. "You see that thin hose?"

"Yeah?"

"Don't worry if it starts to leak."

Jessica raised a concerned eyebrow.

"Worry when it stops leaking."

She gave a pained look as both he and Hector broke out in laughter. Jessica tilted her head back and let out a long exhale. *I'm sitting between juvenile boys.*

The crew chief instructed the team to use the barf bag if they had to vomit, not to make a mess in the toilet at the back of the aircraft, and not to get off the aircraft until they landed at BIAP. She leaned over to Penguin and asked, "What's BIAP?"

"Baghdad International Airport."

Baghdad International Airport. The name rolled smoothly off his tongue as if he'd said it a thousand times.

She slowly nodded as she looked around her, and then it hit her again. *I must be out of my mind! I'm off to a war zone . . . aboard a plane filled with guns, bullets, and explosives.* All that was missing was a pallet of bundled cash to complete their own scene from *Air America.*

The airplane rolled down the runway and, to her surprise, lifted off with ease. It was an odd experience to be sitting sideways as the airplane lifted off, and it was then that it dawned on her that the crew chief hadn't said anything about upright trays and seats, oxygen masks, or seat belts. For that matter, he hadn't given any actual safety instructions regarding an emergency. She turned to ask Hector to ask what to do if something happened, only to find him fast asleep. In fact, the whole team was fast asleep.

We haven't even been fifteen minutes in the air! How in the hell are they asleep already? She let out another sigh. *This flight is going to suck.*

The next six hours slowly ticked by. She watched two movies on her laptop, played games on her phone, and ultimately decided to begin reading her next book. She reached into her backpack and pulled out a copy of Jane Austen's *Persuasion* in Arabic. She'd been saving it for when she had nothing to do at the site, but since she wasn't doing anything now, it suited its purpose.

She got through the first few chapters before the monotone humming of the engines, background white noise, and vibrations emanating from the airframe lulled her to sleep. When she woke, she found her head leaning on Penguin's shoulder. He was warm and smelled nice. She rubbed her eyes and arched in a long, comforting stretch.

She sat up and turned to Hector, who was picking at a stain on his pants. "How long have we been flying?"

He cleared his throat. "We've been flying for about ten hours." He looked down at his watch and smiled. "We still have another thirty-six hours left."

She was about to retort with a complaint when she noticed something off about his smile. "Is everything okay?"

Hector nodded unconvincingly. "Of course. Why do you ask?"

"Because, you seem perplexed about something."

Hector shook his head dismissively. "It's nothing."

"It's about Kel?"

Surprised, he squinted and leaned back.

"Don't look at me like that. I'm a woman, I can tell these things."

Hector looked like he was about to shake his head, but his gaze dropped as soon as their eyes met. "We got into another fight on Friday. A bad one."

Jessica tilted her head and put her hand on his arm. "Oh,

I'm really sorry about that." She examined his expression. Whatever the fight had been about, she could tell it weighed heavily on his mind. "You want to talk about it?"

Hector shook his head. Then, thinking it over, said, "She said that if I went on this mission, I wouldn't be welcome back." His Adam's apple bobbed. "I'm starting to think this might be it for us."

She sighed and squeezed his arm. "I'm so sorry, Hector. I can't even imagine what you're going through." She was reminded about her own fight with Kelly and the things she herself had said. She couldn't help but to feel that, somehow, she bore some responsibility. "Did me coming along have anything to do with it?"

The daggers he stared at her told her everything she needed to know.

She opened her mouth, then closed it. *Don't go down that rabbit hole, Jessica.* She shook off the thought. "Look, Kel and I have a history of unresolved issues. And while I don't know all that she said to you, I can't help but feel that the things I said had something to do with what she told you."

"Jessica . . ."

"Hector, please. Just hear me out." She took a deep breath. "I have always pushed her buttons, and always took it too far. We are both so damned competitive about things that we make an effort to get under each other's skin. The thing you should understand about her is that she's always been insecure about herself around me. She sees things too personally and always takes them too hard. She's her own worst enemy."

She adjusted to look at him directly, making sure he met her gaze. "But the thing of it is this—she loves you so much that she's afraid she's going to lose you to me, and what she said came from a place that is not her true self. That was the Kelly who's still seventeen. The Kel you married is a confident and loving woman. I know that what she said hurt, but believe me when I tell you she regretted those words the second they left her mouth."

Hector rubbed his face.

"Did you say goodbye?"

He ran his hands through his hair and rubbed the back of his neck.

Jessica put her heart to her chest. "Oh, Hector." Her heart ached for him. She had never considered herself a sentimental woman, but this broke her heart. Her feelings and opinions about him had evolved, and she was finally getting to see the man the outside world rarely got to see, including his own wife. The hardened soldier with the cold stare felt the pain of heartache as easily as anyone else. She knew this was killing him inside and that he didn't bear the responsibility alone.

She took his hand in hers, looked him in the eye, and said, "If you still love her, you need to leave the team, Hector. I mean it. You can't do this to her anymore. I understand why she's scared for you, probably more than she does. Despite what she said, I'm sure she'll give you a second chance." She then cautioned, "But if you don't, then you need to let her know. Face the consequences and give her space. Don't make it harder on her too."

The loud humming inside the cargo area filled their quiet void as they kept their eyes on each other. He had really pretty eyes, and a soft face when he wasn't teasing. She smiled. *Oh, Hector, if only Kel wasn't in the way. No—stop that!*

Flushing, she picked up her book and continued reading.

Hector cleared his throat. "What are you reading?"

"*Persuasion*, by Jane Austen."

"In Arabic?"

She glanced at the cover and laughed. "Yeah. It's not quite the same. Some things get lost in translation, but it's a good way to keep up my language skills."

"Yeah! I would imagine so."

Jessica felt her stomach grumble, an odd sensation that

thankfully broke the direction the conversation was going. It'd been almost eleven hours since she had eaten part of the box lunch with a few other snacks the team provided. She opened the box, and her mouth watered at the sight of the crushed roll with its thin layers of ham and cheese. Unable to continue fighting the unrelenting hunger, she unwrapped the sandwich and bit in.

Mmm! I don't care if it's not Kosher, fuck, this is good.

Penguin chuckled at her, and she glared at him like a wolf guarding its kill. She barked, "What?"

"Nothing," said Penguin, shrugging and shaking his head. "I just thought you said you were Jewish."

Jessica took another bite of the half-eaten sandwich and said, "What can I say? I'm a bad Jew."

Penguin laughed and set his own book down. He nodded at her paperback. "How did you learn Arabic? I mean, not just Arabic, but Kurdish too. It's not something you just sign up for in college."

Hector was watching her too, also curious. She swallowed her bite. "Long story short, my paternal grandfather was a professor at Mosul University when he met my grandmother. She was Kurdish *and* his student." She chuckled, recalling the stories her grandmother would tell her as a child. "They married after she graduated and moved to Jordan." She washed the bite down with a gulp of water and went on. "After my father met my mother, an Israeli Jew, they married and moved to the States. So, growing up, I had to learn Arabic, Kurdish, *and* Hebrew." She smiled and said, "Arguments in my house were always interesting."

Hector nodded. "Impressive. Kelly never mentioned your family history. But also—" He cut himself off, embarrassed.

"But also, Kelly never spoke about me if she could avoid it?" Jessica suggested, a smile tugging at her lips. *Typical Kel.*

Penguin scooted closer so he could hear better. "So how did you and Gung Ho's old lady get to be sisters?"

She took another bite and looked up at the ceiling. She chewed slower while deciding how to tell the story. She swallowed.

"I was six when my father passed away." Her face softened. "Heart failure. The man refused to see a doctor unless he was sick." She set the sandwich in her lap and stared at it. "It got rough afterwards. His life insurance refused to pay out the full term because of 'negligence' on his part. I don't remember too much of it, other than seeing my mom cry every night. Anyway, she found a lawyer who empathized with her and took her case."

Jessica lit up at the memory of meeting her stepfather. Hector gave her a small, knowing smile. It was good to know Hector admired him just as much as she did. "He was relentless and eventually got my mom everything we were owed, and then some. He was Kelly's dad—and he's the reason I decided to become a lawyer." She took a bite of her sandwich and mumbled through the bread, "And as they say, the rest is history."

Penguin eventually went back to his manga, but Jessica and Hector went on talking about her childhood, what it was to live in a blended family, and how Christmas and Easter could be highly charged holidays. "And don't even get my mom started about the Easter Bunny. She hated that thing. She'd say, 'Santa Claus I can understand, but a rabbit that lays eggs and hides them! Oy vey! How does that make any sense?'" They both laughed. "And even though she hated it, she still let me have my own basket."

"Do you still keep in touch with your grandparents?"

"I do." She realized something and laughed to herself. *Oh, how ironic.*

"Did I miss something?" asked Hector.

"No." Jessica shook her head. "It just now dawned on me that I'll be in the same time zone as them . . . and Qari."

"Who?"

"Qari Bashir, a friend. We helped each other get through law school. He and I would talk in Arabic to keep up the practice, as well as having something to do to help keep up morale. After the civil war in Syria broke out, he left his job at a prestigious law firm and returned to join the opposition and defend his family against the Assad regime."

"Wow. That's hardcore. Do you still keep in touch with Qari?"

"Yeah, through WhatsApp. But less frequent now than before," she said. "The last time we talked was to wish him a happy Eid al-Fitr after Ramadan, but that was over a year ago."

"Is he from Aleppo?"

"No, he's from Homs, but I guess it doesn't really matter what part of Syria he's from. The whole country is a war zone." She scowled, recalling the training she'd gone through in the past month, thinking how glad she was for her bond with the team. Did Qari have either resource? Was he alone? She looked at Hector and said, "What are the odds of two law school friends finding themselves in the same region doing something that has nothing to do with the law?"

He chuckled. "Yeah, I guess those are pretty rare odds." He checked his watch. "Better get some sleep. You'll want to get rest now, while you can."

Jessica nodded. The exhaustion of the long flight was now enveloping her. She tilted her head back and let the vibration of the fuselage lull her to sleep.

30

Baghdad International Airport
Sunday, 8 June 2014

After a nearly forty-six-hour flight, the final approaching to BIAP was a godsend. For as many times as Hector had been to Iraq, the inbound trip had never felt shorter, and the anticipation never got old. The final approach, known as "the corkscrew," was always a thrill ride. The maneuver was essential for all approaching aircraft, since the threat from SAFIRE—surface-to-air fire—was still very real. It was indeed like a roller coaster, but instead of imparting a cheap thrill, this ride was all about survival.

He turned to Jessica with an ear-to-ear grin and asked, "You like roller coasters?"

"No . . . Why do you ask?" She gasped and reached for his and Penguin's shoulders as the aircraft suddenly banked to one side and then to the other on its downward trajectory.

"You will now!" He laughed as she clung to him for dear life. "Hold on tight, Flash. This is gonna be fun!"

His center of gravity shifted back and forth with each banking maneuver. The cargo straps and tie-downs for the vehicles and gear creaked and groaned. Jessica's wild eyes darted from the potential avalanche of metal to the approaching earth.

Hector leaned past her to yell at Penguin. "It's always fun to see someone pop their corkscrew cherry!" Penguin grinned. He was enjoying Jessica's nearness too, apparently, though, Hector thought, for different reasons.

The maneuvers eventually evened out, and the aircraft resumed its normal landing procedure.

Jessica loosened her viselike grip on his shoulder when they touched down. "Holy shit, that was awesome!" she yelled. The wide-eyed grin on her face said it all.

Hector agreed entirely. The adrenaline rush from the maneuver was like an old friend. It had been far too long.

They taxied down the runway for several minutes before the aircraft came to a stop. The roar of the turboprops dropped to a whine, and the ramp was lowered. The team filed to the rear of the aircraft, grabbed their bags, and hopped off the ramp.

It was dark out. "What time is it here?" Jessica asked.

Hector looked at his watch. "It's quarter past midnight. Come on, get your gear."

Even at night, the heat from the tarmac radiated like an open oven, and the exhaust fumes assaulted their nostrils. Hector took in a deep breath and exhaled hard. *It's good to be home again.* The beast growled in agreement.

Guapo and Cujo rolled the vehicles out while the ground crew unloaded the pallets with forklifts. Similar scenes played across the airport as airplanes landed and took off in the middle of the night.

The team was waved over to a minibus by a blonde woman with hair pulled back into a tight bun. She and Hector smiled and shook hands while the rest of the team filed into the minibus.

"Rachel! I didn't think I'd see you out here again."

"I could say the same thing for you. You doin' another job out here?"

Hector glanced back at the team and nodded. "Yep. Probably my last one, too."

"You?" she asked skeptically. "Never! You ain't happy unless you're out in the field."

He handed her their passports as she began writing on her clipboard. "Well, you're not wrong on that, but I gotta hang it up sometime. This may as well be it."

She was quiet as she finished with the paperwork. "Yeah, I hear you. This might be my last one as well. Besides, if the ISIS situation gets worse, there's a good chance none of us will be back here." She looked up. "I'll get these processed and meet you at the PAX terminal. Good to see you again, Gung Ho."

Hector shook her hand. "And good to see you again, Duchess."

Rachel hopped in the front seat of the minibus next to the driver, while Hector made his way to the back and climbed in.

"So what's with the blonde?" asked Jessica in a lowered voice.

"That's Rachel. She's our facilitator with the Iraqi government. If you think things move slow back home, it's ten times slower here. Nothing happens unless you know somebody, and Rachel knows everybody." He winked. "We're on lockdown until the morning, so she's got time to get us access into the IZ in the morning."

"IZ?"

"The International Zone. You may have heard of it as the Green Zone back in the day."

"Oh, right. And, what's this about a lockdown? What are we supposed to do until then?"

"We're going to the PAX terminal. Or, passenger terminal." He had to remind himself that she was green and didn't know any of the lingo. Jessica might know a lot of languages, but she didn't know the tactical language of his team. He pointed to a hangar in the distance. "That hangar used to house Coalition forces arriving and departing Baghdad during the war. We now lease it for the same purpose . . . but with much better amenities."

Minutes later, they pulled up in front of the hangar, and the team filed in. To Hector's relief, the interior had gotten a much-needed upgrade since the last time he was here. It was adequately fitted with recreation rooms, large screen TVs, computer stations, bathroom and showers, and a fully stocked bar. *Thank you, Rachel!*

The team raced to the bar like kids to an ice cream truck. Hector watched Rachel go up to Jessica, her bubbly and spritely demeanor taking the lawyer by surprise. "Hi, I'm Rachel. Welcome to Baghdad. We don't usually get females, but I managed to get you a separate room." Hector turned his attention to the bar as Rachel led Jessica to the opposite side of the hangar, away from the team, to a room made entirely of unvarnished plywood.

They returned a few minutes later. Jessica was wearing yoga pants and a sweatshirt, and she thanked Rachel.

Rachel handed Hector the passports back, along with a folder. "You're good to go for tomorrow. Passports are in order, and tomorrow's placard is in the folder." She leaned in to hug him. "Good to see you again, Hector. Be careful out there, okay?"

The hug and farewell took him by surprise, but he didn't think much of it. "Thanks again, Rachel. We'll do our best." She left the hangar with a little less pep in her step, turning around one last time before exiting.

"All right, everyone." Hector addressed the team. "Let's finish up the night caps and hit the rack. We've got a busy day tomorrow."

By 10 a.m., the temperature had reached 90 degrees Fahrenheit and they were on the road to the IZ. The drive itself wouldn't take longer than Hector's drive from the house to work, but this was Iraq and anything could happen outside the wire. The team conducted radio checks, and both Hector and Voodoo went over assignments on who would do what if they came in contact with hostiles.

"Is there something I should know, or something I should do?"

From the front passenger seat, Hector turned back to Jessica, who was directly behind him. He showed her a map of Baghdad, outlining the routes that they could take with several lines of varying colors.

He pointed to BIAP. "We're here, and we want to get to the IZ over here." He shifted his finger to a small spot on the map near the center of Baghdad along the Tigris River. "That's where the embassy is." He then drew a line from BIAP to the embassy with his finger, tapping the main road between the two places twice. "This is Route Irish. For a long time, this was the deadliest stretch of road for troops and civilians because of ambushes or IEDs."

Jessica's eyes widened.

"It's gotten better over time, but we're on our own, and occasionally something happens. We're just making sure we're ready for anything. Just remember your training and keep your eyes and ears open."

Minutes later, they cleared the security perimeter at BIAP and were driving east along Route Irish. The drive was so far uneventful, aside from terrible driving by locals and a few glares. Hector couldn't help himself from looking back at Jessica sitting behind him, her dark hair pulled back under her baseball cap and the communications headset on top. Her attention shifted continuously, like a cat following the red dot from a laser pointer, suspicious of any vehicle that came too close or of any objects in between the large cement support pylons under the various overpasses they crossed. She reminded him of his first time outside the wire, back when the roadside attacks were bad. Really bad. And it was because of that empathy that no one in the vehicle gave her a hard time about it.

The inter-vehicle communications crackled, and they heard Pirate Face ask, "Yo, Romeo, when's your next carne asada, bro? I wanna motorboat your sister's tits."

A much-needed laugh erupted in the lead vehicle.

"Shit, you'll drown in those, fucker." The cackle of laughter was heard over the net.

Jessica's laugh resonated over the others. "Boys."

Hector was glad she wasn't the easily offended type. He couldn't imagine Kelly chortling at a joke like that. He leaned his head back. "Sometimes you just have to have time to laugh. Without the humor, the stress alone will wear you down and lead to bad decisions made at very bad times. Sometimes something has to give. Better to be 'pussy hurt' than the alternative."

The convoy reached the fortified checkpoint leading into the IZ, and the team was at its highest alert. There were three lines of vehicles, each with about six or seven vehicles waiting. The team maneuvered to the far-left lane, leaving enough room between their vehicle and the car ahead, should everything go to shit and they had to get out of Dodge. Ahead they could see the security checkpoint, consisting of two armored Humvees with large-caliber machine guns—probably Russian DsKHs—and hardened pillboxes on either side. In between were Iraqi soldiers walking up and down the lines, looking inside the windows with an intensity that would have made the Gestapo proud.

As they crawled forward, the team scanned the Iraqi Security Force positions and the vehicles lining up to enter. Just because the soldiers had uniforms didn't mean they were the good guys. The beast inside Hector thumped its chest like a war drum. This was where it belonged. This was where it was meant to roam free. Hector took a deep breath and exhaled slowly.

Static crackled through the radios, and Guapo said, "We're in the dead zone."

"Dead zone?" asked Jessica.

"Yeah, it's a radio frequency jamming zone. It's supposed to prevent any radio-controlled IEDs from going off but doesn't do crap against command-detonated. Unfortunately, it also cuts the communication between our vehicles. It is what it is."

Jessica put her hand to her forehead. "Oh my God. So anybody here could blow themselves up?"

"Yep."

"Jesus Christ! So how the hell am I supposed to know who's a bad guy and who's not?"

"You just have to look for the signatures. Somebody on the phone, somebody looking around nervously, or somebody praying. It can be any of those things—or more."

"Are you kidding me? Hell, I'm practically all of those right now!"

Hector grinned. It was so easy to mess with her. "Well, are you planning on blowing yourself up?"

"Very funny, Hector!"

The rest of the team laughed. Jessica did not.

When they reached the checkpoint, the tension spiked. Hector pressed a purple placard with the Barcelona Football Club and Scuderia Ferrari symbols next to each other on the windshield. The ISF guard motioned for Guapo to lower the window.

"No fucking way, bro," responded Guapo, pointing to the placard. "This is the fucking signal."

The ISF guard shouted something through the bulletproof glass.

"No, fuck you, Hajji!" Guapo jabbed his finger at the placard, then added, "This is the signal, motherfucker! Now do your goddamned job!"

Jessica gripped the back of Hector's seat. "Hector, what's going on?" she asked nervously.

"This placard is the pass signal of the day. It changes daily, and this is today's signal. The fucking idiot should know this, but the ISF isn't like the US Army." He looked back at Jessica. "These fucking guys probably have no idea what today's placard is, and no matter what, we never lower the windows."

This time the ISF guard shouted something back and raised his AK-47 to the window. A Mexican standoff was about to boil over.

To Hector's surprise, Jessica got up from her seat, stretched her blouse open above the body armor as far as it could go, and leaned on the center console between him and Guapo. She yelled something in Arabic that made her sound like the guard's mother chewing his ass out for something the poor fuck had done. She then pointed to herself, then the gate, and then to the guard. The guard cowered with the look of someone who had been caught with his pants down and repeatedly waved his arm at the guard manning the security gate and let them through.

What the fuck did I just witness? Hector wondered. Apparently, Guapo had the same thought. "What the fuck did you tell him?"

Jessica returned to her seat and said, with a sly smile, "I told him if he refused to allow the ambassador's mistress to pass, I would call his commander and he'd find himself searching for IEDs along the road by the end of the day."

Laughter erupted inside the vehicle.

"Holy shit, that is fucking badass!" said Guapo. "You got some balls, *chica*. Major balls."

Hector raised an eyebrow. "The ambassador's mistress? Good thing he doesn't know the ambassador is a woman."

Jessica shrugged. "Hey, maybe she's into girls."

He had to admit, he was deeply impressed. It was rash, and probably stupid—Jessica may know the customs, though she'd never been in theater or faced situations like this one—but it worked. An instinct like that would keep her alive.

Guapo kept laughing. "Brass fucking balls, Flash. I'll polish those fuckers any day. Just say it, and I'm your bitch."

Jessica looked pleased with herself. "Damned straight, you're my bitch, Guapo."

Penguin, seated beside Jessica, gave her a gentle slug on the arm. "Did you pick that up in law school or negotiator school?"

"It's more of a power thing," she said. "If you can walk around and confidently drop names, there's a lot of things you can get away with. The guard is probably at the bottom of the tribe he belongs to, so chances are he's more receptive to name recognition than placards."

Penguin whistled. "Wow. I'm glad you're on our team."

Traffic lightened once inside the IZ, but security posture remained vigilant. The ISF no longer manned the internal checkpoints. Instead they were replaced by units bearing the presidential guard seal. Things had indeed changed since he was here last. At last they reached the embassy, with its high walls and massive yellow buildings inside the compound. Were it not for the American flag waving, one could easily mistake it for a prison.

They pulled up to the first vehicle entry point. The guard force, consisting of a paramilitary force not unlike Parabellum, were visibly more professional and thorough. Despite having the placard, security in this layer was more scrutinized. Both vehicles were eventually allowed in and parked along with all the other series of armored vehicles belonging to military units and the Diplomatic Security Service.

The team split up, with Hector and Jessica heading to the chancery and the rest of the team going in the opposite direction. "Where are they going?" asked Jessica.

"Probably to the commissary to get us some supplies," said Hector. "That, or they're off to Baghdaddy's for drinks."

"Bag-daddy's?"

"Yep. The embassy bar."

"They have a bar?"

Hector shook his head. "Don't even get me started about their 'Ladies Night.'"

The lush green patch of grass lined with palm trees between the embassy's chancery building and the ambassador's residence had hardly changed. Just as before, it seemed entirely out of place among the plain, sandstone-colored buildings and the concrete service roads that outlined it. Before they got halfway to the chancery, sirens began wailing across the compound. Without a second thought, Hector took Jessica by the hand and dragged her toward one of the many concrete upside-down *U*s that served as bomb shelters.

"In there! Run!"

He shoved Jessica into the shelter. Before she could speak, he barked, "Get down low, open your mouth, and cover your ears!"

She obeyed him unquestioningly. "Jesus Christ! What is that?"

"C-RAM." Hector turned his head to her. "Counter rocket, artillery, and mortar alarm. We're still in a war zone, and the goddamned hajjis like to remind us of that every now and then."

He moved his head from side to side, trying to make out the sounds of any incoming 107mm rockets or mortars. He kept a hand on her, never using enough pressure to startle her, but to show her he was present, should he need to grab her by her blouse and yank her in any direction.

Long seconds passed without incident. Then, a less ominous alarm sounded. "What is that?" she asked in a low voice.

Hector got up and winked down at her as he extended his hand to her. "That was the all-clear. Looks like they missed us." She was still catching her breath, and it probably wasn't because of the running, either. "You okay?"

Jessica rested her hands on her thighs and nodded. "Holy shit! Does that happen a lot?"

Hector grinned. "Yep, pretty normal. Welcome to Baghdad."

31

"Let's get in the chancery, just in case."

Jessica followed Hector out of the shelter, her mind racing as she looked around. No one else seemed bothered by what had just happened. She'd thought the Kobayashi Maru would be the height of her moments of terror. Boy, was she wrong. *Rockets and mortars! You just had to ask, didn't you?*

They speed-walked from the bomb shelter to the two tall glass double doors with tubular handles that were the entrance to the chancery. She reached for the handle and nearly lost her footing trying to open the ridiculously heavy door.

"Oh my God!" she groaned. "What is it with this door?"

Hector reached over her and pulled the handle. "Sorry, I should have mentioned that. Blast-proof doors."

"Huh, I wonder why."

Once that set of doors closed, she opened the second set, which was much lighter. The doors and the near-death episode she had just experienced answered her question as to why the embassy didn't have the regal architectural design of more notable buildings, like the Eisenhower Executive Office Building or one of the many other federal buildings that lined the National Mall. And the answer to that was survivability. Every building was designed to withstand anything from a rocket to a bomb.

And yet they still somehow have a bar. You just can't make this stuff up.

Ahead of them was Post One, the security post built like a mini-bunker, where the US Marine security guard in desert fatigues slid them their visitor badges in a tray under the inches-thick glass. They slipped the lanyards around their necks and made their way into the chancery.

The interior was a different world. An expansive open atrium with granite flooring and art from American artists on display welcomed them, along with an awkwardly sterile scent, like that of a hospital ward. She followed Hector up the granite-lined stairs to the second of four floors where they were met by two men, one taller than the other.

Hector clasped the taller man's hand. "Luis! How the hell are you?"

"I was better before you showed up," he said, chuckling. Luis turned to Jessica and extended his hand. "Luis Gonzales, RSO. It's a pleasure to meet you, Ms. Beaumont." He motioned to the man next to him. "This is Jonathan Hendricks, the Deputy Economic Officer."

Jonathan and Jessica shook hands. His camel-hair blazer with a baby blue shirt and khaki chinos made him look more like an economics professor than a diplomat.

"May I ask, how long have you been in Iraq?" she asked.

"Two years, come October." Jonathan seemed young to her, but his face showed a lifetime's worth of experience in the two years he'd been in Iraq.

Luis gestured for the group to follow him. "We have refreshments ready in the conference room upstairs."

He opened the door and escorted them in. The inside of the second floor was lined with cubicles and hallways that resembled most offices in a New York high-rise. She peeked inside some of the cubicles and found they were no different than those from her own office, with each employee personalizing their own space to make a "home away from home."

Jonathan walked beside Jessica as Hector and Luis chatted ahead of them. "Have you liked it here so far?" Jessica asked.

"I have, but I'm ready to head back to Washington." Jonathan had a tone of urgency in his voice that she found unsettling. He looked her over as if trying to figure her out and asked, "If you don't mind me asking, why do you even want to go up north?"

The question took her by surprise. "Well, I'm the person best suited to represent Norton-Allied. I've successfully negotiated terms with the Gulf states, Nigerians, Angolans, and others."

Jonathan shook his head. "I'm sorry, that's not what I mean. What I'm asking is why do you want to go with those guys? It's going to be rough living, and . . ." He hesitated. "And incredibly dangerous. Aren't you worried?"

Jessica examined him for a moment to see if his question was sexist—but she determined he was sincere. "Um, sure. Yeah, a bit. But I've trained with these guys. I've earned their trust, and they think of me as one of the team. I guess if they feel I'm ready, then sure, why not?"

The answer didn't seem to satisfy him, but he apparently decided to leave it alone.

They reached the conference room, and Jonathan used his badge to release the magnetic lock. Inside was a large conference table surrounded by leather chairs, a large-screen TV, and a computer station. The absence of windows was not lost on her. She and Hector sat at the end of the table, with Jonathan and Luis on the side.

Once they sat, Jessica noted a change in the RSO's demeanor that was impossible to miss, and it wasn't for the better. Luis leaned forward, clapped his hands together, and rubbed them nervously. "You've been traveling, so I'm guessing you haven't heard the latest situation report." When Hector shook his head no, he and Jonathan shared a look. He went on. "Unfortunately, the situation in the north has deteriorated, and your trip may have been for naught." He took a deep breath and just let it out. "Mosul fell to ISIS."

The words struck Jessica like a punch to the gut. She held her composure, a statuesque representation of Norton-Allied's strength and diplomacy. She had always been good at remaining unreadable, when the time was necessary.

Now was necessary.

Luis clicked the TV remote, and Jessica flicked her eyes to the close-up map of northern Iraq.

Hector pushed back on the chair and ran a hand through his hair, staring hard at the map. The crimson red representing ISIS had metastasized over Mosul and the Greater Iraqi–controlled areas. Farther south, the crimson lines resembled an outstretched hand whose crooked fingers grasped for Kirkuk, Tikrit, and finally Baghdad.

"So, what is the Iraqi Army doing about it?" asked Hector. "Where are they engaging?"

Luis sighed. "There is no Iraqi Army."

Hector leaned forward to the table. "What do you mean, there is *no Iraqi army*?"

Jessica glanced from one man to the other. Wasn't the Iraqi Army a large part of their negotiation strategy? She'd need to call Bill.

"What I mean is that they no longer exist. ISIS swept through the second-largest city like the blitzkreig. The Iraqi Army didn't even bother to put up a defense. They—"

"Wait! Stop. Just, stop." Hector pinched the bridge of his nose, inhaling sharply. "Are you telling me that a force of some thirty thousand soldiers with tanks, artillery, and mechanized infantry fell to terrorists with *technicals*?"

Jessica now understood Jonathan's trepidation. She leaned over and whispered, "What's a technical?"

Jonathan whispered back, "A pickup truck with a machine gun in the back."

Luis nodded. "Sixty thousand, including the police. But yes, that's exactly what I'm telling you, Hector. And now those terrorists have all the weaponry that the Iraqi Army left behind . . . including US-made M1 Abrams tanks."

Hector jumped from his seat. He ran his hand through his hair again and again, pacing back and forth.

Luis continued, "The highway north of Baquba is still accessible toward Kirkuk, but as soon as Tikrit falls—and it will—there won't be anything left between ISIS and Baghdad. You'll be on your own." The heavy weight of this news felt suffocating to Jessica. Luis's lips were a thin, grim line. "Whatever elements of the army are left have been pulled back. Their sole job will be to defend Baghdad. And there's more."

Jessica's stomach twisted. *More? How the fuck can it get worse?*

"Tienjing Petroleum's Shia proxies have been wiped out by ISIS, leaving little resistance in the area where the Norton-Allied field is. What's worse is that they have steadily pressed attacks against the Kurds and pushed east toward Kirkuk, south toward Tikrit, and southeast to the Hamrin Mountains. If their projected pace continues unhindered, the Norton-Allied field will be enveloped as ISIS spreads south to Baghdad." He glanced at Jessica. "Your two exfil routes will be cut off."

The twisting sensation in Jessica's stomach stopped, but now it felt like a ball of ice had settled in her gut.

"What about the Peshmerga outpost in Taq Taq? Where are we with that?"

"Hector, I don't—"

He slammed his fist on the conference table. "Goddammit, Luis! Just answer the fucking question."

"Hector!" Jonathan jumped in. "Haven't you heard *anything* he said? Going north is *suicide!*"

Jessica was starting to believe him. But she trusted Hector. He had their best interests at heart, and it was crucial that they successfully establish this oil field. Billions of dollars, her career—all could be lost if they gave up now.

Hector leaned forward and rested his hands flat on the table. He took several calming breaths and looked up. "Luis, I have a team in Taq Taq who arrived before this fucking shit show happened. I am not going to abandon them. Now, we had an understanding that we'd provide infrastructure in exchange for additional shooters. Are the Kurds going to send additional forces to Taq Taq or not?"

Luis nodded. "Yes. We expedited the force protection contract with the Kurds, and a second company already linked up with your advance team while you were en route. Before Mosul fell, the ambassador recognized that, as dangerous as your mission is, it was in the US government's best interest to ensure you're successful. But now . . . everything is different, Hector."

"I understand, but I will not leave my people to fight alone." He paused, giving Jessica a long, hard stare. There was something in his eye that stirred, something Jessica thought was ready for a fight. "Besides, we have an ace up our sleeve."

Jonathan glanced from Hector to her. "I don't mean to doubt you, but what can she do that we haven't already tried?"

Ratcheting up his signature sarcasm, Hector replied, "You really want *me* to answer that?"

Jessica felt her heart sink as she was now put on the spot. She cleared her throat. "The Kurds aren't the Iraqis. They coalesce under a common threat and don't shy away from a fight. But they don't give away their trust, either."

The more she spoke, the more her confidence took over.

This was her element. This was her expertise. They may know about technicals and guns and army movements, but she knew *people*. And without people, there wouldn't be this conversation.

She lifted herself out of her chair and approached the map. "My grandmother is from outside Irbil. What she passed on to me is that there is more to the Kurdish people than what meets the eye." She made eye contact around the room. "I intend to appeal to the Kurds in the region and leverage their support against ISIS. They know the land, they know how to fight, and they've been doing it for generations. I think we can do this."

Luis rubbed his face, considering the options, then nodded. "Fine. I'll bring this up to the ambassador, but she's gonna have a shit fit. I can't tell you not to go, but just know that we may not be able to do much, if anything, from where we are. There won't be any cavalry."

Jessica appreciated his trust. Jonathan, on the other hand, was dumbfounded. "No! You can't just take a woman out there like that. It's . . ." He paused, noticing Jessica's resting-bitch-face-with-a-shot-of-woman-scorned staring back at him. "It's uncivilized."

She leaned forward and rested her curled fists on the conference table. "Listen, Jonathan, I've got a job to do here just like everybody else and am willing to take the same risks as everybody else, including you. Hector and his team saw fit to have me train and deploy with them, so I would hope that you can keep your chauvinistic pretenses to yourself."

Luis turned off the projector. "If you and your team want to spend the night and leave in the morning, you're all more than welcome. We have dorms available."

"Thanks, Luis," said Hector. "I think we'll take that offer. We'll also need use of any spare computers you may have."

Hector motioned to Jessica, and together they headed to the doors to join the rest of the team.

"And Hector," Luis called before they exited. "If you change your mind, you know where to find me."

Hector nodded and closed the door on their way out.

For the first time, Jessica felt the true weight of her responsibility on her shoulders. "All right, what do you need me to do?" A knot tightened in her stomach.

"This went to shit faster than expected, but we can't pull back now." Hector's tone became more intense. "These ISIS fuckers are motivated and they're not scared of anything, so it's going to be on you to not just gain the trust of the Kurds, but also to convince them to put their asses on the line for us if the shit really hits the fan. You might just need to wake up Bill and have him wire a shit ton of money to bribe them with."

Jessica felt the air leave her lungs, but didn't let it affect her. *Resolute. Impassable.* "All right, I can do that. We have slush funds in place for situations like this. Anything else?"

Hector turned back with a stern look. "You're the negotiator, Flash. Use whatever leverage you already have in Irbil and see if they can plus up the forces they're already sending. I'm asking a lot, I know, but I don't want to depend on the embassy alone when our asses are on the line. Make it happen, Flash. You got until morning."

He turned away and strode off down the hall without another word.

Despite feeling the immensity of what Hector was asking, Jessica felt an equal amount of pride that Hector trusted her with this Herculean task. He directed and treated her like a member of the team and expected her to deliver by whatever means necessary.

Well, it's a good thing you're spending the night, Flash, 'cause you've got a lot of phone calls to make.

She smiled and speed-walked to catch up to Hector. "Wait up!"

32

United States Embassy, Baghdad
10 June 2014

The team departed the embassy at dawn as the *al-Fajr*
morning prayers resonated across hundreds of minaret loud-
speakers. They crossed the Tigris by way of the 14th of July
Bridge into the Karada peninsula, or "The Penis" as Jessica
learned it was called by most who were familiar with the
Baghdad geography. They traveled east along the peninsula
and then north on the Al Qassim Highway to make their way
into northeastern Baghdad.

Jessica watched in childlike wonder as old women
hunched over and swept dirt off the sidewalks with wet
brooms, shopkeepers lowered awnings, children helped make
bread for the lunchtime restaurant crowds, and two old men
in tribal attire smoked and drank coffee with a transistor
radio between them. It looked nothing like the alarming
predictions she'd listened to yesterday.

I guess war is just another day in the life.

The scenery became more rural as the convoy left the
outer districts of Baghdad and traveled north on Highway 2

toward Kirkuk. She still couldn't shake off the RSO's account of the fall of Mosul. Sixty thousand soldiers and policemen couldn't stop a fraction of that number—a rounding error with pickups and machine guns—from taking Iraq's second largest city. She was scared. She prayed she didn't show it; no one else seemed to be affected by it, and she didn't want to be the only one.

Hector pulled her out of her thoughts.

"Flash, did you get ahold of Bill, and were you able to make miracles happen with anyone in Irbil?" he asked through the net.

"I did talk to Bill. He saw the news and was worried since we hadn't been in touch. He said he can have as much as five million dollars ready, but getting it physically will be a problem."

Hector nodded.

"As for making miracles, no joy. Everyone is either preparing for ISIS or sending forces to more strategic places. My colleague said Taq Taq isn't even a bleep on their radar." She had reached out to her old friend Qari last night, but the bleak news had dampened their reunion.

"Fuck!"

The northbound traffic was light, but the opposite lanes were jammed with bumper-to-bumper traffic held up at the Iraqi Army checkpoints. Hector warned Jessica, "We shouldn't have any issues until we get to Kirkuk, but if we do, don't be pulling that shit you did at the IZ. It ain't going to work with these guys. You leave that to us, got it?"

Jessica nodded, wondering if he said that because she was a woman and it had worked, or because he hadn't come up with the idea. She shook her head. Jonathan must have gotten to her worse than she'd realized. *Don't be getting all uppity on your feminist study and theory, Flash. This is the real fucking world.*

She startled as the opening chords to Motley Crue's "Kick-start My Heart" blared from a Bluetooth speaker between her and Penguin. The other guys in the vehicle bobbed their heads to the beat, still keeping an eye out for danger. Back home, she would have raised all hell for being startled this way, but this was different. She didn't mind it so much because they were in this all together, and if it meant dealing with loud music to make sure they were at the top of their game, so be it.

However, that didn't mean she couldn't have some music she could enjoy, as well. "Hey, Eric, do you have anything more, you know, current?"

He winked and nodded. "Don't worry, sister, I got you covered."

She wasn't sure what he meant by that, but at least he hadn't verbally assaulted her. True to his word, when the first song ended, her face lit up as she heard Ingrid Michaelson's "Girls Chase Boys," and she started singing the lyrics like she had done so many times with her girlfriends back in DC. When the song came to an end, she grinned as the first notes of "Counting Stars" by OneRepublic played. Heads bobbed, one by one, as the tempo picked up, and eventually everyone joining in the chorus.

Over the next couple of hours, an eclectic playlist shuffled songs from David Bowie, the Gin Blossoms, Katy Perry, Toby Keith, Sam Smith, Tupac, and Stevie Wonder. The ample range in music styles made the nearly five-hour trip much more bearable.

However, there was one awkward yet highly important detail that had somehow been overlooked. The high-capacity fuel tanks in the vehicles made it possible for them to make the five-hour drive without having to refuel, and that was now a problem. Jessica called out, "Hey, guys, can we stop?" She squinted with urgency. "I really have to go."

Hector turned back and scowled like a father on a family trip. "Can you hold it until we get there? We only have some three hours to go, tops."

Jessica brought out her darkest scowl. "Hector! I'm not a child! I'm telling you, I have to go and I can't hold it any longer!"

"Flash, we are in the middle of fucking nowhere, and there are no gas stations or rest stops for you to use. If you need to go, it's gonna be right here at the side of the road. Do you get what I'm saying?"

"Yes, goddammit! I get it. Now pull over!"

"All right then," said Hector. He pulled the microphone boom of his headset closer to his mouth and pushed the talk button. "Spartan Two-One, Spartan Two-Zero. Halt movement for a two-minute security check and keep your eyes open. Over." The convoy slowed down and pulled to the side of the road. Hector laughed at whatever was said on the other end. "Roger. Flash has to go potty."

Jessica slapped his shoulder. "Very funny, Hector!" Once both vehicles stopped, Jessica unlocked her door and stepped out in a hurry. There was nothing but desert and brush for miles, and the noon temperature breached triple digits. She desperately looked for something to hide behind when suddenly Hector and Penguin also stepped out with their weapons at the ready, scanning the area.

She stared at Hector. "Are you kidding me?" Penguin smirked, not looking at her.

"Did you forget your training, Flash?" asked Hector without breaking his sweeping scan in the distance. "We always set up security when we stop. Now hurry the fuck up."

"Fine!" Jessica grunted in protest. She unbuckled, dropped her cargo pants and panties, and did her business right there and then. "And stop laughing, Eric!" she screeched, embarrassed. "I can hear you."

She finished peeing, only now realizing she didn't have any toilet paper with her. She grimaced with disgust and gingerly pulled her pants back up. She shuddered at the grossness of feeling her undies grow wet but got back inside the Land Rover to resume moving.

Four hours after leaving Baghdad, they reached the outskirts of Kirkuk. She'd heard of the refugee crisis, of course, but it was totally different to personally witness the flood of Iraqis leaving the city by any means necessary, a sight reminiscent of the exodus from Egypt. Buses, cargo trucks, cars, mules, bicycles, and anything that could be laden with people or belongings moved past families with young children and elderly grandparents traveling on foot, carrying whatever they were able. The massive line of humanity escaping the scourge of ISIS stretched into the horizon.

Amid the hordes, Jessica witnessed a child, not older than five, crying at the side of the road, tired of walking for hours. Ahead was the father, weeping as he clutched generations-old family heirlooms and photographs. He stood there, forced to decide whether to subjugate the child to continue walking without end or discard the belongings like trash and pick up the crying child. Jessica had seen injustices before, but this one tore into her core, making her eyes well up and her heart break into little pieces in the short ten seconds it took to drive past them.

The rest of the team said nothing. They, too, had witnessed similar injustices, many more than she had, and they showed no outward emotion or voiced outrage. She shook her head as she examined each of their blank faces. *They're completely desensitized.*

Penguin turned to Jessica, as if he could read her mind, and said, "It sucks, and it tears me up inside, but there's nothing that we can do for them, so don't go kicking yourself in the face over this. This ain't the last time you're gonna see this, so steel yourself and carry on. That's about all you can do."

Jessica dried the tears from her eyes and nodded. It wasn't a comforting speech and wasn't meant to be. It was enough to know she wasn't alone in remembering how it felt to be human.

The closer they got to the city, the thicker traffic became. The convoy slowed down to a near halt as vehicles of all types drove in every possible direction, regardless of traffic signs, all making a desperate attempt to leave the city. The junction from the highway to the Sulayman road was impassable with the volume of traffic. Moreover, the bottleneck would make them a sitting target, so they pushed deeper into the city to find an alternate route. Her heart stammered as the sight brought her back to the Kobayashi Maru—only now, this was the real thing. She wiped the sweat of her palms against her cargo pants.

The contrast between driving through Baghdad and Kirkuk was night and day. If ISIS managed to lay siege to Baghdad, what she saw in Kirkuk would be a fraction of the chaos that would erupt in the capital. Jessica covered her mouth as she stared at the absolute chaos around her. *How did all this happen?*

At last, they successfully navigated across the old part of the city. Hector pointed ahead. "There, that's the Kirkuk-Sulayman road." He got on the net and said, "We're crossing through Phase Line Kilo. The hard part's just beginning."

"What now?" asked Jessica.

"We're gonna head northeast toward Taq Taq, then over to the Peshmerga outpost overlooking the oil field. We'll meet up with Alpha Team and the Peshmerga force."

"Is it safe?" Her question was loaded.

Hector looked outside the windows, then said, "Let's

hope. There's a lot of terrain between us and the outpost where ISIS could lay in wait. Just keep your fingers crossed."

Just keep my fingers crossed.

Before she could say anything, Hector keyed the talk button and gave the order. "All Spartan units, deploy guns. I say again, deploy guns. Over."

Penguin immediately cleared the speaker and the other clutter from the middle console, and slid back the false roof that exposed an M2 .50-caliber machine gun on a swivel. He unlatched the two halves of the round hatch, flipped the hydraulics switch that lifted the armor-plated hatches, and raised the spring-loaded swivel to lift the machine gun into a firing position. He pulled a lever unlocking the ring around the hatch and spun it around to ensure a 360-degree rotation. He talked into his mike. "Gun one ready."

The second vehicle reciprocated with its Mk-19, a devastating automatic weapon that fired 40mm high-explosive grenades. If anyone dared test the Parabellum team's resolve to reach their destination, they'd have a nasty surprise waiting for them.

The midafternoon Iraqi sun bore down hard. Jessica wiped the sweat off her brow and drank the last of the water from her second bottle. She crushed it and stuck it in the trash bag with the others. She could only imagine how bad it was for Penguin hanging out of the rooftop, but she understood his discomfort had to be tolerated for the sake of the mission and their survival. Even the few patches of sun that peered through the hatch seared her skin. He was a trooper all right, only breaking his concentration whenever she handed him another bottle of water. He was on his fourth.

The scenery belied the heat wave that assaulted them. She recalled images of the lush green pastures in northern Iraq, but to see them with her own eyes was entirely different. It was like the difference between seeing images of a California sunset and experiencing it in person, watching the orange sun dip into the horizon with the sand at your feet and the salty breeze in your face.

An hour later, they neared the base overseeing the adjacent oil field. Hector keyed the radio. "All Spartan units, halt movement." He switched to the designated frequency of the day and said, "Spartan Base, Spartan Two-Zero. We're at your nine o'clock. Do you copy?"

The radio crackled as the voice on the other end responded, "Lima Charlie, Spartan Two-Zero. Good to hear from you. Glint twice to confirm your visual."

"Roger, Spartan Base. Stand by." Hector switched back to the intercom between the vehicles and relayed, "All Spartan Units, switch frequency to Delta One and glint twice to confirm visual."

Guapo flipped their lights on and off twice and waited for a response. "Roger, Spartan Units, visual confirmed. Approach along designated axis."

"Roger that, Spartan Base. Spartan Two-Zero and Spartan Two-One moving out."

The vehicles crawled along the road leading to the front gate. They zigzagged through concrete chicanes and avoided the intertwined coils of barbed concertina wires and deep ditches on either side of the road that prevented direct access at a high speed, all while under the constant cover of machine-gun nests embedded in the watchtowers. Alpha Team had made very good use of their time.

They crested one of two hills that formed a natural choke point, and Jessica got a better look at her home for the next two months. Hector and the rest of the team would remain for three or more. It looked *nothing* like a fort. It was more like the Alamo, and just as old. The walls were about as high as the training compound but looked as if they would fall apart on their own. Atop one of the two circular castle-style ramparts was a flag with red, white, and green banners and a blazing sun in the center: the unmistakable flag of Kurdistan. When they reached the entrance, the two gates—red from rust rather than paint, most likely—creaked as they opened outward.

"What the fuck is this shit?" asked Guapo as they rolled inside.

"Home sweet home," replied Hector.

The inside was a near replica of the villa back in Texas. Behind the walls were twenty- and forty-foot containers that added an extra layer of protection and served as ramparts, and on top of the castle-like towers were structures resembling deer blinds. But it was the housing area that gave her some semblance of home. In between the three double-stacks of containerized housing units was a courtyard like the one in the villa, minus the bar. Hanging underneath the entrance was a large wooden sign that read WELCOME TO THE ALAMO. Jessica rolled her eyes. "Oh, that's funny, Hector. Real cute." As morbid the thought of making her last stand here was, she had learned to appreciate the team's dark humor—something she would've abhorred in the past.

Hector keyed the radio and ordered the team to dismount, unload the vehicles, and park next to Alpha Team's SUVs and the Peshmerga's Toyota Hilux pickups.

While the team unloaded the vehicles, Voodoo, Jessica, and Hector walked to the command post—the CP—set up inside one of the twenty-foot air-conditioned CHUs. Inside the CP was Spinner, the Alpha Team leader who stood ready to introduce them to the commander of the Peshmerga forces. "Gung Ho, Voodoo, this is Captain Samir. Captain, this is Gung Ho, the Bravo Team leader."

Miffed at being left out of the introductions, Jessica interjected. She put her hand to her heart and said in Kurdish,

"Peace be upon you, Captain Samir. We are honored to stand with those who face death."

Spinner looked from Hector to Voodoo to see if he was the only one who didn't understand what she said.

A wide grin formed under the captain's thick mustache, and he said in English, "The honor is mine, Miss . . . ?"

She extended her hand. "Jessica Beaumont, Captain. It's a pleasure to meet you."

"My apologies, Flash." Spinner cleared his throat and resumed. "Since we don't have T-walls available, we reinforced the interior of the containers with two layers of HESCO barriers to add density against VBIEDs, but I'm hoping we won't have to find out if that would be enough of a buffer against a shock wave that significant. We also established cache sites with fifty-five-gallon water drums and MREs at each wall. We have decent comms, depending on its mood, and we send the TOC a weekly SITREP unless supplemental reports are needed in-between."

He clasped his hands. "So, how about the grand tour?"

Spinner led them on a tour of the not-so-big base and highlighted their logistics. "We've got two twelve-fifty-kilovolt containerized diesel generators running night and day cycles, with a third in reserve. Right now, we have enough stores to meet a four-month cycle, plus emergency food and water rations, but we're finding that buying supplies in Taq Taq is good for making friends and improving the food variety. We'll have to draft a new duty schedule now that you all are here, but it shouldn't be too bad."

"All right," said Hector, looking at Spinner and Samir, "let's talk about the elephant in the room. Where is ISIS in relation to us, and what kind of early warning do we have at the moment?"

Samir pointed northwest toward Mosul and gestured southward. "The reports we are getting is that their main force is focused on taking Tikrit and then moving on to Baghdad." He repeated the same motion and added, "To get to us, they will have to cross between Irbil and Kirkuk"—he hammered his fist into his palm—"and they will bleed heavily if they do."

His bravado was inspiring, but not enough to make Jessica forget the RSO's chilling words.

Jessica listened as the four went on to talk about tactics and patrols and other things outside of her understanding when a sense of clarity and self-reflection hit her like a wave.

She was here, in Iraq, right now.

Events were unfolding in such way that no one could predict what would happen tomorrow, but these events would be studied and analyzed in the years to come.

I am living a historic moment.

If she were back home, she'd probably be arguing with Kelly about who knows what petty thing. But by being here, she was experiencing the things that fueled Hector and the others' spirits, and Kelly was a fool for not understanding that. She was living her own historic moment, and she probably didn't even realize it. She wondered if Paul would be understanding or be more like Kelly . . . *Whoa! Where did that come from?* Did that thought come out of nowhere, or was it because she missed his touch and the way he—*Oh my God, Jessica! You have got to keep it together.*

The craziest part was, all of this was happening because she had seen something she wasn't supposed to. Because she just had to be right, had to stick it to that fat fuck in California. She sighed and rubbed her face. That was something else she'd have to figure out when she returned. What had happened to the journalist? Had she inadvertently led him to his demise? *Ugh, so many questions!* Deep down, she was worried. That unsettling feeling at the bottom of her stomach hadn't left her all these years.

Look at the bright side: at least they don't know you're here.

She snapped out of it when the others stopped talking and

Spinner led them to one of the towers. "Now let's take a look at the oil field."

They followed and stood at the parapet of the tower, observing the oil field below.

Jessica had expected to see massive pieces of machinery, oil pumps, pipes leading in all directions, and anything else that resembled an oil field. Instead, she saw three oil rigs, maybe a dozen pumps, and two burn-off smokestacks. As for storage, there were some twenty floating-top containers and a pitiful bunch of crude oil tank trucks rusting at the truck farm.

Jessica paled. *Bill is going to shit himself when he finds out.*

Hector laughed out loud. "Jesus fucking Christ! This is straight out of *The Road Warrior*!"

Samir grinned happily and gave him two enthusiastic thumbs up. "Yes, Mel Gibson. Very good movie!"

33

Parabellum FOB
Near Taq Taq, Iraq

It was 10 p.m. by the time Hector finished inspecting the ammunition magazines, the "clinic" walk-through with Pirate Face, and all the other administrative requirements that the movies never managed to glorify. Samir had a goat slaughtered, and it was roasted on a spit for his guests, but Hector didn't have time to enjoy the camaraderie with the rest of the team. Regardless of the tedious tasks involved with arrival, Hector felt *alive*. The hot desert air, the frantic energy buzzing like an undercurrent to the daily operations, the constant level of alertness—*this* was home. The beast had purred in contentment as Hector wolfed down his obligatory first plate of roasted goat by the bright fire. Finished but not yet full, he had hurried to finish all the other crap that needed to be done and sent back to Parabellum.

His stomach grumbled as he sat in front of the computer screen waiting for Chuck to answer the Skype call. At least the air was cooling down by now, making it bearable for the team outside to sit by the firepit.

It was noon back in DC, and he hoped Chuck was either eating at his desk or returning soon from lunch. He rubbed his eyes and had a nice long stretch while he waited. It'd been a long day, but it wasn't over yet. The connection came through, and he grudgingly leaned toward the screen.

"Hector! How was the trip?" The VPN made Chuck's movements seem choppy, but the voice was coming through well enough.

"Long. Same as last time and the time before that."

Chuck had a laugh at that. "Well, I'm glad you all are set in. Did you encounter any issues we should know about?"

Hector pinched the bridge of his nose. "That depends on what kind of issues you're talking about. I'm guessing you already know about Mosul."

Chuck forwent the small talk. His voice sobered. "Yeah, we started watching the situation right after you departed. No one expected this to happen so fast. Luis sent me his notes on the situation just before you arrived. So what's your take on the ground truth?"

"Captain Samir is well situated in the information flow from Irbil, so take that any way you like it. He feels confident that the main ISIS force will move south toward Tikrit, but that doesn't mean they won't send forces this way. Either way, he's sure the Peshmerga will put a hurt on any elements that come our way." Hector shrugged. "You know how they are."

Chuck managed to laugh. The old man always saw a way to lighten a tense situation.

Hector cleared his throat and repositioned himself in his chair. "As for my view from the ground, Samir has a force of two hundred fighters, a hundred more than I was expecting, but our defenses are much to be desired. In all honesty, defending this place against the force that sacked Mosul would take a miracle."

"You know, word is that ISIS took Mosul with less than two thousand fighters."

Chuck's comment sent a slow, ice-cold chill down his spine. Hector snickered. "Well, then looks like this will definitely be my last mission, one way or another."

Kelly had always hated his dark humor, but there were times when that's all he had.

Chuck forced a smile. "I'll be sure to light a few hundred candles on Sunday if that's what it takes."

"Hey, Chuck," Hector said, trying to find the right words. "Do you happen to know if Betty talked with Kelly these last couple of days?"

Chuck interlaced his fingers and let out a long sigh. "Not in great detail. Apparently, Kelly's schedule is jam-packed with meetings with the partners about the merger, and Betty has spent most of her time with Heather and Veronica getting the wedding finalized." He rubbed the bald spot on his head. "I can't figure out if it's a good thing or a bad thing that both are happening this summer. Good grief."

Hector's hopes deflated, but he still managed to keep up appearances. "That's fine, I figured I'd just ask."

"Keep your hopes up, Hector. And don't worry too much about Kelly. Betty always makes time to check up on her and keep her sane. By the way, tell Jessica great job for thinking fast about the money. Bill called as soon as he hung up with her and is working some black magic to get it in hard currency. We'll figure out how to get the money to you. It might take an air drop, but you'll get it."

"Thanks, Chuck. I'll let her know. You got anything else for us before I sign off?"

Chuck leaned forward until Hector could see the deep wrinkles around his eyes and forehead. "Yeah. Bill and I had a long talk about it and came to an agreement. If defending that oil field is untenable, do not feel obligated to stay and fight. I know I don't have to say this, but I feel like I should.

Don't make this your last stand, Hector. There's still time to pull chocks and pop smoke."

"Understood. Thanks, Chuck. Spartan Base signing off."

Hector leaned back in the chair, weighing the seriousness of the situation. It gave him a glimpse into the kind of decisions he'd have to make as the Chief of Global Operations, and so far he wasn't liking it. In a way, making judgment calls while on the ground was a lot easier than from behind a desk thousands of miles away. Lives could be forever changed depending on his decision. And then there was the beast. The beast inside him was home, but if he decided to pull the plug on his last mission, could he lock it back in its cage for good?

34

Philadelphia, Pennsylvania
12 June 2014

Paul raced north on 11th and turned left onto Filbert Street, stopping only to wipe the sweat dripping off his brow and suffer the abuse of Philly pedestrians. He caught his breath and looked at his watch again—not that it mattered anymore. Donovan had instructed him to meet at the Reading Terminal Market by 2 p.m. to discuss their "business." But he had stayed up late tossing and turning about his meeting with Donovan, then again by Skyping Jessica on her work trip. With the time difference, her 8 a.m. after-breakfast call was one o' clock in the morning for him—and he had listened to her blather on about how hot and dirty it was, oil rig descriptions, and crying kids on the road. By the time he could finally sleep, his morning alarm was about to go off.

He arrived drenched in sweat, plucking the soaked Charles Tyrwhitt shirt from his chest as he oriented himself. He walked past the Pearl Oyster Bar and Old City Coffee, weaving and pushing his way through until he arrived at the seating area near The Flying Monkey Bakery on the other end of the market. A fat man in a business suit eating a massive cupcake waved at him.

Joseph Donovan, he thought. He was accompanied by a man with long, thick black hair slicked back, dressed in a black sports coat with a deep red button-down shirt. The guy looked like someone straight from the casting call of *Goodfellas*.

"You're late, Paul," said Donovan.

"Yeah, well, I'm here now, aren't I?" said Paul. "So, now what?" He sat opposite Donovan and eyed the Guido wannabe next to him.

Donovan took a bite of the cupcake, wiping the frosting off his double chin. "By the way, this is Konstantin. He represents . . . let's call him them the aggrieved party." He slurped his fingers. "How is the merger going?"

Paul shrugged, trying not to stare too much at this revolting figure of a man. "It's fine. It's just a matter of getting it over with."

"That's good to hear. I understand that there will be a christening ceremony in Philadelphia later this summer. Is that correct?" Donovan raised an eyebrow.

Paul squinted at him. "Yeah, that's right. But you knew this already, so why the question?"

"Again, straight to the point. I like that." Donovan leaned forward and spoke in a low voice. "It's quite simple. We want you to find out where and when the reception will be held as soon as possible. We need precise details."

Paul leaned back and exhaled hard. They may as well have asked him to plan the next merger. "I can't just do that! I'm not even a junior VP, for fuck's sake. How do you expect me to—"

Donovan raised a hand. "You're a bright and resourceful young man, Paul. I don't care how. Just make it happen."

Paul stood up and leaned toward Donovan, about to go off on him, when Konstantin landed a hard hand on his right shoulder and forced him back down. In a thick Russian accent, he commanded, "Sit the fuck down! Enough of this bullshit. Now get on with the plan."

Lunchtime customers in the overcrowded market who'd been walking by stole glances at the outburst, then went about their own business, not wanting a part of whatever was going on. Konstantin rewarded their stares with a glare that shooed them them away.

Paul hadn't been pushed around like that since he was a kid. Anger heated his face.

"Who the fuck are you? I—" Paul yelped. Konstantin had jabbed his thumb hard into the gap behind the clavicle, paralyzing Paul in place and causing him to wince in pain.

Konstantin leaned close to Paul. "It doesn't matter who I am, only that I can prevent—or allow—this from happening to you." With his free hand, he pulled out his phone, manipulating it until a picture of Yuri's charred body on the metal chair came up.

Paul froze as he stared at the ghastly picture.

"Does that satisfy your curiosity?"

Paul couldn't bring himself to look away, despite the sickening details and overt implications. *Oh, God! Who the fuck are these guys?*

Konstantin released his grip, put away his phone, and casually sat back down as if nothing had happened.

Paul rubbed his shoulder and looked at Donovan in disbelief. The image of the charred body was permanently etched into his memory. He asked frantically, "What the fuck did you get me into?"

Donovan rubbed his hands together. "There was no way to describe the alternative over the phone, Paul. But I am glad that you reconsidered without having to resort to more direct methods."

Konstantin jumped in. "Yes, it would be unfortunate for you to end up like that poor bastard."

Paul gulped as he looked from Donovan to Konstantin. "Look, I told you I was in. My word has weight." He jabbed his thumb at Konstantin. "You didn't have to bring along this fucking animal to—"

Konstantin grabbed his thumb and wrenched it. Paul winced in pain, contorting his body in a futile attempt to escape the grip. The Russian leaned in and whispered, "If you call me an animal again, you will meet a real animal. Do you understand?"

Paul nodded twice and quickly pulled his hand back to his chest when Konstantin let go.

"Don't focus on that, Paul," said Donovan. "Focus on the money, power, and respect you'll have when it's all done. You'll have whatever you desire. I can give you that. Can she?" He spread his arms wide. "With all of that, girls like her will flock to you."

"Is true," said Konstantin. "You will have everything at snap of your fingers. Men will fear you and women will want you."

"And Paul," said Donovan with a slithery grin, "you'll never again be referred to as 'Winston's son.'"

Paul hesitated. The nights he had spent with Jessica seemed like a distant memory. His mind went to the countless lectures his father had given him, going on and on about the value of something earned. The old goat was living in a world that no longer existed. Empires weren't built on old rules and decorum. And they certainly weren't built without shedding blood. But he didn't want Jessica to end up like the guy in the photo.

Gah, snap out of it, you pussy!

The fact was, nothing he could do would change what was going to happen to Jessica. He had to think about himself now.

Paul sat up straight, steeling himself before looking both men in the eye. With Donovan, it was easy. With Konstantin . . . "Look, there's another problem. Jessica's in Iraq and won't be back until much—"

"And why the fuck didn't you mention this sooner?" said a blustered Donovan.

"How the fuck was I supposed to know you—"

"Where?" asked Konstantin, his voice cool.

"What?"

"Where in Iraq?"

"I can't remember. Somewhere in the north. Why does it matter?"

"Listen to me very carefully, little mouse," said Konstantin. "Find out *exactly* where she is, who is with her, what kind of weapons they have, and what is size of force. Do you understand me?"

"Yes, but why does it matter? I don't understand."

"Do not worry, little mouse. We have friends everywhere, even in Iraq. Just get us the information. We take care of rest, *da*? If we get her there, no problem for you. If she comes back for party, then plan will be set. Easy."

"All right, I'll do it. I'll get you that information." Paul looked Donovan in the eye. "But you better deliver, Donovan."

Konstantin tapped Paul's shoulder. He flinched. "Very good! This is very helpful. Now, let's go to bar and toast! My treat." Konstantin walked the few steps from the seating area to Molly Malloy's.

A nauseating sensation hit Paul as he stood. He felt like a sheep led to slaughter. He thought about Jessica's naked body on his, only now realizing too late that he actually liked her, but that no longer mattered. Her fate was sealed. *Sorry, babe. You made your bed.*

35

Parabellum FOB near Taq Taq, Iraq
12 July 2014

Jessica's back arched as his mouth worked enthusiastically between her legs. She gripped the pillow with one hand, threatening to rip it to shreds, while the other gripped a fistful of his thick, blond, soaked mane. Her mouth gaped as his whiskers trailed down her inner thighs, and his hands roamed the contours of her sweat-slicked body until they reached her breasts. He massaged them, encircling her nipples with his index finger and sending an electric shudder down to her toes.

"Oh, God, yes!" she moaned. "Just like that! Oh, God, just like that!" Her heart raced and her toes curled as she neared an epic climax. "Don't stop! Please, Paul, don't stop!" she begged, as his tongue probed deeper, curled inside her, and pressed oh so perfectly against—

"Yo, Flash!" a voice called out, followed by a sharp rapping on the door. "You in there?"

Jessica gasped for breath as she startled awake.

"Are you fucking kidding me!" she shouted. "Goddammit. What!" The fury in her voice mercifully masked the unrelenting sexual frustration that had had a grip on her for the last two weeks.

"Easy, killer, don't be giving me no attitude," Eric called from the other side of the door. "You got mission brief coming up at zero-eight-thirty. I'll check back in ten." His footsteps faded as he walked away.

Jessica was still panting when she looked over at the nightstand and saw the digital clock reading 8 a.m., then looked down the length of her bed. She had again kicked the bedsheets off and pulled up her nightshirt to reveal her shimmering skin and the glistening between her legs. She palmed her face and plopped back against the sweat-soaked pillowcase. *Goddammit, Eric! You couldn't have waited five fucking minutes!*

This was the fourth time in ten days that she had the same dream. If she could just fucking climax once during that incredible dream, the humiliation would have been all worth it, but no. She was on the very edge each time she woke or was infuriatingly interrupted, and it was driving her mad.

As if that wasn't bad enough, she was halfway through the second month and this trip had been miserable, at best.

To add to her misery, the incessant humming of the diesel generator was exasperating, the septic tank backed up regularly, she wore days-old clothing because the only two washers and dryers needed parts, there were huge, scary blackflies everywhere, the toilet paper was coarse, and her hair reeked for days after her turn at burning trash. Yes, even the lawyer had to burn trash.

But that wasn't all. Not by a long shot. The Iraqi desert was unrelenting. Scorching heat bore down during the day, to the point that stepping outside was like opening a burning oven, and the comparatively frigid temperatures at night chilled her to the bone. How Hector and the others did this for months at a time, over and over, was beyond her.

Her few comforts came from the fact she at the least had a bathroom in her pod and did not rely on a communal bathroom unit, but even that brought little consolation. Water conservation measures restricted her shower time to no more than ten minutes every other day, leaving no time to shave her legs, which were in desperate need of grooming. Yet even if she could have showered for longer, the hot water didn't last for more than eight minutes.

Despite the many hardships, the Parabellum team managed to provide some manner of comfort in the kitchen. Voodoo made his mama's gumbo, Guapo cooked up Mexican specialties, and Megatron made traditional Middle Eastern meals. Though the most perplexing of all was that they somehow always had cold beer. *How the hell does that happen?*

In turn, Jessica pulled her weight by working in the scullery, after admitting she'd never learned how to cook, as well as volunteering to be another machine gunner if necessary. Everyone in the Alamo was a shooter, even her. And when she wasn't on the road meeting with *maliks* or elders to get them to commit to their cause, or when it was too risky for her to leave the post, she filled it by learning and becoming proficient with the M-2 .50-caliber machine gun, the Mk-19 40mm automatic grenade launcher, the M-240G machine gun, and the M-249 Squad Automatic Weapon. By this point, she was able to break down every weapon system, name every component, identify and remediate every problem, and fire each system with lethal efficiency.

In the evenings, Alpha Team would generally barbecue, giving Bravo Team the opportunity to sit around the firepit like back at the villa. That evening, Hector and Jessica joined the rest of the team already at the firepit, and each grabbed a beer from the bucket. "All right, we got the money counted and secured in the lockbox. We're set for tomorrow."

"I can't believe we still have money left!" said Cujo.

"Yeah, well five million dollars is a huge fucking block. It doesn't even look like we made a dent on that whole pallet."

"Oh, I can tell we did," said Jessica.

"You would," countered Cujo.

"You gotta hand it to the old man," said Hector. "I don't know what strings he pulled to get the money airdropped, and I don't think I want to know."

There was an agreeable laugh around the firepit.

"So, what's on the agenda tomorrow, Flash?" asked Penguin, while he stoked the fire.

Jessica took a quick pull of her beer, pulled out her notebook from her cargo pocket, and flipped the pages. "Tomorrow we're going back to meet with Malik Bilal. His village is the next lucky recipient of the monthly stipend."

"Mmm, I like going there," said Cujo with a devious smile. "He's got some pretty daughters to look at."

"Ew! Cujo!"

"What? I'm just saying! They're easy on the eyes, is all."

"Well," said Hector, "sorry to disappoint you, dirty old man, but you and Megatron are going on a supply run."

Megatron laughed and shook his head. "Does he really have to go? I always end up having to apologize for him."

"Whoa there, amigo! You told me you were saying goodbye for me."

Megatron shrugged, and an easy laugh ensued around the fire.

"Oh, Cujo," sighed Jessica. "Don't ever change."

The following day, on the road to the meeting, Hector caught Jessica looking at him studiously. "Why are you looking at me like that?"

Jessica smirked. "Because, you remind me of Captain Wentworth."

Hector squinted. "Who the hell is that?"

"He's the main male character in *Persuasion*."

He stared blankly.

"Oh, never mind." Jessica adjusted her hijab as they neared the village. Maybe it was a good thing Hector was a little dense at times.

The village was like every other they had visited so far. It barely registered on a topographical map as a cluster of structures, and the name depended on whether you asked someone from the village or a neighboring one. It would have been easy to overlook villages like these and seek larger ones where the population was a triple-digit number, but that would have been a missed golden opportunity. It was in interacting with villages like these where Jessica's true talent shined.

The simple herders and farmers in these villages knew every road, route, trail, and water source within twenty kilometers of Taq Taq. More importantly, the maliks had long memories. They knew the families in the other villages and had the pulse of who did what and who sided with whom when village politics came into play. Malik Bilal was no exception.

When they arrived, Jessica was immediately greeted and surrounded by Malik Bilal's six daughters and ten grandchildren. It was as if the prodigal daughter had returned. Hector, not so much. He was too *Ameriki* to be welcomed in the same way. Jessica presented Malik Bilal with the money in the form of a gift, after which they were led into the compound and sat at a feast consisting of lamb, rice, vegetables, bread, and tea.

As they feasted, Jessica engaged with Malik Bilal with the usual icebreakers that involved talking about the health of the families, recent weddings, and the birth of grandchildren. The topic turned to ISIS as the malik went on a tirade about how they weren't true followers of Islam.

"He says we must stand united against these apostates,"

Jessica translated for Hector. "And that Allah, praised be his name, will lead the true sons of Islam to victory."

"Tell him we stand with him and his people as well, and that we hope our monthly contribution will help Allah's will be done."

"I already did."

"Oh, well carry on then."

The meeting was moving along as usual when a commotion outside caught everyone's attention. Malik Bilal was noticeably annoyed when his eldest daughter stormed in. Jessica listened to the girl, but she was agitated, talking quickly in Kurdish.

"Forgive me, Father, but there is a matter of most urgency." Arwah looked at Jessica, then to her father. "It's the apostates!"

Malik Bilal began shouting commands as he went to retrieve his rifle. Hector stood. "What's going on?"

Arwah collapsed in a seat next to Jessica. "Please, Jessica," she whispered in Kurdish, "you and your husband must leave and return to your base! You are in danger!"

Jessica blinked, trying to process the barrage of words. "Arwah, slow down. I don't understand. Are you telling me we are in danger here?"

"Jessica, what the hell is going on?" asked Hector.

Arwah shook her head and waved her hands. "No, no, no. Not here." She took a deep breath and spoke more slowly. "But you are in danger. They are looking for you, Jessica. You and your husband must return home before it is too late. They know where you live!"

Jessica understood as a cold shudder chilled its way down her spine. *Oh, God! The compound.* "Is it the Daesh?"

"Jessica!" Hector shouted. She waved him to wait a moment as she listened to the girl explain.

Arwah nodded vigorously and said, "Word has come from far by friends. Chechens in Daesh have been asking about a Western woman and showing a picture of you, Jessica. They are very bad and know where you live. They warned the fathers not to help you, and not to come to your aid when they came for you, but you are our friends."

Jessica's face turned pale, conveying to Arwah that she had indeed understood everything. She turned to Hector. "It's ISIS and the Russians! They found me and they're going to attack the compound!"

"Wait, what? Today? Right now? How do they even know?"

"I don't have time to explain!" Jessica grabbed Hector by the arm and led him out of the house, stopping just long enough to say *shokran*, "thank you," to Malik Bilal, who was rallying his fighters.

"What the fuck is going on, Flash?" asked Hector as he ran with her toward the armored Land Rover.

"God, I just hope we're not too late!" She opened the passenger-side door. "We have to get back to the compound!"

Hector ran around to the driver's side. "Will you please tell me what the fuck is going on?" he asked, as he began driving back to the compound.

"I don't know how, but ISIS is working with the Russians looking for me!" Jessica panted. "Arwah told me a Chechen with ISIS has been going around and asking about me. They have a photo of me, Hector! And now they know where we are. They are going to attack the compound today!"

Hector reached for the radio and tried to contact the compound. Static crackled as Hector keyed the talk button. "Spartan Base, Spartan Base. This is Spartan Two-Zero, do you copy?"

There was no response.

"Spartan Base, Spartan Base. This is Spartan Two-Zero, what's your status?"

Again, no answer.

"Goddammit!" He switched frequencies and tried again.

"Any Spartan Unit, any Spartan Unit. This is Spartan Two-Zero, do you copy?"

They let out a collective sigh of relief when they heard the faint response, "Spartan Two-Zero, Spartan Two-One. Lima Charlie. Over."

"Spartan Two-One, what's your status? Over."

"Spartan Two-Zero, we're RTB from a supply run. ETA twenty mikes. Over."

"Fuck! They're just as far out as we are!" said Hector. "Roger, Spartan Two-One. Be advised, there is an immediate threat against Spartan Base. I say again, there's an immediate threat against Spartan Base! Step on it and get your ass back. We can't raise Spartan Base. Try to make contact, and if you can, initiate Condition Red. Do you copy? Over."

There was a short pause on the other end, followed by a somber response. "Roger all, Spartan Two-Zero. Good luck. Over."

The Land Rover jostled over the open and uneven terrain, leaving a wide dust trail behind them. An explosion suddenly lit up behind them. Jessica screamed. Someone behind them had fired an RPG and barely missed.

"Fuck!" shouted Hector.

Before Jessica could figure out where the RPG came from, the sharp pinging of small-arms fire hit the passenger side of the armored Land Rover.

"Contact right! Contact right!" screamed Hector.

"I can't see where it's coming from!" Jessica shouted. "The damn sun's in the way!"

"Our single advantage is that the open terrain makes for a terrible kill zone without adequate planning."

Jessica was about to tell him that now was not the time, but the pinging of the gunfire shifted from the right side to the rear.

"Fuck!" Hector cursed. "That's no ambush, we just happened to cross their path on their way to the compound."

Jessica looked back, putting a hand over the blinding sun and trying to make out vehicle silhouettes through the dust. "I can't see how many of them are back there."

Hector huffed. "If we're lucky, this is a scouting element. We need to buy time while I try to get the base on the radio." He pointed up and said, "Flash, get on that Mk-19 and return fire!"

"You want me to do *what*?" She stared at him, mouth agape. Sure, she'd played around with the weapons systems for the past few weeks, but he'd just asked her to be an active participant in the fight. No way.

Hector gnashed his teeth, glared at her, and repeated his command. "Get up on that fucking gun and start pouring fire on those motherfuckers!"

Jessica snapped out of it and moved without delay, fearing his wrath more than those chasing them. It was as if the devil himself had possessed Hector and commanded the legions of hell through him.

She got up from her seat, donned the ballistic helmet and headset, and unlatched the hatches. She flipped the hydraulic switch and propped up the Mk-19 on its spring-loaded swivel, then unlocked the turret and rotated it until the barrel aimed behind them. Bullets whizzed past her with a loud, high-pitched snapping, causing her to duck and scream. In that moment, she felt a fear that paralyzed her to the core.

A voice deep inside her lashed back with a force stronger than the fear.

Get up on that fucking gun. Do. Your. Job!

She wiped her tears and forced herself to open the gun's cover assembly. She fed the high-explosive 40mm linked rounds from the ammo can into the tray in spite of the jarring movement from racing across the uneven terrain. *Come on, Flash, you can do this!* She grabbed the charging handles on either side of the machinegun and grunted as she struggled to pull back the bolt, the powerful spring offering heavy resistance. At last, she pulled it all the way back, only to remember that she had to pull the trigger to send the bolt forward and repeat the same thing again to finally get the gun to shoot. *Goddammit!*

"What the fuck is taking so long? Fire that goddamned weapon . . . now!"

"I'm trying, goddammit!" She yelled back. "Leave me the fuck alone!" The anger was just what she needed as she pulled the charging handles a second time and locked them to the rear.

All right, you bastards. You messed with the wrong chick!

Jessica pressed the butterfly trigger and sent round after round through the dust cloud. *Thud-thud-thud-thud-thud.* She didn't see the faint flashing of the impacts, but she heard them in the distance. More importantly, she saw and heard the secondary explosions of enemy vehicles she'd struck. "Yeah, motherfuckers!"

She fired the gun again, feeling the blowback and hearing the slow rhythmic bursts of fire—*thud-thud-thud-thud-thud*—destroying several of the vehicles giving chase.

"Flash! Contact right, technicals!" yelled Hector.

She saw them: three small white pickup trucks with machine guns in the cargo bed racing to engage them. Each had a black flag mounted on a pole.

Oh no you don't, you bastards!

Jessica swiveled the turret to the right and fired, but the rounds were impacting behind them. Their trucks were lighter and faster but were no match to the Mk-19's high-explosive rounds. She adjusted the turret, aiming ahead of the trucks, and fired three bursts, swiveling the machine gun from truck to truck. *Thud-thud-thud-thud . . . Thud-thud-thud-thud . . . Thud-thud-thud-thud.*

Without the dust cloud to conceal her targets, Jessica witnessed the devastating effect of the HE rounds as they exploded on impact, enveloping the enemy trucks in a maelstrom of death that tore the gunners apart and mangled the vehicles like crushed aluminum before they exploded in a fireball.

Jessica stared in awe with a wicked smile at the havoc she wreaked. Excitement and a rush of adrenaline pumped through her veins. "Holy shit! Did you see that? I nailed those motherfuckers!"

"That's fantastic!" Hector yelled back. "Now finish them off!"

Hector tried to hail the base again while Jessica continued firing the Mk-19 in a sweeping motion, destroying anything that dared to continue the chase. Their pursuers backed off, preferring to avoid the deadly steel curtain she created.

"Spartan Base, Spartan Base, this is Spartan Two-Zero, do you copy?"

"Spartan Two-Zero, Spartan Base, Lima Charlie. What's your status? Over."

Jessica could hear the relief in Hector's voice from the rooftop. "About fucking time!" Hector keyed the talk button and relayed the dire warning. "Spartan Base, set Condition Red. I say again, set Condition Red! Spartan Two-Zero and Spartan Two-One coming in hot! Be advised, enemy forces of unknown size and direction are en route!"

"Roger, Spartan Two-Zero. Engage duress visual sign at five-hundred-meter marker to confirm your position. Over."

"Roger, Spartan Base. We'll be in your sights in three mikes. Spartan Two-Zero out."

They eventually cleared the narrow choke point formed by two hills and stopped once they were in sight of the compound. Jessica collapsed back into the passenger seat of the Land Rover, shivering with adrenaline. Hector flickered his high beams three times, followed by flashing the hazard lights three times.

"Spartan Two-Zero, your visual is confirmed. Spartan Two-One is inbound. We got your six."

36

Hector zigzagged around the chicanes, narrowly avoiding getting the tires tangled in the waves of concertina wire. He slowed only when the gate opened and they were inside the compound, parking haphazardly next to the other armored SUVs. He left Jessica behind and raced to the CP, passing the makeshift desks with laptops, radios, printers, maps, and a large-scale map printer that lined the walls. He reached Voodoo and Spinner, who were already plotting out positions on a wall map, and updated them on the situation.

"I don't know the full size of the enemy force, but we encountered an ISIS scouting element of approximately twenty technicals." Hector wiped the sweat off his face. "We took out a significant number of them—I just don't know how many more are there."

"How did you manage to do that?" asked Voodoo.

Hector smiled. "Flash lit them the fuck up with the Mk-19."

"Flash did that?" Voodoo nodded approvingly. "*Ma chérie!*"

Spinner drew attention to a point on the map north of their position. "Is this where you came in contact?"

Hector nodded. "Yeah, roughly twenty minutes away."

Spinner acknowledged, then pointed to a position south-west of the base. "Spartan Two-One spotted a checkpoint on the bridge in Altun Kupri and a column of vehicles approaching from there, exact numbers unknown." He shifted his finger to the south. "A Peshmerga patrol reported a second element north of Kirkuk near Baba Gurgur, but we haven't received further reports from them." He then swept his fingers to the right. "We still have a second Peshmerga patrol scouting the eastern approach from Chamchamal, but we've received no reports." He looked at Hector with a somber expression. "I'm deploying the remaining platoon from the first Peshmerga company to secure reinforcements in the north. I think Flash should go with them."

Spinner didn't need to spell it out for him. If the compound was overrun by the ISIS savages, they'd be killed —or worse—and he didn't dare imagine what her fate would be at their hands, especially since they wanted her. "All right, send her."

"We got enemy forces spotted from the west!" reported a member of Alpha Team. He was maneuvering a commercial quad-copter that relayed real-time video to the CP. "Looks like the element from Altun." The drone served as their eyes from above, and despite its limited range, it flew far and high enough to detect dust trails as dozens of black flags approached, bearing down on their position.

Hector and Voodoo looked at the drone operator's monitor just in time to see the vehicles stop at the side of the road before the gap between the hills.

"What the hell are they doing?" asked Voodoo.

Hector just shrugged. "Can you get an approximate count on the number of vehicles?"

The drone maneuvered toward the vehicles, then stopped as the camera zoomed in. The aftermarket HD camera with a powerful zoom was proving to be a worthwhile investment.

Hector could clearly make out the black figures climbing off the trucks and forming around one individual.

"Shit, they're dismounting," Spinner said. "That's probably about fifty to sixty of those fuckers."

"Yeah, and looks like they're waiting on orders." Hector focused on the leader of the group. He was much taller than the others, but what drew his attention was how much paler he was than the others. He tapped the controller on the shoulder. "There! Can you get any lower and focus on the leader? He looks too pale. Probably the fucking Chechen hunting Flash."

He shook his head. "No, not without letting them know we're watching."

"Fuck!" He thought for a moment, then asked, "Can you scan around the compound and see if other enemy elements are approaching?"

The controller maneuvered the quad-copter around to scan the areas beyond the protective berms and hills that formed natural defenses. So far, nothing had approached from the south, but they still didn't know if it meant that the first Peshmerga patrol was still engaged with the enemy, or if they had won the day.

The controller said, "The bird is running out of juice. I need to bring it back and change out the batteries." Bringing the drone back would leave them blind, but there was nothing to be done.

A radio crackled as a transmission in Kurdish came in. The Peshmerga communicator jotted down the information transmitted, responded, then brought it to Hector and Voodoo. "The scouts from the south reported a Daesh patrol approaching and are requesting to engage." He spoke in a thick accent. "They think they can kill them all but ask what you want to do."

Hector smirked and shook his head. The Peshmerga were fierce, but as brave and capable as they were, he needed every able body to defend the compound. "Tell them not to engage. Tell them we need everyone back here."

The communicator nodded and turned back to relay the order, but the other end of the transmission crackled first. "Sir, it is too late. They engaged the enemy!"

Voodoo let out a long string of French curses.

"Goddammit!" cursed Hector. "Fine, you tell them they better win, or I'm going to be really pissed. Oh, also, see if they can take a prisoner. We just need one to know who how many of these fuckers are there."

The communicator nodded again and relayed the message. Hector turned to another Alpha Team member. "Send a flash message to the TOC and give them our SITREP."

He took a deep breath and looked at Voodoo. Both nodded in unison. Hector was about to make the one call he had hoped never to make. "Let them know we're declaring a Castle Keep."

The term was an internal code letting the TOC know a position was under siege and about to be overrun, and every possible effort should be made available to assist. The thing about a Castle Keep here was that the closest support was still in Baghdad, and that just wasn't enough.

Hector and Voodoo exited the CP and ran out to the court-yard. Hector whistled loudly. He waited until all eyes were on him before addressing the crowd. "Listen up! Shit's about to get real. We have approximately sixty enemy combatants with maybe thirty technicals west of here"—he pointed toward the direction they came in from—"another element to the east, and probably have a third coming from the south. In all, we're looking at maybe two hundred fighters . . . and that's without reinforcements or other elements. The Peshmerga scouts are now in contact with an enemy force in the south, but we need to plan for the worst."

He turned to the Bravo Team, gathered together. He tried

not to focus on Jessica, huddled in the middle with wide eyes, her pretty face white with fear, mouth opened slightly. He focused instead on Romeo's face beside her. "Megatron, Romeo, and Guido, break out the ammo and dispense accordingly. Pirate Face, set up a casualty collection point and get your docs ready. Alpha Team, disperse water cans and MREs at intervals along perimeter. We're in for a long night, folks. Now let's make these fuckers bleed!"

The men dispersed, leaving Jessica alone. Hector met her gaze. "Flash, I need you to go with Captain Samir's men and get help. Find someone to join the fight, 'cause we're gonna need it." Jessica was about to protest, but he raised a hand, cutting her off. "I don't want to hear it, Flash. Just do your job."

He turned to leave, but Jessica gave chase.

"Hector," she called out, but he kept walking. "*Gung Ho!* Don't walk away from me! I'm talking to you!"

Hector wheeled about and strode toward her. "They're hunting you, Jessica! And if we can't hold them back . . . I just don't need that on my conscience right now. So please go!"

"No! I'm not going, and you better not try to make me. You know the maliks aren't going to help. And even if they did, by the time they organize their fighters, this thing is going to be over. I feel safer *here*, please let me stay. I can help."

Hector took a deep breath as his mind searched for how to say what he needed, to make her understand why she couldn't stay here, but before he got the chance, Penguin had run over to them.

"I got this, man." Hector nodded and stepped back. But he watched. He couldn't leave until he knew she'd be safe. If she wouldn't listen to him, she'd listen to Penguin.

Penguin grasped her shoulders tenderly as he looked her in the eye. "Jessica, I need you to do this."

She stared back, confused.

"I . . ." His voice started breaking and his eyes began to well up. He pursed his lips, as if holding back what he truly wanted to say. "I won't be able to live with myself if something happens to you, so please go."

Ah, so he's choosing this moment. The beast inside Hector roared with jealousy, but he kept it back. Why shouldn't Penguin get to say his piece to her? Hector had no claim on her, besides being family.

Jessica covered her mouth and gasped, finally understanding. Penguin reached to embrace her, but she began pounding on his chest over and over as she cursed him. "Goddamn you, Eric! Why did you have to tell me this now?" She let out her frustrations, but finally embraced him. "I can't leave you! I can't leave my family."

Hector felt his heart pull for her. He understood that completely. He was about to comfort her, but Captain Samir came up to him, drawing him away. "I can't delay my men any longer. If the Daesh block our route to the north, we'll be completely surrounded." He looked over at Jessica, then back at Hector. "So what will it be?"

Deep down, Hector knew Jessica was right. Even if the maliks did muster some semblance of a fighting force, by the time they arrived it all would be too late. Perhaps Captain Samir's men could maybe, just maybe, get another Peshmerga group over to relieve the siege, at best, or collect enough of their bodies to give them a decent burial.

I better not live to regret this. He nodded. "Very well, tell your scouts to depart."

Captain Samir nodded and turned. He gave an order in Kurdish, and the two Hilux pickups loaded with Peshmerga drove out the gates. In the distance, the faint sound of gunfire crackled, like an ominous darkness coming their way.

37

Hector stood behind the decrepit rampart of the south-facing tower, sweeping the horizon with his binoculars in search of any movement. He spotted dust trails coming from the south and recognized the Peshmerga trucks. *I'll be damned—score one for the good guys.* Outside the wire, the last of the demolition teams emplaced infrared beacons, signaling a safe path for the returning Peshmerga. Once they crossed through that pass, the demolition team would activate the mines and explosive charges, destroying anything that crossed after.

The crest of the sun dipped below the horizon, giving way to the night sky that slowly expanded. Minutes later, Hector's radio crackled. "Enemy movement observed. Whatever the dismounted element was waiting for happened and they're moving out."

Here goes nothing. Hector exhaled hard and hurried down the tower. The too-familiar surge of adrenaline began pumping through him, feeding the beast before battle.

A fireball flashed in the distance, then another, the booms following immediately. The advancing ISIS forces had hit pre-positioned land mines that tore through metal and flesh alike, warning the base of the coming onslaught. The element of surprise was lost. It wasn't long before the war cries of the advancing horde resonated in the dark, seemingly in every direction, as they drew closer to the compound.

Gunfire blinked in the darkness while more fireballs and booms appeared from another direction, then another. The mines continued eating into the enemy's numbers, and yet they kept coming, firing their machine guns and rifles, slowly chipping away at the walls of the compound. The shipping containers and HESCO barriers absorbed the impacts, but even they could only take so much punishment.

And then the moment Hector had been waiting for came.

The attackers in the open became entangled in layers of crisscrossed tanglefoot and concertina wire, and anti-vehicle obstacles blocked the technicals, making them sitting targets. Their movement slowed to a crawl.

Now free from its shackles, the beast looked through Hector's eyes and roared through his mouth. "Kill them all!"

The combined force of the Parabellum teams and Peshmerga forces unleashed hell.

A blaze of fire erupted from the ramparts as red- and white-hot streaks dashed across the darkness, laying waste to the attackers below. The war cries faded, giving way to screams of death, agony, and despair. Bodies were ripped to shreds by gunfire, unable to escape the maze of razor-sharp wire at their feet.

The green scene visible through Hector's night-vision goggles was surreal. It was he who was seeing through the beast's eyes as it repeatedly took aim and fired, killing everything the infrared laser at the end of his rifle pointed at. The beast fired round after round, stopping only to reload before firing again, sating its bloodthirst. The euphoria from the adrenaline rush was intoxicating. A high unlike any other took over as the beast killed again and again. This was where he belonged. This was why he couldn't take the job. This was why he *needed* the missions.

Hector's peripheral vision caught movement away from the raiding horde, and the beast instinctively moved the weapon there and fired. The attacker pulled the trigger just as he dropped, sending an errant RPG over their heads.

"RPGs! Pick up the RPGs and drop them before they can fire!"

A massive explosion sent a shock wave into the compound as a section of the wall crumbled, exposing a deep dent on the container filled with HESCO barriers. Attackers with suicide vests were getting too close.

"SVESTs! They're bringing up SVESTs. Don't let them get near the perimeter!"

Hector took a step back, separating himself from the beast, and considered the tactical situation. The ISIS force didn't have the anti-aircraft and anti-tank guns they used as ground weapons. *Thank God.* But they had greater numbers, plenty of cannon fodder, fighters with SVESTS, explosive-laden vehicles that would cut holes in the perimeter and take out dozens of his defenders, and plenty of RPGs. All they had to do was wait it out while he was forced to expend their ammunition. Even without reinforcements, the attackers outnumbered the remaining defenders almost three to one. For ISIS, this, in the end, was a numbers game, and as the battle continued into the night, Hector's numbers slowly dwindled.

38

Jessica ran from position to position, replenishing ammunition and water, but mostly helping carry the dead and wounded to the casualty collection point that was becoming more crowded as the battle raged on. The sight was both frightening and heartbreaking as the number of dead surpassed the wounded. Her clothes were soaked in sweat and blood. All she wanted to do was escape the madness and wash the blood and sweat and disgust away.

The various liquids smeared across her hands, plus the trembling from the adrenaline, made it a struggle to open her canteen and take a goddamned sip of water. Why couldn't she just have one sip of water?

"Flash! I need you over here!" shouted PF as he worked feverishly to hold a man down and apply a tourniquet. She groaned as she stood and made her way over. "How can I—"

"Hold him down and apply pressure here!" He pointed to the bandage on the man's chest that was quickly turning red.

She did as told and was rewarded with the man's ghastly screams. He struggled against her, but she kept the pressure on while PF tightened the tourniquet on what was left of the man's upper leg. The screams and gore churned her stomach.

She didn't have to be a military strategist to understand their odds.

She might not live to see tomorrow.

It was impossible to tell how many hours had elapsed since the attack began, but it felt like an eternity as she went on with her duties without pause. The drain of adrenaline was taking its toll. She was weary, running on fumes. The constant gunfire had stopped being deafening long ago, to the point she was sure she could sleep through it all. *Sleep.* What she wouldn't give to have just five minutes of sleep.

Come on, Jessica. Your family needs you. She wiped the blood, sweat, and soot from her forehead and trudged on. She coughed from the gun smoke and dust in the air as she carried the ammunition cans that became heavier with each trip.

By then, the temperature had dropped, and she shivered as fresh sweat soaked her already wet clothes. She couldn't understand how ISIS kept attacking without pause. For sure, they had to have killed so many that only a few remained. But evidence to the contrary was everywhere. Wave after wave of attackers swarmed from one side to the other and the other, each wave weakening their defenses further. *They have to be tired too. They have to be near their end!*

She winced from the burning aches in her back, shoulders, and arms. Her knees and palms felt as if they had been scraped raw from crawling every time she moved from rampart to rampart. She had never experienced such prolonged exhaustion. She was drunk with fatigue and making simple mistakes that she knew could get her killed.

At one point, she was pouring fresh water into a five-gallon can and was startled awake by water overflowing on her foot. She couldn't tell if she'd dozed for three seconds or three minutes. Never had she wanted to sleep so much. *Come on, Flash. These guys are depending on you.* She had taken a deep breath and forced herself up, wincing as she lifted the water cans and shuffled as fast as her body allowed her to.

She went over to Penguin on the north wall to deliver the water and collapsed on one of the cans. "Eric, I can't do this anymore. I just can't," she cried. "We're all going to die here, and it'll be my fault." She began sobbing, feeling herself losing her edge.

Penguin paused firing his weapon to stow fresh magazines in his plate carrier and refill his canteen. His red hair was black with soot. "Hey, come on now. They keep charging and they keep dying. Just hold on. We're going to get through this, all right?"

He took three massive gulps, then wiped the soot from her cheek and tenderly held her chin. "We're gonna make it. You're gonna make it. I promise, we won't let you down."

Jessica tried smiling between sobs. She couldn't understand how he could remain so positive and so energetic—but then, that's what these brave men did. They somehow kept going, and she had to force herself to go on as well.

Come on, Jessica. You've managed to survive this long. You can make it through.

She took several large gulps of water, handed the canteen back to Penguin, and went on with her duties.

39

"RPG!" The words came too late as the rocket streaked across the night sky and exploded against the exposed western wall, sending ripped, burning bodies and searing hot debris in Hector's direction. He checked himself for shrapnel wounds or burnt skin but was miraculously unharmed. The same could not be said for the five or more defenders killed.

He groaned as he went up on one knee and assessed the situation. ISIS was hammering the exposed wall with everything they had. What remained of the containers wouldn't last long, and then the real fighting would ensue.

He rallied the fighters around him, getting them to give it everything they had again. He began firing his own weapon and screamed, "I need fire superiority now!"

The other fighters around him poured more fire on the attackers, and soon they repelled the ISIS line, trying to take advantage of the situation. It was another back-and-forth that had been going on all night: keep finding another weak point to exploit.

He tapped Voodoo on the shoulder. "Keep up the fire! I'm going to check on the north wall!"

Voodoo nodded and continued directing fire.

Hector jumped off the rampart, groaning and cursing his knees as he stood and began to run. He looked up at the ramparts as he ran to them, trying to figure out how to solve the next problem. The number of defenders was dwindling dangerously low.

He keyed his radio. "Cujo, I need you to send five shooters to the western wall!"

"I don't have five guys to spare, Gung Ho! We're low enough as—"

"Just fucking do it! We're about to lose the wall if—"

"Fine, goddammit!"

Hector climbed up to the ramparts and joined Penguin and the fighters there. "What's the word? Talk to me!"

"We're fucking running low on everything, bro. Ammo, water, and shooters."

They ducked as automatic PKMs fired on them. Penguin waited for a break in the shooting and returned fire, killing one of the two machine gunners firing on them. "You see the shit I've had to deal with?"

"Hang on, Penguin. Just hold—"

"SVEST! SVEST!"

Penguin's eyes widened. Hector spun to see a group of fighters running to the wall, not bothering to shoot or take cover.

The defenders focused their fire on the suicide bombers. They were racing to the wall, opening their arms to splay themselves against the wall and clack off their SVESTs. One of the fighters went up in an explosive fireball, taking others with him.

Hector and Penguin could only laugh as they continued pouring fire on the attackers.

The radio crackled. "SVEST! SVE—"

A series of explosions erupted from the western wall. Hector turned just as the center of the container buckled and collapsed into itself. The sound of metal bending reverberated throughout the compound. It didn't take long before black-clad figures began pouring from the gap and going berserk. Hector had men on those ramparts. *Fuck.*

Waves of shahids with suicide vests charged the wall. ISIS now had the upper hand and were on the brink of finally breaching the hard-fought defenses.

"Hold the line! Keep up the fire!" he said to Penguin before jumping off the rampart and dropping fighters as he made his way to cover.

The scene around Hector was bedlam. Attackers and defenders clashed in close quarters and hand-to-hand combat, making it nearly impossible to fire without hitting a friendly. The beast wanted to charge and destroy, but Hector had to reel it in; *be smart.* Guapo came up beside him, and both peeked out from their cover behind pallets of cement bags.

"Okay, boss man, how the hell are you gonna get us out of this one?" Guapo peeked out again to return fire.

Hector loaded a fresh magazine. "I'll let you know when I pull something out of my ass!"

Savage screams mixed with the sound of gunfire resonated inside the compound. Fire that once poured outward now focused inward as waves of drug-infused fighters fought their way inside. Near the CP was a group of Peshmerga fighters that had managed to form some semblance of a squad and were now maneuvering to suppress the enemy and attack.

Hector pointed to them. "Go rally some stragglers and link up with those guys. I'll do the same, and we can hit them from three sides. That should help plug the hole and buy us some time!"

Guapo nodded, waited for a break in the fire, then ran like the devil.

This might just fucking work! He couldn't worry about the guys on the ramparts. They had their own jobs to do, and now he had his. They would defend this compound to the last man. This *was* his Alamo. He took another deep breath, then fired as he moved.

He ran to a group of four Peshmerga who all seemed to be doing their own thing. When he reached them, he pointed and gestured at each one individually. "You, you, you, and you. Come with me. We're going to link up with those guys over there and take back this base, do you understand?"

The four nodded like schoolchildren, and he gave them a thumbs-up. Hector loaded his second-to-last magazine, gave them a quick countdown, and charged forward, taking careful aim and firing. He moved to cover and avoided the hail of bullets that followed. He breathed hard, feeling as if his body armor was constricting him as they moved from cover to cover, returning fire and dropping three more ISIS fighters.

Opposite him, Guapo did the same with the group of six he had managed to wrangle up. The third squad of Peshmerga followed suit. The enemy was everywhere, but they were the ones now dealing with chaos.

The fighting lulled for a brief moment when the attackers formed a cohesive line and tried suppressing them. Hector had to do something. If he couldn't break the stalemate, ISIS reinforcements would certainly pour in and shift the momentum.

Out of nowhere, a line of subdued headlights and muzzle flashes advanced from the north and rushed through the gaps. Hector loaded his last magazine and keyed his radio. "Who the fuck is that? Anybody? Anyone have eyes on that element?"

Fuck! It had to be ISIS reinforcements from Mosul.

This was it. This was the end, and he'd go down fighting.

He thought of Kelly just then. *I'm sorry, babe. I'm sorry for not being the man you needed. The husband you deserved. I'm sorry for not placing you above everything else.*

Goddammit. Why was it now, at the very end, that he realized just how much he still loved her? And now she would never know. He'd die leaving her to wonder if he ever truly loved her.

He was brought back into the fight when the ISIS fighters turned to engage the fresh troops.

They're Peshmerga!

Hector's throat closed as a tidal wave of emotion overwhelmed him. He aimed at the fighters scampering to escape through the gap. He and the beast screamed a triumphant roar that echoed amid the others across the compound with renewed enthusiasm. An intensified ferocity beat back the demoralized attackers who turned away to escape the ensuing Peshmerga force that now pursued with extreme prejudice.

The fight shifted from inside the compound to the perimeter and the terrain around the compound. Hector's knees buckled and he dropped to the ground. He had given every last ounce of strength, and any effort to hold back his tears was futile. God had seen fit to give him this one opportunity to go home to his wife, profess his love for her, and tell her she was right. He had lived through the night of nights, and all was crystal clear to him now. He was determined to return to her and take the desk job without a second thought.

The cries of the wounded and dying brought him back to the moment. The fight was won, but what did they gain? The oil field was indefensible against ISIS, and his hubris had cost many good men their lives, including his own. He rubbed his face as the gravity of the losses assaulted him. His team had been ripped apart, and it was all on him. No one else. As he reflected, he remembered something very important.

Shit. Jessica! He had to find her.

40

Jessica huddled in a corner, surrounded by the dead and wounded, her unfiltered emotions pouring out. The compound was being overrun. Pirate Face had left her alone in the makeshift clinic to help fight the overwhelming tides. She stared at the Glock in her hand and cried like never before. She'd seen what ISIS did to their prisoners, what happened to the women. *And should they find out I'm a Jew—!* The fear of what would happen to her terrified her to the core. She clutched the gun tight against her chest and determined she would die by her own hand. The alternative was too horrid to allow.

She perked up. The sounds outside the clinic had changed. *Is that . . . cheering?* It was. The faint sounds grew louder. But who was cheering? Her mind began conjuring the worst possible outcomes, but logic finally took hold. If it was ISIS cheering, she'd hear *"Allahu Akhbar."* No, that wasn't what she heard. Renewed hope swelled through her.

Her thoughts turned to her team, praying they would reunite and return home, get the fuck out of here. She slowly made her way out of the clinic, taking purchase along the way to avoid falling. Her legs were like gelatin.

The medic team was back to their frantic work. As she passed through the clinic, she caught glances of the dozens of bodies, both Peshmerga and Parabellum, spread throughout the collection point. The screams of men in agony were everywhere, and the scene was beyond revolting. Pirate Face and his medics worked on bloodied stumps and exposed internal organs. The scent of charred flesh assaulted her senses, and she dry-heaved. She dared not look directly at the wounded, and silently she thanked God that none was familiar. She hated herself for thinking as much, but it was what it was.

She left the clinic and scanned the ramparts for her team. Bodies and parts were littered everywhere. Bloodied and exhausted defenders, cigarettes dangling from their mouths, were lethargic. Some sat, others stood, and some grouped together in morning prayer. She reached what remained of the west wall, where the fighting was the fiercest, and all the air left her lungs.

The sight was grotesque. Floorboards were slick with blood, thick metal contorted like crushed tinfoil, and piles of bodies lay in the gap formed within the container. Corpses and limbs lay like discarded trash, strewn about and oozing as hundreds of brass shells glinted like gold dust on the dirt. She saw PF and another medic tending to a screaming Cujo, a bloodied stump flailing wildly where his left arm used to be.

Shaking, she climbed up the tattered ramparts and stepped delicately over the red-stained floorboards on her search for her team, careful not to disturb the wounded, the dying, or the dead. What Jessica saw next wrenched her stomach.

She found Voodoo—or rather, what remained of him. And beyond him were both halves of Romeo. Megatron's horribly charred body was slumped against the rampart next to Guido's decapitated head, which resembled more of a smashed melon than the jokester she met in Texas. Their bodies, bloodied and torn, were almost unidentifiable to anyone but her.

Her heart sank to the pit of her stomach and her breath caught in her lungs. She inched toward them, clawing at her chest, desperate to breathe. The tears blurred her vision, and she wept like a lost child.

Jessica finally gasped precious air and let out a primal scream that erupted from deep in her core. She stumbled, her limbs unwilling to hold her up any longer. She shook her head in refusal of what her eyes saw.

She knelt next to them while the world went on around her, existing in some separate plane of time and space. She felt as if a fist had punched through her chest and crushed her soul.

It's not fair! It's not fair!

The fight was won, but victory came at a price. Too high a price, in her view. One by one, what remained of Bravo Team gathered around her, paying silent tribute to their fallen comrades. They bore their pain in full view of her, the same crushing her inside. She saw no machismo, no stiff upper lip, and no pushing past the pain. She saw plainly how fragile these rough men could be. They weren't indestructible, emotionless beings.

Someone crouched down beside her and wrapped his arms around her shoulders. Jessica leaned into Eric's chest, sobbing violently. His own tears dripped down on her cheek, mingling with hers.

She recalled Vicky's words, the manner she looked at them with motherly care, and how she called them "my boys." *Oh God, Vicky!* Her heart ached for her as well, and she wondered how many of "her boys" she'd lost over time. Jessica wept, unable to bear the thought of facing her after losing so many.

41

Dulles International Airport
Tuesday, 15 July 2014

In the aftermath, Parabellum had moved heaven and earth to pull everyone out through Irbil, with the dead and wounded given prioritization before what remained of Bravo Team could return home. The experiment in oil exploration and production in the new Iraq ended in disaster, with tragic losses for both Americans and Kurds, in a part of the country that would barely register this tragedy as a side note in the history books.

Jessica had searched the news channels and online newspapers for any validation of their stand against the forces of ISIS, but the most tragic and impactful event in her life hadn't made a bleep in the current news cycle. She didn't know why she needed such validation by someone who could barely find Kirkuk on a map—much less pronouncing it without the aid of a prompter—but the absence of it felt like a slap to the face.

Her days in the field were at an end. She'd return home having accomplished little of what she came out to do, if anything at all. The hardest part was the call with her boss the morning they headed back to the airport, away from the godforsaken base. Bill had known what had happened already, from Chuck probably, but having to talk about what had just happened . . . It was tough.

"Yes, thank you, Bill. I know. And please do send my regards to everyone, as well."

"Of course, of course. Again, I am so thankful to hear your voice, Jessica. I can't tell you how many sleepless nights Gretchen and I had the past few days. Are you sure there isn't anything else we can do for you?"

"I'm sure, Bill. But I'll be sure to let you know if I change my mind." She gripped the phone tighter as she took a deep breath. "Bill, there is one more thing."

She could not in good conscience endorse her firm's push to occupy the site and have others sacrifice themselves, knowing that the tsunami of black flags would swallow everything in its path. There was so much to say, but she was too exhausted to find the right words for it. "I'm going to recommend that we do not pursue operations in this area. At least not until some stability returns to the area, if ever."

There was a pause on the other end.

"I understand, Jessica. We can talk about it with the board when you return. I know that is a tough and painful call to make, but know that I understand and have your back. Come home soon, kiddo. And job well done."

The rush of emotions hit her like a truck. She pulled the phone away from her ear and let everything out. She tightened her grip around her knees and rocked as her tears soaked her pants. She wanted so hard to get ahold of herself, but she couldn't do it. The memory of it all rushed back, and as hard as she tried, she could not unsee what had been done to her family.

A dreaded silence filled the air while they waited at baggage claim at Dulles International. Her mind went from the team to her former life—her real life, rather. She'd return to her comfortable chair behind her comfortable desk in her comfortable air-conditioned office. She grimaced at the thought, tasting the acrid bile that filled her mouth. She couldn't imagine herself at meetings in lavish conference rooms wearing her tailored business suits anymore. Not after living, fighting, surviving, and suffering along with her team. *My team.* Her heart fluttered and the lump in her throat hardened. Hector leaned over and wrapped a comforting arm around her.

One by one, their bags appeared on the carousel. She and what remained of the team stood solemnly side by side while other passengers went on about their business and cursed the latency of the baggage delivery, blissfully unaware of the goings-on half a world away.

Jessica snickered and smiled, turning to Hector. "Remember the first time you met me at the airport?"

Hector chuckled, allowing it to turn into a modest laugh, and then into a belly-aching laugh. Jessica joined in as both bent over and wiped their eyes while other passengers looked on at the two laughing lunatics.

It was a well-deserved laugh, a healing laugh. "Thank you, Flash," he said as he recovered. "I needed that."

One by one, the team collected their bags and said their goodbyes. When it was Eric's turn, Jessica met his eyes and felt the tightness in her chest, the flutter at the pit of her stomach. She'd felt the loss of each teammate, but if it had been Eric . . . She reached out and hugged him, tightening her embrace as his arms enveloped her. "I don't think I could stand it if it had been you," she said into his chest.

"Jessica, I . . ." He struggled to speak.

Jessica sniffed and lifted her head. "Eric?" She smiled reassuringly through her tears. "What is it?"

Eric smiled. "I love you, Jessica Beaumont. I love you and want to be with you. I want to see you again no matter how far apart we are."

The wave of sensation that overcame her was more than she had expected. She smiled, she cried, she laughed. She felt relief and hesitation at the same time. What they shared had been fun, but she was returning as a changed woman. One who needed to figure out where her heart lay. She felt the warmth of his hands as he cupped her cheeks and leaned in to kiss her goodbye.

"I can't stay, but I will come back. I promise. I don't want to lose you, Jessica."

Her heart fluttered as she felt his hands slide from her face. He slowly made his way up the escalator, never taking his eyes off her.

No sooner had she lost sight of him than the wave of euphoria came crashing down. She missed him already.

She turned and saw that, at long last, she and Hector were the only ones left. They retrieved their bags and looked at each other, unsure of what to say, though Eric's words lingered in her mind.

"I'm going to miss you, Flash. You have a place at Parabellum anytime you want."

Jessica choked up, wiped the tears rolling down her face, and said, "Thank you, Gung Ho. I'll miss you too. All of you." She stood on the tips of her toes and wrapped her arms around his neck. "Be careful out there," she whispered. She let go, then added, "And watch my boys, okay?"

Hector sobbed and held her tight as tears at last escaped him. "I will," he whispered back. "You got someone picking you up?"

They broke their embrace, and Jessica wiped his tears with her thumb, wondering if any of them would ever be whole again. "Yeah. Paul." It was going to be awkward to see him again, especially since she'd agreed to go with him to the unveiling party. She searched Hector's eyes, unsure of what, if anything, she could say. So she said the easiest thing she could say. "Goodbye, Hector."

She locked eyes with Hector and gave a small smile, then proceeded to the ramp leading up to the arrivals level. Even now, as she lost sight of him, she longed to be with her team. Soon, she'd be back home in her chic home.

Home. She scoffed at the word.

42

Hector took a cab to the Parabellum building where he spent the next several hours at the casualty affairs office, filling out the forms that allowed family members to receive the remains and expedite death benefits. Filing this paperwork was another painful and tedious necessity that reminded him of his failures.

He thought of Jessica and the look in her eyes. He knew her pain. He had felt it before, of course, but this was different. With her, it felt like his first time. The most painful of all. Half the team was gone, and it was his fault. If he hadn't been so goddamned cocky, so damned self-assured, they'd all be home. Alive.

If you had only listened to Kelly and taken the damn job.

The weight of it all was crushing. He ran his hands through his hair and clasped them behind his neck, battling back the waves of emotion that battered over him.

And because he wasn't quite done torturing himself, his thoughts drifted to the lingering anxiety of returning home after the last fight with Kelly.

Her final words rang in his ears. *Don't bother coming home.* Too late had he realized that he did love Kelly, but he had no idea how to reconcile after so much had happened. The task seemed daunting, like trying to put together a shattered crystal.

But Jessica . . .

She entered his thoughts, unbidden, churning something other than dread or anxiety about his uncertain future. She was ever-present in his mind, even when he didn't think he was thinking about her. Her fiery spirit, her clever wit, her deep empathy, her dark hair, her toned skin— He shook off the thoughts. *You need to fix your situation with Kelly . . . your wife.*

And so, when all the administrative work was done, he made his way to his Jeep in the underground parking garage. His vehicle, along with those of Voodoo, Megatron, Guido, and Romeo, were the last ones still there. He took one last long look, then headed home. Where he was supposed to be.

The drive to Leesburg was excruciating as he played over and over what he would say to Kelly, to the point of second-guessing his tone and wording and anticipating every possible reaction to whichever response she gave. It was hard to focus. His mind was fractured, split in so many directions and bruised by so many recent hurts.

Before long, he arrived and parked on the driveway, sitting and waiting, as if something was to happen that would let him know everything was all right. He looked out at the porch. Its light was on. He hesitated, building up the courage to go and ring the doorbell.

It's your house too, you know. He wondered why it was that he hadn't opened the garage door and walked in. He heard her words again. *Don't bother coming home. You'll not be welcome.* His head slumped forward, resting on the steering wheel, and his heart dropped to his stomach. There was no coming back from that. He could tell her why he came home earlier than expected, but she'd just throw it back in his face, gloating with an "I told you so."

He shook his head. She wouldn't do that . . . would she?

The fact was that he couldn't think straight. He'd been through hell, he was exhausted, and perhaps talking to her tonight was not ideal. Yet deep down he needed comforting, even if he wasn't willing to admit it. *Suck it up, buttercup.*

He clicked the garage door opener, but nothing happened. He pulled it from the visor, tapped it against the palm of his hand and clicked it again. Nothing. He exited the Jeep and made his way to the front door. He inserted the house key, noting the resistance, and tried turning the lock once the key was seated all the way in. The lock didn't budge.

Things could, in fact, get worse. Much worse. Kelly had changed the locks.

A sickening feeling of utter helplessness and abandonment swam through him. She meant what she said, and now he was alone. He went back to the Jeep and drove to the only other place where he could feel welcomed.

Brenda was putting away the beer mugs when Hector entered the bar. "Hey, Hector! It's been a while! How're you doin'?"

He went to his stool without offering so much as a greeting. "Get me the bourbon."

Brenda grew somber and her skin turned paler, if that was possible. She paid no mind to the other customers and reached for the half-empty bottle of Staggs deep in the center top shelf, one that was well out of sight unless you knew to look for it. The same one she pointed out the day of the party, so long ago.

The only time Hector or Chuck ever asked for it was to toast a fallen comrade, and this was the first time he'd asked for it without Chuck. She set the bottle and a shot glass gently down in front of him, and asked softly, "Hey, Hector, is everything okay?"

Hector snatched the bottle and barked, "Just give me the damn bottle and mind your own business."

Brenda shuddered from the sting and backed off, returning to the other customers in a failed attempt at pretending all was fine.

"I'm sorry," he said heavily, looking up at her with pleading eyes.

Brenda stopped and turned around. With a deep breath, she asked, "Was it . . . Chuck?" She sighed when Hector shook his head. She leaned forward against the bar. "You want to talk about it?"

Hector thought for a moment, then shook his head without a word.

"All right, just know that I'm here for you." She left him and went to tend to the other customers, glancing back at him one more time.

Three steep drinks later, Jessica again seeped into his thoughts. Specifically, the night of Kelly's party. That felt like a lifetime ago. The way she had flirted and how it made him feel. The way she had sighed as he carried her to the guest room.

He dragged his hands down his face, groaning at his inability to get her out of his head. Why was she there? Why wasn't he thinking about Kelly? The answer never came to him. His memories of that night, the team, and the alcohol monopolized his thoughts. Jessica had been through the worst of it with him and the team. She had seen and lived through the horrors of it all. And even more importantly, she understood him. She got what it was like for him. For all of them.

He thought about her going through her own demons. After everything that happened, she didn't deserve to face them alone. At last, he paid the tab and said good night to Brenda. He stumbled as he tried to get out of his stool, focusing on the door and putting one foot perfectly in front of the other until he made it to the Jeep. He slumped into the driver's seat, fumbled with the key until he got it in the ignition, and instinctively drove east until he eventually reached the junction to the beltway. Then he headed south, to Old Town Alexandria.

Hector shook his head, thinking of every possible reason why following this juvenile impulse was dramatic, idiotic even. *What the hell are you going to do when you get there?* Yet he kept driving in her direction as the last rays of sun dipped behind him and night slowly emerged. Deep down, he didn't want to be alone. Not after the hell he'd been through. He cursed himself for leaving her on her own. She was unexperienced and uninitiated in what he knew all too well would come next. But in truth, what could he do? The boyfriend, Paul, would be there with her, but that wasn't the same. She'd need someone who understood that once everything grows quiet, the demons come haunting— because they would, and they'd condemn you for what you did and did not do. And Paul sure as hell wasn't that person.

Before he knew it, Hector was at Jessica's door. *Did I ring the bell?* He honestly couldn't remember. Worse yet, he had no idea what he would do. *Fantastic job, commando. Perfectly planned.*

He was about to leave when the door opened. Jessica stood there, putting in a dangling earring and wearing a strapless royal blue cocktail dress that made Hector's heart race. He grinned ear to ear. She may have been through hell too, but in that doorway, she looked like the same woman he'd met a lifetime ago. He fidgeted with his hands as he struggled to get the words out.

Jessica smiled at him, but hers with perfect red-colored

lips did not reach her eyes. "Hector, what are you doing here? Is everything okay?"

His face went blank, devoid of all emotion. He looked away. "I'm sorry. This . . . this was a mistake." He turned to leave, refusing to make a fool of himself any further.

"Hector, wait!" She closed the door carefully behind her, grabbed his shoulder, and turned him to face her. "What's up? Why aren't you home with Kelly?" Her voice was genuinely concerned.

Hector couldn't meet her eyes. The effort to try to explain was exhausting. He took a deep breath and said, "I came because I needed someone to talk to. Someone who understood people like us."

Jessica put her fingers to her mouth and asked, "But what about Kelly?"

"She changed the locks." He hesitated, then lifted his eyes to hers and added, "I just didn't want to be alone tonight. Not after everything that happened." He hesitated at saying the words, feeling both guilt and relief at the same time. "I . . . wanted—needed—to talk to you."

Jessica was quiet. She turned around, looking past the closed door, as if waiting for something, then turned back to him.

Hector gulped. "Look, I'm obviously keeping you from something, so I'll just—" He was interrupted by her door opening.

"What's going on, babe?" Paul stepped out in a sports jacket and chinos. He looked at Hector and slipped his arm around Jessica's waist, pulling her to him. He nodded with a smug grin. "Hey there, champ, what brings you over here?"

Jessica looked away, trying to pry his grip from around her waist, but he was intent on holding on to her, making it a point that she was his prize. It wasn't a side of Jessica that Hector was used to seeing. He frowned.

Still staring at Jessica, his voice cracked as he said, "I'm sorry. I shouldn't have. I just needed to . . ." He shook his head, trying to come up with the words. Why were words so hard to find?

"You just need to turn around and walk away, champ," interjected Paul. He stroked his hand up and down Jessica's waist. "She's with me now. I'll take good care of her, so—"

"Shut the fuck up!" the beast responded. An unmistakable glare radiated from him that said, *I will fucking kill you.* He took a step forward. "I'm talking to her." He took another step forward, causing Paul to flinch. "Interrupt or call me 'champ' again, and I will cut out your fucking tongue."

All of Paul's cocky confidence was replaced with fear. Jessica took a small step between them, lightly placing a hand on Paul's chest. "Paul, please. I told you I didn't want to go out tonight anyway. We can do this another night."

Paul puffed out his chest, trying to regain some of his lost bravado. "Absolutely not! Do you have any idea how hard it was to get us a table so quickly?"

Jessica turned fierce. "Not tonight, Paul! I told you earlier I wasn't in the mood! Now if you don't mind, this is important."

That's the woman I know. Hector relaxed a little.

"So you can be with this drunk loser? He's pathetic, Jessica!" He held her chin between his fingers. "Just tell him to leave and—"

Jessica snapped her head from his grasp and tore herself away from his grip. "You're such an asshole, Paul." Her voice cracked. "I'm doing this. And if you think you can control me, you're greatly mistaken! Either let it go or we're done."

Hector caught a vision of her cleavage rising and falling with each breath. That and the fire in her made her irresistible.

Paul threw his hands in the air. "Fine!" He glared at Hector. "No need to get my stuff right now. Call me when you've finished . . . whatever it is." He gave Hector a wide berth as he stormed off down the road.

Jessica's eyes followed him, then she ran a hand across her forehead. "Paul, don't be like that!" He disappeared without looking back. She turned to Hector, no longer empathetic, and groaned, "Come on. I need a fucking drink."

43

Old Town Alexandria, Virginia

Jessica gestured at her door. "Please, come in." Hector did as he was told, and she followed him in, closing and locking the door behind her. "Make yourself at home. I'll be just a few more minutes. There's beer in the refrigerator, if you like."

Hector thanked her and scanned the interior as she disappeared upstairs. It was modern, well-kept, and furnished with decorations he never would have considered. The white leather living room set was arranged in a nontraditional angle, offset with elaborate floor lamps, a glass-top coffee table, and a matching white bookshelf filled with books of varying sizes and thicknesses, giving the room a cosmopolitan feel to it.

Just like in Kelly's magazines. He shook his head, shuffling the thoughts out of place. *Jesus Christ, man! Don't start this shit now!* At a second glance, he noticed something. There were no photographs. Nothing personal like portraits, photos of Kelly or their parents, life events like graduations or vacation spots. Not even a frame with a smiling generic family.

She called from upstairs, "Okay, I'm ready." The clicking of her heels on the wooden stairs grew closer.

Hector couldn't help gawking at her legs as she descended. He had grown so accustomed to seeing her in khakis and dirty T-shirts, he'd forgotten what heels could do to a woman's figure. "You look amazing!"

She gave him the same beguiling smile from the party, but it quickly morphed into a forced one. "I'm glad you're here. I needed someone to talk to, and Paul just wanted to . . ."

"You don't have to explain it. I've been there many a time."

Jessica leaned in and wrapped her arms around him. He reciprocated. God, her body felt good pressed against his. It was impossible to put everything into one emotion. It was consolation, regret, gratitude, and lust. He ran his hands softly across her upper back, feeling the smoothness of her skin while taking in the intoxicating scent of her perfume. *You can't, Hector.*

Why not? It's over with Kelly. She kicked you out of your own home.

Because she's your teammate. That's why.

He sighed with disillusion, put his hands on her shoulders, and tried to pull her away. She didn't budge.

She sniffed. Muffled from where her head was buried in his neck, she whispered, "Just hold me, please."

He nodded and enveloped her in his arms once more. The lust gave way to something more comforting and healing. The moment lasted until she was ready to let go. They separated, and she swiped under her eyes, checking her fingers for mascara.

She sniffed again and laughed softly. She then looked into his eyes, holding them a moment, and smiled. "I don't know about you, but I'm famished."

He nodded. "Me too."

She took him by the hand and led him outside. "Come on.

We may as well make use of the reservation. It's an excellent restaurant at the waterfront that I think you'll like."

He looked down at his jeans and simple button-down shirt, then gestured at her—well, all of her. "I'm not dressed for—"

"Doesn't matter," she cut him off. "We have the table, and I have the cash. They can deal with it."

Together they exited the Harborside community and made their way north on Union Street. She took his hand as they walked in the dark. "How did things go with Kelly?"

Hector hesitated, unsure if he should burden her with his own problems.

Jessica looked at him with concern. She cocked her head to him and said softly, "Look, you're the one who came over, remember? So, let's talk."

Hector hesitated to answer, but her smile and demeanor were very disarming. He said with a resigned tone, "She changed the locks."

She opened her mouth, but then closed it. "Oh my God. I'm really sorry, Hector."

They walked past the Torpedo Factory to the Blackwall Hitch, a restaurant on the marina with large-pane windows, twin glass-sided cupolas on either end, and various rose bushes and hanging arrangements that adorned the exterior, reminding him of an old European conservatory. Hector could see why the asshole chose to come here. It had a very appealing exterior and offered a magnificent view of the Potomac and National Harbor.

They spent an hour talking over dinner, more time than either of them had expected. They talked about the team, the moments around the firepit that would stay with them forever, and they wondered what the others were doing tonight. When the conversation became too nostalgic and painful, he changed topics.

"So do you think you'll stay with Norton-Allied?"

She stirred her cosmo as she pondered the question, giving it ample thought. "I don't know. I love Bill and enjoy the work, but I don't know if I feel the same about it now." She looked up. "You know what I mean?"

He sipped on his whiskey and soda and nodded. "All too well. But the thing of it is that if you felt this was your calling before we met, then it was meant to be."

"Yeah, maybe you're right. And besides, I've grown tired of moving around."

"Would you go back to San Francisco?"

"No." Her answer came quick and decisive.

"But I thought you loved the Bay Area."

"I did, and I do. But that would mean going back to my past, and I don't want to do that. I can't do that." She stared out at the lights of National Harbor and the Wilson Bridge.

A memory came back to him. A story from the firepit all those nights ago. "Right. The Russian mafia. I can only hope that they think you were killed in the attack. If not, we can protect you, I hope you know that. But still, have you thought about where you would go next?"

She shook her head. "No. I pray that episode in my life is finally behind me. I don't ever want to relive it. But if I had to run again, I'd go to St. Louis."

"St. Louis? Why there?"

"I was born there. I don't remember much, but my father always spoke fondly of it. I think that if I had to make a fresh start, St. Louis would be it."

Hector nodded as he sipped his drink. "And it wouldn't have anything to do with the fact that Penguin is from St. Louis?

Jessica perked up. "Is that where he went?"

Hector chuckled. "Yeah, I thought you knew."

"No, he never said anything about it." A smile formed from ear to ear. "Thank you for letting me know."

"Don't mention it."

"If you don't mind me asking, what are *you* going to do?"

He let out a long exhale and stared out into the Potomac. "I don't know. During the fight, it became crystal clear that I still want to be with Kelly for the rest of my life, and that I wouldn't go back out again." He took another gulp of his drink. "But I'm afraid it's all too little too late. I don't even want to think about a divorce lawyer, but that may be out of my hands." He looked at Jessica. "She's your sister. You know her better than anyone else. What do you think?"

She smirked. "She's my *step*sister, to be clear, and as far as knowing her . . . I don't know how true that is now. We've changed a lot over the years, but the one constant about her is she tends to be overemotional about things and keeps her grudges for a long time."

Hector leaned back against his chair, all his hopes deflated.

"But like I said, we've both changed over the years."

He watched the lit-up reflection of National Harbor's observation wheel twinkle and spin. Maybe things would have turned out differently if he had bothered to pay attention to the things Kelly enjoyed, and less about what mission came next. He let out a long sigh. "Kelly talked me into joining Parabellum so we could have a better future." He looked down at his tumbler, swiping away a rolling dew drop as if wiping away his own inner tears. "But it was my same old desires from before Parabellum that ruined our marriage." He shrugged. "It's over."

Jessica reached across the table and clasped his hand. They continued talking for a while longer, genuinely enjoying each other's company. At the end, they both walked outside, unsure of where the night went on from there. She took his hand into hers again and rested her head on his shoulder. This was the most enjoyable evening Hector had had with a woman in a very long time.

They reached the street corner, and Jessica said, "I know a really good bar close by."

Hector weighed the options. He'd already had a lot to drink tonight. The responsible thing would be to go home. There was that word again. But there was no *home* to go to, not anymore. He sighed. "All right, but let's not close the place down, okay?"

She smiled, hooked her arm around his elbow, and led the way to the Union Street Public House, a bar a few blocks down the street.

The main room of the bar was small, with booths and tables that surrounded the square bar on all sides. It had an intimate feel. Fortunately for them, a cozy corner booth had just been cleared. The drinks flowed as the night went on, bringing the underlying sexual attraction to surface as the alcohol wore down their inhibitions.

In a moment of spontaneity, Jessica moved to his side of the booth, sitting precipitously close to him. Hector instinctively put his arm around her, breathing in her intoxicating perfume. He found himself lost in her eyes.

In that moment, as if by some outside force, he lifted her chin and his lips met hers. The last of their inhibitions melted, damning whatever consequences may come.

She let out a moan as their tongues drifted into each other's mouths, which excited Hector, encouraging him. Their movements became more agitated. Her hand slid between his legs, feeling his hardness and pressing against it. The passion between them reached a boiling point that neither wanted to back away from.

His hand slid down from her chin to her neck, feeling the silkiness of her skin, the contours of her neck and the growing pulse of her heartbeats. He curled his fingers slightly, feeling the dip between her neck and collarbone, then slid them down to her heaving chest. He cupped his hand on her breasts, forcing another moan from her. He felt her hand groping and rubbing wantonly against his hardness. The months without release or the touch of a woman had been too much.

Then without warning, he broke their kiss.

"What is it?" she asked with alarm.

He fixated on one of the large windows by the door, searching for something that had spiked his senses to life. He turned to scan the people mingling in the bar, searching for anything out of place. His heart was beating fast as his senses continued tingling. "We need to leave. Now."

She wrung her arm from his tight grasp, clasped his face between the palms of her hands, and forced his eyes to focus on hers. "Hey! Look at me . . . look at me. Focus on me." She held his gaze until the thousand-yard stare faded. She slowed her speech and lowered her tone. "We're okay here. Nothing's going to happen. We're just at a bar, that's all."

She stroked his chest gently, calming him until his heart quit trying to punch through his chest. She pressed her lips against his ear, her breath sweet with fruity vodka, and whispered, "Let's get out of here."

Hector wiped the sweat off his forehead and nodded. "I'm really sorry, Jessica. This . . . this isn't normal for me. Not here." She said nothing as they exited the booth. He reached for his wallet and left enough cash to cover their drinks and a tip, still trying to figure out why his spidey senses had gone off.

Jesus, Hector. Get a fucking hold of yourself!

He took her hand and left the bar without looking back. He scanned the street when they stepped outside, searching again for whatever caused his senses to spike, and trying to find anything out of place.

Before he could finish, Jessica pulled him to the right. "Come on, let's go back to my place."

He was back in control, and again confident as before. His outburst was quickly fading from his mind as he focused on Jessica and how gorgeous she looked in the moonlight. His lust from earlier in the night reemerged. Despite what had just happened, he still wanted her. She interlaced her fingers with his, tucked her head into his shoulder, and led him away down the avenue.

A moment later, a head crept up from below the dashboard of a car parked just across the street from the bar. Paul was still breathing hard from racing back to his car, barely making it in time, wondering if the loser had spotted him.

How the fuck did he know?

Paul peeked out, waiting for the savage to turn around and head straight for him. Instead, the two continued down the street. Paul gripped the steering wheel, clenching his teeth as he watched Jessica holding hands with the loser and resting her head on his shoulder. He knew where they were going and what was going to happen. The bitch had been having an affair with that guy this whole time. Fine by him. It justified his own tryst with some of the other girls in the office —not that he felt troubled by it. But it still made his blood boil that she had the nerve to cheat on him. He slammed his hand against the steering wheel. *Bitch deserves everything coming to her.*

Paul raised his camera above the dashboard and focused the zoom. He snapped several photos in rapid succession, seething with jealousy at their closeness. *Fucking slut.*

He started the BMW, flooding the street with his cool white headlights, and inched forward. His mind conjured up every irrational way he could make the guy pay and teach her the price of cheating on him.

To think I almost defended her. I hope they make the bitch suffer.

Hector pressed Jessica against the door, his rigidness aching for her as she breathed heavily. His mouth slid from her bare shoulder to her exposed neck, kissing hungrily, while he massaged her breasts from behind. She at last got the door unlocked, and both stumbled inside as the door gave way. He closed the door behind them, watching her like a lion watches its prey. He strode forward, pinning her to the wall and pulling her hands over her head. He pressed his lips to hers and kissed with an insatiable desire for her.

She broke their heated kiss and gasped for air, meeting his eyes. Her gaze held the same need as his own. She slipped from between him and the wall and led him up the stairs to her bedroom. There, inside her inner sanctum, she ripped his buttoned shirt open and pulled it halfway down, locking his arms in place and exposing his chiseled chest and sculpted abs.

Hector watched her through a hazy intensity as she examined him, admiring his masculine physique and exploring his hot skin and hard muscles with her hands. She pushed his head up with her forehead and sank her lips into his neck while her hands roamed over his broad shoulders and flowed down to his chest until she reached the upper edge of his jeans. She opened his belt buckle and unzipped his jeans to let loose the animal inside.

She turned around, presenting her back, and gasped, "Unzip me!"

He pulled her zipper down immediately, relishing how her back muscles twitched at his touch as he slipped his hands beneath the dress. With the dress loose around her torso, he slid his hands up to her shoulders, feeling her tight, soft skin against the roughness of his hands. He caressed down her arms, grasping her hands and forcing them up and behind his neck. He gently traced his fingertips down her arms and slipped his hands in the void between her skin and the dress, letting his hands roam down her body, sliding the dress off until it fell to the floor.

She stepped out of her dress and turned to him. He took her roughly in his arms, then stopped. Here, in this moment, the transition from fantasy to reality hit him like a cold splash of water.

Jessica paused too, her brows knitting together with concern. "What's wrong?"

Hector released his grip, and he rubbed his face as if waking from a deep slumber. "I'm sorry. I can't do this." He took a step back. "I can't do this to you or to Kelly. I'm sorry."

Jessica stared at him with shock etched on her face. "Are you serious right now?" She pointed to herself. "Look at me, Hector! Look at how I am." She then pointed at him. "Look at yourself! You came here, remember? We're consenting adults, for fuck's sake!"

Hector looked away, unable to look at the woman he couldn't stop thinking of, and pulled his shirt back on as he turned to leave. He murmured, "I'm really sorry about this. I truly am." Then he left her room.

Jessica chased him to the doorway. "Please! Don't leave!" There was desperation and doubt in her voice.

The last thing he saw as he got in his Jeep was her standing in the front door, her dress clutched against her naked form and black streaks running down her face. Hector hated himself for causing her the degradation and humiliation of being "the other woman."

[44]

Parabellum Headquarters
Wednesday, 16 July 2014

Hector had almost committed the cardinal sin of affairs by
sleeping with his wife's sister. If his marriage wasn't already
irrevocably ruined, for sure it would have been then. But the
fact was that he had felt something for Jessica he hadn't felt
with his own wife in a long time. Jessica understood that part
of him that needed to feed the black hole to keep it from
crushing everything else around it, and now he had soured
that relationship as well. Worse yet, he felt like he had
betrayed a teammate—just another in the list of things that
tore him inside.

But you both bled together, the connection there— No, that
connection was for naught, even if it was over with Kelly. She
and Kelly were again part of each other's lives, and even if he
had stopped himself from making that mistake, he had fool-
ishly put them both in that predicament. If the truth of that
came to light, like a body in a shallow grave, the consequences would be devastating.

Leaving her house had been more complicated than he'd

expected. He couldn't stay there, obviously, and he couldn't go home. So he'd headed to the Parabellum building and his stocked dorm room. He expected to be there for the coming weeks, or until he figured out what he would do next.

He had garnered strange glances from those on duty, all offering their condolences until he mercifully escaped into his room. Once inside, he dropped his phone and keys on the nightstand, changed out of his clothes that still bore the scent of Jessica's perfume, and slipped under the covers. The stiff mattress was a blunt reminder of the comfortable bed he wouldn't be sharing with Jessica that night. He had stared at the ceiling as the demons emerged with the soft noise of the air conditioning. But blissfully, the alcohol in his system at last caught up with him, and his eyelids had grown heavy.

He now woke in what felt mere minutes to find the alarm clock next to him showing 8:17 a.m. He had a killer headache from drinking the night before. The few hours of sleep had done nothing to put his mind at ease, so he did what he thought was the next best thing: he changed into some workout clothes and headed to the gym in the complex. He mounted a treadmill near the middle of the room and pushed the start button, increasing the speed and incline until he reached a pace that could keep up with the speed of his thoughts.

An hour later, he was breathing hard. His mind was still trying to come to terms with everything that had transpired. Was Kelly really throwing it all away because of one mission? Was his career in the field over after that devastating failure? How did Jessica cope after he left her heartbroken? How ruthless had her demons been her first night home? Was his marriage truly over? What exactly did he feel for Jessica? Did he still love Kelly, or just the idea of a happy marriage?

At the end of the seven-mile run, no real answers had materialized. He slowed the pace and decreased the incline until he was at a walking pace. One thought lingered above the others. *Do I still love Kelly?*

He showered in the gym after the run, leaning against the white tile wall of the confining shower stall and letting the hot water run down his back, wishing it could wash away all the anxieties and burdens he carried. The thought persisted.

Do I still love Kelly?

Hector turned his face up to the showerhead and let the water run down his long hair, his short, unkempt beard, and down the bruises and scars that covered his weary and aching body. It reminded him of the many times Kelly had tended to his wounds, the care and devotion she gave to each and the gentle touch of her fingers on them even after they healed. But what he remembered the most was how she hugged and held him for so long each time he returned. He missed that about her. God, how he missed her right now.

Jessica stirred something in him he thought he desired, but that was all a fantasy. What an idiot he had been. So they couldn't have a family. Was that any reason to throw it all away and leave the woman who loved him so much it hurt? The fog of it all was starting to lift, and he was at last able to see what was in front of him. He wrapped a towel around himself and exited the steam-filled stall. He walked to the line of sinks and wiped the fog from the mirror, staring at his own reflection.

I do. I still love her. But is that enough?

The hot shower had been refreshing in more ways than one. He still had things to figure out, but he felt some sense of clarity. He brushed his teeth, shaved, and automatically did all the other things of his morning routine. *I still love her!* The revelation that he still loved his wife was invigorating. *Did I have to endure all that pain and hardship to realize this, in the end?* The answer was obvious. He did. Jessica had been right about that.

He entered his room, towel still wrapped around his

waist, and reached into the metal-and-wood dresser to pull fresh clothes out, when something caught his attention. On the nightstand, his phone lit up with a notification. He picked it up, and his heart dropped to the pit of his stomach. It was a text from Kelly, but it was her message that sent a jolt coursing through him.

I know you're back. We need to talk.

A mix of fear and relief surged through him, like a surrounded fugitive exhausted from endless running. But the fear of what had almost happened last night overshadowed any relief. He unlocked the phone and exhaled hard, his thumb lingering above the keyboard, trying to decide what to text back—or if he wanted to text back. He took a deep breath and messaged her back.

Yes, I am. It's a long story. Where do you want to meet?

The screen remained static for several long seconds, extending his torment like a convict awaiting the pronouncement of his punishment. Then he saw the three-dotted bubble marking her response.

Home.

The single word sent a cold chill down his spine. He hoped she'd pick some public place, like a coffeehouse, but he was unsure why. Perhaps it was because he hoped an argument would be negated by the crowds. He texted back.

OK. I'll be there in an hour.

He sighed heavily. *Maybe it's better this way.* They could say what they needed to say, leave their past, and get on with their lives. He dropped the phone and began dressing, all the while trying to think about what he truly wanted in the end. He still loved her, yes, but did he still believe in their marriage?

Hector pulled into the driveway an hour later and felt the heavy dread return. He made his way to the porch, each step feeling heavier than the last until he stood at the front door. He hesitated. Should he ring? Try the handle? The decision was snapped away when Kelly opened the door, leaning against it, looking disheveled, like she hadn't slept a wink last night. Her hair was a mess, and she clearly hadn't bothered to remove yesterday's makeup. She stared at him blankly, not greeting him in any manner, and simply tilted her head, gesturing him in.

Hector followed her into the sitting room at the right of the foyer. She sat on her reading chair by the window, head down and knees together, deep in her own thoughts. In front of her on the coffee table was a box of tissues surrounded by a cluster of wadded-up ones. He sat opposite her in his plush brown leather chair that clashed with the sleek mid-century modern décor, a defiant claim that had once screamed, "This is my chair."

As if on cue, Kelly raised her head and asked, "Why didn't you come home yesterday?"

The question came like a hook to the head, but it was the pain in her expression that hurt the most. He searched for an answer, but Kelly didn't wait for one.

"Why didn't you call?" Her expression was not that of an indifferent ex but of a loving wife not understanding why she was punished without cause. It was the expression of a broken heart, one that seared into his soul.

Defenseless, Hector opened his hands, cleared his throat,

and said softly, "I did come home. You changed the locks. *You* made it clear I was not welcome."

Kelly didn't move. Tears rolled freely down her face, following a trail of dark stains her mascara had left. She pointed at her chest with both hands. "I'm your *wife*, Hector." Her voice cracked as it pushed past the thick lump in her throat. "I love you! Why would you ever think I didn't?" Her eyebrows twitched as if trying to understand.

Hector wiped his face with both hands, clasping them together in the end. "You made it clear, Kelly. You told me it was you or the mission. I tried begging with you to let me go this one last time. Not because I wanted to, but because I had to. And then I come home to find the locks *changed*."

He wanted to find a way to tell her that he still loved her, but the opportunity was again snatched away.

"I was angry, Hector. You should know I didn't mean that. And if you had bothered to call me *once*, I would have told you about the locks. But you didn't. Instead you left, with my slut of a *sister*!" Kelly reached for two fresh tissues, shaking her head. She wiped the tears and added, "I thought you knew me better than that. Worse yet, I thought you cared about us, but clearly I was mistaken."

Her tone was accusatory, immediately sending him on the defense. "Dammit, Kelly! I do care about us! But we fight all the time!" He clenched his fists, trying to contain the anger brewing inside. "All. The. Time! I can't remember a day when we didn't fight about anything and everything. So how was I supposed to take your ultimatum? Or the fact that you changed the locks? Why would I bother to call after you clearly told me it was you or the mission?" He regretted his words as soon as he said them, letting the conversation go farther from where he wanted it. He balled his hands in front of his lips, trying to find another way of telling her that he loved her and wanted to stop fighting, but then the unexpected happened.

"I see. So that made it all right for you to take my skank of a sister with you?"

"Goddammit, Kelly! Why do you keep—"

"Did you sleep with her?" The question came, brash and unapologetic. She watched him knowingly. Spite, hurt, anger, and disappointment all emanated from within. Her lower lip quivered and her eyes welled up again, but she remained focused on his response.

Hector's heart beat against his chest as the same cold fear from the text shrouded him. "What? No. I . . ." He paused, trying to figure out how she knew that he had come back yesterday, wondering if she knew about the failed mission and how she had known he'd gone to see Jessica instead of his own wife. "No, I didn't. She was a teammate, Kelly! I would never—"

"Don't fucking lie to me, Hector!" Kelly burst out, spittle exploding with her accusation. "Don't you fucking dare lie to me! I know you did! I know you fucked my bitch of a sister! I know you fucked her over there, and I know you fucked her last night!"

Fresh tears spilled down her cheeks, but she didn't bother dabbing or wiping them. She pulled her phone out, manipulating it until a picture appeared on the screen. She thrust it in his face. "You are a lying, cheating bastard, Hector! And I'm done with you! You hear me? I'm done with you!"

Hector drew back in shock. Her rage was one he'd never seen from her, nor imagined her capable of. Her face was red with fierce, penetrating eyes. Her hand trembled from the rage coursing through her, barely able to keep the phone steady. In that moment, he wasn't in front of his wife. He was facing a warrior. He took the phone from her hand and looked at the picture. His heart sank to the bottom as he recognized himself and Jessica, kissing passionately at her doorstep. He flipped to the next picture, showing him pressing against her at the door, and the following, showing them going inside.

They had been followed. Who? Why?

"Kelly, I swear to God, I didn't sleep with Jessica!"

Kelly jumped from her seat, pouncing on him like a lioness, and slapped him hard, to the point he saw stars. "Don't lie to me!" She slapped his other cheek, opening a scab from the battle and letting blood dribble out.

Hector touched his cheek while holding Kelly's hand. "Yes, I went to see her, but I swear I didn't sleep with her! I've never cheated on you, Kelly, I promise! I love you! As God is my witness, I love you. I don't know why it took me so long to realize that I still love you, but I do!"

Kelly paused, her chest heaving against her blouse. There was an intense rage in her eyes, her own beast raging against its chains.

She brushed her hair away from her face. "I'm going to Philadelphia next Friday for the new firm's official recognition party." She sniffed and wiped her mouth. "When I come back on Sunday, I expect you to be out of the house and gone. I don't care where you go. Just don't be here." She slumped onto her chair in defeat, covering her face as she gave in to her pain. "I don't want to do this anymore. I don't want to fight, and I don't want to be hurt anymore. Go to that whore if that's what you want."

Hector's heart ached. He lifted himself out of his chair and took a step toward her, but she stopped him with a raised hand. "No. Don't. You don't get to come near me. You don't get to tell me you love me. Just go. That's what you're good at. Go to that fucking slut."

Hector became light-headed, feeling as though he was having an out-of-body experience, unable to wrap his head around what had just happened. He rubbed his face, only then noticing his own tears escaping, and he ran his hands through his hair. He had realized too late what he truly felt for her and had thrown it all away with a moment of weakness, even if his choices didn't end the way Kelly assumed. In a matter of days, he'd lost everything that was of importance to him. His friends, his wife, his marriage. And each was lost because of his wants. Because he wanted to go on the mission, and because he wanted Jessica.

He looked at Kelly, slumped in her chair, crying unconsolably. There was nothing he could do about it. He turned and slowly walked to the foyer and grabbed the door handle. He turned to her one more time, wishing he could take it all back, to turn the clock back, but that was impossible. He opened the door and walked out, knowing this was possibly the last time he'd call Kelly his wife.

45

Norton-Allied building, Washington, DC
Friday, 18 July 2014

Inside the Norton-Allied conference room on the seventh floor, lawyers and board members faced off on either side of a polished rectangular mahogany field of battle, dressed in their English-tailored suits of finely woven armor and seven-fold silk-tie banners. The war cry of springing briefcase locks resounded in the conference room, each side ready to wage war once more and end the weeks-long stalemate regarding the oil field.

The Kabuki dance held no interest to Jessica. She rolled her eyes at the pretend hardened faces of the K Street heroes who would call for a medic at the sight of the first paper cut. Instead, she shifted her unfocused gaze out across the other office buildings along Pennsylvania Avenue. Her thoughts were with the rest of Bravo Team, smiling as she imagined them sitting around the villa firepit, probably telling the same stripper story to the new guys . . . the replacements. She laughed to herself and dabbed a tear from her eye; she had to keep her immaculate makeup from being ruined. Her heart ached for them. For the ones they lost, and the ones who remained.

"Jessica . . . Jessica!"

She snapped her head around, coming back to the board room and finding Ben Warner, the senior VP for operations at Norton-Allied, scowling at her.

"What's the matter with you? Quit daydreaming and get your head in the game."

She rolled her eyes again. "I already told you. I'm not changing my mind. I will not endorse operations in that oil field."

"Look, I know we had some setbacks, but—"

"Fifteen brave Americans and dozens of Kurds lost their lives, Ben!" Jessica said, springing to her feet. "At least have the common decency to call their sacrifices more than just a setback."

Ben steepled his fingers before him, his voice cool. "Yes, of course. We all feel for their loss, but I don't need to remind you that this firm needs to produce energy to survive. In the end, we need to make money and satisfy our shareholders." He then added condescendingly, "Unless you know of something more important."

Jessica laughed to herself, then quoted one of Cujo's many rants, a bad imitation from *Conan the Barbarian*. "Yeah, Ben, it's crushing your enemies, seeing them driven before you, and hearing the lamentation of their women."

A single laugh came from the opposite side of the table.

Ben was about to respond when Bill raised his hand, ending the discourse. "She's right, Ben," he said in his Texas drawl. "What happened out there is nothing short of a tragedy. We're only blessed that the good Lord saw fit to spare Jessica and the rest of those brave men."

"Bill," Ben started, but he was quieted with another raise of the hand.

"I don't want to hear it, Ben. I'm not going to sacrifice

more lives for a single oil field when we still don't know how much it will yield. There are plenty of other places in the world that we can compete in, including our very own country."

Low murmurs erupted around the table. Ben rested his elbows on the table, rubbing his temples. "Bill, I understand your sentiment, I do, but the new firm will be unveiled next Friday, a week from now! What are we going to tell the people on the Columbia side? We can't possibly keep them in the dark about this."

"Ben." Bill met his eyes, then those of everyone around the room. "That is exactly what we are going to do."

A stunned silence filled the room. Jessica sat up, reinterested in the meeting.

"Bill," said Marsha Perales, the Norton-Allied CFO, "we can't do that. There will be hell to pay if—"

"You let me worry about that, Marsha."

"Bill!" interjected Ben. "We cannot jeopardize this deal just because a bunch of knuckle-draggers were killed. They won the day in the end, right?" He looked around the room. "Let's at the very least say we're considering sending reinforcements, or something."

Jessica's eyes welled, and it took everything within her not to break down. She uncrossed her legs and stood, striding across the room without so much as excusing herself. She would not give them the satisfaction of seeing her break down, even if the pain of it all was insurmountable.

"Jessica! Where the hell are you going?" asked Ben as she passed him.

"I need a moment, Ben. It's important," she retorted condescendingly.

Ben, who looked like he was about to have an apoplectic seizure, reached out and grabbed her by the bicep.

"You will sit down or—" He shut up immediately at the glare she gave him, a death stare he'd not soon forget.

"Ben—" Jessica's voice was like a wolf's growl. "If you do not let go of my arm, I will break your wrist and elbow, and slam your head through the table."

Ben released her immediately. The stories about her facing off against and killing a hoard of ISIS fighters seemed to have circulated the office gossip chain all the way up to him. *Good.* Now she just needed a moment to mourn her fellow "knuckle-draggers."

46

Morris House Hotel, Philadelphia, Pennsylvania
Friday, 25 July 2014

Kelly gripped her clutch tight as she entered the reception
area, alone and unescorted, with guests standing and
applauding her. Here she was, the architect of the merger,
celebrated on the eve of her crowning achievement without
her "beloved" husband at her side—a cruel symbolism that
summarized her past few years.

She felt all eyes on her as she made her way through the
crowd, imagining the whispers being about her unescorted
entrance instead of the magnificent royal blue satin off-the-
shoulder dress with matching gloves she'd eagerly waited
months to wear. Her gloved hands pressed against her chest
as she bowed in appreciation, willing herself to hold back the
tears that would ruin her perfectly applied makeup.

She was overcome with emotion from admiration by her
peers, but also by the heartbreaking disappointment from
Hector. If asked, she'd say that Hector was away on business,
which would have been the case if all had gone as expected,

but he had robbed her of the grand entrance she had secretly desired: to be escorted by the man she still loved. And knowing that he had returned, only to cheat on her with her own stepsister that same night, cheapened her experience. More than embarrassing her, it insulted her.

But the party was, otherwise, magnificent. The celebration for the newly christened Cygnus Investments was being held in Philadelphia, the site of the new hub. The choice for the Morris House Hotel, a boutique hotel near Washington Square, had been a well-guarded secret, and that secrecy paid off. The smaller venue wooed the exclusive list guests and made the event feel even larger, somehow.

In the middle of a conversation, Kelly heard a familiar laugh that sent a shudder down her body. *Jessica.* She tried to resist the impulse to turn and look, not wanting to give her the satisfaction, but the urge to see the woman who had destroyed her marriage was too much.

And there she was, putting her pretentious charms on Alex Portman as his eyes took in her burgundy spaghetti-strap dress with the slit provocatively high on her right thigh. *Slut*, Kelly scoffed as Jessica touched Alex's arm before walking off with her elbow around the arm of Paul Monroe, the brown-nosing little prick. Kelly quickly faced forward as Jessica looked in her direction, hoping to avoid eye contact, but she knew it was too late. If Jessica hadn't noticed, the sway of Kelly's dangling earrings would have given her away.

The emcee stepped up to the podium and announced the formal start of the evening's events. Kelly took a deep breath and followed the other managing partners of the combined firm behind the podium, as practiced beforehand. Alex Portman went up to the podium and gave some amusing anecdotes about the lead-up to the merger.

"But of course, none of this could have happened without

the fine work and effort that our very own Kelly Vidal, the chief architect of this merger, put into making this happen."

Kelly bowed as the room broke into applause. She was enjoying the spotlight.

Alex looked at her and went on. "Kelly, I know the countless hours and many sacrifices you put into making the merger appear seamless. That was no small task." He lifted an intricately cut crystal monolith, its prismed facets projecting rainbows as the lights hit it. In the center was her name etched into the crystal along with a citation for excellence. "For that, we are happy to present you with this award as a small token of our appreciation." He gestured for her to come to the podium and accept the award.

She took the monolith from Alex and shook his hand. As she looked out into the room, her eyes went to her table with two empty chairs directly in front of the podium. Hector was supposed to be sitting there. He was supposed to be her most enthusiastic supporter, but all that was a dream now. She choked up as she looked at the award, trying to think of some appreciative words, but her mind faltered. Her heartbreak robbed her of her words.

"Thank you, Alex," she managed to say. "But I must also thank the amazing team that worked with me every day." She choked up in mid-sentence. "This is as much yours as it is mine."

With that, she finished and returned to her seat at the head table, setting the award in the empty chair beside her.

After the ceremony, and two glasses of wine later, Kelly saw Jessica approaching with Paul in tow. She rolled her eyes.

"Hey, Kel," said Jessica. "Congratulations on the award. You look beautiful." Her tone was bubbly, almost forced, despite the obvious attempt to avoid eye contact a few seconds ago.

"Thanks. You too," Kelly responded flatly. She swigged another sip of wine, not bothering to look Jessica in the eye.

Jessica paused for just a heartbeat, then cleared her throat. Somewhat hesitantly, she asked, "Do you mind if we join you?"

Kelly kept her eyes on the music trio, watching the youngest pluck the strings of the double bass as his feet tapped along with the deep tones. She shrugged. "If you insist."

Jessica smoothed the back of her dress and sat, crossing her legs and exposing her visibly pampered leg through the dress slit in the process. She tilted her head back to Paul and said, "Would you mind getting us some drinks? Thanks." She then turned her attention to Kelly, her instructions more like an order than a request.

Kelly glanced at the couple, noting Paul's lips pursing and nostrils flaring at her not-so-sweet stepsister. He gave a stiff nod and left, his steps too measured to be casual. Kelly's initial instincts were being proven right. In all the years since graduating, Jessica hadn't changed at all. She was still the manipulative bitch who always got her way. It was only a matter of time before she discarded him like the others, unless he had enough of her first.

"I see he's still hanging around," Kelly said with a hint of disdain.

Jessica leaned back against her chair, her brows knitted in confusion. "What is it with you today? This is supposed to be your big day. I thought you'd be over the moon."

"Yeah, well, it isn't. No thanks to you," snapped Kelly, crossing her arms sharply.

"What is that supposed to mean?"

"Nothing," said Kelly, shaking her head. She took another gulp of wine. "Forget I said anything."

Jessica opened her mouth to snap a retort when Paul returned with the drinks. He was about to pull out his chair, but she stopped him. "Would you mind giving us a moment? We need to talk in private."

Paul balled his hands into fists, but quickly loosened them. "Of course," he said with a gentle smile. "I'll be over with the guys." He turned and walked off without so much as reaching for a kiss.

As soon as he was out of earshot, Jessica leaned in to Kelly and said in her lowest voice possible, "What the fuck did you mean by that, Kel?"

Kelly leaned back, glaring at her adulterous sister. "Oh, please. Like you don't know."

Jessica rolled her eyes.

Kelly cocked her head, her demeanor like stone. "You two came back from the mission early. I guess it didn't go well, huh? Tell me, did you find comfort in each other's arms? Or were you already with him before you came home?" Her tone was cold and unfeeling, even though she knew lives had been lost.

She regretted the words as soon as she said them, but throwing that in Jessica's face felt so good. She stared, searching her face for shock or feigned surprise, daring her *step*sister to lie to her face just like her cheating husband had.

Jessica shuddered, and her chest heaved. Her lower lip quivered and her eyes watered. "I never imagined you could be so cold, Kel." Her voice croaked. She looked away, barely managing to blink the tears away. But when she turned back, Kelly recognized the resting bitch face. "I can see how you drove Hector away."

"Did you sleep with him?" Kelly's blood boiled beneath her skin and her heart throbbed against her chest, racing as she awaited the answer she already knew.

"D-did I sleep with him?" Jessica sputtered. "God, Kel! No! I wouldn't—"

Kelly scoffed. "Oh, really!" Her voice was getting louder. "Then what did you do with my husband that night you returned, hmm? Because he sure didn't come home to my bed." She jabbed an angry finger at her. "I knew I should have kept you far away from me, but no, clearly I was too stupid to recognize that you'll never change! I should have known the lengths you'd go to steal a man from me. Going in person on a mission . . . yeah, right. That could have been a Skype call, Jess. But it was all part of your little plan, am I right?" She shook her head, looking at Jessica with disgust. "You'll always be the manipulating little *bitch*!"

Jessica rolled her eyes. "Whatever, Kel. You changed the fucking locks on him! Clearly you didn't want him to go back to you. And why would he? You never gave a shit about his work. Never bothered to understand or care about the things that really happen on his missions. The toll it takes on him." Her chest was heaving, and her hands were balled into fists. "I wish he'd leave you for someone who truly appreciates him, unlike you, you ungrateful bitch."

"No, Jessica, you don't get to do that!" Kelly's voice was loud enough that others took notice of the argument now, but she didn't care. "You don't turn this around on me." Jessica's words had set off a fuse that she didn't expect. "You flirted with him the night of the party, like the little whore that you are. You couldn't keep yourself from taking another man from me, could you? And don't give me that sanctimonious bull-shit, Jessica. I know you too damn well. You only ever give a damn about yourself and no one else."

"Fuck you, Kelly!" Jessica shouted back, crossing her arms as she leaned back on her chair. More heads turned in their direction. "I care about him. About him and the other men in his team because we really are a family. One you care *nothing* about!"

Jessica dabbed her eyes with a tissue. "And for the record,

he came over because I was the only one who could understand him, and he me."

"You poor thing!" mocked Kelly. "You were so distraught that you took my husband back to your place and fucked him." People were murmuring around them. Kelly was aware of at least one young associate pulling out his phone to film them. "That must have been so terrible for you."

Jessica's mouth gaped, and she leaned forward. "You know what, I never asked you to invite me, much less 'reconnect.' I didn't sleep with him, and I sure as hell didn't steal him from you. You pushed him away, sweetie." She flicked her index finger at her. "You did that all on your own. And look at you now. Sitting here all alone, with only your grand award to keep you company. How pathetic."

She cocked her head and grinned mockingly. "Way to go, Kel." She turned on her heels and headed to the bar. Kelly seethed as she watched her go, Paul chasing after her like a whipped puppy.

"Can we head out early to Talula's? I need a change in scenery."

Paul's ears perked at Jessica's request, and a pulse of fear coursed through him as his mind raced to think. The timetable was key, and leaving now would push it forward too much. More importantly, they were supposed to wait for the number of guests to dwindle so as not to raise much suspicion. His eyes widened, and he felt the hair on the back of his neck stand up. He looked around, expecting FBI agents and police officers to come out of nowhere and arrest him.

Keep it cool, man. Just keep it cool.

"Um, sure," he said nervously. "Let me just finish something, okay?" He turned away from her and texted.

She wants to leave now. MAKE IT HAPPEN NOW!!

He stowed his phone and turned back to her. He slipped his hand around her bare shoulders, needing to buy some time, and asked, "Are you sure you want to leave now? I mean, I'm part of the planning committee. I still have some duties to fulfill."

Jessica tilted her head back and huffed. "Seriously, Paul? Did you not hear what just happened in there?" She pointed to Kelly, then dropped her arms to her sides. "I don't want to be here anymore. It doesn't matter anyway. I'm not working for these shitbags much longer. You can stay if you want, but I'm leaving."

She started walking past him, but he held her by the arm. "Okay, I'll go with you."

He wrapped his arm around her shoulders, hoping she wouldn't sense his nervousness, and led her out onto St. James Street. The plan was to take a walk in Washington Park before heading to the restaurant. Konstantin was supposed to have created a dead spot by "magically" putting out lights to mask the kidnapping in darkness. But now that the plan changed, he had no idea if he should still go to the park. He scanned left and right, hoping to see some signal to direct him. Many of the lights in the narrow street were out, making the north side much darker than usual.

He spotted a series of parked panel vans and led Jessica in that direction. He caressed her back to put her at ease, or rather put himself at ease. He goaded her to talk about what had just happened and how she was feeling, anything to keep her from noticing the enveloping darkness—especially from noticing the lone panel van with the engine still running.

Still sitting at the table, Kelly felt her blood rising to a boil as her rage steeped. It had taken all of her self-control not to chase after the bitch and slap her across the face, lest she cause a dramatic scene that would eclipse the rest of the evening and make the catfight the one thing everyone talked about for days. But now she regretted not getting the satisfaction.

She faced forward, still seething, and took another sip of wine. She had to let it go. Jessica was immature, self-absorbed, and manipulative, and Kelly just had to stay as far away from her as possible.

But that bitch needs someone to put her in her place!

In every argument that her memory could conjure, Jessica always ended up with the last words, regardless of winning the argument or not, and that had always gotten under Kelly's skin. No, she didn't deserve to walk out carefree and unrepentant. *Not this time, Jessica. You don't get to walk away like that this time.*

Kelly left her clutch and award at the table and gave chase. She was determined to finally have the last word. She followed the path some guests outside pointed to, but they were nowhere in sight. Their head start was negligible; they should've been just outside the hotel. She heard the distant clicking of heels and followed it. As she closed in on the sound, a turning car flashed momentarily on the pair and she spotted the glint of Jessica's earrings.

Jessica pressed her head against Paul's shoulder as she walked deeper into the darkness with him, unaware of the danger that lurked only a few feet ahead of her. "I tried, you know. I really tried to be a better sister, but she has such impossible expectations that only set people up for failure."

"Yeah, I get it," Paul said as he caressed her shoulder, but he couldn't care less about her yapping. He was getting more nervous as they passed the van, still unsure of what was supposed to happen, when he suddenly felt his phone vibrating. He stopped, pulling Jessica to a halt beside him. He was about to pull the phone out when Jessica gasped, stiffening in his arms.

Konstantin manifested from the darkness. He had jabbed a stun gun on her upper back and paralyzed every voluntary muscle. The only thing she could do now was succumb to the chloroform and intense shock before falling helplessly against Paul.

Konstantin pointed. "Don't just stand there. Get her in the van!"

Paul scooped her body before it hit the sidewalk. The van's side panel opened, revealing a horrified and profusely sweating Joseph Donovan. Konstantin motioned for Paul to move faster as he turned his attention elsewhere.

The act had happened in a matter of seconds, its efficiency unsettling. Whatever ethical doubt remained in Paul's mind evaporated in the time it took to get Jessica in the van. The reality that it could easily have been him sent another chill down his spine.

"Jessica? Paul? What's going on over there?"

Paul turned to find Kelly slowly walking toward them. *Fuck!* He recognized her look of terror as she grasped what was happening. Just as he was about to blurt out some excuse, Konstantin whipped out a yellow Taser and fired it at Kelly. A half-second later, her body grew rigid. Konstantin quickly descended upon her with a chloroform rag, and a moment later she was limp on the ground.

"What the fuck are you doing?" Paul grunted at Konstantin.

In turn, Konstantin stood, dusting the knees of his pants and pointed at Kelly's body on the ground, her legs folded beneath her like a rag doll. "No witnesses."

Paul ran his hands through his hair, yanking at the roots and feeling the world collapsing around him. People would eventually notice Jessica was missing, but they'd surely notice very soon that both sisters were missing. Especially after that little scene in the reception hall.

Having no choice, he ran to Kelly, relieved that she was only unconscious, and picked her up. He staggered back to the van where Jessica was now bound and slid Kelly inside.

In the van, Paul and Donovan secured Kelly's body, then Konstantin pointed at Paul. "Remember the plan. Go to party and act normal. You saw nothing. Understand?"

Paul weighed his actions in his mind. Everything had gone so fast that he didn't have time to process that it was all done. He looked at Konstantin and nodded. "I understand."

The sliding door closed and the van drove off, disappearing around the corner. Paul glanced around nervously, praying no one had witnessed the act. Finding the area clear, he casually made his way to Talula's Garden on the opposite side of the block.

47

Donovan focused on the road, heading south on I-95, as was the plan. He sighed when he passed mile marker 15 and took the exit ramp to Enterprise Avenue. Their destination was at last within view, and he could now breathe more easily. He parked in front of the private aircraft terminal on the west end of Philadelphia International Airport, where two massive men in ill-fitting suits met them, each pushing a wheelchair. They placed the unconscious women in the chairs and escorted them into the terminal.

Donovan gingerly lowered himself out of the van and waddled toward the terminal. He had a sinking feeling his deal with the devil was not done yet.

Konstantin wrapped his arm around him, laughing as if they had just played the best prank ever. "Excellent job! See, I told you you could do it. Come, our airplane is ready. It's okay, everything is taken care off. We will celebrate."

Two new guards, equally massive brutes, escorted Donovan out of the terminal and into the Gulfstream 550 that awaited them. The inside of the aircraft was lavish with its leather seating, cream-colored sofas at the front of the fuselage and four swivel chairs surrounding a round chestnut table on either side of the aisle. Donovan watched the guards carry the women to the rear of the aircraft and place them in separate cabins, one on each side of the aircraft. An attractive flight attendant, a young brunette, held out a silver tray with champagne flutes for him and Konstantin, as if this were just another normal flight. He took one, having no real alternative, and sat on the leather sofa opposite Konstantin. He was unsure if he'd return from this trip alive.

The guards nodded to Konstantin before taking their seats at the front of the cabin. The Russian acknowledged them, then raised his drink to Donovan. "To success! You have done well, my friend, and you will be handsomely rewarded."

Somehow, Donovan was beginning to doubt that. They raised their toast and drank the vodka without fanfare. Minutes later, the G5 was in the air.

48

Not America
26 July 2014

Jessica awoke to the sensation of being turned on her stomach as her eyes fluttered with lethargy. Her wrists were forced behind her, and she yelped as cold, hard metal squeezed down and rubbed against them. Now fully awake, her mind raced back to her last memories, putting them together and assessing her current state. She recalled leaving the reception, walking in the odd darkness, then the attack and . . . *Oh God, Paul.*

The realization hit her like a wave. He hadn't fought back, yelled, or done anything to help her. *He was in on it.* In a single synapse, everything fell into place. The late-night phone calls, his obsession with learning the party's secret location, how easily he had agreed to still be her escort despite their fight last week, his nervousness about leaving early . . .

A sudden discomfort in her shoulders brought her back to the present. She was lifted upright by her arms, torquing them in a direction nature hadn't intended. She winced and yelped again. The strain eased once she was upright, and she took the opportunity to scan the strange setting. There had to be something that would fill the gap between the attack and now, but more importantly, hopefully something that would tell her where she was. She recognized the sound of turbine engines powering down and saw daylight peeking around the closed airplane shade.

I'm on a jet, but . . . where?

Bear-paw-sized hands grasped her shoulders and spun her, like an admonished child, and Jessica found herself facing a massive beast of a man with arms as big as her thighs and broad shoulders that stretched his suit jacket. She tilted her head back until she saw his squat, bald head with thick, protruding eyebrows, small eyes, a jagged nose over pouty lips, and a scruffy, square jaw over a thick neck, which was barely contained in the white oxford shirt with black necktie. His face was expressionless, indifferent to her predicament. He pointed down to her heels by the side of the bed and in a thick Russian accent said, "On. Put on."

Recognition sent a cold chill down her spine. She froze in place, staring at him, and the only thought that occupied her mind was that the Russians had caught up to her. A bear paw grabbed a fistful of hair, and she yelped as he pulled her head back. "Shoes! Put on. Fast!"

Jessica winced and yelled back, "Okay! All right! I'll put the damn shoes on!"

The man-beast loosened his fist. She balanced on one leg as she tried setting the shoe upright to slip her foot in. It turned out to be much harder than she expected, and she nearly fell sideways until the man-beast gripped her arm tightly and pushed her back upright, as if she were a fence post that needed setting. She had barely gotten the second shoe on when he again grabbed a fistful of her hair and shoved her out the door and through the main cabin of the aircraft.

She had never felt more alone and afraid.

She struggled to get a solid footing, only to be rewarded by having her bound wrists pulled up toward the guard, which forced her body to arch awkwardly. She sobbed as she stumbled forward. She had spent sleepless nights thinking about what had almost happened to her at the hands of ISIS. A new fear wrapped its cold shroud around her as the unknown but predictable conclusions of this march became more real than Iraq.

Dear God, please, I don't want to die!

Dry heat touched her skin as she neared the jet door. Jessica locked eyes with the flight attendant standing by the captain's cabin who wore a mindless grin on her face. Jessica hoped to find sympathy or a sign of solidarity in her sapphire-blue eyes, but she saw nothing but a Stepford smile—a *smile*, the girl holding the stupid tray out to her even as she could see her hands were bound behind her back.

Jessica got to the door and squinted, pausing to let her eyes adjust to the bright sun. The guard wrenched her arms up again and pulled her head back, adding pressure to her already straining shoulders. She winced as her foot searched for the first step.

"Move!" ordered the guard.

"I'm trying, asshole! But I can't see where—" She yelped as the guard wrenched her arms almost parallel to the ground.

He again pulled her hair back like reins on a horse. "Move or fall."

She thought he was about to push her out when she heard an angered yell in Russian from a man with long black hair. But it was the fat man next to the Russian who got her attention. Joseph Donovan, still as fat and disgusting as before. It all made sense now. He and the Russians had never stopped hunting her, and Paul had delivered her to them.

The guard grunted and released his grip on her head, but his hold on her wrists didn't relent. She struggled to walk down the stairs, each step making her shoulders burn with pain. The fact that she didn't fall or twist her ankles while wearing four-inch stilettos and contorted in an awkward position was a feat unappreciated by anyone else.

Seconds later, she heard more shoes clacking down the steps. Two sets, the light click-clack of high heels mixed with the heavy stomping of boots. Unexpectedly, she saw Kelly lurch forward, now standing at her side, looking disheveled. Her hair was a mess, her dress was wrinkled and slightly askew, and her makeup smudged. Jessica's heart skipped. *Oh God! No. He got her too!*

The two sisters glanced at each other, understanding their dire predicament in that single look. All the transgressions from before melted between them in the scorching heat of the midday sun, doubly intensified by the heat radiating off the tarmac.

"Where are we?" asked a shaken Kelly.

Jessica scanned the area, recognizing the patterns of flags flying and the writing on the sides of some of the aircraft in view. She gulped. "I—I think we're in Syria."

Their attention turned toward a line of black sedans parked near the plane. A Middle Eastern man in a military uniform opened the rear door of the third vehicle, and a man stepped out. He was taller, his blond hair as long and thick as that of the Russian at Jessica's side. He, too, was dressed European-style, with black skinny pants, a slim matching jacket, and a white shirt beneath with the top three buttons undone. In other circumstances, she might have considered him handsome, but all potential appeal was lost when he removed his sunglasses and fixated his icy blue eyes on her, like a viper on its prey.

Jessica's heart raced, and she trembled uncontrollably as the man with the Slavic cheeks and cold eyes approached them and stood mere inches from her. His eyes bored deep into her, but it was the twisted grin that haunted her. Her lip quivered and at last she broke down, sobbing as the reality of her situation set in. They would not be going back home, ever, and what remained of her life would be nothing less than agonized torment.

He said something she couldn't understand, but the tone succeeded in sending the frightening message, made worse with the men's laughter that followed.

The blond man held her chin between his thumb and index finger, pushing her head up to meet his eyes, taking in the sight of her tears and the dark mascara trails on her cheeks. He smiled with satisfaction.

"You are scared, aren't you?" he asked with an eager edge to his lightly accented voice.

When she didn't respond, he pulled her chin closer to him. "You should be scared, *bitch*." Spittle escaped his mouth. "I am going to torture and ravage you for weeks, my sweet."

Jessica tried to break away, but he formed a vise grip on her cheeks, forcing her to look into his eyes. "You'll wish for death, but I won't be so kind." He released his grip, then traced his finger up along her cheek, letting her tears coat the back of his finger. "This is the wish of Mr. Fedorovich," he said softly. "And when I tire of you, I'll give you to these animals." He tilted his head in the direction of his detail. "These savages prefer American women even more than I do." He ran his fingers down her face, then her neck, coming to her collarbones. "Tell me," he said, as his hand slid to her trembling body, "have you heard about the Shabiha?"

Jessica whimpered and nodded. She'd learned plenty about the Assad regime's thugs and how they were let loose like wild dogs on those who opposed the regime. Their brutality, especially to women and children, was well and horrifically documented.

"Good, because you and your lovely friend here will be spending a lot of time with them when I tire of you. You will make a lot of money for us, but not before I am through with you."

Kelly erupted in hysterical sobs beside her at these words. Jessica fought to control her own hysteria, grasping for any hope from the horrors that awaited them.

The man turned to Kelly, appraising her. He grabbed a fistful of hair and pulled her head back, earning a yelp and grimace from her. He examined her with glee, drinking in how her wild, unfettered look of horror was highlighted by her ruined makeup. He spoke to Jessica. "She's right to be afraid. The last Western girls we gave them for entertainment lasted a few weeks before they tried to kill themselves." A maniacal grin formed on his face, and he added, "They failed."

Jessica closed her eyes, horrific images flashing across her mind.

Without warning, he slapped Jessica hard. Her head whipped to the side from the force of the blow. "Fucking bitch! You think that by telling Yuri, you could destroy our arrangement with the Syrians? I'm going to enjoy making an example out of you."

Jessica's thoughts immediately went to her training, to the things Hector had tried to teach her, like remaining calm and observant—neither of which she was being right now. She cursed herself for it. She desperately needed to shake all those horrific visions of the Shabiha and focus on something else.

Think, Jessica, think. What do you know? The Russians had a small naval base on the Syrian coast because it was the only base they had with consistent warm waters. It meant they were near Tartus. The trafficked women pleasured the Russians as much as the Syrians. That was what the reporter shared with her. That was why her information was so crucial. Fedorovich had access to the area through his military connections, which was how the women were smuggled from Europe to Syria. Cold fear slithered around her and constricted, squeezing away all hope of salvation. If she had only left well enough alone, turned her head at the money laundering and trafficking like any other sensible employee would do. But no, she had to be the hero, and now look where she was.

"Antonin," said the dark-haired Russian brute holding Kelly's arms, "can we get moving? It's fucking hot here."

Antonin waved at the Shabiha detail and gave an order in poor Arabic to move the women to his car, never taking his eyes of Jessica. Swiftly, two men with thick black beards, bushy eyebrows, and olive-colored skin took Jessica and Kelly and marched her to the lead sedan.

Jessica fought her captors, screaming and yelling, praying for some semblance of a Hollywood plot twist where she was miraculously rescued, but that didn't happen. The men were strong, and her struggles didn't even slow their pace. This was her reality, and she sensed it would be far worse than anything she had ever imagined.

Antonin slid into the sedan next to Jessica. Konstantin— the man who had grabbed Jessica back in Philly—leaned on the doorframe, resting his arm on the roof of the car. "You have the informant and another whore to use as you wish, Antonin," he said. "My obligation to Sacha is complete. I'm washing my hands of this mess."

Antonin smiled and put his hand on Konstantin's shoulder. "Come on now, Konstantin. You know it doesn't work that way. You're done when Sacha says you're done." He then tapped his open hand on Konstantin's face, a little too hard. "And he hasn't said anything of the sort."

Jessica's car led the convoy to a nearby apron where a converted Mi-17 helicopter was ready for departure. A Syrian military officer in a flight suit received them, and in short order all climbed into the helicopter with its caramel-colored interior and leather seats. Kelly and Jessica shared a horrified look, but Jessica forced herself to look out the window instead of seeking comfort from her sister. She needed to know where they were, but, more importantly, where they were going.

The helicopter took flight northward, in the direction of the port city of Tartus, just this side of the Lebanon-Syria border, a stronghold of the Syrian regime. It took them past Tartus and continued over the water. As the flight wore on, a small island with a prominent medieval fortress on its western side came into view. The four-sided fortress with round turrets commanded the high ground, and on the south-west turret was a makeshift helipad raised on a scaffolding platform where the helicopter made its final approach and landed.

With the blades still turning, the crew chief opened the side door, allowing Antonin to exit first and walk down metal stairs that connected with the battlement. Jessica followed, coughing as she breathed in the exhaust from the rotor wash and feeling its heat against her face. She felt the jab of something hard against the middle of her back as one of the guards pushed her forward.

One by one, they reached the bottom of the stairs, and Antonin led them across the narrow walkway to the north-eastern battlement, where a guard opened a barred door without hesitation. The doorway was narrow and arched, with just enough daylight peeking in for Jessica to see the downward spiral of more stairs. She hesitated, fear taking hold of her, which earned her a prod from behind. She stepped gingerly forward, sinking lower into the darkness. Their footsteps echoed inside the narrow, dimly lit, and claustrophobic descent without rhythm. Jessica and Kelly's heel-clad feet wobbled on the short, narrow steps until they reached level ground.

There, Antonin gestured around himself and spoke excitedly. "In these dungeons beneath the fortress, crude torture techniques were applied to great effect." The twisted grin again reappeared, grislier in the amber light of the bare bulbs above. "I have vastly improved on them, as you two will soon find out."

Opposite the stairs was a simple metal door. A guard pulled it open with a metallic groan that resonated in the enclosed space. Kelly's whimper echoed under the arched entrance. Jessica's own body trembled uncontrollably as she stared into darkness beyond the door. The guard behind her grunted as he again prodded her, but she resisted his push, ardently shaking her head. She didn't want to move an inch closer. A second guard joined as they tried to force her onward, and to her credit, she stood firm for several seconds. But in the end, her heels didn't offer any traction, and the sheer strength of the guards won. Once on the other side, the door slammed shut with the finality of a tomb closing before being pushed deeper into the tunnel.

Jessica turned her head back, searching for Kelly. She desperately wished she could hold hands with her sister, like they had done when they were little and scared. They found each other's eyes, Kelly looking as frightened as Jessica felt.

Beyond the door was a narrow, dimly lit hall that led to a black mass. Jessica's heart pounded against her chest, and she felt her pulse in her ears with every step she was forced to take into the darkness, as if she was descending into hell. The scuffle of feet, boots, and the click of high heels echoed as they plunged into the darkness until a single red light revealed a modern steel door. The guard at the door slid a card into a magnetic strip reader and waited for the colors to change, releasing the magnetic lock.

A chorus of bloodcurdling screams escaped from inside when the door cracked open, growing louder as the opening widened. The indistinguishable shrieks of agony reverberated in her ears.

Jessica flashed back to her earliest nightmares of abuse when the fifth-grade boys dragged her to the dark closet, laughing as she had begged for any modicum of mercy. She shook her head and dropped like dead weight, clawing like a wild animal.

"I don't want to go in there! I don't want to go in there! Please, God! I don't want to go in there!"

The guards struggled to get a grip on her, eventually lifting her off the floor, but Jessica wouldn't submit easily. Self-preservation dictated she scream, rage, and fight.

Fed up with her antics, a guard raised the butt of his rifle to strike her, but Antonin raised his hand. He gripped Jessica's terrified face with a single hand and grinned lustfully. He watched her tears glisten in the low red light and said, "You'll scream louder than that, I promise you." He squeezed her cheeks hard. "The place I'm taking you is much worse."

Jessica dropped her head, sobbing, silently reciting the Hashkiveinu prayer her mother had taught her so long ago. The same she had recited in that closet. *Hashkiveinu Adonai eloheinu l'shalom—*

She was half carried down the hall, past arched cast-iron doors where shrills of unimaginable suffering permeated. They reached the end of the hall, coming to a wider metal door with two other guards in place, apathetic to the anguish taking place inside the arched cells.

Ufros aleinu sukat sh'lomecha . . .

A guard swiped a key card into an electronic device and opened the door. Jessica was shoved inside. The group followed behind her, and the door slammed shut behind them, muffling the shrills in the hall but doing little to comfort her. A second set of narrow stairs hugged the wall, leading down to a lower yet modernized section of the old fortress.

This section was shaped in a semicircle, with five steel doors spaced at intervals.

"Welcome to my play area," said Antonin with manic glee. "You'll be here for a very long time. I promise you that." The fluorescent lights cast deep shadows over Antonin's eyes, turning them into black coals. "I want you to meet someone."

He took a key card from his jacket pocket and slid it into the middle cell to unlock the door.

[49]

Kelly shivered beside Jessica, peering into the brightly lit room beyond the middle cell's thick door. The room, roughly the size of her living room and kitchen combined, was covered from floor to ceiling in white tile with fluorescent lights above. Kelly's eyes shifted to a pale-skinned figure that skittered across the floor, moving to a makeshift bed of plywood and soiled sheets. The young woman curled into a ball of quaking, white naked skin and grimy blonde hair. Her wide, piercing hazel eyes peeked above her crossed forearms.

"No! Not again! Not again!" the girl screeched hysterically.

Kelly gasped in dismay. *She's just a girl! An American!*

The girl appeared to be in her late teens or early twenties. It was impossible to tell in her state. She struggled half-heartedly against the guards, like a broken animal beaten into submission. The guards dragged her out by both arms to Antonin. Kelly's heart hammered at the sight of the girl's body. Her torso was awash in lurid bruises. Raw purple and red marks crisscrossed her back, distorted scars marked her bruised nipples, and there were untreated sores on her lips and uniform raw marks on her wrists and ankles.

The girl winced as Antonin grabbed a fistful of grimy hair and pulled her head back. He looked at Jessica and Kelly and said, "This is Whitney." Then he turned his attention to the girl. "I have enjoyed her so much. Haven't I, Whitney?" He released her hair and stared wantonly at the two sisters. "But you are here now, and I can't wait to hear your screams."

Kelly shut her eyes, bawling harder, with the image of Whitney's tortured body seared in her mind. Her nerves were frayed to the point that every sensory detail terrified her. Where the hell were they? Why were they even here? Everything seemed so surreal. She wasn't supposed to be here—this was like the plot of some horror film. Nothing made sense to her, and when logic fled, all that reigned over Kelly was her unbridled panic.

Kelly tried to look away, her vision blurry with tears, but a guard grabbed a fistful of her hair and forced her to look. The man grinned down at her, revealing rotted, yellow-stained teeth.

Antonin stroked Whitney's face and wiped her tears almost lovingly. "Don't worry, my pet—I'm not through with you just yet. I'm letting those Syrian animals have you next." A malevolent grin stretched from ear to ear. "A beautiful young girl like you . . . I don't think you'll survive long with those savages."

Whitney's eyes bulged, and her mouth opened in a silent scream. Despite everything she'd been through, she had not seen the worst of it.

Antonin's grip on her hair slackened, and the guards took that as their cue to release her. Whitney slumped to the floor, the girl doing nothing to cushion her impact against the cold tile.

Fear, helplessness, and hatred flashed in Kelly. Antonin noticed this, licking his lips in hunger and delight as he studied her from head to toe. "Ah, a fighter emerges. I'm going to enjoy taking my time breaking you. And when I'm done, you, too, will beg me for death."

He paused for a moment, his thoughtful gaze turning to Jessica. He clapped his hands, the sound ringing sharply in the small place. "But why delay the fun? Let's begin now." He waved at the guards holding the women and led all three to the far-left door of the semicircle.

Kelly shrieked when the door opened.

If she thought she was in a horror film before, the scene that unfolded inside was the source of those nightmarish visions. Meat hooks dangled from chains over a stained water drain on the floor, while a blood-stained metal gurney with restraints and a nauseating array of surgical instruments were set under a bare light bulb near the center of the room.

Suddenly, a guard tore at Jessica's dress, snapping the thin spaghetti straps from her shoulders and splitting the garment in two as he busted the zipper with his bare hands. Jessica screamed, the ruined dress pooled in a heap around her feet, leaving her exposed save for her undergarments.

"No! God, no!" she pleaded.

The guard ripped the remaining clothing from her body, seemingly taking her will to fight along with it.

Kelly and Whitney were forced to watch the guards uncuff Jessica and pull her by each arm to a metal gurney with gynecological stirrups on one end and a pair of worn leather restraints on the other. Jessica fought hard, clawing, scratching, and kicking, but all was useless. They forced her down on the table, and she struggled pathetically as they tightened the restraints around her wrists. Her legs were forced on the stirrups, and they strapped down her shins.

Kelly turned away, and for a second, her eyes met Whitney's. The girl's expression left no doubt as to what would come next.

Kelly's heart sank deeper than ever at Jessica's cries. "Wait, wait, wait! No! Oh God, oh dear God, no!" She wailed louder, shaking her head as their worst nightmares were materializing all at once. "Please, no! Please, not that! Dear God Almighty, please, not that!"

Antonin paced slowly around the gurney as an overhead light illuminated every aspect of her naked, writhing body. He looked her over with lust, his fingers dragging across her trembling skin. Coming full circle, he placed his hand on her bare breast, groping it cruelly. He delighted in the sounds of her whimpers and the feel of her body quivering with fear and revulsion before moving to the other side.

"Yes, beautiful. I'm going to take my time with you tonight. I may even play nice and share you with my friends." He finished with a malicious laugh.

Kelly was helpless as the brutality began . . . and went on, over and over. She looked away from it all to Whitney, wondering how many times the savages had used this mere girl until fatigued. She would learn the answer soon enough.

Antonin had finished for the moment, but his men were ready and eager to take his place. Kelly was nauseous and dizzy. Her stomach twisted, causing her to dry heave until she was left exhausted and broken. She desperately wanted to bring her hands to her ears, but there was no relief to be found. Antonin left them to the Shabiha. Behind her, the door clanged shut while Jessica's screams continued to echo inside the room.

50

Talula's Garden, Philadelphia, Pennsylvania
29 July 2014

Hector sipped his bourbon and gazed at the ornate hand-blown glass lights that hung from exposed wood beams. They gave the bar the same unique semi-rustic garden home feel as the rest of the boutique restaurant. *Kelly would like it here.* He wondered if she'd made it here after the party. His feet bounced nervously on the stool's footrest like pistons, his fingers tapping the glass like piano keys as his imagination once again offered him the worst possible outcomes.

Why the fuck did he let her come here alone? He should have been here, with her. He should have . . . The list of could-haves, would-haves, and should-haves went on.

Hector's head had grown cloudy with fear and concern after Alex informed him Kelly had left her clutch and award and asked if she was with him. So Kelly hadn't returned Sunday evening, and these had only become worse as news of Jessica's disappearance in the same evening reached him. He had needed to think straight, to make good judgments if he was to get answers and find her. Instantly, he'd thought of

Chuck. He was a good sounding board and someone who could help him keep his cool.

He and Chuck had come to Philly looking for answers. They had spent most of yesterday with the Philly police trying to find out what leads they had and if there had been any reported sightings at any of the points of entry and exit—like the airport, train stations, ferries, and even bridges—but they'd gotten nothing for their troubles. Now that the girls had been missing for four days, they were told their hopes of finding the women were quickly vanishing.

Today, they had decided to take matters into their own hands. They had spent the earlier part of the day at the hotel repeating questions and had only left after the manager grew tired of explaining in every imaginable way that he had no idea what had happened to Kelly or Jessica. They had simply vanished, and he was not responsible for occurrences outside the hotel.

The last person to see them was Paul, and he had already given multiple statements to the police saying that the women had a falling-out and were no longer on speaking terms. Then, just before he and Jessica were to go to Talula's Garden, Jessica had broken things off with him. That was the last time he'd seen her. Now Hector and Chuck were here, at Talula's Garden, in search of answers.

The manager approached them at the bar. She wore an elegant black peasant top with skin-tight white pants and lots of jewelry. It fit the place's aesthetic. "I'm sorry, gentlemen, I'm afraid no one recalls seeing either young lady." She nodded at the hostess and waited for her to leave before continuing. "I was the manager on duty that night, and I would definitely remember seeing either of them." She smiled, studying Jessica's picture Hector had given her, and raised an eyebrow with a smile. "Oh yes, I would definitely remember."

Chuck and Hector exchanged a look. Chuck cleared his throat. "Thank you for your time, Miss . . . ?"

"Simone," said the manager, extending a slender hand with multiple bangles on the wrist. "And should you find her, tell her to call or come by and ask for me," she added with a wink.

Hector forced a smile, hiding the gravity of the situation. "We'll be sure to do that, Simone. Thanks for your time."

Hector sighed and gulped the bourbon, eyeing the manager as she left. "Another damn dry hole," he said, exasperated.

Chuck sat beside him, taking his own drink in hand. "Tell me again what Jessica told you about what happened in California."

Hector let out a deep exhale and repeated the story. He then said, "I know it's pretty far-fetched, but I have a strong suspicion that they have something to do with this."

"What makes you say that?" asked Chuck as he sipped his drink.

"My spidey senses. I can't back it up, but I have a feeling that the attack on the compound had something to do with Jessica and the Russians, too." The memory of the pale European outside the base came back to his mind.

"That's more than far-fetched—you know that."

"I do, but the tip we got about the attack also mentioned that Chechens were specifically looking for Jessica. And now both Kelly and Jessica disappear? That can't be a coincidence."

"And that little shit Paul Monroe?"

Hector scratched his five-day scruff and grimaced. "That piece of shit knows something, I just fucking know it. But he's lawyered up and is untouchable." Hector leaned over and murmured, "I tasked the Parabellum Ops chief to run his social media profile and other open sources to discover Paul's pattern of life."

He hesitated, knowing that he'd broken every possible civil rights law. He wasn't sure how far Chuck would want to be dragged down this rabbit hole.

Chuck's eyes flared at the comment, then he rubbed his face. He shook his head, exasperated. "Ah, Hector. Fine. All right, what did you find out from Paul's POL?"

Hector unlocked his phone and opened the document he'd received earlier that morning. "We identified a time and place where he'd be vulnerable to interdiction. His POL shows he'll be playing racquetball at some fancy sports club on K Street tonight."

Chuck scowled. "Racquetball? What kind of pansy-ass pattern of life is that?"

Hector shrugged. "I don't know, maybe it involves some fucking Ivy League circle jerk while singing their alma matter."

Chuck laughed.

Hector pointed to the screen. "Dickhead posts every fucking thing he does, where he does it, and with whom. Hell, I'm surprised he hasn't posted when he takes a shit."

Chuck rolled his eyes. "Fucking millennials."

That evening, Chuck and Hector entered the Ivy League Association Sports Club on K Street. True to form, Paul stuck to his POL like clockwork. Chuck had used his connection with Senator Stevens to gain access to the club, and on the way to the racquetball courts, they made their way past the grand exercise room, the sauna, and the basketball court. They found Paul inside a Plexiglas-enclosed court, racing back and forth with another player, each swinging their racquets and sending the ball bouncing to and from the far wall.

Hector sighed. "Well, no circle jerk." They both chortled.

Outside the court were two other young men watching the game. All four were dressed in white shorts and shirts with matching blue logos. The only thing missing were pullover V-necks tied around their shoulders to complete the Ivy League poster child picture. These two saw them coming and approached them. The first swung his racquet up to his shoulder, as if that were some menacing overture, and asked, "Are you gentlemen part of this club?"

Chuck sized him up. "Take a hike, Billie Jean King."

The two were obviously confused at the tennis reference, staring at Chuck as if he were some crazy old man.

Chuck leaned closer and bared his teeth. "I said take a fucking hike, sweetheart!"

The two glanced at each other, tapped the enclosure as a warning, and ran without another word.

Hector tapped Chuck on the shoulder and gave him a nod. Both had been through a lot together, and they'd reached a point where they anticipated each other's actions. And just now, Chuck had cleared an opening for Hector to move in and conduct the interrogation. More than a mentor, Chuck was deferring to him as a friend.

Hector stepped into the court. Paul and the other guy stopped their game, gawking at him like he'd just walked into first class from coach. Before either said anything, Hector pointed at the other guy. "Beat it, precious. Your boyfriend and I need to have a chat."

Flabbergasted, the other guy said, "Dude, that is totally not sensitive, bro! And we're not gay."

Hector snatched the racquet from him, raised it like a club, and took a step in his direction. The guy gasped and made a run for the door, nearly taking a spill as he tried to jump out of Chuck's way.

Paul was about to say something, but not before Hector grabbed him by the throat and slammed him against the wall.

"What the fuck, man?" gasped Paul.

"Shut the fuck up and listen, you little bitch." Hector leaned in closer and increased the pressure on his neck. He was looking through the beast's eyes as it growled, "I want to know what happened to Jessica and my wife, and if you don't tell me in the next three seconds, I'm going to smash this racquet into your kneecaps until something shatters, do you understand me?"

Paul's eyes bulged. He looked over at Chuck, who simply shrugged.

"Don't look at me, sweetheart," said Chuck. "I ain't holding his leash."

"Hey!" Hector dug his thumb up into the tender spot between the jaw and throat. "Look at me! He can't help you. No one can. I'm going to count to three and then I'm going to start smashing." He brought the tip of the racquet just above Paul's left kneecap, hard enough to make the leg reflex. "And I'm going to start with this one."

The beast inside roared, smelling blood and thirsting for it.

Hector raised the racquet, but Paul screeched, "Wait! Jesus Christ! Just fucking wait!"

His descent into tears was predictable. It didn't take Hector long to coax him to talk, and he spilled everything from the phone calls in the middle of the night to the trip to Philly, the Russians, the kidnapping, and their eventual destination.

"What the fuck do you mean 'Syria'?"

Paul's face went from red to purple as Hector squeezed his throat harder, earning a tap from Chuck on his shoulder to loosen his grip.

Paul coughed and gasped, then answered, "That's what the guy with the scar said, man! I didn't ask more! I swear!"

"Syria is a big fucking country, dickhead! Give me something to work with, or I will make you hurt in ways that you didn't know existed." The beast focused on its prey, ready to pounce.

"Look, all I know is that they talked about Syria. Something about an island . . . started with an A, or something? But that's all I know, man! I swear! That's all I know!" Paul sniveled, raising his hands in surrender.

As much as Hector wanted to shatter Paul's femur into pieces, time was against them. His mind drifted to whatever horrors his wife was enduring—and, yes, Jessica too. It was almost five days since their disappearance, and the likeliness of their survival, much less a rescue, seemed nonexistent. He let go of Paul's throat and watched him reach for it with both hands as he gasped for air. He grabbed the handle of the racquet like a baton and jabbed it into Paul's stomach with all the force he could muster.

Paul doubled over and spewed liquids from his stomach before dropping into a fetal position, whining in pain.

Hector turned to Chuck. "I need to go get them. I need to find them and get them. For Kelly, and for Flash. I need Bravo Team." To find them and dare a rescue would mean pulling Parabellum's significant resources for a rogue mission with odds stacked overwhelmingly against them. *Please*, he begged in his mind. *Please, God, please.*

Chuck met his pleading gaze with a steady nod. "Kelly is family, and Jessica is one of us now. I'll get you what you need." He then smiled and said with a wink, "Good thing I got some pull with the boss."

51

Arwad Castle, Syria
5 August 2014

The door buzzed. Whitney crouched behind Jessica, who lay motionless on the makeshift cot. She burrowed low, as low as she could, trying to be invisible to the men who were about to enter through that door. The men were coming more and more, ever since Kelly and Jessica had been brought here. In a way, she was glad that they were the new playthings. As terrible as the thought was, at least Antonin wasn't as interested in her. But she couldn't tell time anymore. She never knew if it was day or night, but she could tell when they would be coming for her next. It was all different now. She peeked out from her burrow just enough to see the door open.

Two guards walked in, holding Kelly between them. She was shuddering and crying. They tossed her on the floor like soiled laundry. Her body hit the tile, hard, and they closed the door without so much as a second look. She laid on the floor, crying, unable or unwilling to move.

Whitney observed the redness of contact marks from the electric prods and the fresh purple-red streaks on her back, sides, and legs. That was how they always started with the ones they would sell to the general. At one time, they'd said they were going to sell her to him, but Antonin had changed his mind.

Kelly groaned, her arms and legs quivering as she struggled to lift herself up on all fours. Whitney stayed in her burrow, watching silently. The new woman's hair hung down, clumped together in strands, weighed down by sweat and grime. She remained there, panting and sobbing, as if trying to decide whether to move or slump back down and wait to die. She then used one hand to wipe the tears away, got her legs beneath her, and stood as best as she could. The crimson-red burn marks, intermingled with purplish streaks, were there as well: across her stomach and breasts and between her thighs. She took a single step and nearly collapsed, cupping her hands between her legs and crying out in pain.

Whitney rose to a low crouch. She looked at Kelly, then the door. She wanted to go help Kelly, but a cold terror kept her frozen in place. She knew, just knew, that as soon as she moved to Kelly the door would buzz open and Antonin would walk in and take her to be punished.

She whimpered and sobbed as she watched Kelly. She wanted to help. She wanted to let something good happen in this horrible place, but she just couldn't do it. Kelly had tried being a protector, a mother figure in this godforsaken place. When Antonin had reached for her, Kelly had stood between her and Antonin. She had even gone so far as to scream at Antonin not to touch her, and it had earned her a heavy-handed reprisal.

Whitney wiped the tears from her eyes and slowly, so slowly, moved a hand forward. Then the other. She was determined to return the kindness. She crawled with catlike movements until she reached Kelly, always keeping her eyes on the door.

When she reached Kelly, she gingerly put her hands where there were no marks or streaks and slowly helped her up. Kelly, she noticed, still had her figure. That would change soon. Her ribs were only now beginning to show. She helped Kelly over to the cot, laying her behind Jessica, then she nestled down behind her. Her dignity about her nakedness was something Antonin took from her long ago.

Kelly brushed the hair from her face and asked, between sobs, "How did you end up in this place?"

Whitney rested her head on her hands and thought for a moment. When had she gotten here? It felt like any life before this dungeon was a childhood dream.

"I talked my parents into letting me backpack through Europe with my best friend after graduation," she whispered. "It was Melissa's idea. My parents didn't want me to go, but Melissa showed them the list of all the places where we would be staying. They thought it over and changed their minds." She choked on a regret-filled sob. "It was all bullshit! It had been some crap she found on the internet and used to talk both our parents into it."

She sniffled and went on. "We met some boys in Austria who invited us to stay with them in their apartment. We blew so much of our money and were so hungry and tired that we thought anything would be better than sleeping in another hostel, or worse, on the street again. But I was wrong. They . . ." She cried as the memory blossomed. "They raped us and drugged us. When we woke up, we were here."

Kelly reached behind her head and gently scratched Whitney's hair. "Where's Melissa now?"

Whitney bawled at the question. "I don't know." Her crying filled the room, echoing off the tile walls.

"Do—do you know when they took you?" asked Kelly in a low voice.

"I . . . can't remember," said Whitney. "I just remember they were about to celebrate D-Day, or something like that."

She sniffled and asked in earnest, "Do you know how long I've been here?"

Kelly winced as she slowly rolled to face Whitney. She brushed the hair off Whitney's face and held her hand against her cheek. "Oh, sweetheart. I'm so sorry about everything. You must've been here almost two months."

Whitney wailed. The hurt went deep into her soul, and she felt nothing but despair. "I'm going to die here!"

"No, honey, don't say that. Please. You have to hold on to hope. Just hold on."

"She's right," said a groggy Jessica. "If you lose hope, you lose everything." She groaned as she crawled over the pile to the other side of Whitney, aiming to offer some measure of reprieve, even if it was imagined.

Whitney felt a warmth that she'd forgotten about entirely. One that lit a tiny spark of hope. The three cried together until blissful sleep came to them.

Whitney startled awake when the door buzzed. She froze in place, like a cornered rabbit, and trembled as the footsteps grew closer until her eyes shifted to see Antonin standing in front of them with that twisted grin that filled her with terror.

"My, isn't this absolutely delightful. My three pretties lying together, getting to know each other much better." He took two steps forward, making the other two flinch and startle. "It makes me very hard to see that."

He pointed at Jessica, and three of his Shabiha guards pounced on her. She screamed and fought like a caged lioness until they had her up on her feet. "No! No! Please! Not again!" she pleaded all the way to the door. Whitney could still hear her screams after the metal door closed.

Antonin looked back and pointed at Whitney. "Don't think I've forgotten about you, my sweet. I have something very special for you." He took slow, methodical steps toward her. "My friends have won a major victory against the rebels, and I have promised them a very special treat." He reached for her and knelt down to her level, holding her gaze. "You'll wish to be with me before they're done with you, my beautiful." He looked her over, the twisted smile returning. "Maybe I should enjoy you one last time, huh? What do you think, my sweet?"

Whitney shook her head, crying like a little girl fearing her father's belt. Satisfied with tormenting her, he stood and turned, laughing as he left the room and the door shut once more.

Kelly pulled Whitney to her, embracing her as she cried heartily.

"I don't want to be here anymore! I don't want to be here anymore! I want to go home!" Whitney's cries were muffled by Kelly's embrace. "I just want to go home! Please! Let me go home!"

Kelly swayed back and forth as she stroked Whitney's thick blonde hair, her fingers occasionally getting entangled.

Whitney struggled and pushed away from her. She looked about the room as if for the first time. "I need to get out of here! I need to find a way out! I—I can't be here anymore!"

Kelly pulled her in closer, caressing her hair faster and longer. "Shh, calm down, honey. Please calm down! Please!"

Whitney gave in at last, sinking into Kelly's arms. She cried until she had nothing left.

52

Kelly was startled awake by Whitney's warmth jerking away, then she heard the buzzing of the door. She huddled closer to Whitney when the door opened, and both gasped in horror as Jessica was dragged in. What she saw sent cold waves of terror through her. Someone had reapplied makeup on her, only to have Jessica's tears run black streaks down her face. Solid purple-and-red horizontal streaks marked her midsection, but the true horror of it was the blood smeared between her legs.

The guards dropped her on the floor, and Jessica let out a scream that sent chills through their collective bodies.

As soon as the door closed, Kelly raced to Jessica, gingerly helping her onto the cot, but nothing kept her from wailing in agony. She screamed like a possessed woman, filling the room with her shrieks and terrifying the souls out of her only two friends. Even Whitney, who seemed to have experienced it all, was horrified by her condition.

"Oh, dear God, what did they do to her?" asked Kelly.

Whitney sniffled. "They sent her to the general."

"The general?"

Whitney nodded. "He's some old, gross fat guy. A general

in the army, or something. He likes to dress girls up. To make you think nothing bad is going to happen, but . . ." Her voice trailed off. "He's really bad."

She wiped her tears and added, "He's the one who picks the girls who are to be given to his men."

Kelly swallowed. "Were you . . ."

Whitney shook her head. "No, Antonin was going to give me to him, but he changed his mind." She broke down again. "He gave Melissa to him, instead."

Kelly lay next to Jessica, wanting to hold her and try to calm her, but Jessica thrashed at the slightest touch, screaming something akin to "don't touch me" and other pleas in languages Kelly didn't recognize. Kelly feared that whatever had happened had caused her to lose her sanity. *Oh, God, will this be my own fate as well?*

There was no salvation from this hell. There was none for Melissa or Whitney, nor the other poor girls before them—and none for her. Her thoughts turned to Hector. He fought men like this. Buf if she didn't even know where she was, what hope was there that he would? If there was a God in heaven, she prayed He would make Hector her savior. But right now, it was impossible to believe there was such a benevolent being. In that moment, Kelly regretted every instance she had ever felt of selfishness toward her husband. If his missions had led him to places like this to rescue people from horrors all too real . . . How could she have asked him not to go? She wondered if he even knew she was missing, if he would ever find out what became of her.

After all, they *were* going to die here. She would never have the chance to tell Hector all the things she now regretted, or how much she still loved him. Oh, God, how much she missed him. Her last words to him hurt deeply, adding to the physical pain and misery she was forced to endure.

53

Royal Air Force Akrotiri, Cyprus
5 August 2014

The G6 arrived at RAF Akrotiri in the early evening and taxied to the terminal of the British air base in southwestern Cyprus. The arrival was highly unusual, but Parabellum's partnership with Anglia Security Enterprises allowed special access for the aircraft on loan from Bill Carson. By landing there instead of Larnaca International Airport, they saved precious time.

The Parabellum team entered the terminal and were met by Chester "Cheshire" Titchmarch, the British representative from Anglia Security, who stood with his chin up, hands clasped behind him, sporting an unmistakable British officer's mustache. Were he in uniform, Cheshire would have painted the perfect image of the proper British officer. His stiff demeanor softened as Chuck approached, and the two clasped hands, their knuckles turning white as each hand became a vise.

"Welcome, gentlemen," Cheshire said. "Chuck, it's a pleasure to see you again, old chap, though I do wish it were under better circumstances."

"Same here, Cheshire. Maybe we'll have a few pints after this is all over. If I may, I'd like to introduce you to the rest of the team." He turned and gestured. "These men are Gung Ho, Penguin, Guapo, and Pirate Face."

"Pirate Face! Good heavens, mate, who did you piss off?" The laugh broke some of the pre-mission tension.

Cheshire shook hands with each, then led them to a private briefing room while the G6 was unloaded outside.

"Thanks again for helping make this happen," Chuck said, bringing the group back to business. "Hector's wife and one of our team members are the women held in some prison inside Arwad Castle."

Cheshire nodded. "You know, I've been stationed here four years and I'd never heard of a secret prison inside the old fortress. You might as well have told me you needed to raid Narnia."

Chuck gave a small, tight smile. "I apologize for being light on the details, but I appreciate your assistance with a speedy execution. The island fortress is operated by members of the Russian mafia, and we have reason to believe they keep a company of Shabiha in their employ."

Cheshire was surprised. "The Russian mafia, you say?"

"Correct. It's where we presume they hold Western women they kidnap from Europe. God knows what happens in there, but they are ultimately sold to regime officers and other elements."

Chester's demeanor grew solemn. "Yes, of course." He turned to Hector. "You have my full support, Hector. I'm truly sorry about your wife." He turned to the full team and said, "Whilst we didn't detect a Russian presence, we were able pull reports from multiple sources regarding the fortress itself. The lower levels were modified for . . . other purposes. Originally, we thought it was another site like those seen in the 'Caesar photos,' but we could never confirm."

"You mean they torture people there?" asked a frantic Penguin.

"I'm afraid so, chap. And if your ladies are held there, I'm afraid to think what may have already happened."

Penguin ran his hand through his hair and paced back and forth.

Hector put his hand on his shoulder. "Hey, we don't know anything, Eric. Keep your cool, brother."

Penguin nodded.

"We have some limited information on the layout of the fortress, mostly from old tourist blogs long before the civil war, but I'm afraid that any reports about the deep interior are dodgy at best." He looked the team over and said, "We took the liberty of developing an infil and exfil plan, including allocating air assets, which we'll adjust accordingly. Now, if you'll follow me, I'll take you to our operations centre."

Soon, the team was inside the Anglia Security Operations Centre, where the hastily planned and highly dangerous rescue operation had been hatched up in the time since Parabellum had made contact, thirty-six hours earlier. The building was older than Hector had expected. They walked along narrow, whitewashed hallways with polished linoleum tiles on the floor and exposed pipes and tubes of varying diameters above them that occasionally bent and disappeared into walls on either side. The hallway widened as they reached a set of metal, battleship-gray double doors that opened with a simple push-button-combination cipher lock.

Beyond the door was an area half the size of Parabellum's TOC and twice as old. They followed Cheshire through a door at the far end, into a room that seemed entirely out of place with the rest of the dated vault. Inside were mounted flat-screen televisions, computer stations with double monitors staggered along the side walls, four different types of military radios along the far wall, and a backlit rectangular surface in the center of the room where maps of various scales and aerial photographs of the island were set, including a hand-drawn schematic of Arwad Castle made by a tourist in the early 2000s. The schematic wasn't a masterpiece, but it did lay out parts of the interior not available on old tourist maps.

Hector and the team gathered around a large-scale print of the schematic along with the rest of the maps and photos, slowly piecing together the jigsaw puzzle that was to be the rescue plan.

The clock showed the local time was nearing three in the morning when the Frankenstein plan was at last patched together. Hector yawned and stretched, then stood to go put the half-empty Styrofoam coffee cup in the room's only waste bin. It was overflowing with cups, beer bottles, and carryout baskets of curry and kebabs, whose scent filled the room. He was mentally and physically exhausted. He reclined on the swivel chair, his feet up and hands clasped on the crown of his head. His eyes were closed, but he wasn't sleeping. His brow twitched and scrunched, and his lips pursed off and on. He was trying to focus on the mission and not imagine what Kelly or Jessica were enduring while they planned.

They were all quiet and pensive, each trying to identify the anything they hadn't thought about. One mistake could cause the mission to fail—or worse, get them killed. Chuck and Cheshire were by one of the computer stations, likely going over the very last details.

Chuck stood, stretched, and filled two cups with black coffee. He walked over to Hector and set the cup on the table. "How're you doing, Hector?"

Hector put his feet down, stretched long and slow, and

groaned as he reached for the cup. "I can't stop thinking about them. I want to get my mind in the mission, but . . ." He took a long sip of the coffee and grimaced. "Jesus, Chuck! Did you put the whole damn can in this pot?"

Chuck chortled. "I'm sorry, princess. Would you like me to add some caramel and fancy shit in it to make it taste better?"

Hector smirked. "No, it's just fine." He took another sip, and the smile left his face. "I'm scared, Chuck. I don't know if I can face what's happened to them. Or what's become of them. We've seen our own fair share of sick shit, but this . . ." He rubbed his face. "This is Kelly and Jessica."

Chuck tapped his knee. "And that's why we can't fail. Whatever may have become of them, they still deserve the opportunity to come back from it."

"I know, I know. I just wish I hadn't been such an asshole to—"

"Hey," interrupted Chuck. "You can't think like that. You know better."

"You're right." Hector sighed. "I can't think of anything else. We might have missed something, but if we did, I can't think of it. My brain is fried."

Chuck nodded in agreement. "Me either. I think we've done about as much as we can do, all things considered. I'm sure we all would have preferred a dry run and a walk-through, but this is going to have to do."

Together they surveyed the rest of the room. Hector's gaze lingered on each of the team members who sat hunched in concentration and fatigue, consumed with thoughts on how to get their Flash back.

"We all do this willingly and without reservation," Chuck said. "We never leave someone behind, no matter where, no matter the cost. No sacrifice too big, no task too small." Everyone nodded in agreement. Chuck paused, making eye contact with every member. "Tomorrow we bring Kelly and Jessica home. We've done all we can for now, and the plan is as good as it's going to get. So, let's get some sleep and kick ass tomorrow."

A jolt of electricity coursed in the room as spirits were renewed and optimism filled the air. By the next period of darkness, the mission would be underway.

When dusk settled across the clear sky the following evening, Chuck, Hector, Penguin, PF, and Guapo boarded an AS332 Super Puma helicopter, compliments of Anglia Security. Weapons, ammunition, and communications were all loaded and ready. A rubber-hulled inflatable boat was attached to the bottom of the helicopter by a steel cable.

As the helicopter readied to depart, Cheshire spoke into the headset that connected him to the rest of the team. "Now, remember, you have only a six-hour window to infiltrate, conduct the rescue, and get out of there. The exfil helicopter will leave five hours after you depart unless you rescue them before then and hit jackpot. Now, whilst it has a sufficient fuel capacity, if you haven't hit jackpot by then, it will have to loiter outside the range of the Syrian early warning radar until you declare 'jackpot' and will have a short amount of time before it reaches bingo. Do you understand?" The four men gave the thumbs-up signal. "Godspeed, gentlemen. Tallyho!" With that said, he removed his headset and slid the side door closed.

"All right, gents," said Chuck, "here we go." Chuck gave his thumbs-up to the pilot, and the helicopter was soon off the tarmac and on its way.

54

Hector rested his head against the hull of the helicopter, coughing every now and then from the occasional exhaust fumes that penetrated the side gunner's open window. He relished the lulling massage of the vibrations that traveled up from his boots to his ballistic helmet. Other than the bouncing of his knees and his fingers rapping on the stock of his suppressed short-barreled HK-416, he portrayed a calm demeanor.

Inside, however, was the complete opposite. The pre-mission jitters that sat at the bottom of his stomach were worse than ever. He and his team—no, his *friends*—were headed into their most dangerous mission yet, to rescue the two people who meant the most to him personally, and it had all been patched together like an episode of *The A-Team*. This was no way to prepare for a mission, but time, intelligence, dry runs, and ground truth were luxuries he could not afford. It was bad enough they were going in practically blind to rescue his wife and Jessica from . . . God, he didn't even want to begin to think about it.

On top of all that, he was putting his friends' lives at stake. Yes, they came willingly, but the fact that he *needed* their help made the knot in his stomach tighten. He had pleaded with Chuck to stay back and oversee the mission from the TOC, to which Chuck had taken personal offense. When Hector protested that Betty and the girls needed him back home, Chuck had responded with, "Betty would be very disappointed with me if I didn't go. Kelly is like family to her as well."

Hector's spidey senses made him open his eyes as the crew chief, wearing night vision devices, raised his hand showing five fingers, indicating they would reach the splash-down zone in as much time. The fluorescent lime-green rings from the NVGs formed circles over the crew chief's eyes.

Hector's stomach tightened even more, if that were possible, as he mentally went through each step they would take from now until they reached the island, and beyond. Each man did a quick equipment check before checking one another. Hector looked at his watch, noting the time was nearing 2 a.m. The red light inside the cabin turned green.

The helicopter slowed and descended, hovering just over the water. The crew chief gave a hand signal, and the cable carrying the boat disengaged and the rubber-hulled boat splashed on the water. He counted down to zero with his fingers. At zero, Hector and the team jumped out from both side doors into the water and swam to the rubber-hulled Zodiac. The helicopter maneuvered sideways away from them and soon disappeared into the darkness, save for the thumping doppler effect of the rotor blades.

Hector climbed into the boat and opened one of the Pelican cases fastened to the side of the boat. This one held climbing rope and equipment, medical gear, two combat shotguns, flash-bangs, grenades, and explosives. Around him, the soft *clicks* of the others doing the same was the only unnatural sound in the dark waters. Guapo passed the medical gear to Pirate Face and stowed the roll of explosive breaching tape and blasting caps in his own backpack. Penguin moved to the rear of the boat, started the outboard motor, and piloted their careful approach to the island.

Reaching the island took longer than Hector desired, but absolute stealth demanded it. The boat edged toward the western side of the island, their approach masked by the jagged sea wall, with the added benefit that no one would imagine someone trying to get onto the island from there. Penguin switched to the silent electric outboard motor once they were less than a kilometer away from the island. The underpowered motor made reaching the island a slow progress, but it was silent.

As the boat inched closer to the sea wall, PF reached out and looped a line over a rock outcropping and moored the boat. If the plan went well, they'd never have to come back to the boat, but if everything went to hell, the boat might be their only lifeline to safety. Guapo disembarked and set up security as each member followed and did the same until all were off the boat. Hector glanced at his watch. *Fuck!* They were twenty minutes behind schedule. The waves had been much choppier than anticipated. *Fucking great!*

The team sneaked along the western walkway of the island, keeping close to the walls of unevenly built houses and structures that masked their approach from anyone standing guard over the citadel walls. Hector knelt and peeked around the end of a house and down a narrow alley that zigzagged to the citadel. He wiped the sweat dripping down his face and searched for movement or illumination from cigarette smoke. There was none.

He sighed in relief. *Okay, one thing at a time.*

He waved his hand in the direction of the alley, and the team rounded the corner, moving their weapons in gentle arches, keeping aim wherever their eyes moved. Once they were ahead, Hector caught up to them, walking backward for a short distance and bringing up the rear.

The choreographed movement repeated itself until they reached the outer wall of the citadel itself. It wasn't a massive structure like other historic fortresses on the mainland, but it was still going to be a challenge to climb without being seen by either guards or civilians. Even at this hour, some locals were still awake, smoking hookahs, watching television, or talking about whatever people on the island talked about.

The plan was to break in through the former visitor's entrance, the only entrance they were aware of. Old photos from travelogues showed a small guard shack at the gate. If it was manned during the night, chances were that it would be a single guard, most likely asleep at this hour. *Let's hope.* Even if there was a lone guard, it wouldn't take much for him to set off an alarm.

As small as the island of Arwad was, the houses were densely built next to each other, making progress toward the citadel that much slower. The narrow alleys were long, with doors and windows facing into the alley. A person exiting into the alley to smoke could quickly end the mission. Were that to happen, the judgment call to take lethal force or not was up to whomever was at point. Each time it was Hector's turn at point, he felt his heart thumping against his chest, desperately hoping whoever was inside couldn't hear the rapid staccato of his heartbeat. *Please don't come out. Please, please, please.*

At last, the team reached the citadel, but they were now forty minutes behind schedule. *Goddammit!*

Hector had wanted to cover ground faster, but in missions like these, speed most definitely killed. He peeked around the corner of the last house to get a view of the shack. A guard was slumped on a chair inside, his head back, snoring. Hector let out a slow, stuttered exhale.

He raised his hand over his head and waved it forward slowly, giving Chuck his cue to move. He kept the laser sight, visible only with night vision goggles, pointed at the guard's head while Chuck crossed the wide, cobblestone street to the guard shack. If the guard so much as did anything other than snore, he'd split his skull with the squeeze of the trigger. *Come on, come on, come on.* Sweat dripped down Hector's soaked balaclava onto the bridge of his nose, but he let it go. He focused entirely on the guard's head.

Chuck reached his hand into the open window of the sheet-metal door and unlocked it. Hector adjusted his grip on his weapon. Chuck slowly turned the handle to open it, and Hector held his breath as the door inched opened wide enough for Chuck to slip in without getting caught on it or making any unnecessary sounds. Hector exhaled.

He watched Chuck move behind the snoozing guard and slip his arm around his neck, pressing the guard's head forward into the *V* formed by his bicep and forearm, keeping steady pressure. The guard woke to a startle. His eyes bulged and his mouth gaped as he tried to breathe and escape the choke hold, but it was too late. The blood flow to his brain stopped, and soon he fell still again. Chuck returned him to his slumped position and cuffed his wrists to each side of the chair before injecting him with a sedative. It would be hours before he would wake up again. Meanwhile, he was in almost the same position, which would keep anyone from suspecting anything odd or too different.

Hector signaled for Penguin, PF, and Guapo to follow. Once they were all inside, Chuck snipped a cable leading to the alarm and rendered it useless. Everyone gave a collective sigh; the first phase of the rescue operation was complete.

Behind the guard post was a door that accessed the court-yard of the citadel, as the travelogue had correctly described. To their luck and surprise, the door was left open, probably to allow air circulation into the musky room. But that luck formed a tight knot in the pit of his stomach. *No fucking way. This is way too goddamned easy.* They all *hated* the easy missions. It was just one more opportunity for Murphy to rear his ugly head and turn everything into a shit show.

He again flipped down his NVGs and scanned the court-yard, the enclosing high walls, and the rooftops, searching for any sign of movement or a light source. Two guards stood at a door on the far right side of the courtyard with two others on the rooftop above, and two more approaching the ones at the door. All six guards were on the right side of the citadel, making it easy to figure out where the key areas were. The difficult part was going to be getting to the door without any of the guards spotting them and setting off possible secondary alarms. In a disturbing way, the difficulty was welcoming. The only cover the courtyard provided was behind two palm trees in the center, but both were a signifi-cant distance apart.

Just then, the last two guards separated from the group and walked along the perimeter of the courtyard, heading right in their direction. That in itself created an opening for them, though a high-risk one. If timed properly, they could take those two out and take their place. The distance and moonless night would make it difficult to distinguish them from the regular guards until it was too late.

Hector looked around at his team, who also saw the opportunity. They all nodded in agreement. The guards kept talking as they neared the doorway, oblivious to the lethal team of commandos lurking in the dark.

As soon as they were hidden from the other guards' view, Hector and Chuck fired their weapons. Their heads snapped back and they dropped to the ground like sacks of potatoes. As soon as they did, Guapo and Penguin exited cover and resumed the path the guards had been taking, keeping their pace deliberately slow. Hector watched for any alert move-ment from the others and exhaled when nothing happened. He keyed his radio and whispered, "No spikes detected. Proceed."

Getting the message, Guapo and Penguin rounded their turn at the far side of the courtyard and moved toward the guards. PF kept his weapon trained on the group while Hector and Chuck moved out as quickly and quietly as possible, keeping to the walls in a low crouch and also keeping their weapons trained on the guards.

One of the two guards on the roof strained his neck in the direction of Penguin and Guapo, as if detecting something was amiss. Hector made a split-second decision and fired two suppressed rounds to his head, exploding it in a dark mist. In a fraction of a second, the same was repeated with the other guards above and below. *Fuck, that was close!*

With all threats down, the team converged on the door. Hector went through their pockets and found only a key card. The others grabbed the bodies and hid them within the shadows formed by an archway near the door.

From here on out, they would have to exercise extreme caution and figure *everything* out on their own. Hector slid the key card through the reader, and the light turned green. He raised his hand, counting down to zero, then opened the door slowly. The metal door's creak sent a cold shiver down his spine. He opened it wide enough for the team to file in and clear the dimly lit hallway. Ahead were stairs spiraling down into the unknown.

Once again at point, Hector took a deep breath, readjusted the grip on his weapon, and descended slowly. His feet moved in a delicate dance as each searched for the next step down, all the while keeping his weapon ready to identify and take out any threats lying in wait.

The stairs continued spiraling until they had nearly come full circle. Then he abruptly froze in place. His heart thundered against his chest. There, poking out from the next bend, was the elbow of a guard who had shifted in place. He heard the guard say something he didn't understand, but that didn't matter. What mattered was that it meant the guard wasn't alone. Hector raised his left hand and shaped it in the form of an upside-down gun. *Enemy sighted.*

For now, they had the element of surprise. *For now.* But how long would that last?

Hector and Chuck inched forward slowly, side by side, each dividing the narrow stairs into two imaginary sectors in the event the guards were on either side of the door. Hector was on the outside of the spiral and would likely be the first to make contact. Chuck canted his weapon to get the best angle possible while Hector looked directly ahead, trying to gauge Chuck's actions with his peripheral vision.

The guard's head came into view, and the man's eyes widened. Hector fired two shots into the guard; Chuck fired less than a second after him, dropping the second guard who came into view.

The bodies made a clattering noise as their belts and weapons hit the floor, sounding like a drum set that had just been kicked down the stairs. Hector and the team hurried to the bottom of the stairs with their fingers on their triggers, ready to fire again, if necessary. Hector's pulse raced in anticipation. He was aware of his palms sweating inside his tactical gloves.

And then . . . nothing happened.

Hector let out a long exhale, feeling the hot breath trapped in the balaclavas against his eyes as it escaped his nostrils. *Jesus fucking Christ!*

Penguin searched the guards and found a key card similar to the first. This door, however, was much different than the last. It was solid and thick. Whatever was behind that door was important and possibly heavily guarded.

Hector let his nerves settle, again checking his weapon and kit. He nodded to Penguin, who slid the key card into the reader, opening the door when the light turned green.

Soul-ripping screams erupted as the door cracked open, sending ice-cold shivers down Hector's spine. The screams only grew louder the more it opened, making him hyper-tense as the horror-movie soundtrack echoed through the corridor. Hector immediately noted that the hall was unguarded, but more importantly, that the screams were all male. *Thank God.* Even so, the screams sent his imagination into overdrive.

Dungeon-like doors lined each side of the hall, and the screams were coming from inside two of the cells: one on the left, close to them, and one on the right near the middle. Kelly and Jessica could be inside any of those cells. *Please, God, don't let them be here.* After taking several long seconds, forcing himself to block out the screams, Hector and the team moved to cover each side and peek in the slits in search of the women.

Hector reached the first door, where the screams were coming from, and instantly wished he hadn't looked. Inside was a man—or what once was a man—strapped to a bloodied gurney. His skeletal body convulsed like a trapped rat while the torturer flayed the skin off his shins. His feet flailed pathetically, strapped to the gurney, oozing red where skin had once been on the soles of his feet.

Hector gagged in revulsion, the scene rivaling that of any horror film. *Fuck, I'm going to have nightmares about this for weeks.* The victim's howls echoed in the room as he struggled like a wild beast trying to escape his horrific fate.

He thought of Kelly and immediately shook off the horrid thoughts. *No, they need them alive,* he told himself. But that sent a different shiver down his spine. *Oh, God, that isn't better.*

Instead, he pushed forward. There was nothing he could do for the poor bastard now. If he dropped the torturer, he might alert others and set off a chain reaction that could end up with Hector strapped to that same gurney.

At the other door, where there were muffled screams, Hector watched Chuck peek inside the room, then yank his head back, leaning against the wall to catch his breath. Angst took hold of Hector, and he made his way to the door, needing to look inside. A prisoner was strapped to a dental chair with only his feet and hands able to flail about helplessly. The torturer twisted pliers inside the victim's mouth, ripping teeth out one by one and disposing of them in a chamber pot to the side.

Goddammit! Why? Why did you have to look in there?

Penguin peered inside the first door and, like Chuck, yanked his head back in disgust. Guapo went to see, too, but Penguin put his hand on his shoulder, shaking his head.

Desperate to get past this horrifying sight, they continued until they reached the last cell door at the end of the hall. The women weren't here. *Thank God.* They collectively looked at the second heavy door.

Kelly and Jessica would be somewhere beyond that door, and Hector secretly prayed that whatever was on the other side wouldn't be as horrible as what they'd seen. Like every other disturbing thing he'd witnessed, he quickly buried the images into his personal chest of nightmares and proceeded with the mission. *Mission first, personal second. Keep it straight and stay alive.*

Hector again checked his watch. They were almost an hour behind schedule. *Motherfucker!* He nodded at the rest of the team as he slid the key card into the reader. The light flickered between red and green a few painfully long seconds, then turned solid green. The magnetic lock released, and Hector opened the door.

55

A lone amber light scarcely illuminated the narrow stairs that descended into a dark abyss. The team instinctively lowered their NVGs as they made their way down. Below they could see the far end of the room was a semicircle cut into the side of the fortress, with metal doors at equal intervals. There was something inhuman about it that made Hector shudder. A sudden high-pitched shrill echoed from behind one of the doors.

The horrors from the cells above flashed through Hector's mind, and he imagined Kelly suffering agonizing horrors. The beast took control without his consent, and he rushed down the rest of the way, paying no mind to hidden dangers below.

"Hector, wait," Chuck whispered, but a new set of screams echoed again, this time longer and more frequent. Hector reached the bottom and scanned from one side to the other. He heard what sounded like rapid gasps and whimpers coming from the far side of the semicircle. He slowed, scanning the last three doors and listened, but the rapid heartbeats pulsating in his ears made it that much more difficult.

He wiped the sweat from his eyes, breathing heavily through the balaclava, and waited. He felt the gentle squeeze from Chuck behind him, letting him know they were there and ready. The screams erupted again, long, agonizing screams that guided them to the second-to-the-last door. Hector's pulse quickened, and he searched for a handle, only to discover this door, too, used a key card.

The screams were loud and in faster succession now. Hector fumbled with the key card, finally sliding it into the reader and watching the light flicker between red and green. Then the light stayed red.

Motherfucker!

He tried again, waiting as the light flickered, but again it remained red. The screams were more desperate, turning into howls of agony and terror.

They would have to fall back to Plan B.

Hector gestured for Guapo to turn around. He pulled out the roll of green breaching tape, yellow detonation cord, and detonator from Guapo's backpack. Despite the need to move quickly, he carefully unrolled the thin, sticky, green clay-like explosive material. The key would be to use just enough explosives to sever the hinges from the door. If they used too much, the door could warp or act as a projectile and risk killing Kelly.

But no matter what, their stealthy rescue mission ended there. Once the explosion was heard—and it would be—the enemy forces would mobilize against them.

Penguin set up security while Hector, Chuck, and Guapo cut the tape into four sections, one for each hinge and the lock, pulled the clear lining to expose the sticky side, and put them in place. PF, in turn, took his backpack off, ready to take out any medical equipment that might be needed.

While Hector and Guapo placed the breaching tape, Chuck spliced four segments of detonation cord to one long enough to clear any debris or shock wave from the coming blast.

Guapo crimped the blasting caps onto the ends of the det-cord and embedded each into the sections of breaching tape. He twisted the other ends of the det-cord into a thin brass cylinder with a pull ring at the end, and they got into position. Once pulled, the detonator would ignite the cord and set off the explosive tape.

The beast was unshackled, ready to destroy anything he didn't love. *Do it. Do it do it do it.*

Guapo nodded, then pulled the ring. In the amount of time it took to exhale, the breach tape exploded with a bright flash and a deafening bang that resonated inside the semicircular room. The explosion tore the door off the frame. Hector and the others wasted no time breaching to clear the room.

The room was entirely lined with steel, like one massive metal box embedded into the rock. The mellow light from the two flickering fluorescent lights cast a shimmer on a woman, hung by her wrists in the center of the room.

Jessica.

She swayed slowly, her head slumped forward. She was naked, more frail and thin than he had last seen her. Instead of the toned, confident build she had been so proud of, her skin was marred and her ribs jutted out in stark relief in the dim light. A stream of water came from above and covered her naked form.

Three men writhed on the floor with wounds from the blast. Near them was a hand truck with a car battery fastened to it. Wires leading from the posts attached to two metal tubes wrapped in leather. The bastards had been delivering electric shocks to her body.

Penguin rushed to her, lifting her up so her wrists could clear the meat hook at the end of the chain. Hector went to help and shuddered as ice-cold water poured down on them. Together, they moved her away from the water.

"Those fucking bastards! What have they done to you?" asked Penguin.

Jessica's arms fell around his neck, unable to lift them on will alone, and he lowered her so that her body could rest on his knee while he removed the binds from her wrists. Her skin was ice-cold to the touch. PF moved in and inspected her body for any wounds produced from the breach while Chuck covered their only exit atop the stairs.

Hector wondered how long she'd been forced to hang and endure this torment. He couldn't help staring at the patchwork of marks that riddled her body. There were purple-red streaks, bruising around her ankles and wrists, redness and bruising in her pubic area, and the burn marks from the shocks.

PF brushed the wet, grimy hair matted against her face to check her vitals. He whispered, "Jessica, can you hear me?"

Jessica slowly opened her eyes, focusing on Penguin. She blinked once, twice, then flung her arms around him. "Eric!" She pulled him closer, as best she could. He gripped her as tightly as he dared, obviously not willing to let her go again. Jessica bawled as she clung to him. "I thought I was going to die here! Thank you! Thank you!"

Hector squatted down beside them and stroked her hair. He wanted to give her all the time she needed, but they didn't have a lot of time, and he needed to know about Kelly. "Hey, hard charger."

She looked up at him, eyes and nose red. She sniffled and touched his face. "Thank you, Hector."

PF moved in, already packing his medical equipment back in his bag. "She's severely dehydrated. She needs an IV, but we don't have that much time. We need to get her out now."

Hector gulped and asked her, "Is Kelly here? Do you know what happened to her?"

"Th . . . the other . . . rooms." Jessica gestured at the blond man writhing on the floor. "He has the key." Her voice was low and weak.

Penguin lifted Jessica effortlessly off his lap and handed her off to Hector before rounding on the man nearest the makeshift torture device. He lunged at the blond with a ferocity Hector had never seen before and pulled him up by his hair, ripping a piece of his scalp in the process.

The man winced and screamed something in Russian.

"Yeah, it hurts, don't it, you piece of shit!" Penguin growled. He unholstered his Glock and pressed it against his temple.

The man smirked, exposing blood-coated teeth, blood oozing from his lips, nose, and ears. In a Russian accent, he said, "You will die here, but not for long time."

"You first, motherfucker!" Penguin let him fall to the floor, then fired a suppressed round into his chest—then another, and a third into his skull. His head burst like a watermelon meeting a baseball bat. Guapo gave him a questioning look. Penguin snarled. "That piece of shit had it coming."

PF gestured to Jessica, who had fainted at the gore. "I need to get her out of here, now!"

"Guapo, can you help him?" Hector asked.

Guapo nodded. PF wrapped Jessica in an emergency blanket from his backpack, then he and Guapo led her out of the nightmare room.

Seconds later, the faint sound of klaxons reached the team at the bottom. Hector looked at his watch. "Shit! We're on the clock." He turned to Penguin. "Go call for the exfil."

Penguin ran out of the room as he spoke into his headset. "Freedom One, this is Spartan Two-Two, do you read?"

Hector searched through Antonin's pockets and pulled out a blood-stained card key, one different from the others. He looked at Chuck, and both hurried out of the room and slid the key into the lock of the next room. The light immediately turned solid green, and the magnetic lock released. Both raised their weapons and entered the room.

The room was white-tiled and filled with all kinds of horrific medical devices. Their focus shifted to the naked woman trembling in the corner of the room. A girl, really. Hector stared in shock once more. Never in all his missions had he seen something so horrible that hit so close to home. He eased back, trying not to reveal his shock at the sight of the girl's scarred and abused body.

Chuck wiped his hand down his face and shook his head. "Jesus," he whispered, "how many of these poor girls are there?"

Chuck slowly approached the girl, easing toward her like one to a skittish horse. Hector's eyes watered as tears rolled down with a blink. His heart ached for what Chuck must be feeling now. *My God, she's Veronica's age.*

Chuck moved with smooth, slow motions, talking soft and gently, until he was close enough to cradle her and stroke her grimy, clumped hair. "Shh. It's all right, sweetheart. It's all over." Chuck took off his body armor and blouse, wrapping it around her and enveloping her body with his top. He took her in his arms with care, as if she were his own daughter, and they walked her out of the room.

Hector frantically opened one door after another in search for Kelly. His fear took a greater hold with each empty room, until he reached the second-to-last room. *Oh my God!*

She was at the back of the room. Like the others, she was naked and badly beaten. Her arms were locked above and behind her, forcing her to double over. He rushed over to her but stopped as she shrieked.

"No! No! Please! No more!" She sobbed and wailed in a frenzy, desperate to avoid whatever horrors were intended for her.

Hector took off his helmet and balaclava. "Kelly, it's me,

Hector." He moved slowly toward her. "It's me, it's all right. I'm going to get you out of here."

Kelly strained to look up, still shivering in terror, and stared. She looked at him strangely, then sobbed with relief. "Oh, God, Hector. Thank God it's you! Thank you!"

He rushed to her and unbuckled the leather restraints around her wrists. Once free, she sank her face into his shoulder and bawled.

He pulled her in close, though tenderly. The sight of her abused body was crushing, but she was alive. *Thank you, God.* He stroked her hair thick with grime and held her. He felt every one of her sobs like a hot poker to his chest. He wiped his own tears away on his shoulder and held her face in his hands. He looked her in her eyes as he swiped her hair behind her ears.

"I'm taking you home, baby." He didn't remember the last time he had called her baby, but by the smile on her face, she did. "I love you."

She smiled like he'd never seen her do before. "I love you too."

He wrapped his own top around her and led her outside with the others.

As soon as they joined the others in the outer hall, the three women rushed to one another in a heap of sobbing joy.

Hector watched with renewed hope, then joined the team huddled near the stairs. "What's the status on the exfil?"

They looked at each other, then Penguin said, "We got a big problem, and it isn't that I can't get a signal. We're getting the Bell 212, not the Super Puma. We won't make it." Penguin summarized what Hector had feared, and all shared a collective expression that relayed they were knee-deep in shit and sinking fast.

Kelly and Jessica remained huddled with the young girl, rejoicing at the unexpected but welcome turn of events. That is, until Kelly looked to her husband, her savior. She recognized his look. Something was terribly wrong.

"Hector," Kelly asked cautiously, "what's wrong?" The words came out slow and careful.

Hector turned, trying to decide if . . . no, how he would tell her. He gulped and pointed at the other girl. With a lump in his throat, he croaked, "She can't come with us."

56

Konstantin was stirred awake by the wailing sirens coming from the citadel. *What the hell is going on?* He threw the covers off, put on his trousers and shirt, and threw open the window blinds. It was pitch-dark outside. He stared out from his upstairs room across from the fortress. He expected to see spotlights, gunfire, and other sporadic sources of light, but as best as he could tell, guards were running around with flashlights in no particular pattern. *The damn idiots have no idea what to do.* He picked up his phone from the nightstand and dialed Antonin. The phone rang without an answer.

He dialed a different number and waited. "Hello, Joseph? It's Konstantin. Meet me at the lobby immediately."

He paused as he listened to the response, all the while shaking his head. "No, no, no. I don't know either. Now stop asking stupid questions and meet me in the lobby." He was about to end the call, but he added for good measure, "And Joseph, do not make me come find you. You will regret it if you do."

He ended the call and dialed a final number. "General Farhad, there are sirens going off at the citadel." He looked outside the window once more at the confused panic. "No. If you want those girls, you're going to want to send *everyone*. And I suggest you send them now!"

He felt his skin crawl. His business with Sacha wasn't over yet, and if whatever was happening at the fortress had anything to do with him, he'd have to find someone else to take the fall for it. But would Donovan be enough?

57

"Please! Don't leave me here! Please!" The girl wrung her hands over and over and shifted her weight from one foot to the other. She looked from Kelly to Hector as her lower lip quivered and her eyes welled with tears. Kelly and Jessica wrapped their arms around her, and Kelly pressed the girl's head against her chest, comforting her just as she glared at Hector with rage in her eyes. "What do you mean, she's not coming?"

The girl's wails, her quivering lips, puffy red eyes, and sniffling could have broken the hardest, most frigid heart. She took a step forward and began opening the blouse, crying as she offered her body with tears trickling down her cheeks. "I'll do anything you want. Anything. You, you can do anything you want with me! Just please, don't leave me!"

Hector turned away, unable to look her in the eye as his soul crushed. It tore him apart to offer her salvation just to rip it away, as if the girl hadn't suffered enough. He gnashed his teeth, wiping the tears from his eyes, and turned back, hating himself for having to say it again. "She can't go, Kelly. We'll be overweight!"

"Look at her, Hector!" Kelly yelled back, pointing at her thin, emaciated frame. "Tell me, how is she overweight?"

"Kelly . . ." Hector balled his hands into fists. How could he explain it differently?

"What he means," said Chuck, struggling with his own emotion, "is that we're getting a smaller helicopter with a lesser fuel range than the one we expected. And has been flying and burning fuel at a rate that can't exceed a certain weight." He wiped his tears. "If she comes with us, we'll crash in the sea before reaching Cyprus."

The rest of the team watched in silence, none of them finding the words to say to help the situation.

Despite the surmounting cold, hard facts about physics and the rescue helicopter, Kelly stubbornly shook her head. She closed the blouse around the girl and held her tighter. "If she doesn't go, I won't go."

"I won't either, Hector," said Jessica. "You have no idea what this poor girl has gone through. What we all have gone through. I'm begging you. Please don't do this!" The three women held tight to each other, refusing to be separated.

"Goddammit, Kelly! Don't fucking do this! Not now. We're leaving"—Hector pointed at the girl—"and she's not coming!" He choked back the tears as he reached for his pistol. His hand trembled in protest. He gulped. "I promise you she won't suffer any longer, but she can't come."

Kelly and Jessica stared in horror as he rested his hand on his Glock. Kelly cradled the girl's head against her chest and cried, "Don't you dare, Hector. Please!"

Jessica kissed the girl's forehead. "She's just a child, for God's sake. She's an American. Her name is Whitney, and . . ."

Hector's eyes welled up, struggling to hold back the emotions tearing him up inside, unable to unholster his Glock. "Goddammit! You're not listening! We can't all make it. I wish to God we could, but not everyone gets to go home. That's the harsh reality."

Kelly's voice trembled, still shaking her head in denial. "She'll be twenty-one in October. Her father's a minister, and her mother's a—"

"It's all right, Kelly," Chuck said softly. They all turned to him.

"Chuck," Hector started to say.

"She's right. We can't just leave her any more than I could leave one of my girls to die in this place. As a father, I'd want someone to bring my little girl home." A fatherly smile brightened his face. "She'll come with us. We'll figure something out." He walked up to her and wrapped his arms around Whitney. "Come on, princess. No one is leaving you behind. We're going home. All of us." Whitney propped her head on Chuck's shoulder and wrapped her arms around him.

Hector didn't know how the old man planned to pull off a miracle, but they didn't have time to argue. He started back up the stairs without another word. Once at the door upstairs, he waited for Penguin and Guapo to get in position to clear the hall. As soon as he cracked the door open, a hail of bullets shot out from across the hall.

"Fucking hell!" He slammed the door shut. Bullets pinged at the steel door. "Well, they know where we are now."

Penguin took out a fragmentary grenade and handed it to Hector. They waited for a pause when the guards reloaded their magazines, then Hector pulled the pin of the grenade and shouted, "Frag out!"

In one quick motion, he opened the door, threw the grenade hard on the floor, and shut the door immediately. A few screams let out seconds before the grenade exploded. Hector waited a few seconds more, then opened the door and sprayed the hall with his weapon. Whoever was unlucky enough to be in the hall was dead now. He proceeded forward, keeping his weapon at the ready to drop anyone who got in their way.

Chuck led the women across the hall and said, "Close your eyes, girls!" Despite surviving unspeakable horrors, they didn't need to add to the vivid nightmares that would soon haunt their sleep.

In short order, they made their way back up to the rooftop under the cover of darkness, only to find that the helicopter had not arrived and house lights all across the island were on now. Penguin keyed his radio. "Freedom One, Freedom One, this is Spartan Two-Two, do you copy?"

"Spartan Two-Two, this is Freedom One. What's your status?"

"Thank God!" muttered Hector.

"Freedom One, Spartan Two-Two, we got jackpot. I say again, we got jackpot!" Penguin looked at the others, took a deep breath, and again keyed his mike. "Freedom One, be advised, we have jackpot plus one. I say again, we have jackpot plus one."

There was a long silence.

The radio crackled, and a less-than-jovial voice responded. "Roger, Spartan Two-Two. ETA ten mikes, do you copy?"

Penguin and Hector exchanged a look, then Penguin responded in an unenthusiastic tone, "I copy, Freedom One. We are standing by. Spartan Two-Two out."

The pilot's tone conveyed that they were truly screwed. A commercial version of the UH-1 Huey, the Bell 212 had been the last resort for the mission because of its reduced range even under ideal conditions. Now that Whitney was with them, their chances of making it back safely plummeted. Hector had to chuckle at his own dark pun.

Penguin and Hector made their way to Chuck, who was providing security while Jessica, Kelly, and Whitney huddled together, shivering from the cool Mediterranean breeze. "Grumpy," PF said, "we have a problem."

"No shit, imagine that," said Chuck. "What is it?"

"We're about to have company! Maybe two platoons!"

The team caught sight of blinking lights out on the water. Smaller boats were arriving from the mainland and docking inside the breakwater.

Guapo then called out, "Rotors inbound from the mainland! Mi-17s!"

Hector looked at the three women huddled together, then at the boats arriving and the inbound helicopters. At this rate, everything would be over in five minutes. *Any-fucking-time, lads.*

"All right, gents," said Chuck. "Let's get our sectors of fire and get ready to rumble."

Hector ran over to the two dead guards on the rooftop and grabbed their AK-47s and ammunition vests, then ran back and placed the rifles in between them. "Hey, why leave them to the enemy, right?"

Chuck smirked. He walked over to Jessica and gave her his suppressed pistol. "Here. Just in case you need it." He gulped, then added, "Remember to save one for yourselves."

PF spotted figures now running up from the dock through the maze of houses. "Shit! We got enemy coming up!"

Hector frowned. Since when did the Shabiha have boats and helicopters? *There's too many of them.* The Parabellum team formed up into a defensive perimeter and prayed they wouldn't be overrun. If they were lucky, they'd all be killed in the shootout.

The enemy force was unorganized. "I think they're trying to figure out what to do," said Guapo. Their lack of training and leadership would probably improve their chances, but just barely.

The guards charged at them in groups of two or three and were cut down immediately. A second wave did the same and were cut down just as fast. "It won't be long until they figure some shit out!" said Penguin.

No sooner had he said that when the guards all charged at the same time from different directions. The team put out a hail of fire in an effort to suppress their movements and any returning fire, but they were too quickly going through their ammunition. And then the Mi-17s dropped fresh troops: in the courtyard, outside the citadel, and on the tower opposite them.

"Troops!" yelled Guapo.

They were now suppressed by the reinforcements. Hector peeked out and fired, dropping one or two but having other rounds go stray, before he crouched again for cover. More reinforcements had made their way up to the roof and were slowly gaining ground.

Hector yelled out to the team, "They're crowding to our north and east! Let's take them out with grenades!"

The other men nodded, each taking a grenade in hand, and in unison they lobbed them in both directions.

Frantic cries were heard in the seconds before the grenades went off, followed by cries of agony.

Hector noticed a shadow moving across the water, and before he could call out to the team, the rescue helicopter swooped up from below, barely missing the house rooftops before climbing up and hovering over them. Just then, the rooftop access door opened, and reinforcements burst through both the door and the citadel gates below. The helicopter's door gunner swung his M134 minigun out and sprayed a white stream of rounds, cutting down all in its path.

Chuck climbed up the skid on the side opposite the gunner and helped the women climb up the skids and into the cabin of the helicopter while Hector helped from below. The interior was much smaller than that of the Super Puma. The two facing canvas benches could support six passengers, including the door gunner and crew chief, making for a very crowded cabin. And now it would be impossibly crowded.

For Hector, the only scenario where the helicopter made it with everyone on board was if God somehow miracled them back to base. Short of that, they'd end up in the middle of the Mediterranean for sure. The only question was, just how close would they be to Cyprus.

Hector helped Whitney into the helicopter, watching the crew chief gritting his teeth as synapses pulsed instant calculations in his head. He shook his head and shouted, "All right, lass! Hop on!"

Meanwhile, the door gunner continued firing the minigun at the approaching enemy below. The steady yellow streak cutting them down by the dozens kept the smart ones behind some form of cover. The loud, rapid hum sounded like a weed eater on steroids as it cut down Shabiha reinforcements on the rooftop.

Guapo climbed up next and took a position by the door gunner. He fired his own weapon, killing the exposed fighters and keeping others from firing back. Penguin continued providing cover while the others pulled back and loaded on the helicopter. He began bounding away, still providing covering fire, when a fighter popped out of his position and fired. Penguin fell back, writhing in pain and desperately trying to crawl toward the helicopter, leaving a trail of blood behind him.

Hector quickly dropped the two guards pouncing for Penguin. By now, the helicopter was taking a significant amount of fire as rounds impacted on the fuselage. More fighters emerged like ants from a kicked-over mound, and if any of them had RPGs or hit the fuel tank or tail boom, they would be done for.

Hector and PF raced after Penguin, braving the hail of gunfire coming their direction.

"Come on, time to go, buddy." They dragged Penguin by the strap of his body armor while he kept returning fire. He was bleeding bad and fading rapidly. If he didn't get on the helo and get some immediate combat casualty care, he'd bleed out, for sure.

Chuck reached out, and together they all hauled Penguin up and laid him on the deck. "Oh, God, it's Eric!" Screamed Jessica. She reached for him but was held back by Kelly and Chuck.

Hector assessed the situation in the blink of an eye. They weren't going to make it. Not like this. The helicopter would be shot up before it had a chance to make it off the island. And if they did, there was no way in hell they'd make it back to Cyprus. At the very least, Penguin would die. At worst, they all would.

In the same blink of an eye and in the midst of chaos, the solution became perfectly clear. Hector turned to Chuck, still standing on the skid, and said, "Give me your ammo!"

Chuck stared at him quizzically. He turned somber when he recognized Hector's plan.

"No fucking way! Get your ass up on the chopper!" Chuck barked. "We're all going home!"

Hector paused, coming to terms with what needed to be done. He made peace with his demons and gazed up at his friends, at his wife, one last time. He studied her face, as if to memorize every feature, recalling the dimples that formed in her cheeks when she smiled, the way she bit her lower lip when something devious came to mind, and the cute way her nose scrunched when she sneezed.

He cleared the lump in his throat. "It's the right thing to do . . . for them." He locked eyes with Kelly and gave a resigned, peaceful smile, then stepped away from the hovering skid and gave a thumbs-up to the crew chief. He turned to Chuck. "I'll make my own way out. Just give me your ammo." He gulped as he looked at Kelly one last time. "And take care of her. Please."

Chuck put his hand on Hector's shoulder. "Get out any

way you can. I don't want to have to come back to this place to save your ass."

The crew chief gave a solemn salute, then signaled the pilot.

Hector took the extra magazines from the others, looked at Kelly one last time, and yelled into the cabin, "I love you!" Then he stepped off the skid.

The pilot pulled up on the collective and twisted the throttle, the helicopter struggling as it prepared to lift off under the strain.

58

Every second they delayed sent a new wave of terror through Kelly, as she feared the rescue would all fall apart and she'd end up back in the hell she had just escaped. *Come on, guys, what is taking so long?* She peeked out of the helicopter after the guys were hoisted into the cabin, one bleeding heavily. Another guy worked quickly to try to stop the bleeding.

Kelly tapped repeatedly on her lap. "Please, guys! Let's go!" She again peeked out to see what was taking so long. Chuck was putting his hand on Hector's shoulder. *What are they saying?* In that moment, she locked eyes with Hector. The look in his eyes made her heart sink to the pit of her stomach. *Oh God, Hector. No!*

He shouted, "I love you," and she understood.

She grasped Jessica's arm and let out a pain-filled scream, "No!" She shook her head, refusing to believe what she was seeing. "Please! Sweetheart! No! Don't leave me!" He held her stare with a look she'd never forget.

Then he stepped off.

She let out a primal scream as she burrowed her face into Jessica's shoulder. He'd been right all along. Not all of them would make it home—so he was sacrificing himself so that the rest of them could make it back.

She tried to breathe as her heart sank deeper. This wasn't right. This wasn't how things were supposed to end. Too late did she appreciate what his work truly entailed. She leaned toward the door, feeling as though her world was shattering, and yelled out, "I love you, too!"

But it was too late. She clutched at her chest while the lump in her throat hardened. If he climbed back in, and if they made it back home, she knew that they could conquer anything together. There would be nothing separating them anymore . . . if only he would climb back in.

Please God, grant me this one thing.

Chuck watched Hector step away from the rotor wash. He turned slowly back to face Kelly, Jessica, and the others. "We almost made it out together."

Kelly felt the regret in his tone. But then his expression changed, and she feared what would happen next.

He looked at the women, at PF and Guapo giving first aid to Penguin, and sighed. "Goddammit, Betty is gonna fucking kill me for this." He leaned over to give Whitney a kiss on the cheek, then said to Kelly, "Tell Betty I'm sorry, and that I love her."

Kelly looked at him with disbelief, and then her heart dropped a thousand feet as Chuck hopped off the helicopter. "Chuck! No!" The helicopter lifted with ease and began maneuvering to its outward route.

Guapo tapped on the gunner's shoulder. "Lay down suppressing fire on those motherfuckers, and take out as many as you can! We're not going to leave those guys without a fighting chance!" He then yelled at the crew chief, "You, tell the pilot to circle around and give the gunner a good field of fire to buy those guys time! It's the least we can do." The crew chief nodded and relayed the message.

As they circled, Kelly could see Hector and Chuck gathering weapons and ammunition before running toward the edge of the citadel. Her hopes for a happily ever after disintegrated as the helicopter took flight.

59

Hector and Chuck moved away from the sound of gunfire. When they reached the edge of the fortress, Chuck said, "Well, it could have been higher."

It was still dark on this side of the citadel, and Hector wasted no time taking out the climbing rope from his back-pack. He anchored the rope to the ancient masonry, then cast it down over the side. The air felt cooler as they descended. The sound of the minigun and rotor blades cutting through the air grew more distant the lower they got. Once on the ground, they set up security while deciding what their next move would be. Above them, the helicopter continued circling, reducing the enemy numbers significantly.

Hector scanned the long alley that offered the most direct route to the docks. It was the perfect death funnel. The question was, for whom?

"All right, old man," said Hector, "what's your recommendation?"

Chuck considered their options aloud. "Well, the Zodiac is on the other side of the island, so that's out of the question. Let's see what our chances are of getting to one of the boats on the docks."

Hector turned on his infrared beacon, switched channels, and keyed his radio. "Freedom One, Spartan Two-Zero, we have beacons on. What's the enemy situation on the docks? Over."

"Roger Spartan Two-Zero, I see your beacon. The docks are lightly defended, and the enemy is spread out. We can clear a path to the dock and take out the enemy force's boats, clearing your escape, but we'll be calling attention to you, and I have no bloody idea where you'll go from there, mate. Over."

"Roger, Freedom One. Clear a path. We'll figure out from there. Thanks for the assist. Spartan Two-Zero out." Hector turned to Chuck and relayed, "The helo is gonna clear a path down this alley and kill everything in between us and the dock, but that's going to put a huge spotlight on us. Are you ready for this?"

Chuck checked his weapon and kit, turned on his infrared beacon, and then nodded.

"Freedom One, Spartan Two-Zero, we move on your go. Over."

"Roger, Spartan Two-Zero, stand by."

The helicopter circled around to give the gunner a perfect field of fire. Anything that didn't blink with the infrared beacon denoting Hector and Chuck's position was met with the gunner's fire. White-hot lead streamed from the gun, shredding any enemies in the open or advancing toward them.

Hector and Chuck raced past the carnage that littered the alley, hearing the rounds shredding into flesh. Fifteen yards ahead, the destructive stream forced all other enemies to split like the Red Sea. The helicopter circled around and turned to escape in the opposite direction while still giving the gunner a field of fire.

The path to the dock was clear when Chuck and Hector reached it. The smell of smoke and burning fuel and oil was thick as the torn enemy boats burned and slowly sank into the water, all save one.

"Looks like that's our ride," said Hector. He keyed his radio and said, "Freedom One, Spartan Two-Zero, thanks for the assist. We got it from here. Spartan Two-Zero out."

"Roger, Spartan Two-Zero. Godspeed, lads. Freedom One out." The rotor of Freedom One faded away as it flew back toward Cyprus.

Hector sighed in relief when the outboard engines started. Chuck pushed the boat off the dock, and they were on their way out to the breakwater. Once they cleared it, they discussed their options. "We could go out into international waters, call for help, and wait it out," said Hector.

"No good. Those helos will be out searching for us. We'd be in open water, exposed, with nothing to drink. Besides, I don't think we have enough fuel to make it that far."

Both looked out to the dim sliver of light just now cresting over the horizon, their minds in agreement about where to go. Their only option would be to go deeper into the lion's den: they'd go into Syria.

60

Somewhere off the coast of Syria
7 August 2014

The first glimmer of dawn was just stretching beyond the horizon when the boat slowed to an idle outside the break-water of a marina somewhere along the Syrian coast, where the Assad regime still reigned supreme. Hector scanned the shore with a pair of binoculars. In view were folded beach chairs, closed beach umbrellas, shuttered shopping stands, and a multistory building farther back that was likely a hotel.

"It looks like some beach resort." He continued scanning and reported, "I don't see any military or otherwise armed presence. It's practically empty."

"Yeah, well, let's hope." Chuck drove the boat into the breakwater, always on the alert in case they needed to turn and throttle out of the marina.

"The port is probably about five miles north from us, so my guess is we're just a few miles south of Tartus, but no way of telling where from here."

Once they were close enough to the shore, Chuck shut off

the engine. The boat bobbed close to the beach, and Hector jumped off, pulling the boat and grounding it on the shore. They moved swiftly off the beach and sought cover behind one of the closed stands as the calls for morning prayer echoed in the distance. People would soon be moving about. Hector peeked out from the side of the stand and listened for any unusual noise or any form of movement.

"I think I found our ride." Chuck pointed to an old Toyota Carina parked near the hotel.

"Not bad, old man. Now we just need to decide which way to go."

They crouched behind the stand and considered their options. Chuck tilted his head to the north. "There's the route north to the Turkish border, but we'd have to go through the raging battleground that is Aleppo." He then tilted south. "And then there's the route south to the Jordanian border, but that would mean crossing through Damascus."

Neither was a palatable option. "What if we pushed east to Homs?" asked Hector. "The opposition still has control over it, and we might be able to link up with Jessica's friend Qari Bashir. He's with the opposition in some high-up capacity."

Chuck grimaced as he brushed his hand over his face. "Well, that's the best of all the bad ideas, I suppose." He huffed and said, "All right. Let's see what happens. Maybe we'll stick our heads out of the windows and yell, 'We're Americans!'"

They chuckled at the *Spies Like Us* reference, a laugh that was much needed given their predicament.

In short order, they crept to the car, hot-wired it, and drove along the highway, passing signs that conveniently pointed to Homs. So far, they hadn't seen any checkpoints or a military presence of any kind, either regime or opposition. But the longer they went without any contact, an unsettled weariness reinforced their belief that Murphy had something spectacularly catastrophic in store for them.

They drove nearly an hour along the open road before they spotted the first visible checkpoint, well beyond the populated areas. Hector parked the car below the crest of a rolling hill. With the aid of the binoculars, Chuck scanned the checkpoint, then handed the binoculars to Hector. "That's an opposition checkpoint."

Hector took a look for himself. The checkpoint was a substantial size that extended well beyond either side of the highway. In essence, it was a small outpost dropped in the middle of the highway. There would be no bypassing it. It consisted of concentric layers of Jersey and HESCO barriers, concertina wire, and concrete blocks. There were sandbagged machine gun positions at various intervals. Atop what looked like a shanty at the center of the checkpoint flew a flag of green, white, and black horizontal bands with three red stars —the flag of the Free Syrian Army.

Chuck inched the car forward until they crested the hill. The checkpoint suddenly became alive with activity. Alerted to their presence, soldiers rushed to man their machine gun positions, with others shouting as they pointed their weapons. They rolled at turtle speed to the checkpoint, avoiding any overt indications of being a threat, and waited as a group of soldiers surrounded them. Most were in their late teens or early twenties, wearing clothes that looked as if they had been handed down no less than five times. The leader, not older than thirty, shouted off questions that neither could understand.

Hector smiled and said, "*Marhaba!*" He tapped on his chest. "*Ameriki!*"

The soldiers looked at each other, trying to figure out what to do. One of the younger ones asked something, to which the oldest one simply shrugged. It didn't take a translator to figure out that one was asking what to do with these guys, and the other was saying something to the effect of, "Hell if I know." It was evident this was their first time encountering Americans. The leader lowered his weapon, extended his hands calmly, and slowly waved for the two to follow him. Hector and Chuck glanced at each other. *Here we go.*

They exited the vehicle, relieved that their weapons weren't confiscated. They were escorted beyond the walls to a shanty with a corrugated metal roof that was supposed to be a command post. There, their escort said something to another soldier, the communicator, who then got on an old US-made PRC-77 radio and presumably called someone in charge.

For over an hour, Hector and Chuck took turns trying to communicate with the commander, with no success. "Qari Bashir," Hector said, with slow and exaggerated enunciation. "Do-you-know-Qari-Bashir?" His efforts were rewarded by jovial laughs from the soldiers, who clearly found it comical.

"I don't think these guys know who the hell that is. Hell, he may even be dead."

The radio operator had several kind-of conversations with others on the radio, frequently using Qari's name and "Ameriki" in the same sentence, but it was difficult to say if any progress was being made. This, along with the increasing heat inside the shanty, made the situation more frustrating.

Their sad attempt at communication was interrupted by an alarm coming from an old crank-handle siren, followed by outgoing fire. Hector took the commander by the shoulder and asked, "What the hell is going on?"

The commander broke Hector's grip, grabbed his weapon, and moved to the door. He shouted a bunch of words as he went, of which the only ones Hector understood were *jaysh*—"army," in Arabic—and *Assad*.

Hector turned to Chuck. "It's the Syrian army!"

Seconds later, explosions shook the shanty, and returning fire ripped through the walls. Hector and Chuck dove instinctively, but not before some soldiers had dropped dead on the floor, including the radio man, whose face was now covered by destroyed radio components. Hector and Chuck grabbed their weapons and ran outside, moving from cover to cover to identify the threat. They met up with the young commander at the wall overlooking the road Hector and Chuck had arrived on.

Three BTR-60 armored personnel carriers and six technicals were now spreading over the rolling terrain on either side of the M1 highway. Above them were three Mi-17s escorting the convoy split in either direction as they approached. The commander stood, pointing at the two helicopters that were landing and deploying troops at either flank of the checkpoint. Then another hail of bullets dropped the young man in the blink of an eye.

"Jesus Christ, these fuckers are everywhere!" said Hector.

Hector rushed to the long-barreled 12.7mm DShK machine gun and dragged the dead soldier from that position, while Chuck made his way to the much larger 14.5mm ZPU antiaircraft machine gun cradled in a tubular frame. He pulled the dead soldier from that seat and opened fire as well.

All right, motherfuckers! It's showtime!

Hector pointed the weapon at the rapidly approaching technicals south of the highway and fired a five-second burst, then another. Inside Hector, the beast roared, its bloodthirst being sated as the rounds hit the cabin of the lead technical, tearing the driver apart and causing the truck to turn erratically. It crashed into the second, and both flipped over, crushing the gunners in the process. The third technical banked right in a futile effort to flee. The beast smiled with satisfaction. He fired at that one, ripping through the broad side of the truck and igniting it. The gunner, covered in flames, jumped off and flailed on the ground, but he was unable to escape his gruesome death.

Chuck concentrated his fire on the approaching BTR-60s. A rocket flew from behind him and, striking it, sent the attached turret into the air like a bottle rocket. The mangled BTR came to a halt. Its occupants tried to open the doors but were unable to escape the inferno. A celebratory roar erupted from the opposition soldiers.

"The fight's not over yet, guys!" yelled Hector. He shifted his fire to the approaching troops offloaded by one of the helicopters. "Chuck! Take out those helos!"

Chuck swiveled the ZPU and cranked the cradle to shift his fire upward, toward one of the three helicopters. The ZPU fired at a slower rate than the DShK, but the larger-caliber rounds were enough to pierce the thicker armor of the helicopter's floor plates. Antiaircraft rounds pierced through the skin of one of the Mi-17s, forcing it to bank out of the cone of fire of the ZPUs as it left a trail of smoke behind it.

"That's right, pussies," yelled Chuck, "run away."

Hector saw a second helicopter coming around and moving into position above them, creeping closer while gaining altitude. The dark cabin appeared as the side door opened, and Hector realized what they were about to do.

"Barrel bomb!" He turned the DShK toward the Mi-17 and fired.

Chuck, in turn, spun the elevation wheel, gasping as his forearms burned from the exertion of adjusting the elevation higher. The glowing rounds of the ZPU barely missed the bottom of the helicopter. He let out a battle roar, commanding his tiring arms as he fired. Just then, an explosion flashed outside the door to the helicopter, followed by a secondary explosion that swallowed the helicopter in a massive fireball and sent the burning hulk crashing down over the troops approaching on the ground.

The opposition soldiers again roared victoriously as the assault was halted. But their celebrations were short-lived. A faint trail of vehicles approached from the near horizon in their direction. The battle wasn't over yet.

61

Somewhere west of Homs, Syria

The blistering midday Syrian sun neared its apogee as the relentless Syrian Arab Army attacks raged on. Hector, Chuck, and the dwindling number of opposition fighters so far had repelled five assaults, yet the enemy kept coming in still greater numbers. Warped hulks of destroyed vehicles and baking corpses crammed the battlefield. The number of enemy dead neared two hundred, almost triple that of the remaining opposition force, and yet they kept coming.

Their last act on the defensive came at a high price. The FSA took even more casualties and expended more ammunition, including the last of the RPGs and the DShK and ZPU rounds. Hector and Chuck used the lull in the fighting to help treat the wounded who could still fight, take stock of what little supplies remained, and refill empty magazines. Whatever food or water was left wouldn't last much longer. They all were hot, parched, hungry, and exhausted.

Hector shook the upside-down bottle, forcing the last drops of water to fall into his dry mouth, and when there was nothing more to drink, he dropped it at his feet.

"It's only a matter of time before we bleed dry and are overrun, Chuck." Hector's voice was hoarse and dry. "You should have stayed on the helo, old man."

"Nonsense," retorted Chuck. "I never leave a man behind." His voice was coarser than usual, and he was visibly fatigued. "Besides, these bastards have to be near their end too. They can't keep this up."

Hector refilled a stack of magazines and looked up at Chuck, his face covered in sweat and smudged with black patches of burnt gunpowder. "I chose to stay behind. I had no expectations of anyone following me."

Chuck consolidated their medical supplies and cut strips of cloth for spare bandages. "Betty wouldn't have expected any less from me. Especially after what those girls went through." His eyes began to tear up, making Hector wish he'd turned away. "I think of my girls going through that nightmare, and I feel myself losing control." He ripped another strip of cloth, then met Hector's gaze with steely eyes. "Those animals needed to fucking die, and that's what's getting me through this. If we die, then we die. But I'm taking as many of these bastards with me as I can." His voice was determined, resolute as ever.

Hector nodded in agreement. He put the magazine and rounds down and said, "I can't stop seeing the image of Kelly's scarred body. I keep thinking of her, helpless in that cell, and I wonder if she will ever return to be the woman she was before. I don't know. Maybe it's this goddamned place, but I know I want to make it back home. I want to be with her."

"Me too, Hector. Me too."

Outside, the lookout sounded the alarm. Hector and Chuck grabbed their weapons and supplies and hurried to the lookout's position. Like the previous attacks, the doppler effect from the approaching Mi-17's rotor clued the defenders in of the oncoming attack, and they braced for another assault.

Hector scanned the avenue of approach and froze in place. The color drained from his face. Without a word, he handed Chuck the binoculars.

"They have fucking tanks." He exhaled hard. "We're screwed."

Approaching along the highway was a column of six BTR-60s, a fleet of technicals, and a platoon of three T-55 tanks. They had no weapons or ammunition remaining that could counter the armor of a tank. Together, Hector and Chuck raced from position to position, tapping each soldier on the arm and giving them a thumbs-up in an effort to rally them and make sure they were ready for the fight. The soldiers didn't need to know it was hopeless.

Plumes of smoke appeared from the T-55 turrets, followed by the whoosh of inbound tank shells that exploded within the perimeter of the checkpoint. The fleet of technicals split on each side of the road as they raced forward, dodging destroyed hulks, crushing corpses, and firing DShKs on the fortified position. The BTR-60s opened fire from their enclosed turrets.

In all, the combined enemy force laid down a thick wall of lead that kept Chuck and Hector from returning fire or moving positions. Under such an overwhelming barrage, they wouldn't last long. All they could do was sit and wait until the enemy broke through and dismounted, then fight in close-quarters combat, where they'd at least fight on almost equal terms.

Hector knelt behind a block of concrete, crouching as low as possible to the ground to minimize his profile. The Jersey barriers, concrete blocks, and sandbags could absorb the impact from heavy machine guns to a point, but they were useless against the explosive damage of a tank round.

The repeated booms from the tank rounds resonated

across the battlefield, followed by an ear-piercing blast that destroyed a position a few yards from him, catapulting smoldering bodies like rag dolls.

Hector gnashed his teeth from the concussive waves and quaked in terror, waiting for his turn to be torn apart like the others. In all the combat he'd experienced, never had he been as terrified or as helpless as he was now. Why the fuck did he keep wanting to do this? To feel "alive"? He had felt *alive* just being with Kelly once again; he didn't need the terror that now gripped him like a vise. It was being with her again that mattered the most. What a fool he'd been all along. The sensation of a warm smile, the touch of her skin, and the taste of her lips. That was what he desired. To come home to someone who loved him.

And she did love him. In his last sight of her, she had said, "I love you too." The thing that mattered the most had always been right there, but he'd been too blind to see it, too stupid to acknowledge it—and now it was too late. He would die here, never able to show her just how much she meant to him.

The stench of diesel fumes and the discordant squealing of the tank's heavy wheels broke him from his thoughts. His heart hammered as the ground rumbled beneath him. Nearby, ghastly cries were swallowed up by the crunching of bodies under the weight of the tank. The electric motor hummed as the turret turned, and he gripped his weapon tightly, bracing for his gruesome death to come.

62

The tank fired. The projectile shook the ground as it left the turret, but it whooshed away from Hector, hitting something far in the distance. Hector gasped for air, as if breaking the surface of the water. By some miracle, he was still alive. But now there was a new sound: the high-velocity whoosh of an incoming round, followed by the distinct sound of armor exploding.

The tank's turret cast a shadow over Hector's cover as it flipped in the air like a coin. A high-pitched snapping of supersonic bullets met with flesh and metal somewhere behind Hector. Chaos erupted around him, and screaming ensued.

The advancing Syrian soldiers ran away in droves as they were cut down by an unknown force. Hector peeked around the brittle remaining layer of concrete that was his cover and saw BTR-60s being destroyed, one after another, along with the burning chassis of the T-55. *What . . . ?* Hector scanned in the direction of the incoming fire and saw opposition reinforcements arriving from Homs.

"Holy shit!" he yelled. "The cavalry's here!"

A column of T-55 and T-62 tanks flying the Free Syrian

Army flag flanked the checkpoint position, destroying the remaining enemy BTR-60s as if they were made of wet paper and mowing down the remaining forces fleeing in mass confusion. The two remaining Syrian T-55s sped in reverse, crushing anything dead or alive while in retreat. One tank took a direct hit to the side, mangling it, as the tank rounds inside cooked off and engulfed it in flames. The remaining tank turned its turret to fire, but not before being hit again and again, until the burning hulk stood still.

Yes! Hector felt his entire body tingle as an old yet familiar sensation overcame him. Endorphins rushed through him like electricity. He opened his mouth and the beast roared through him. *Holy shit, it feels good to be alive!* They had held back the repeated attacks for twelve excruciating hours, fearing each attack would be their last. Now that their own reinforcements had arrived, it was payback time.

He sprinted to Chuck's position and pointed at the men they had fought with for so long. "They're mounting a counterassault without any leadership, Chuck. We need to get in there!"

Chuck rested his head against the concrete block. "Yeah, I know," he said, wiping the sweat off his forehead. "They're running around like lost children. I . . . I just need to catch my breath."

"Hey, I can get to them while you find some comms and get us in touch with Chester."

Chuck waved his hand. "No, it's all right. Let's go finish these bastards off." He put his hands on his knees and groaned as he pushed himself up.

Hector and Chuck joined the counterattack where the remaining army troops had massed near an old opposition fortification and prepared a hasty defense. They bounded forward from cover to cover, taking aim and firing as they moved. This dance repeated as they slowly gained ground.

Chuck bounded forward when he suddenly dropped

backwards and writhed in pain, as though he had hit an invisible wall.

"Chuck!" Hector ran to him but stopped abruptly as the ground below him popped repeatedly from enemy gunfire. He fired his own weapon in the direction of the incoming fire, then sprinted to Chuck. He grabbed Chuck by the shoulder strap of his vest and pulled him while firing in the direction of the incoming fire.

Hector felt what seemed like a sledgehammer to the chest and dropped back. All the air was knocked out of his lungs, which felt like a clear bag had been wrapped over his head. He lay still, exhausted and reeling from the pain that throbbed throughout his body. The last of his energy was spent.

Get. The fuck. Up, the beast growled. At last, precious air returned, and he clutched at his chest. He opened his eyes, and a second wave of energy flowed from someplace deep inside him.

Get the fuck up. Now! Get up! Grab your fucking weapon and return fire!

Rage coursed through him. He reached for his weapon, but not before a Syrian soldier landed on him and plunged a combat knife toward him. He moved in the nick of time, and the knife got caught in the webbing of his plate carrier vest, breaking the momentum of the stab—but it still slid into his left shoulder. Hector thrust a backfist against the man's face, striking him on the temple and sending him off-balance. Hector pulled his own combat knife as both men took a fighting stance.

The soldier again lunged at him, but this time Hector was ready for him. Using the attacker's own momentum, Hector twisted his arm and flipped his body to the ground. He stabbed downward, but not before the soldier grasped his wrist. Using his legs to build momentum, the enemy hooked a leg around Hector's neck and threw him off.

The soldier jumped to his feet and lunged again at Hector, landing a knee on his body armor plate. Again, the air was sucked from Hector's lungs. Hector saw the knife reach its peak, the attacker ready to thrust down, but the beast would not die today.

He plunged his fingers deep into the man's eyes, feeling the orbs pop and spill ocular fluid down his hand and wrist. With rage still fueling him, Hector plunged his knife into the attacker's throat and sawed at the muscles and arteries with both hands.

The soldier gargled, blood oozing like an oil well as he lay writhing on the ground.

Hector rested his hands on his knees, gasping for breath. The enemy soldier was still. Now that this fucking thing was dead, Hector struggled up and stumbled to Chuck. He was exhausted beyond measure and reeling from the searing pain in his shoulder, but he was resolved to get to his best friend. He detached the front armor plate and patted Chuck front and back, searching for the source of his injury, sweeping his hands along Chuck's torso. He stopped when he found the hot, sticky liquid under Chuck's arm. *Oh, God!*

Hector groaned as he cut away the clothing. "Come on, Chuck, stay with me!" He exposed the torso and lifted the arm to inspect further, finding the entry wound inches from his armpit. *Please, God, no!*

Chuck was still breathing, but barely. Hector wiped the blood off on his pants and fumbled through Chuck's first aid pack. He pulled a pack of QuikClot, but the blood had slickened his hands, making it a challenge to open the package. He resorted to using his teeth to rip it open, and he fed the cloth into the wound, packing it in tight while talking to Chuck.

"Come on, old man, stay with me!" His voice trembled as he sobbed without holding back. "You have to walk Heather down the aisle, remember? You can't let her down, Chuck."

He sniffled as he continued packing and blubbered, "Please! Just hang on!"

Chuck's eyes opened slowly and shifted to Hector. Blotches of dirt, blood, and soot mixed with sweat were smeared across his face. The corners of his mouth twitched into a faint smile, then the deep crow's-feet around his soot-covered eyes wrinkled. He winced and began gasping like a fish out of water. His throat distended to the side of his neck.

"Shit! Fuck! Stay with me, Chuck! Stay with me!" Hector fumbled for a red and white tube from Chuck's first aid kit and extracted what looked like a thick needle.

He looked around and let out a primal scream. "Medic! I need a medic!" Opposition soldiers all stared at him and exchanged looks, unsure of what to do. "A doctor, goddammit! I need a fucking doctor!"

He couldn't wait any longer. He put his index finger on Chuck's collarbone and used his other fingers to feel their way down to find the gap between his third and fourth rib. He lifted the needle and was about to plunge down, but hesitated. *Fuck! Is it third and fourth rib, or fourth and fifth?* He couldn't recall. *Fuck it.*

He jabbed the needle between the ribs. A horrid frothing sound came from the tube poking from his chest. He held his breath, watching for a response. He let out a long exhale as Chuck breathed in, as if coming up for air.

He took Chuck's hand, pulling it close to him and holding it like a sacred relic. But Chuck did not reciprocate. The virile white-knuckle squeeze so commonplace of his friend and mentor was replaced by one so fragile and unfitting of the man who commanded respect among titans. Chuck's lips parted slightly as he mouthed, "Betty." His piercing blue eyes watered, tears rolling down in clean streaks on his dirtied cheeks as he closed his eyes. Chuck's grip loosened, and his hand went limp.

"No, no, no! Please! Come on, Chuck! Please!" Hector

bawled and begged, "Please don't fucking do this to me, old man! Don't do this to Betty. You're stronger than that! Please! We need you!"

Hector lifted his head, keeping his eyes on Chuck, and screamed for dear life, "Medic! I need a goddamned medic right now!"

Chuck had slipped away.

Hector quivered as a storm of emotions descended on him all at once. Fear, rage, loneliness, regret, sorrow, hatred, and desperation all pummeled him mercilessly. He pressed his forehead on Chuck's, and his tears found the lines in the old weathered face.

"I'm sorry," he whispered. "This was all my fault."

Time slowed in that moment, dragging out his pathetic existence in this purgatory. He didn't care about the potshots in the distance or the groaning of others around him.

He felt a hand at his shoulder and lashed out like a rabid dog. "What!"

A young man in his mid-thirties gingerly knelt beside him. In clear English, he said, "Are you Hector?"

Hector nodded, staring blankly at Chuck's body.

"I'm Qari. I got a message through my command that some American was looking for me. What can—"

"What the fuck took you so long?" Hector's voice was low but harsh.

Qari paused, then let out a slow exhale. "I'm sorry for your loss. I deeply am. And I'm sorry we didn't get here sooner, but we were engaged in a regime attack on our way to you. Death is everywhere, my friend."

It should have been me! Memories flashed by in a dizzying array—like the many times Betty had laughed at Chuck's musings, the way she looked at him in endless love, and the way she had watched him and Heather dancing at her engagement party. That one tortured him the most. He choked, unable to breathe while drowning in his own sorrow.

In the middle of the pain, sorrow, and exhaustion, the memory of Chuck's infectious smile after dancing with Heather at her engagement party waded through the fog like a beacon. He had never seen Chuck so happy, so . . . unreserved. He would never see that smile again. None of them would. Hector dropped his soot-covered face on his blood-soaked hands and cried. *I want to go home.*

Hector passed the unmarked time motionless, staring blankly at the place where Chuck's body had rested before Bravo Team had carried him in a body bag into the Super Puma.

Cheshire rested his hand on Hector's shoulder and whispered, "Time to go, mate."

Still in a daze, Hector rose and unsteadily followed. Before getting into the helicopter, he walked over to Qari. "Thank you. I'm sorry for—"

Qari raised a hand and shook his head. "You risked your life in the aid of my brothers. And you saved my friend's life. For that, you will forever be my brother. Your apology is not needed."

Hector pursed his lips and nodded. He extended his hand "You have very brave fighters. I wish you success."

Qari smiled and put his hand to his heart. "Thank you, my friend. Inshallah, we will be victorious."

Hector climbed in the helicopter and looked out as they lifted off the ground. Only then did he see the full extent of the carnage. Dozens of mangled heaps of metal and hundreds of bodies littered the battlefield. The sight sent a rush of emotions that overtook him again, and he wept. He had survived the day, but he cursed himself for living through it.

He then looked at the black body bag with Chuck inside,

willing for him to start jabbing at the bag and screaming, "All right, goddammit, who's the fucking idiot that thought it'd be cute to put me in this fucking thing?"

He wouldn't hear Chuck's raspy, angry voice anymore. Hector covered his face, no longer able to hold so much pain, sorrow, and overwhelming regret inside.

63

Old Town Alexandria, Virginia
16 August 2014

The lobby of the Hilton in Old Town Alexandria was bustling
with activity as guests traversed the lobby, going from the
front desk to the elevators and back. Whitney sat between
Jessica and Kelly, resting her head on Jessica's shoulder,
content to have her silky, shiny blonde hair stroked. Their
transformation since Hector had first seen them in the prison
was a godsend. Their quarantine period at RAF Akrotiri was
restorative, physically at least. Color had again returned to
their skin, and the bruising around their wrists was barely
visible now. Mentally, however, he would have to wait and
see. For now, they just waited for Whitney Clark's parents to
arrive and take their little girl home.

Hector sat opposite them, his eyes fixed on Kelly, taking in
the smoothness of her skin, the contour of her neck from
jawline to collarbone. She caught his stare and blushed, then
brushed her hair behind her ear. God, how he had missed
that, making her blush in public. Why had that changed?
There were many issues still left for them to address, but

divorce didn't seem to be one of them anymore. What he knew for sure was that he'd be there to help her deal with the demons that would haunt her for a long time to come.

A middle-aged couple and a younger girl, the spitting image of Whitney, burst through the hotel doors in a frantic search. Whitney popped up immediately upon seeing them. "Mom! Dad! Kayleigh!" Her parents and sister searched for their voices. The four reunited and hugged together tightly, unwilling to be away pulled away from each other.

Hector, with Kelly and Jessica, followed the girl at a slower pace, standing side by side and not daring to disturb the reunion.

"Thank you! Thank you for bringing my little girl home." Mr. Clark's voice cracked. He wiped his eyes. "I can never thank you enough for what you have done for our family, but I know our Lord Almighty will reward you with eternal life."

"No thanks needed, Mr. Clark," said Hector.

"There is something you can do," Jessica spoke up, caressing Whitney's hair one last time. "You can start by being very patient and being there for Whitney. She's going to need your love and prayers for what's next. You won't want to hear what she has gone through, but you have to take it in . . . for her sake." Her words served as a warning to Whitney's parents.

Mr. Clark nodded. The family, still huddled in a loving embrace, headed toward the exit. Before leaving the hotel, Whitney ran back to Kelly and Jessica. She hugged them one last time and said, "Thank you for being there for me. Thank you for not leaving me behind."

They hugged tighter and cried over shared experiences they couldn't yet put into words, experiences that no one else would ever understand. Whitney wiped her tears, then hugged Hector last. "Thank you for saving my life. I am so very sorry for Mr. Masters. You're all are my heroes, now and forever."

Hector leaned in and kissed the crown of her forehead. The cowardly shame of even considering leaving her in that hell, for the sake of the mission, still loomed heavily over him. It would follow him for the rest of his days.

The Clarks exited the hotel, leaving the three in an awkward silence. Whitney's journey was on its way to a conclusion—but where did they go from here?

Hector cleared his throat. "I don't know if it matters, but I thought you should know that Paul was—"

"I know," said Jessica, trying to choke back the tears, but failing. "I trusted him."

"The feds picked him up and charged him with a whole slew of felony charges, including kidnapping and conspiring with terrorist groups. He lawyered up, but I don't think that will do him any good."

"He wasn't alone in this. Joseph Donovan, the worthless piece of shit I worked for back in San Francisco, was in on it too." Jessica wiped her tears. "Do you know what happened to him?"

Hector shook his head. "No, I'm sorry. The feds are looking for him, as well. Apparently, he just fell off the face of the earth. They think the Russians may have taken care of him, one way or another."

She crossed her arms and nodded. "I just hope that son of a bitch gets what's coming to him."

Kelly rubbed her arm.

"I don't know if this is the right time to say this," said Hector, "but the offer is still on the table."

"You mean . . ." Jessica's face brightened.

"Yep. It's yours if you'll take it."

Kelly looked from Jessica to Hector. "What offer?"

"To join Parabellum," said Jessica.

Kelly's mouth gaped, and renewed concern filled her features. "You two are going to keep doing missions? After all that?"

"The team's gonna need to be reconstituted," said Hector. "Especially since they'll need a new team lead with me back at TOC."

Kelly cupped her nose and mouth and gasped with joy. Her eyes watered once again, then she wrapped her arms around him, pressing her head against his chest. "I wish it was under better circumstances, sweetheart. But thank you."

Hector wrapped his arms around her and swayed with her. He was never going to leave her side again, and he was never going to let his team down again. He would do Chuck proud and take care of the family.

Jessica stepped back slowly. She was happy for them, truly, and wished she had someone right now who would hold her like Hector did Kelly. She thought of Eric, still healing back at the Parabellum building, and how she had nearly lost him a second time. She thought of his declaration of love for her, how his words to her got her through her darkest times, and how he had been there to save her from that nightmare.

Kelly lifted her head from Hector's shoulder and wiped her tears. "Chuck's funeral is tomorrow. Will you be there?"

Jessica smiled. "Yes, of course. I want to pay my respects." She reached out and touched Hector's arm. "He was very brave, Hector. He was a true friend."

Twice had she seen the tears fall from his eyes. Tears shed over lost brethren.

She hugged Kelly and Hector, savoring their embrace before taking her turn to exit to the portico of the hotel.

Kelly called after her, "I love you, sis!"

"And I love you, Kel." She smiled, then passed through the hotel doors.

A tropical storm had been battering the mid-Atlantic for the last three days, and it would rain for another two.

Passersby hurried along the cobbled sidewalks with umbrellas and ponchos donned to protect against the wall of rain. At the portico, Jessica buttoned her raincoat, cinched the belt around her waist, and braved the storm as she stepped out to start her way home.

On her way, she stopped in the middle of the sidewalk. She closed her eyes and tilted her head back to feel the rain on her face. Never had the sensation of rain against her skin made her feel so alive. The moment inspired her. She pulled her phone from her pocket, thumbed the screen a few times, then put the phone to her ear and waited. "Hi, Eric." She brushed her hair behind her ear as a smile curled upward. "It's good to hear your voice too. I wanted to ask, can I see you tonight?"

Kelly nuzzled her head against Hector's chest, savoring the scent of his cologne and listening to the steady beating of his heart. She slid her hand to his, examining both—one with old scars, the other with new—and slowly interlaced her fingers into his. He closed his fingers around hers, and a rush of emotion overwhelmed her. She held him tighter with her other hand and let her fears, hopes, trepidations, and prayers out. Her body shuddered against his with each sob. "I love you so much!"

A finger from his free hand reached her chin and gently lifted it up. She saw his tears and ached for him. Despite his sadness, he formed a smile, one that she had long forgotten about. "And I love you too, babe."

She buried her head against his chest again, wanting nothing but to let this moment last for an eternity.

64

Church of St. John the Apostle, Leesburg,
Virginia
17 August 2014

Chuck would have been proud of the funeral service at St.
John the Apostle in Leesburg. He would have been happy to
see it was an open casket funeral, but even happier to hear the
litany of personal stories shared by those who knew him best.

Hector knew Chuck would have wanted him to share one
of their countless memories from the bar, the outdoor kitchen,
or some godforsaken place thousands of miles away, but he
couldn't bear to face Betty or the girls.

He sat in the back of the church during the service, with
Kelly at his side. Next to them were Penguin, his arm in a
sling, and Jessica beside him. Guapo, PF, and Cujo sat
solemnly in the pew behind them.

The church became eerily silent when Heather stepped up
to the podium, wearing a sleek black dress and a black veil
that came halfway down her face. She took a moment to
collect herself, then pulled the microphone close.

She cleared her throat. "I loved my father." Her voice

cracked. "Yes, he was gone a lot when I was younger, and I h . . . hated him for it." She tightened her grip on the podium and steadied herself. "It wasn't until much later, and after a horrible fight we had, that I realized who my father really was, and why he had to go so many times. I went away to college, and for a while, we went our separate ways. Or so I thought. I never knew that he kept watch over me. He was there, making sure I was safe. He was there when I was comfortable and happy, and when I made my own mistakes and cried for days over them. Had I needed him that second, he would have been there in half the time. I never knew that about him."

She released a thick sob, which turned into a short, happy laugh. "We made our peace at my engagement party. I let him know that I loved him. I can't remember the last time before then that I did." She covered her mouth below the veil, but the shuddering of her shoulders betrayed her silence. In the pause, Betty's own sobs echoed in the quiet church.

Heather sniffed, wiped her eyes and nose with a white handkerchief, and looked up into the heavens. "I love you, Daddy. You're *my* hero. And I know you'll be with me walking down that aisle."

She looked down at his casket and said with unfiltered heartbreak, "I miss you, Daddy!"

Heather stepped off the podium and walked to the casket. She dropped to her knees, weeping like the little girl who had tugged at her father's arm with all her might to keep him from going off to war. Hector's heart broke for her. Today, like then, she needed her daddy home.

When the service ended, Hector joined the end of the line of those giving their condolences to Betty, or at least the shell of who Betty had once been. Even from afar, he could see that she was broken. The always jovial and confident woman was no more. That Betty had died along with Chuck, another consequence of Hector's failure to keep him safe.

Hector tried to think about what he would say to Betty when he reached her, but words failed him. He took a deep breath, and his stomach tightened as he neared. Her haunting, tear-filled eyes stared into his. Before he could speak, he felt the stinging slap across his face that made him see stars.

"How dare you show up!" Betty's voice trembled with rage. "It should have been you!" Her fury echoed in the church, and again she accused, "It should have been you!" A second slap struck his other cheek. A third, a fourth, and a fifth. "I wish it had been you!"

Kelly tried to hold her back, to console her, but Betty shrugged her off. "Get off me! And get him out of my sight!"

Heather and Veronica arrived just in time to wrap their arms around their mother and escort her away. All the while, Betty's vile assaults persisted. "I hate you! I *hate* you!"

Hector's cheeks were bright red from her ferocity. Instead of prolonging her agony, he took his leave. Betty's verbal assault followed him all the way out, drilling deep inside him and tearing away at him. "You took my Chuck from me! I hate you!"

He exited the church and stared out at Union Cemetery across the street, a persistent reminder of his constant failures. He had lost half of his team and his best friend. He had almost lost his marriage. This was all his doing. His inability to keep those closest to him from pain or suffering was his legacy. How was he supposed to be the Chief of Global Operations if he couldn't even protect his personal teams?

Kelly stood next to Hector, the rain now coming down on both of them. She slipped her hand into his and rested her head on his shoulder. "It really wasn't your fault, you know." Her voice was soft and gentle. "If it wasn't for you, none of us would have survived."

Hector shook his head. "I should have jumped out later. Chuck would have stayed on board and he'd be alive now."

Kelly pressed her body against him. "He would have followed you no matter what. That's just who he was. But, Hector . . ." She raised her head and looked him in the eye. "If he hadn't, you would have ended up in his place, and I don't think I could live with myself knowing that."

Her tears mixed with the rain. "When you looked at me, that day you left the helicopter, I feared we would never see each other again. My heart broke, and I was coming apart." Her lower lip quivered. "I hate that Chuck died. I do. But he'd be heartbroken too. And . . ." She paused. "I wouldn't have you here with me. He did it for all of us. Yes, Betty is in pain, and will forever be, but she'll see that what he did made him the Chuck we knew."

Hector's eyes searched her face. He was seeing her anew. In front of him was a woman who was willing to be strong for him when he needed it. The same kind of woman Betty had been many times over. She lifted an insurmountable weight off his shoulders by helping carry the burden. His best friend, his mentor, was gone. But in dying, Chuck had given him a second chance at life. He would work to earn it ten times over. He smiled down at his wife. Everything would be all right.

In Moscow, Sacha Fedorovich moaned in delight as the beautiful girl practicing her soothing art massaged his full body. She was an absolute nervous wreck. Forced against her will into service, she knew refusal or abysmal performance would earn her an untimely and brutal demise, the same as her predecessor.

A bodyguard burst into the room, and the girl startled, breaking Sacha's relaxation.

"Misha!" Sacha barked. "I told you, no interruptions."

"I'm sorry, sir, but I think you'll want to take this." He extended a mobile phone in his hand.

Sacha snatched the phone from him. "I don't pay you to think, idiot." He put the phone to his ear. "*Da.*"

"Mr. Fedorovich . . . It's about our operation in Syria." The voice on the other end was nervous. "Someone killed Antonin and took the girls. News about our operation has spread. We've been compromised. You need to be ready, Pacha."

Sacha waved off the masseuse and propped himself up on his elbows. "What the fuck do you mean, we need to be ready?" he screamed into the phone. "What about Konstantin? Where is that idiot?"

"We don't know. He—he disappeared."

Sacha sat back down, snapping his fingers at the frightened masseuse. She timidly returned to her post and continued his massage. "What do you mean he disappeared? *I* make others disappear. And no one makes it happen without my say-so."

The person on the other end gulped. "Yes, sir."

"Now, go make yourself useful and find Konstantin, Dimitry."

He ended the call and turned to the girl. "I didn't tell you to stop!"

She immediately resumed, the relaxing strokes and rubs tainted slightly by her trembling. He lay back down, again moaning at her touch. He had to think what he would do next. He had to make an example of Konstantin. He had to do it quickly, and it had to be even more brutal. Once he made an example of Konstantin, everyone would fall in line, and all would be like before. Perhaps even better.

Days later, Jessica badged into Parabellum's TOC and found the workforce had gathered. She spotted her teammates, including Hector, who wore . . . a shirt and tie? *Oh, dear God!* She made her way over and greeted everyone individually.

"Hey, Jessica!" said a very jovial Eric. "I'm glad you made it. And thank you for coming by again yesterday. I've really enjoyed spending these last few days with you."

She leaned in and hugged him. Damn the peering eyes. "Hi, Eric." Her voice was maybe more than just friendly. "Me too. I'm glad to see the sling came off," she said, touching his arm where the sling had been.

They held each other's gaze. In that moment, as she looked into his eyes, all she wanted was for him to lean down and kiss her.

"Hey, hard charger. How are you doing?" asked Hector from behind.

Jessica turned around and hugged him, as well. "I'm good, Hector. Real good." She glanced up at Eric and smiled. She turned back to Hector and asked, "So what is this all about?"

"I'm not entirely sure. Our new CEO called for an all-hands. I know about as much as you do."

No sooner had he said this than Betty walked into the TOC with Heather, Veronica, and—*Kelly*? Betty shook several hands before standing in front of the television screens and addressing the Parabellum workforce.

"With the passing of my dear Chuck, I inherited his shares of the company. And with my own shares, I now control a vast majority. As many of you know, two days ago I became the new CEO of Parabellum Risk and Security Enterprises."

A round of applause broke out from the assembled crowd. Betty paced back and forth, thinking about what she would say next. "The animals that began this ordeal and led to the death of my dear Chuck are still out there." She stopped her pacing. "Before, I was but a silent majority partner in this enterprise. I am choosing to no longer remain silent. I have decided to make some changes to Parabellum.

"As the new president of this organization, I am designating the creation of a task force that will bring home those taken and held against their will. No longer will young women suffer in darkness at the hands of evil men, nor will families cower in fear from bands of thugs that prey on the weak. This task force will deliver that salvation, and heaven help those who stand in our way, for they will feel our wrath."

She paused to let her words sink in, then said, "I will spare no expense to subsidize this effort. There are many in need of justice, and Parabellum will be there to deliver it. Are there any questions?"

A murmur rolled throughout the TOC as people discussed among themselves, but no hands were raised.

"Details regarding this task force will be forthcoming, and I thank you all for your support and understanding."

With that, she made her way to Jessica, Hector, and the rest of Bravo Team. She gently touched the place on Hector's cheek where she had struck him some days ago. "I am so sorry about what I said, Hector. I was angry and grieving, but it was misplaced." He shook his head, but she cut him off. "No, it's not all right. I was in a lot of pain. I still am, but I should never have said those things." The remorse in her voice was genuine. "You sacrificed yourself to save those girls, and I should have remembered that. As much as I wish Chuck was still with us, I don't know if I could look at him the same way if he had left you on your own."

She got up on the tips of her toes and kissed each cheek as many times as she had slapped them. Betty then turned and smiled at the small group. "Can you all meet me in the conference room?"

Hector nodded. "Of course. We'll follow you."

Once inside the conference room, Betty asked that everyone have a seat. It was a small gathering, consisting only of Jessica, Hector, Kelly, Penguin, Guapo, Pirate Face, and Betty. She clicked a remote, and the light on the speaker in the middle of the table turned green. "Chester, can you hear us?"

"Loud and clear, Betty," came Cheshire's unmistakable proper British voice.

"Excellent. I have called you all in here because I would like for you all to be part of this new task force." Everyone exchanged looks of surprise. "And Hector, I would like for you to lead it."

Hector cleared his throat. "I for one am honored, Betty. But, I made a promise to—"

"It was my idea, sweetheart," said Kelly.

Hector looked puzzled.

"I've given this a lot of thought, and the fact is that if it were not for you"—Kelly looked around the room—"for all of you, Jessica and I would have died in that place. And I just don't think I could live with myself if other women suffered as we did because of my selfishness."

"Kelly—"

"I've made up my mind, Hector."

Jessica was overjoyed at this turn of events. This was exactly what Hector and Kelly needed, and what Bravo Team needed.

Hector turned to Betty. "What do you want us to do? How do you want us to run this task force? There are thousands of women in this same predicament. How are we to pick and choose? And those who prey on the weak, are we to destroy them with extreme prejudice?"

"Let me worry about those who we choose to go after. As for those who prey on them, do whatever is necessary." She leaned forward on the table and said with conviction, "Unleash hell with a savage joy."

Hector turned to Jessica. "Are you up for the challenge?"

Jessica grinned. "When do we start?"

ABOUT THE AUTHOR

 Luis is a veteran of the United States Marine Corps and has served overseas in the Middle East, South Asia, Africa, and Latin America. He graduated from St. Mary's University in San Antonio, Texas, with a degree in International Relations and was a member of the Lambda Chi Alpha fraternity.

He was inspired to write by the imagery, prose, and themes of classics like *Sherlock Holmes, Atlas Shrugged,* and *The Old Man and the Sea.* His interests reading and writing in the thriller genre were influenced by the works of great authors like Tom Clancy, David Baldacci, Jack Carr, Lisa Gardner, Hank Phillipi Ryan, and Jason Matthews, among others. His debut novel, *A Savage Joy*, reflects unique elements brought into the printed word from the authors mentioned and the emotions evoked by inspirational classics.

Luis has lived in the Washington, DC, region and the United Kingdom, but he's still proud of his Texas roots and his birth city of Laredo. Luis currently lives in St. Louis, Missouri, with his wife and children.

facebook.com/LuisRosasBooks

twitter.com/LERosasAuthor

instagram.com/LuisRosasBooks

WOULD YOU WRITE A REVIEW?

If you enjoyed reading *A Savage Joy*, would you consider writing a review on your platform of choice? Reviews help indie authors get more readers like you.

Thanks!